Lost Hope

Book Four in The Redstone Chronicles
J. T. Bishop

Eudoran Press LLC

Eudoran Press LLC

6009 W. Parker Rd. Su. 149-193

Dallas, TX 75093

www.jtbishopauthor.com

Publisher's Note: This is a work of fiction. Names, characters, places, and incidents are a product of the author's imagination. Locales and public names are sometimes used for atmospheric purposes. Any resemblance to actual people, living or dead, or to businesses, companies, events, institutions, or locales is completely coincidental.

Author Photos by Nick Bishop and Mayza Clark Photography

Book Editing by P. Creeden and G. Enstam, C. Marquis and C. McGuire.

Updated Cover Design by J.T. Bishop

Lost Hope/ J.T. Bishop -- 1st ed.

Paperback ISBN 978-1-955370-19-6

Hardback ISBN 978-1-955370-36-3

I would like to dedicate this book to Taylor, my beloved nephew. Without your wise cracks, annoying habits, and constant harassment, my life would be a lot less interesting. Whether you like it or not, I love you tons, and, let's be honest, I know you love me, too.

Other Books by J. T. Bishop

Chapter One

THE CRICKETS CHIRPED, A soft, cool breeze blew, and the city lights twinkled in the distance. Appreciating the view, Jag sat by himself on a bench at the overlook. After leaving work at two a.m., he'd come here because he knew he'd have the place to himself. As a bartender, he could sleep in, and he liked the quiet of the early morning hours. Needing to decompress before returning home, he would frequently visit this spot in the hills, where he could look down on humanity and feel some distance from it. His job, while entertaining, also exposed him to the seedier side of life, and not wanting to take it home with him, he'd stop at the overlook, where he'd go quiet, relax, and focus on the positive. That wasn't always easy since he was broke, his girlfriend had broken up with him, and his attempts at making it big as a singer had so far failed. He'd left L.A. because he couldn't take the rejection anymore and his friend had offered him a job. It had seemed like a reasonable alternative at the time, but now he wondered if he needed to return to L.A. and try again. Maybe he'd licked his wounds long enough. And after tonight, maybe the universe was giving him the signs that his luck was turning.

He eyed the time and wondered if his new friend would show. Thinking back on his shift, Jag smiled. He'd met a woman at the bar, which wasn't unusual. Women gave him their numbers all the time. It was his job to schmooze and flirt to get them to buy more drinks, and he was good at it. Listening and smiling were attributes that served him well. He rarely acted on any of the interest though, mainly because he'd had a girlfriend and also knew the women were drunk and would likely forget about him the next day. Tonight, though, had been different.

A woman had arrived around midnight, had sat at the bar, and ordered a gin and tonic. He'd made her drink and they'd started talking. The bar had been slower than usual, and he'd had more opportunity to talk. She'd introduced herself as Eleanor and had an easy laugh and a pretty smile. Her hair was up in a bun and loose tendrils framed her face. She'd told him how she'd left her boyfriend and family in Ohio six months earlier and had come to San Diego to start a new life. She was also a singer and had found a job singing at a local bar. Jag had told his story, too. They had an easy camaraderie, and she had a charisma he rarely found in others. Since breaking up with his girlfriend, he hadn't made much of an effort to date, but Eleanor made his stomach flutter, and he'd found himself telling her about where he'd come at night to overlook the city. When the bar closed, he'd invited her to meet him out here. She'd hesitated, and he'd promised he wasn't a stalker or serial killer. After a thoughtful moment, she'd told him a firm maybe, and she'd left.

Jag didn't know whether she'd join him or not and she hadn't given him her number, so if she didn't show, he might never see her again. He understood. Not many great romances were born in bars between a bartender and a customer, although it would be a cool story if they did.

Deciding he'd wait a few more minutes, he settled back on the bench and enjoyed the peaceful panorama, telling himself that no matter what happened, it would be for the best. Thinking about L.A. and what was next for him, he contemplated his future when he heard the sound of an approaching car. He turned and squinted at headlights that turned off the road and saw a car pull into a rocky space and stop.

His heart thumping, he waited. The car engine turned off, the door opened, and he grinned when he saw Eleanor step out. She smiled and closed the door.

Jag stood from the bench. "Glad you could make it."

Taking a deep breath and blowing it out, Eleanor walked over to him and widened her eyes at the view. "You weren't kidding. It's beautiful."

"It's one of my favorite places," he said. "Most people hang out here during the day or evening, but I like it when it's just me."

She set her purse down on the bench. "I can see why." The breeze blew and the tendrils around her face fluttered.

"What made you decide to come?"

She shrugged. "I knew I wouldn't be able to sleep. And you seemed like a nice guy, and I haven't met many of those." She glanced sideways at him. "And you're cute."

Jag felt his cheeks warm. "You're pretty cute yourself."

She sat on the bench. "Thank you."

"You're welcome." He sat beside her.

They didn't talk for a minute and Jag enjoyed the moment. He pondered whether his great love story would start with serving a pretty lady in a bar.

"How long do you normally stay out here?" she asked, draping an arm over the back of the bench.

"I don't know. Depends on the night. Thirty minutes? By then, the fatigue sets in and I go home to sleep."

"You ever bring your ex here?"

He shook his head. "No. She's in L.A. Had no interest in coming to San Diego. She's still hoping to hit it big as an actress."

"Good for her. That's a tough gig."

"It is, especially since she's terrible at acting. Can't remember lines to save her life. She got fired from her waitress job because she couldn't remember the menu."

Eleanor giggled. "Oh, dear."

Jag shifted to face her. "I know."

Eleanor crossed her legs. "Maybe she'll get lucky. Some do, you know."

He nodded. "Some do."

They stared for a moment, and she turned slightly toward him. "You hoping you might get lucky, too?"

Jag chuckled. "It crossed my mind."

She smiled and scooted closer. "It crossed my mind, too. I just don't want you to think I'm the kind of person that meets and makes out with strangers every night."

"Definitely not." His heart thumped faster. "Maybe just once a week."

Her smile grew. "More like once a month."

Jag moved closer. "I can live with that." He looked into her eyes and saw her gaze travel to his mouth. He lowered his head and let his lips graze over hers. The sensation was electric, and he heard her take a breath. "I really like you," he whispered.

"I really like you, too," she whispered back. She pressed her lips against his and the kiss deepened.

He felt her hand on his thigh and he brought his to her cheek, where he cupped her jaw and moved his lips over hers, slow at first, but then the pace picked up. He opened his mouth and their tongues touched. His whole body tingled, and he told himself to go slow, but Eleanor was picking up speed. She slid her hand up his leg and nipped his lips with her teeth. She moved her body closer, and her other hand slid into his hair.

Trying to catch his breath, Jag slid his lips from her mouth and trailed a path to her jaw. He heard her moan and his body responded to the sound. He moved his hand down to her shoulder and then cupped her breast. She gasped and gripped his hip, pulling him close.

Her head fell back, and he nibbled her ear and kissed her soft skin. "You taste so good," he said between kisses.

Eleanor grasped his hair and pulled him away. She raised her head and stared into his eyes. "I bet you do, too." She kissed him hard, swiveled, and slid her leg over his until she straddled him on the bench. The move thrilled him, and he put his hands on her thighs.

She moaned and rocked her body against his, dragging her mouth from his lips to his throat, where she teased him with her tongue. His heart was thudding so fast, he hoped it wouldn't stop from shock. She ran her hands over his chest, and up to his neck, where she grazed her lips just above his collarbone. "I want you," she said against his skin.

"I want you, too," he said, although he could barely speak. Everything was happening so fast. He cupped her buttocks with his hands, wanting to yank her clothes off, when he heard an ear-splitting shriek from behind and she abruptly shot away from him. Frightened, Jag stood as she jumped up. A man, bellowing and holding a wicked knife, stood beside the bench, his face a mask of fury. He'd swung at them, narrowly missing Eleanor's head and Jag's face.

Terrified and shocked by the unexpected attack, Jag froze, realizing how close he'd come to dying, and realizing he still might.

The man wore jeans and a dirty t-shirt, and holding his long knife, he glared. His muscled shoulders and arms bunched beneath the fabric and his dark and menacing eyes bore into Jag's. Jag didn't know what to do. He was too scared to move. Eleanor stood still and didn't speak or scream. She simply glared back.

Jag raised a hand. "Lis...listen. We don't want any trouble. Ju...Just leave us alone." His breath came in short gasps.

The man took a step closer, and Jag stepped away. Eleanor didn't move. "Go," said the man, in a gravelly voice.

Jag assumed he spoke to Eleanor. "Run to the trees," said Jag. "I'll try and fight him off while you get help." He didn't think for a second he could defeat this man, but he wouldn't sacrifice Eleanor to save himself.

"He's not talking to me," said Eleanor.

The man waved his free hand toward Jag. "Go. Now. And don't return."

Jag looked between the man and Eleanor, not understanding. "What?"

"I said go," screamed the man, his face stern.

His tone and volume broke through Jag's fear, and since Eleanor made no effort to do anything but glare, Jag ran.

His adrenaline propelled him down the dusty road. On his right was the steep embankment and on his left was the pebbled road that led from the street, where he'd parked, down to the overlook. If he could get up it and back to his car where he'd left his phone, he could call for help if he could stop shaking long enough to use it. Running as fast as he could, he debated going back. He'd left Eleanor alone with a crazy man and his knife. She would be murdered, and Jag would be the loser who'd let it happen. For a second, he almost slowed and turned around, when he heard a guttural yell which morphed into a shriek, and then a terrible gut-wrenching wail that abruptly stopped.

His terror ramping up further, Jag forced himself to run faster. The loose rocks made his feet skip and slide and he almost fell. Gasping for air, he could see his car and raced toward it.

Hearing a scraping sound and what sounded like rapid footsteps behind him, he had the horrifying feeling he was being followed. Something was chasing him. Too terrified to look behind him, he scrambled up the small hill, praying to get to his vehicle in time. His feet slid and he fell forward but righted himself. Desperate, he heard whimpering and realized it was him.

Reaching his car, a small kernel of hope bloomed when he realized he might survive this, when something slammed against him from behind. His body was thrown into his car with a hard thump and another blow sent him over the hood. His mind and extremities went numb. After hitting the pavement, his vision spun. His legs wouldn't move and although he wanted to scream, nothing emerged. And then it was on him, and helpless to stop it, he was dragged into the brush.

Chapter Two

MASON REDSTONE ENTERED SCOPE. Tired, he dropped his hat on the sofa, sat and leaned his head back. His head flared with a headache, and he sighed.

"Let me guess," said his sister Mikey, who sat at the desk she shared with Mason with her laptop open. "It didn't go well."

Mason thought back on his two appointments–one with a client and the second with his addiction therapist, Tarina. "It's been a long morning." He raised his head and noted the empty desk on the other side of the office. "Where's Trick?"

"Meeting with Janice Trammel, our new client. He should be back soon."

Mason nodded and laid his head back again. He heard movement and then someone sat beside him. He opened his eyes and saw Mikey holding out two aspirin and a glass of water. "I suspect you need it," she said.

Mikey could always sense when Mason was on the verge of or had a headache. He took the water and swallowed the pills. "Thanks."

"You're welcome." She rested her arm on the back of the sofa. The side of her fitted black t-shirt rose and he could see her narrow frame and that her normally snug jeans were looser. "Did you eat the bagels I brought you this morning?"

"I ate one."

He stared at her.

"Okay. Maybe half of one."

"Not hungry?"

"You know me and stress. I lose my appetite."

He nodded at her and worried a little. "It's been four weeks."

She flopped back against the couch. "I miss him."

"Rem's got some decisions to make and he's dealing with a lot."

"I know."

He patted her knee. "How are things between you and Kyle?"

"You mean since I told him we could only be friends? You know Kyle. He's all rainbows and lollipops. I could tell him I was moving to Kansas, and he would never see me again, and he'd understand."

"He was disappointed at first."

"I suppose, but he's bounced back pretty quickly. I guess I'm not the heartbreaker I thought I was."

"Rem's not doing so hot. I think you've got plenty of heartbreaker in you."

She sighed. "That was his doing. Not mine."

"Still. He's missing you, too."

"Not that I would know. I've barely spoken to him since he quit the force last month."

"After everything that's happened, he's got to figure things out. Give him time."

She sat up and rested her elbows on her knees. "How much time is enough before I go over there and kick his ass."

"You've done it before, and it worked."

"I was just getting to know him then. Now...it just seems harder. There's more at stake."

"Because you know how you feel about him."

She glanced at him with weary eyes. "Mom told me once that love isn't always enough. She loved Dad and look how that turned out."

Mason groaned. "Let's not compare Rem to Dad, okay? That comparison is like night and day. You're both just in a funk. It will pass."

Mikey eyed the floor. "Can we talk about something else? My life is depressing. How's Tarina?"

Mason's head flared again. "She pushed me again about the day of Mom's funeral and how I handled it. God. I hate talking about that." He massaged his temples. "I met with Mrs. Carmichael, too. She insists there is a spirit in her house when I've told her numerous times there isn't. She keeps insisting that things are happening, but all of it has a reasonable explanation."

"I keep telling you. She's lonely. Her husband passed last year and then her mother not long after. You're easy on the eyes and you talk to her. She likes your company."

Mason snorted and smoothed his handlebar mustache. "I think it's the mustache."

"That and your hunky good looks. It certainly got Valerie's attention."

Mason smiled, thinking of Val, his girlfriend. "No. She got mine. We're supposed to go to dinner tonight."

"Good. It will be nice for you to get out and relax, and not think about Tarina or Mrs. Carmichael."

"You okay with being home alone?"

Mikey frowned. "I'm fine."

"You sure? After what happened with Oswald? You haven't really been alone in the house since."

"Mason, you and I can't be glued to the hip forever. Go out and see Val. Spend the night at her place if you want. I'll bake cookies, eat loads of ice cream, watch dumb movies and wallow in my sadness. It will be fun."

"You know what I mean."

"And you know what I mean. I know Margaret's still a risk, but we have to live our lives. Val misses you, too, you know?"

Mason nodded. "She's been a trooper to put up with me."

"She deserves an award. I'm your sister. I don't have a choice. But she could have left you months ago."

Mason had to admit that was true. "I'll consider it. It would be nice to spend extended time with her."

They heard the door open and shut and Trick entered the inner office. He waved his hat at Mason and Mikey. "I hope y'all's day is going better than mine." He tossed his hat on the chair and sat on the other side of Mason.

"Did you meet with Mrs. Trammel?" asked Mikey.

"I did," said Trick, leaning back and putting a booted foot on the coffee table. "After I changed a flat tire on the side of the road." He huffed and smacked at a smudge of dirt on his jeans. "Then I get to the appointment, and I tried to pay for the coffee and my card declined. Apparently, somebody tried to use it to buy sneakers in Korea. Now I have to wait for a new one and Mrs. Trammel had to pay for my drink."

"I bet it was that club you went to the other night," said Mikey. "Bars are notorious for stealing credit card numbers."

Trick snorted. "I guess I should have bought fewer drinks, but the lovely lady I was talking to kept dancing with me, and then her friend joined us, and well, after that..." He grinned.

"You don't have to say any more," said Mason, raising a hand.

Trick settled into the couch. "Let's just say Mickey Mouse could have taken my card and treated Minnie to dinner and I wouldn't have noticed."

Mikey shook her head. "At least someone around here is having a good time."

Trick glanced over at her. "Still singing the Remalla blues?"

"She doesn't want to talk about it," said Mason.

"I'm sick of talking," said Mikey.

"Then don't," said Trick. "Go over there, shove him against the wall and kiss his brains out. That will get him moving."

Mason stared at his partner in disbelief, and Mikey dropped her jaw. "Seriously?" she asked.

Trick chuckled. "I remember when Beatrice Cullen came over to my place back when we were Rangers. You remember, Red?"

Mason's head pounded some more. "I'm sure I blocked it from my mind."

"I'd never really noticed her before. She worked in the Records department, and we flirted on occasion, but I didn't think she was my type." Trick stared off, a smile on his face. "Then, on my day off, she showed up at my door, wearing nothing but a trench coat. I let her in, she slammed me against the fridge and told me she was sick of waiting on me to make a move, and she kissed me, and well, I kissed her back, and then the coat came off—"

"Okay. Okay," said Mikey. "We get the picture."

"I hope it's imaginative because that was a fun afternoon," said Trick, resting his head back with a smirk.

"That's the advice you have for Mikey?" asked Mason. "Based on your sexual encounter with Beatrice Cullen, the woman from the Records department?"

"She got my attention," said Trick.

"Did you ever see her again?" asked Mikey.

"Once or twice. She ended up marrying Donald, one of the guys in Records. I always suspected she went after me to make him jealous."

"And that was okay with you?" asked Mikey.

Trick closed his eyes and rested his hands on his stomach. "I'm here to serve." He cracked an eye open. "Trust me. You should stop waiting on Remalla. The man needs a hot poker up his ass."

Mason raised a brow at Trick and glanced at Mikey. "Please don't listen to him."

"Maybe he's right." Mikey leaned back next to Mason.

"I know I'm right," said Trick.

Mason sat up. "Be quiet, Trick." He shot a look at Mikey. "And before you go over and ravage Remalla, maybe take into consideration that you are not Beatrice Cullen."

"She's not far from it," said Trick.

"Shut up, Trick," replied Mason. He spoke to Mikey. "And Remalla is not Trick in this scenario."

"Thank God," said Mikey.

"Hey...," said Trick, narrowing his eyes.

Mason bit back his impatience. "Just trust your gut, Mikey. You'll know what to do and when to do it." He shot a thumb toward Trick. "And please don't take advice from a man who once told a suspect to soak his feet in ice to prevent foot odor."

"My grandma Bellavina always told me that," added Trick.

Mason rolled his eyes. "Grandma Bellavina was ninety-three years old. She ate squirrel meat and didn't have running water until she was sixty."

"Still," said Trick.

"Our suspect tried it and almost lost two toes to frostbite," said Mason.

"Those were the days," said Trick with a sigh.

Mikey raised the side of her lip. "I hear you. I won't ravage Rem without some serious thought about it first." She ran a hand down her black jeans. "But man, something better happen soon to distract me or I'm going to go a little crazy."

"Nothing a little ravaging won't cure," said Trick with another smirk.

Mason frowned. "Why don't you go do something useful."

The buzzer sounded, and Mikey straightened.

"We have another appointment?" asked Mason.

"No. We don't." Mikey stood and went to the computer on the desk. "Maybe it's a package." She shook the mouse and the screen brightened.

"I hope that's all it is," said Mason. "I'm beat. I just want to go home, get cleaned up and go see Val."

Trick dropped his foot from the coffee table. "Apparently, Mikey's not the only one thinking of ravaging someone."

Mason shot him a dirty look and was about to add a colorful comment when Mikey sucked in a breath. Mason looked over to see her pale face and wide eyes. He stood. "What is it? What's wrong?"

"I was just kidding," she said to the monitor. "I didn't mean it. I don't need any more distractions."

Fearing it was Margaret, Mason walked up beside her and checked the cameras. Seeing the person out front, his stomach dropped, and his heart thumped. "Shit."

Trick, stood, too. "What is it?" He joined them at the desk and stared over Mikey's shoulder. "Holy Toledo, Red. Is that who I think it is?"

Mason couldn't believe his eyes. Neither he nor Mikey had talked to the man standing outside SCOPE's door since their mother's funeral.

"It's Dad," said Mikey, her voice soft. She paused. "What do you want to do, Mason?"

The man pushed the button and the buzzer sounded again.

"Martin Redstone. The patriarch," said Trick. "Never been much of a fan."

"Join the club," said Mason. He swallowed as his father rang the buzzer again and then banged on the door. Mason heard a muffled hello and then a "Michaela? Mason? You in there? Open the damn door." He banged again.

"Hell," said Mikey. "We're going to have to talk to him, aren't we?"

Mason curled his fingers into fists and then shook out his hands. He exhaled sharply and mentally prepared himself. Watching the screen with dread, he leaned over, hit the button, and held his breath as his dad entered SCOPE.

Chapter Three

Mikey held her stomach, recalling the last time she'd seen her father at her mom's funeral. He'd gotten drunk, and Mason had thrown him out. Max, their older brother, who'd always been more accepting of their father's misbehavior, had not interfered, but didn't agree that Dad should have been asked to leave.

Margaret had made a brief appearance, but she'd left soon after Dad had stomped out with his latest girlfriend at the time who'd also been a friend of their mom's. Max had stayed in touch with their father, but Mikey and Mason had not spoken to him since.

Mikey heard the outer door open. None of them went to the inner door to open it and they waited. It opened, too, and Martin Redstone entered.

Seeing him, Mikey hid her surprise. Her father had always been a self-indulgent man. He liked his beer and his women and marriage hadn't curtailed him from either. While he'd had moments of promise as a husband and father, usually after Mom threatened to leave him and he'd told her he'd straighten up, they'd never lasted long. Mom had finally divorced him when Mikey was a teenager, but he'd continued to come around, and their mother had somehow remained friendly with him. She'd never been one to tolerate fools, but she'd always had a soft spot for Martin Redstone.

When her dad had showed at the funeral, Mikey could see his indulgences were showing their effects. He'd gained weight, his skin had looked gray and his eyes sunken. Mikey had wondered how much longer it would be before both her parents were gone.

Looking at him now, though, she was shocked. His extra weight was gone, his skin was a healthy color and he looked fit. His hair even looked thicker.

He stood and stared at them, and they stared back. Mikey didn't know what to say, and apparently neither did anyone else.

"Well," Martin finally said. "Don't rush to welcome me all at once."

He wore his usual jeans, but they weren't the typical saggy worn ones with the holes in them. These were dark, well-fitted jeans which accentuated his narrow waist. He wore his customary boots and a belt with a silver belt buckle, and his long-sleeved shirt looked ironed. The only thing missing was his cowboy hat, which he rarely took off in Texas, not even at Mom's funeral, which had been another point of contention between Mason and Martin.

"What do you want?" asked Mason.

Martin narrowed his eyes. "Still the hard ass, I see. I've never known someone who could hold a grudge as long as you."

Mikey detected the stiffening of Mason's back. "Probably because I take after you, Dad," said Mason.

Martin opened his mouth to respond, and Mikey slapped a smile on her face, determined to keep things peaceful. She stepped forward. "Hi, Dad." She walked over and gave him a hug. "You look good." Her father gave her a half-hearted hug.

"At least Michaela is glad to see me." Her father eyed Mason with a hard gaze.

Mikey moved back. "You can call me Mikey, Dad."

Her father glanced at her. "Michaela is the name I gave you and that's what I'll call you. You're my daughter, not my son."

Mikey knew arguing was pointless. Her father looked her over. "You look good. You married yet?"

Mason grunted. "What do you want?"

Martin frowned at Mikey. "I'm not seeing a ring, so I guess the answer is no."

Uncomfortable with her father's appraisal, Mikey gripped her elbows and rounded her shoulders. Martin glanced at Trick with a scowl. "I'd heard the rumors that you two were working together again but didn't want to believe them. I guess I don't have a choice now." He looked at Mason. "I told you he was bad news. But as usual, you follow your own trail."

Trick snickered. "Hello, Mr. Redstone. Long time, no see. I believe the last time I spoke to you was when I said goodbye as Mason kicked you out of Martha's funeral."

"That was the last time I spoke to him too, Trick," said Mason. "And I thought it would be the last."

"Bad pennies have a way of turning up," said Trick.

Martin looked between the two of them and spoke to Trick. "I came here to talk to my son and daughter. Maybe you can take that smart mouth of yours somewhere else."

Mikey clenched her fingers and Mason glared. "The only one who's going anywhere is you," said Mason. "Trick and I are closer than you and I have ever been or ever will be. So if you came here to say something, say it and leave. Trick is not going anywhere."

Martin hardened his stare. "Fine. It's your rodeo." He stepped further into the office and looked around. "SCOPE is a catchy name. You still doing that paranormal crap? Or have you finally smartened up and taken your brother's advice?"

Mikey forced herself to engage. "Don't start, Dad. Max and Mason are finally talking and getting along. Max supports Mason."

Martin sneered. "Max is the only one in this family with some sense. He may say one thing, but he thinks another." He walked to the window and looked outside. "I don't know how I got one practical child and the rest are a damn mess."

Tense, Mikey bit her lip. "Mason and I are doing just fine. Business is booming." She could never understand her need to prove herself to her father.

Martin looked away from the window. "Well, you're in California with the wackos, so that makes sense. You two would never survive with this woo-woo crap in Texas."

"We'd do just fine wherever we went," said Mason. "The biggest advantage of leaving Texas was getting some distance from you."

Martin chuckled. "I believe the reason you left was that wacky friend of yours, Victor. Not me." He scoffed. "And we all know where that got you."

Mikey raised a brow. Her father had known about Mason's friendship with Victor and about Mikey's and Margaret's involvement in Victor's cult, but she didn't think he'd known what had happened since.

"You didn't come here to discuss Victor, nor do I intend to justify what I do or who I spend time with." Mason crossed his arms. "So if you've got something to say, say it."

Martin straightened and held Mason's look. Mikey half expected her father to curse at Mason and tell him all the ways he'd been a disappointment. Her father didn't say a word, though, and instead, walked to the door and opened it. He stepped into the outer office and disappeared for a few seconds. Mikey wondered if he'd left, and hoped he had. She heard footsteps though, and her father returned, holding the hand of a woman who wasn't much older than Mikey's sister Margaret. She was taller, had straight black hair that ran down her back, and pale skin. She was beautiful but young and looked at them with anxious eyes.

"This is Vicki," said Martin. "We're getting married."

Mikey dropped her jaw.

"Married?" asked Mason. "Are you kidding?"

Trick furrowed his brow. "No offense, ma'am, but you seem far too young and pretty to marry Martin Redstone."

Startled, Mikey had no idea what to say.

"Did he tell you he has money, Vicki?" asked Mason. "Because if he did, he is lying. Money runs through his fingers like water."

Mikey sensed Vicki's discomfort and could only imagine what the woman was thinking. She stepped forward. "Hi. I'm Mikey." She pointed. "And this is my brother Mason and his partner Trick Monroe. Don't mind Mason and Trick. In case you haven't noticed, Dad puts us in a bad mood." She offered her hand and Vicki shook it.

"Nice to meet you," said Vicki.

Martin snorted. "At least somebody has some manners."

Mikey tried to calm the tension in the room. "This just took us by surprise. How long have you two known each other?"

Vicki glanced at Martin. "Three months," said Martin.

"What?" asked Mason. "Are you serious?"

"You got a problem with that?" asked Martin. He squeezed Vicki's fingers. "When you know, you know."

Mason stared in surprise. "Considering your track record with your first wife and your relationships since, yes, I have a problem with that. You barely know each other."

"I didn't come here to ask for your permission. I just thought you should know." Martin spoke to Vicki. "We can go whenever you want."

Vicki shook her head. "No. I wanted to meet your family. All of them. That's what we came here to do." She looked at Mason and Mikey. "I know this sounds fast and you don't know me, but Martin and I love each other. He's been good to me, and I think I'm good for him. He told me you've been estranged, and I understand how me coming into the picture so suddenly is difficult, but I thought you all needed to know."

Mikey did her best to act casually. "When are you getting married?"

"We haven't set a date yet," said Vicki. "Martin just popped the question last week and we're in no hurry."

Mikey spoke to her dad. "Have you told Max?"

"We're having lunch with Max tomorrow. I'll tell him then." Martin looked at Vicki. "Max will be much nicer. You'll like him."

Vicki nodded. "I'm sure once I get to know Mason and Mikey, I'll like them too."

"Don't count on it," said Martin. "They've been difficult since the day they were born."

"Honey," said Vicki, "you haven't seen them in years, and when you finally do, you drop this bomb on them. How do you expect them to react?"

"Better than spoiled brats," said Martin.

"Do yourself a favor, Vicki," said Mason, "and give yourself a long engagement. The longer, the better."

Looking uncomfortable, Vicki shifted on her feet and Mikey tried again to break the tension. "How long have you been in town?" asked Mikey. "Did Max know you were planning to visit?" Max had not said a word to her or Mason about Dad coming to San Diego. She could imagine his reaction to the news, and she doubted it would be as positive as her father hoped.

"Of course he does," said Martin. "I told him not to tell you though, because I know how you two can get."

"We've been in town for a little over a week," said Vicki. "We've been seeing the sights. Your father has never been to California. I lived here for a short time before I moved to Texas. So I'm familiar with the area. Plus, it's been nice to see your sister."

Mikey wasn't sure she heard right. "Sister?"

Mason went still. "Do you mean Margaret?"

"Course she does," said Martin. "You got another sister?"

Vicki smiled. "Yes. Margaret's been so kind. She introduced us."

Feeling the blood leave her face and her legs wobble, Mikey sat in the desk chair.

Chapter Four

MASON TRIED NOT TO yell, but still raised his voice. "Margaret? You've seen Margaret?"

Martin nodded. "Sure have. What's the problem?"

Mason gaped at his father. "What's the problem? Did you seriously just ask me that? You know Margaret's wanted by the law."

Martin rolled his eyes. "That nonsense? Your sister said the only reason they're looking for her is because of the lies you and Mikey have told about her. Your older sister may have a few screws loose, but she could never do the things you've accused her of."

"She told us she was working things out with the authorities and not to worry," said Vicki. "Is that not true?"

Mason couldn't prevent a laugh. "Margaret is a psychopath. Whatever she told you is a flat-out lie. She almost killed Mikey and is responsible for more deaths since, plus assaulting and almost killing a detective. The police have been looking for her for months." He had an uncomfortable thought. "Has she been staying with you all this time?"

Martin glowered at Mason. "Watch what you say about your sister. She's still family."

"Pardon me, Mr. Redstone," said Trick, "but Margaret is not a family member you want to hang around with. She's dangerous, and if you've been harboring her, you could go to jail."

"Mind your business, Monroe. This is between family," said Martin. "And I know Margaret's wanted by the law, but she is still my daughter."

"She escaped from a psychiatric facility, you idiot," yelled Mason. "How long was she in Texas?" He had every intention of notifying his Texas Ranger connections and telling them to be on the lookout for Margaret.

"She's not in Texas anymore, you jackass," spat Martin. "She showed up three months ago and we caught up. She knew Vicki from Vicki's time in California and looked her up. That's how we met. Marge stayed a few days and then left."

Vicki stared with wide eyes. "We had lunch with her after we arrived. She picked us up at the airport."

Mason couldn't believe his ears. "Are you kidding me?" He wondered what the hell law enforcement was doing with their time.

Mikey, her face pale, finally spoke after sitting in the chair. "Where did you eat?" She couldn't imagine Margaret taking Vicki and their dad to some crowded and popular place to enjoy a meal.

Vicki glanced at Martin. "She took us to a small restaurant without much light. "Your father didn't like it because he likes his big windows and sunshine, but Margaret insisted, and the food was excellent." She paused. "Afterward, we went back to the hotel. Martin went down to the bar to have a beer and Margaret and I hung out and caught up. Then she left, and we haven't seen her since."

Still in shock, Mason cursed. "I need to know exactly where you went, who you saw, and what Margaret did or said. We have to find her."

"Can you call her?" asked Trick. "Ask her to meet you somewhere?"

"She contacts us," said Vicki. "I have a number for her, but she never answers, so I leave a message. She didn't give me a new one."

Martin sneered. "If you think we're going to help you catch her, you're wrong. Your sister is innocent."

"Then what I've always suspected has now been confirmed," said Mason. "Margaret got her insanity from you."

Mikey stood. "Dad, she's lying to you. She does not have your best in-terests at heart. If you know where she is, you need to tell us. Her intention is to hurt me and Mason. Everything she's accused of is true." Mikey spoke to Vicki. "Despite what my father says, you have to believe us. Trick's right. Margaret is dangerous. She'll use you to get what she wants."

Vicki's mouth fell open. "It's just so hard to believe. She's been so nice to us."

"If you see her again," said Mikey, "call the police. Immediately."

Martin put his arm around Vicki. "You're scaring her."

"You should both be scared." Frustrated, Mason ran a hand through his hair. "Margaret doesn't do anything without a reason. She could be targeting you."

Martin snorted. "Your sister isn't going to hurt me or Vicki, and she's not going to hurt you either. She's had her issues, but she's better now. Says she wants to repair her relationships." Martin squeezed Vicki's shoulder. "And I believe her."

Mason's anger flared. "Then you're a fool."

"Red is right, Martin," said Trick. "If you want to protect Vicki, then keep her away from Margaret."

Martin scowled again. "When I want your advice, Monroe, I'll ask for it. Until then, keep your mouth shut. Like I said, this is between family."

Mason had heard enough. "Trick is more of a family member to us than you or Margaret will ever be. You're in my place of business so show a little respect. I'm not in your house anymore and you don't pay the bills, so you no longer have any say over me, or Mikey." Mason did his best to soften the edge in his voice. "You've said what you had to say, and we've warned you both. So unless you've got any more shocking news you'd like to share, then the door is right behind you. I suggest you use it."

His face taut, Martin stared at Mason. "Your sister was right about you. She told me a few things. I've heard some things from your brother, but Margaret gave me the full story. She told me how you'd been popping pills for years before you finally got treatment for it. I always knew you were weak since you were a kid. Max had all the smarts, and you were just like your mother." He gestured toward Mikey. "And now you've got her all turned around. Margaret tried to help Michaela when Michaela got out from under your buddy's cult, but you butted in and now she's stuck in a dead-end job and in love with a man who doesn't love her but loves Margaret instead." He pointed. "That's on you, Mason. If Michaela ends up alone and destitute, it'll be your fault."

Mason heard Mikey's intake of breath.

Trick chuckled. "Boy, Martin. When God handed out the smarts, you were obviously at the end of the line."

Mason set his jaw and forced himself to stay cool. He thought of his therapy sessions with Tarina. He wondered what she'd advise him to do in this situation. "Listen to me," said Mason. "For some reason, our mother found something worth loving in you and because of that, I'm not going to physically throw you out." He looked at Vicki. "It was nice meeting you and I hope to God you come to your senses and don't marry this man. And if either one of you has any brains, do not listen to Margaret. If she contacts you, do yourself a favor and call the police." He waved a hand. "You need to leave. Now."

Martin's face tightened, and Vicki swallowed. "Come on, honey," said Vicki. "We should go." She pulled on Martin's arm.

Martin looked at her. "I told you this was a waste of time. Mason and Michaela are a lost cause."

"Dad," said Mikey, her voice soft, "you're our father and we love you, but we saw how you treated Mom and now you treat us the same. I'm glad you and Max are close and I'm even glad you saw Margaret. Maybe in some crazy way, she does want to reconnect. But what she told you about me and Mason was cruel and untrue. She doesn't love us, and I doubt she ever did. I'm not sure she even knows how to love. Which is why you have to be careful."

Martin walked to the door, holding Vicki's hand, and turned toward Mikey. "Michaela, you've always been a good girl, but you're easily manipulated. If you ever decide to make a different choice my door is always open in Texas. But I still play by my rules, and if you choose to join me, you'd be expected to do the same." He paused. "Which might be the best thing for you." He eyed Mason.

"I appreciate that, but I'll be staying here." Mikey's eyes welled with tears, and she nodded. "You have a nice life, Dad. I wish you both well."

Martin studied her and shook his head. "Let's go, Vicki." He started out the door.

"Remember what we said, Vicki," said Mason. "Take it to heart."

Martin held the door for Vicki, glanced back, and followed Vicki out. Before leaving, he stopped and turned. "I'll pray for you both."

"Save your prayers for Vicki," said Mason. "She's gonna need 'em."

Glaring again, Martin hesitated, and left.

Chapter Five

His heart thumping, Mason waited until he heard the outer door close, and cursed again. He couldn't believe what had just happened. His father had showed up with a fiancée half his age and had told them he'd been spending time with Margaret, who'd been filling his head with lies about him and Mikey. The whole thing pissed him off.

"You two okay?" asked Trick.

Mikey returned to sit in the desk chair. She looked like she'd been forced to eat beets, which their mom had loved, but her offspring had hated. "No. Not really."

Mason empathized with her. He didn't feel too great, either.

"Both of you sit on the couch," said Trick. "I'll get us something to take the edge off. After that little visit, we need it."

Mason didn't move at first until Trick tugged on his arm. "On the couch, Red. Let's go. You, too, Mikey."

Mikey stood, and Mason headed toward the sofa, feeling like he was on autopilot. He sat and Mikey sat beside him.

Trick went to his desk and opened a drawer. He pulled out a bottle of liquor and set it on his desk. "Nothing like a little Kentucky bourbon to settle the nerves." He went to the back closet and brought back three plastic cups. He poured some liquor in each and brought them to Mason and Mikey, who each took one.

Mikey stared at hers. "I feel a little sick to my stomach."

"All the more reason to drink it," said Trick. "This will cure everything." He sat next to Mason and raised his cup. "Bottom's up."

Mason roused himself and raised his glass. Mikey did the same and they downed the liquor. Feeling the heat, Mason grimaced, and Mikey gasped.

"Ugh," said Mikey, putting the cup on the coffee table. "That's awful."

"Couple more of these and you won't care anymore," said Trick.

"I will when I puke it up." Mikey wiped her lips.

"That would be a sad waste of good liquor, so we'll stop here." Trick set his cup next to Mikey's. "But if you change your mind, let me know. Something tells me the workday is over. I'll refrain and can be the designated driver if needed."

Mason studied his empty glass. "I'm still in shock. But I'm not sure more booze is going to help."

Mikey held her head. "I can't believe that just happened."

Mason couldn't help but chuckle sadly. "I guess we shouldn't be surprised. It is Dad after all."

Trick nodded. "You think Max knows that your father has been talking to Margaret?"

Mikey looked up. "There's no way. He'd never put up with that. He knows what Margaret's capable of. If Dad tells him tomorrow that he's been talking to her, Max will go off on him."

"You think Max knows about Vicki?" asked Trick.

Mason shook his head. "I doubt it. He'd have told us. I can't imagine what he's going to say when he finds out."

"She's so young," said Mikey. "She's got to be around Margaret's age."

"What woman in her right mind would want to marry Martin Redstone?" asked Trick.

Mason's heart fell. "Our mother did."

"Your mother," said Trick, "God rest her soul, married a man her age who at the time probably showed a lot more promise." He sat back. "The current Martin Redstone shows no such promise." He tipped his head. "Although he is looking pretty good. That was a surprise."

"Vicki obviously has some positive effect on him. Dad looks better than he has in years." Mikey sat back against the cushions and studied the ceiling.

"She hasn't had much effect on his personality," said Mason. "If anything, he's meaner."

"That happens with old age," said Trick. "You lose your filter. My great uncle Jasper was mean as a hornet when he died. I thought he was bad when I was a kid, but I was wrong."

Mason sighed. "I can see why Dad would want Vicki, but Vicki falling for Dad? It makes no sense."

"Margaret introduced them," said Trick. "Makes me wonder why."

"Why would Margaret want to introduce a friend of hers to Dad?" asked Mikey. "What would be the purpose?"

Mason thought about it. "What if this is a ruse? Are Margaret and Vicki playing some cruel joke on Dad? Making him think this pretty lady wants him, and then he'll get dumped at the last minute?"

"Sadly," said Mikey, "that makes more sense than this marriage. Margaret and Dad were never close." Mikey paused. "But why would any friend do this for Margaret? A practical joke is one thing but pretending to be in a relationship with a surly man twice your age that you don't love is something else. I don't know anyone who'd sacrifice this much of their life just to get back at her friend's father." Mikey put a hand on her head. "Besides, could you sense her emotions, Mason?" She glanced at her brother. "I could. It felt to me like she cares for him and genuinely wanted us to reconnect."

Mason had a fleeting recollection of Vicki's emotional state. "Yeah. I felt it too. I wouldn't say it was love, but there was something there." He sighed. "If this is a practical joke, Vicki has jumped in with both feet."

Trick shifted on the sofa to face Mason. "What do you want to do about Margaret?" He rested his elbow on a couch cushion. "You want me to contact Texas?"

Mason nodded. "Damn straight I do. They need eyes on Dad's house. Pronto. If Margaret returns, they need to be ready."

"What about here?" asked Mikey. "Should we call Captain Lozano and let him know?"

"Of course we should," said Mason.

Mikey groaned. "That means we'll have to tell him about Dad's involvement. They'll likely question or even follow him."

"I hope they do." His headache growing despite the aspirin, Mason squeezed his temples. "Dad knows the circumstances. It's not our problem. If he is the best way to catch Margaret, then so be it." He paused. "It's not like we have to worry about making him mad."

"You should contact Max," said Trick. "We need to find out where Vicki and Martin are staying. That way the police can keep an eye out."

"I should tell Daniels, too," said Mikey. "He'll want to know."

"What about Remalla?" asked Trick. "You think he should know that Margaret's telling people that he's in love with her?"

"I think I'll keep that to myself," said Mikey. "Although, I'm a little unnerved that Margaret knows how I feel about Rem."

"Don't be too unnerved," said Trick. "It wasn't that hard to figure out."

Mikey looked over at him. "Maybe for you, but you see me every day. Margaret doesn't, or does she?"

"Margaret is empathic just like us," said Mason. "She'd pick up on it whether she's around you are not. Plus, she knows Rem likes you and doesn't like her. She planned for that comment to Dad to get back to you."

"That's just it," said Trick. "She knew your father was in town, and probably knew he was going to visit you two. It would be logical to assume Martin would tell you about seeing her. She knows we'll contact the police. But she obviously doesn't care. The question is, where is she now? And what's next on her agenda?" He looked at Mason. "You think your dad is in danger?"

Mason shrugged. "Maybe. When it comes to Margaret, who knows? Maybe Vicki is, too. All we can do is notify the authorities and hope for the best."

Trick pointed. "That means that you both better be careful. Margaret could still be in the vicinity. Maybe she plans to hit all of you at once."

Mason considered that. "It's unlikely. She's using our father to get to us. As long as Dad is in her corner, she'll play that to her advantage."

"And what if Dad is in danger?" asked Mikey. "What if he was in trouble and needed our help. You think Margaret would use that to lure us in?"

Mason didn't hesitate. "No. That implies we'd want to help him." He stood. "And Margaret isn't that stupid." He picked up his glass. "I'm getting another. Anyone care to join me?"

Chapter Six

TRICK OPENED THE TRAY table and placed it in front of his couch. He put the bag of food down, grabbed the remote and flipped on the TV. A *Seinfeld* episode began to play, and he smiled when he recognized it as one of his favorites. He headed to the kitchen and grabbed a beer from the fridge. After opening it, he returned, sat on the couch, and reached into the bag. Watching the episode, he pulled out his two Taco del Fuegos, settled back on the sofa and started to eat.

Chuckling at something a character named Kramer said, he thought back on his day. After Martin Redstone's visit, Mason and Mikey had imbibed a bit more bourbon, and after they'd relaxed and vented more about Martin and discussed what else to do about Margaret, Trick had driven them back to Mason's house. Mikey had been staying with Mason since Margaret's escape and Trick had to wonder if Mikey would ever be able to return to her own apartment. As long as Margaret was a threat, Mason would not let his sister live alone. Trick suspected Mason didn't enjoy being alone either and had welcomed Mikey's presence.

Recalling their conversation about Martin, Trick sipped his beer and ate his tacos. He couldn't help but worry. Margaret had been in the area recently and likely hadn't left. Trick had no doubt Mason and Mikey's older sister had something up her sleeve. Could she have gone to see her father out of a true need to make amends? Trick shook his head, not believing that. He knew Margaret Redstone well enough to understand that her motives were never altruistic. Based on what Margaret had told her father about Mikey and Mason, he believed her intentions didn't bode well for anyone.

He picked up his napkin and wiped his fingers. He understood Mikey and Mason's frustration and felt his own. At this rate, Margaret would never be caught, and they would never feel safe. And worse, there was little they could do, except wait.

Grateful to be at SCOPE and able to offer whatever help he could, he made a mental note of what needed to be done the next day. He'd have to pick up Mikey and Mason to take them to work and then he'd follow up on Janice Trammel's case. She'd been kind enough to buy the coffee after Trick's card declined and he'd shown up late and dusty after changing his tire. To her credit, she'd ignored all of that and had told him she was looking for her son. He'd disappeared three days earlier and the authorities had done little to search for him. Jackson Trammel, or Jag as they called him, had moved to San Diego from LA to take a bartending job after his singing career had faltered. He talked to his mom frequently and would always call her back if she left a voicemail. After not hearing from him, his mother had contacted the bar where Jag worked and had learned he'd missed work for the last two days. She'd immediately called the police, and they'd opened a missing persons report, but she didn't detect the urgency in them she'd hoped for. She'd made a few phone calls, and Trick had been referred to her. She'd called Mikey to set up the appointment and after meeting Mrs. Trammel that morning, Trick had agreed to do some initial research and then update her about what to do next.

Since the rest of the afternoon had been a wash after Martin's visit, Trick planned to get started on Jackson's case the next morning. He would start at Jackson's apartment and then go to the bar where he worked. Then he'd contact Mrs. Trammel before going further.

Trick thought of Kyle and wondered if he'd want to join in on the investigation. Kyle had expressed interest in learning more about the non-paranormal side of investigating and Trick had agreed to teach him. This would be a good case to start that training. Kyle had shown a lot of promise on the paranormal side of SCOPE. Although his hopes to date Mikey had failed, Kyle had still shown that his reliability, smarts, and friendliness were assets that served SCOPE well. Plus, he was a good investigator.

Trick watched the rest of the episode and finished his tacos. After taking the last sip of his beer, he stood, grabbed his trash, and threw it away. He grabbed another beer from the fridge, popped it open, returned to his living area where he sat in his recliner, pushed it back and relaxed. He thought again of Mikey and Mason and debated calling them to be sure they were okay. The visit from their father had rattled all of them and he knew how family troubles could mess with your head. Trick didn't know his biological father, but he'd had plenty of stepfathers to compensate. His mother had fought addiction all her life and while currently sober, she was now on her fifth husband. Other than his mother, Trick knew of no other biological family, but he'd had plenty of step siblings and step grandparents. He was close to some, but not others. His upbringing had been unsettled at best and abusive at worst. He recalled how, at the age of ten, his mother had taken off with a new boyfriend and had left him alone. A week had passed with Trick walking himself to school and scrounging through what little was left in the fridge when the mother of his previous stepfather had knocked on the door. Trick had answered and she'd quickly deduced the problem, packed a bag for him, and had taken him home with her. His mom had eventually returned, picked Trick up, and before leaving with Trick, his step grandmother had laid into his mother about her parenting skills. Trick had heard every word.

He often wondered how close he'd come to being removed from his home by child services and put in foster care, but it had never happened. At the age of eighteen, he'd packed a bag and left his mother's house and never returned. He and his mom had a complicated relationship. As a Texas Ranger, he'd done his best to help her, and she'd been through several drug treatment programs. Some had stuck for a while, but others hadn't. Her current husband seemed more stable and supportive and Trick could only hope his mother would stay sober. Her struggles had been the reason Trick had been so determined to get Mason help when Trick had discovered his best friend had an addiction to pain pills. Trick had suffered enough through his mother's illness, and he'd seen what it had done to her, and Trick was not going to allow that to happen to Mason, even if it meant losing their friendship.

Mason had come through it, though, better than ever and seemed more at peace with himself than Trick had ever known him to be. Their friendship had strengthened because of it. They were like brothers and as close as Remalla and Daniels. Trick gave thanks every day that he had at least one stable relationship in his life.

Not that he didn't hope to settle down and get married one day, but after seeing his mother and her failed attempts at finding the right person, he often wondered if he'd have the guts to marry anyone, much less fall in love. Besides, he thought to himself, he was having too much fun playing the field. He thought of his date last week with a woman named Linda he'd met at Biggie's bar. They'd had plenty of drinks, danced to the music from the jukebox, and he'd gone home with her for a raucous night. He grinned at the memory.

Sipping his beer, he watched as the *Seinfeld* credits rolled across the screen and the news began. He reached for the remote to change the channel, when the top story flashed on the screen. A reporter stood on the side of the road near an overlook. There were police behind her and she mentioned how the body of a man had been found in the brush. The death had been violent, and police were investigating. After authorities had notified the family, they'd identified the victim as Jackson Trammel, a native out of L.A. who'd recently moved to San Diego.

Staring at the screen, Trick pushed up in his recliner, gripped his beer bottle, and cursed.

• • • • • • • • • •

The next morning, Trick pulled up near the overlook where Jackson's body had been found and parked on the side of the road. He spotted the crime scene tape encircling the area as he unbuckled his seatbelt and got out of his truck. The area, which had been bustling with police activity the prior evening, was now quiet. Trick spotted a police car parked further up the road and as he followed the perimeter of the scene, a car door opened, and an officer stepped out. Trick had anticipated that, and he waved as the officer approached.

"Can I help you, sir?" asked the officer. He was tall and thin, and he studied Trick with suspicious eyes.

Trick feigned innocence. "Hello, officer. I was coming to the overlook to check out the lovely view, but I see this." He waved a hand toward the tape. "What's going on?"

"This is a crime scene, sir. You can't enter the area."

"Crime scene?" Trick flashed an appropriately shocked look on his face. "You mind if I ask what happened?"

The officer tipped his head. "What's your name, sir?"

Trick smiled. "Name is Trick. I'm visiting from Texas. Friend of mine told me about this place and I had some time to kill, so thought I'd stop by."

The officer appeared to think but then nodded. "There was a murder, sir. This overlook will be closed until the police are ready to open it again. Sorry, but you will have to move along."

Trick dropped his jaw. "A murder? Up here? My friend told me this place was safe." He shook his head. "I'm from a small town and I'm not used to this big city crime." He put a hand to his chest. "Was it gang-related?"

"No, sir. We don't believe so. In all likelihood, it was probably a drug deal gone bad." He lowered his voice. "But you didn't hear that from me."

"Drugs?" asked Trick. "That was my next guess. Can't seem to go anywhere anymore without needing a police escort, huh?" He made a tsk-tsk sound. "That's why I like my small-town living. Don't lock the doors at night and everyone knows each other."

The officer nodded. "There aren't many places like that left. Especially not around here. You have a nice day, sir."

Trick got the message. "Thank you, officer. I guess I'll have to find another place to enjoy the view."

The officer returned to his car, and Trick headed to his truck. He got in, started it up, and did a U-turn. He drove down the road until he was out of sight of the police. Then he turned again and pulled into a rocky space off the side of the road. He made a quick deduction that if he stuck to the brush and trees, he could come up to the crime scene from below and the officer sitting in his vehicle would not see him unless he got out to look.

Satisfied he was in the best possible spot and not wanting to take long, Trick got out of his truck, darted into the trees and up the embankment. He was careful to stay away from the drop-off below him but followed it closely enough so he would recognize the overlook when he neared it. The day was cool, but the sun was out, and as he jogged up the hill, sweat popped out on his skin. The trees thinned and the brush became less dense, and knowing he had to be close, he spotted crime scene tape that cordoned off the area. He slowed his pace and dipped beneath it. Stopping to catch his breath, he noted his surroundings. Looking through the trees, he could see the city in the distance. He stepped closer to admire the view when he spotted a drop of something dark on the ground. Squatting, he touched it and confirmed it was blood. Looking around, he saw another droplet and then another beyond that. He followed the drops and stopped cold when he came across a large puddle of blood. The dirt and grass around the scene were disturbed and he saw footprints. The scene had obviously been processed by the police and he wondered if this is where the body had been found. Thinking back on the footage from the news, though, Trick recalled seeing officers milling around an area closer to the road. Were there two crime scenes? Had Jackson been attacked in one area and killed in another? Trick straightened and looked around, knowing he had to move further toward the overlook. He kept walking and it wasn't long before he spotted the bench at the viewpoint. He double-checked the area but saw no one. The patrol car was still up on the road and the overlook was just below it. Careful to stay out of sight, Trick passed a couple of rocky parking spots and approached the bench. He did a quick scan of the area and spotted a few more drops of blood near the bench that led back toward the bloody scene he'd just left. Obviously, something had happened here. The victim had been injured and had either run into the woods or had been taken into the woods and killed.

Trick spotted more crime scene tape that included an area beyond the other side of the bench. It ran up the embankment and back to the road near where the patrol car sat. He suspected this was the area focused on by police in the news footage. Ensuring he couldn't be seen, he crouched low and jogged back into the woods. Climbing uphill, he followed the dusty path toward the street near the patrol car. He stayed aware and kept his eyes open for another crime scene. It didn't take long before he found it. Blood droplets spattered an area of brush and Trick found additional blood sprayed on tree trunks and shrubs. Dropping low, he found another puddle of blood. Surveying the gruesome scene, he realized that whatever had happened here had been brutal. Squatting and studying the space, he felt slightly ill. If this is where Jackson Trammel had died, then it had been a violent death. He couldn't imagine what had happened or what Jackson had gotten himself into. Nothing about this scene implied a drug deal gone bad. This scene and the one below it implied rage.

Hearing another car from above, Trick shrank back. Hiding behind a bush, Trick peered out and saw a second vehicle stop behind the patrol car. Trick watched the officer he'd spoken to leave his car and approach the second vehicle. The doors opened and a man and a woman stepped out. Trick groaned to himself when he realized he recognized them. It was Detectives Bevins and Winkler. Two detectives whose history with Trick and Mason had been problematic at best. Winkler, the female detective, was decent enough, but Bevins, in Trick's experience, was a pain in the ass.

Muttering a curse, Trick scooted back behind the shrub, guessing that Bevins and Winkler must've been assigned to Jackson Trammel's murder case.

"Of course, it has to be Bevins and Winkler," he muttered to himself. Hearing the muffled voices from above, he figured he should get out of there before the detectives found him wandering through their crime scene. That would definitely not improve their strained relationship. Careful to move quietly, he backtracked over his steps, returned to the overlook, passed the additional pool of blood, and made it back to his truck.

Chapter Seven

SITTING AT HER DESK at SCOPE, Mikey hung up the phone. She opened her drawer, found a bottle of aspirin, and shook out two pills. She popped them in her mouth and swallowed them down with water. Although the alcohol had helped calm her after Dad's visit, that morning she'd woken up with a slight hangover. Mason hadn't felt much better.

Trick had picked them up, dropped them at work and had left, saying he had to do something related to his new case and he'd fill them in later. Mason and Mikey had simply nodded and waved when Trick had driven off. Needing food, Mason had left to get coffee and donuts while Mikey made phone calls.

The office door opened, and Mason entered, carrying a coffee tray and a paper bag. He walked to the table and set them both down. "Come and get it."

Mikey stood. "Thanks." She sat on the sofa and opened the bag. Seeing napkins, she pulled them out and set them on the table.

"How's your headache?" asked Mason, who'd sat beside her.

"Just took some aspirin. How's yours?"

"I may steal some of your aspirin."

"Feel free. Hopefully, the coffee will help." She grabbed a chocolate donut, bit into it, and sighed. "That's good."

Mason grabbed his own donut. "You get the calls made?"

Mikey nodded. "I talked to Max and prepared him for Dad's visit. I asked him to find out where they're staying so we can tell Daniels."

"What did he say about Dad?"

"Just that Dad had told him he'd planned to come to California, but Max didn't think he actually would. Then Dad had called Max a couple of days ago and had set up the lunch. Max didn't tell us because he didn't want to argue about it."

"What did he say about Vicki and Margaret?"

Mikey shrugged. "I'm not really sure he believed me. I figured he'll get confirmation when he sees Dad for himself."

Mason chuckled. "That will be a fun lunch."

"Too bad we can't film it." She sipped her coffee. "I talked to Daniels, too. Told him what we knew. He said he'd fill Lozano in and once we know where Dad is staying, they can watch the place for Margaret."

Mason nodded. "Good. How's he doing?"

Mikey took another bite, thinking about her conversation with Daniels. "Okay, I guess. But not great." She swallowed. "He and Marjorie are still separated, but I think they've had a few counseling sessions and are working on things."

Mason shook his head. "I hope they can figure it out. They've always seemed so happy."

Mikey hated the separation. She'd always liked Marjorie and had witnessed how much Daniels and his wife loved and supported each other during the worst of times. Daniels' cases had taken their toll though, and Marjorie had left after what had happened with Oswald Fry. Not that Mikey could blame her. Being married to a detective had to be hard enough. But dealing with everything Daniels had faced over the last year, it wasn't surprising Marjorie needed some time to reevaluate. "I hope so, too. Between Rem and Marjorie, Daniels has had a rough month. Now he's got that new partner Lozano wants him to train."

Mason raised a brow. "He's got a new partner?"

"Supposedly it's just temporary until Rem comes to his senses and returns to the force."

"But he resigned."

"Lozano didn't submit the resignation. He put it in as a leave of absence. So, technically, Rem still has the option to return."

"Smart," said Mason, "assuming he does." He picked up a donut. "I wonder how he's spending his time. He doesn't strike me as the sort to sit around all day." He bit into his donut.

Mikey wiped her lips with a napkin. "Get this. Daniels told me Rem's working at the zoo. His cousin got him a job there."

Mason coughed and swallowed his bite. "The zoo? What's he doing at the zoo?"

"Maintenance stuff, I guess. Cleaning cages, stocking food, whatever odd jobs they need done."

"I can't imagine that will be long term."

"Who knows?" Thinking of Rem, Mikey couldn't help but worry. She'd tried calling him, but he hadn't answered, and she didn't leave a message. Rem needed to know about Margaret, and Mikey also wanted to tell him about her father's visit. Rem was always good at talking things through with her. She'd been there for him after difficult situations, and he'd done the same for her. He was the rare friend she could say anything to and not fear judgement. Despite all that had occurred over the last few months, she and Rem had finally admitted their feelings for each other, but Margaret's antics, and Allison and her baby's death had halted everything and caused Rem to leave the force. He and Mikey had spoken a few times since, but Rem had not been in any place to discuss their relationship. If anything, he'd pulled away, and not just from her, but from Daniels, too. She'd been trying not to take it personally. Mikey had found herself in some dark places, too, and it had taken time to reemerge into the light. She was doing her damnedest to give him space, but at the same time, she wanted to give him a swift kick in the pants.

"I can't imagine he'll stay for long," she said. "I suspect after he's cleaned enough monkey and zebra poop, even police work would be more appealing." She played with the lid of her coffee cup and sighed, recalling their last evening together at Rem's place. She'd been rattled after Oswald Fry's attack and Rem had comforted her and confided in her about Allison's threat against him. Allison had offered to turn over the parental rights of her unborn child, Chloe, to Rem if he agreed not to testify against Allison. If he did testify, she'd told him he'd never see Chloe and neither he nor Chloe would ever be safe. Mikey had seen and felt Rem's struggle and if circumstances had been different, Mikey had no doubt Rem would have kissed her that night. Mikey had almost kissed him herself, but Rem had been correct. The timing hadn't been right.

Holding his napkin, Mason glanced at her. "Why don't you go see him?"

She came back to the present. "See him? You mean at the zoo?"

"Sure. Why not? You haven't been there in a while. You can go see the animals and talk to Remalla."

Mikey scrunched her face. "This coming from the man who doesn't want me to be alone and bitches every time I leave SCOPE to get the mail?"

"I'm not that bad."

"You kinda, sorta are."

Mason rolled his eyes. "I doubt Margaret will be lying in wait for you at the zoo. Plus, it's a lousy place to go after someone. Too many people. But if you want to do it, we can figure it out."

Mikey thought about it.

"Sometimes, a face-to-face meeting is all it takes to knock some sense into someone." He smiled at her.

"I'll think about it."

"Don't think too long. I know how much you miss him."

Mikey crumpled her napkin. "More than I care to admit."

"He'd probably like to see you, too. As much as he tries to hide from the world, it's only going to get harder. Loneliness is tough, and Rem won't stomach it for long." He pulled off a piece of donut. "Maybe seeing you will get him to realize that he needs to rejoin the world. Mourning is understandable, but at some point, you need to resume your life."

"I suspect he's waiting for the lab results. He's still stuck on whether Chloe was his child, and until he knows either way, he's going to retreat."

"He should know soon and that will help." Mason popped his bite of donut into his mouth.

Mikey wasn't so sure. "If that baby was his, it might make it worse." Her appetite waning, she set her donut down.

"No, you don't," said Mason. "Eat that. You need some food and worrying about Rem is making you waste away."

Mikey made a face and reluctantly picked up her donut. "I can't believe I have to be cajoled into eating. Especially something chocolate."

"Maybe it's a sign of the second coming."

"Considering everything that's happened, I wouldn't be surprised." Mikey heard the outer office door open, footsteps approach, and then the inner door opened. Trick walked in, his clothes dusty and holding his hat.

He saw them and walked over. "Jag Trammel was murdered, Bevins and Winkler are investigating and if it's a drug deal gone bad, I'll eat my hat."

Mikey frowned and sipped some coffee. Chewing, Mason stared and picked up the bag. "Would you like a donut?"

• • • • • • • • • •

Trick eyed the bag and the coffee they were sipping. "I'd love one." He took the bag. "Did you get me a coffee?" He pulled out a donut.

"Sorry. I didn't know when to expect you back," said Mason.

"That's fine. I'll make my own." Holding a donut, he set the bag down.

"I'm assuming whatever you're talking about has to do with the Trammel case," said Mikey. "Aren't they looking for someone?"

Trick went to the coffee machine. "Mrs. Trammel is. Her son. But his body was found yesterday at an overlook of the city. I saw it on the news. That's where I headed after I dropped you off." Holding the coffeepot, he went to the closet to fill it with water from the dispenser.

"You went to the crime scene?" asked Mikey.

"I did." Trick poked his head out of the closet as he filled the pot. "Jag's mother has questions she needs answered. I spoke to her on the way back. The police questioned her about Jag and wanted to know if he had a drug problem. Apparently, that overlook is the sight of past drug activity, and Bevins and Winkler, our brainiac detectives, obviously assume that's why he died and are ignoring everything else."

Mason swiveled on the couch. "How do you know it didn't have to do with drugs? Maybe you're assuming the worst, when the obvious reason is the truth."

The pot filled, Trick returned to the machine and added the water. "Give me some credit, Red. You and I are familiar with drug deals gone bad. Those players bring guns to the table, not knives. And they don't leave a bloodbath behind."

Mikey grimaced. "A bloodbath? How do you know that?"

Trick raised an eyebrow at her.

"Sorry I asked," said Mikey.

"Please tell me no one saw you," said Mason. "Especially Bevins and Winkler."

Holding the donut in his mouth, Trick added a filter and grounds and flipped on the machine. "Noonsame."

"What?" asked Mikey.

"He said 'no one saw me,'" said Mason. "I occasionally speak Trick."

Trick bit into the donut and took the rest out of his mouth. "I saw Bevins and Winkler though." He chewed, returned to the sofa and sat. "That's how I know they're on this case."

"Bevins and Winkler," said Mason with a sigh. "I thought they'd been reassigned to another division."

"Apparently, they're back," said Trick. "Maybe our division is short-handed."

"Lucky us," said Mikey. "Does Mrs. Trammel want you to investigate?"

"Hell, yes," said Trick. "She's devastated by her son's death and the last thing she wants is to have it look like her son was involved in something illegal. I told her I'd do some digging, but that there had to be more to it than drugs." His stomach still churned at the memory of the crime scene, but he still ate the donut.

"You can't be sure of that," said Mason. "Don't get her hopes up if you're not sure."

Trick set the remains of his donut on a napkin he'd grabbed from the bag. "You didn't see what I did. Whoever killed Jag wasn't pissed about drugs. They were in a rage. There was blood everywhere. Plus, there was a second crime scene, which means there was a second body the news didn't mention."

"A second body?" asked Mikey. "How do you know that?"

"Two separate locations, two pools of blood, both distinct from each other, with no blood trail leading from one to the other."

"If that's true, then where's the second body?" asked Mason. "Why wouldn't the news mention it?"

"Maybe they haven't found it," said Trick.

"Haven't found it?" asked Mikey. "What do you think happened out there?"

Wondering that himself, Trick rested his elbows on his knees. "Maybe Jag wasn't the only one at the overlook. Maybe he brought a friend. They could have been followed and someone attacked both of them."

"And left Jag's body but took the other?" asked Mason. "Why?"

"Don't know," said Trick. "But I'm going to find out." He glanced at his watch. "I figure I'll go to the bar where Jag worked and ask some questions.

See what I can learn. Then go to his apartment." He looked up. "You're welcome to join me and Kyle."

"Kyle?' asked Mikey.

Trick nodded. "He wants to learn the ropes. No time like the present."

"I would go," said Mason, "but I have an appointment with Tarina."

Trick frowned. "Didn't you just meet with her?"

Mason interlaced his fingers. "I did. But after Dad's visit, I thought it wouldn't hurt to see her again."

Trick eyed his friend, noting Red's pale face, which he'd attributed to the hangover. "You okay?"

Mason paused. "I'll admit, Dad's visit threw me. I called Tarina this morning and she advised me to come in today."

"Probably a good idea," said Mikey. "Can't hurt to talk about it."

"I'm glad you called her, Red," said Trick. "I'll take Kyle and let you know how it goes."

"Just be careful, okay?" asked Mikey. "The last thing we need is for Kyle's first case to endanger him. All this talk of bloodbaths and bodies makes me nervous."

Trick raised his hands. "Hey. He's with me. What could possibly happen?"

Mikey frowned and exchanged a look with Mason. "I'll make sure Daniels is on speed dial," she said.

"Call nine-one-one while you're at it and give them a heads up," said Mason.

"Good idea." Mikey took another bite of her donut and smiled when Trick smirked at them.

Chapter Eight

MASON SHIFTED UNCOMFORTABLY IN his seat. He eyed Tarina Phelps who sat across from him. Her short red hair framed her round face and her gold hoop earrings bounced when she spoke. He'd just finished telling her about the incident with his dad.

"How did you feel when your father left?" asked Tarina.

"I felt angry and frustrated. Plus..."

"Plus what?"

Mason expelled a long breath. "I don't know. Disappointed. Lacking."

Tarina nodded. "What do you mean by lacking?"

Mason poked at the armrest of his chair. "Dad has the unique ability of making me feel small. I guess there's some part of me that will always seek his approval. Since I hadn't seen him in a while, his obvious dislike of me had faded but when I saw him again, that feeling of being a disappointment brought back a lot of memories I'd rather forget."

"Sometimes, it's better to face the past rather than try to ignore it. Why do you think it is so important for you to have his approval?"

Mason's annoyance rose and he raised his voice. "Because he's my father. Everybody wants their father's approval." He softened his tone. "I could see it on Mikey's face, too. She wants his approval just as much as I do. And that pained me. I hate it that Dad makes her feel as rotten as he makes me feel, and that I can't do anything about it."

"So, not only do you feel that you don't measure up to your dad's standards, but you also feel guilty for the way Mikey feels?"

Mason rolled his eyes. "I wouldn't say that my dad has standards. I just wish he could look at me with some pride. The way he does Max. I want the same for Mikey."

Tarina crossed her legs. "Why do you think he's proud of Max?"

"Because Max followed the path Dad considers successful." He leaned back in his chair, trying to relax. "Max does what Dad wants. Has since he was a kid."

"You told me that growing up, your older brother would never reveal his abilities to your father. Then, Max leaves the house, goes to school, opens his business, and makes a lot of money. How much of that do you think comes from wanting his father's approval?"

"All of it."

Tarina rested an elbow on the edge of her cushioned chair. "Would you rather do what you're called to do and be who you are meant to be, and suffer your father's disapproval? Or would you rather be like Max?"

Mason shook his head. "I could never be like Max."

She paused. "Are you proud of yourself?"

Mason hesitated at the question and had to think about it. "I don't know. I know I'm not proud of some of the things I've done."

"Are you proud of how you've handled some of the things you've done?"

Mason shrugged. "I guess so."

Tarina bobbed her foot up and down. "Mason. You grew up in a house with a difficult and unsupportive father. Despite that, you became a police officer and then a Texas Ranger. You eventually embraced your gifts and moved to a different state to pursue a new career. You started a new life, faced your addiction, got treatment for it, and in the meantime, you pulled your sister out of a cult, reestablished a relationship with your former partner, dismantled a conspiracy at Windhaven, and let's not forget, put up with a psychotic older sister." She tipped her head. "I'm sure there are other things I could add to the list. Are you going to tell me you are not proud of that?"

Mason cleared his throat. "When you put it like that..."

"Maybe it's time you reevaluate whose opinion is worth considering and whose isn't. I have no doubt I could bring Mikey, Trick, Valerie, or Max into this room and they would tell you that they are proud of you."

Mason picked at the armrest again.

"Maybe it's also time you realize your father is not the man you've always wished he could be. It's hard for him to be proud of someone when he's not proud of himself. He can't give you what he doesn't have to give."

Mason squirmed. "I often wonder how his father treated him."

Tarina tapped her jaw with a finger. "That's a good observation. Perhaps the very thing you want from him is the very thing he wanted from his own father."

The thought made Mason sad. "That would explain a lot."

"It would." She paused and played with an earring. "You want to talk about the other reason you called me?"

Mason set his jaw and tensed in his seat.

"Are you still craving a pill?"

Mason wanted to shrink. He'd dreaded this conversation but knew he had to have it. The moment he'd woken that morning, the familiar craving had plagued him. In the past, the first thing he'd do after waking was pop a pill, but it hadn't been an issue since leaving Windhaven. He'd had moments where he'd considered using, but never an intense craving. The minute he'd opened his eyes that morning, though, he'd felt shaky and uncomfortable. He'd told Mikey it was due to the bourbon, but he knew it was more than that. It scared Mason to think that if there'd been a pill bottle in the house, he would've used again.

After discovering Windhaven's abuse of its patients and how they'd administered drugs without consent, Mason had attributed his successful recovery to the drug he'd been given. The Montes family, owners of a billion-dollar pharmaceutical company, had taken advantage of patients in treatment facilities to test a drug designed to end addiction and prevent further usage. One of the sons, Ruben, who'd supposedly left the company and was now a wealthy donor and philanthropist, had instigated the testing, but his family had taken the fall. Some patients had died and most of those involved in distributing the drugs had been arrested. The FBI had investigated, the treatment centers were closed, and Mason had gone home. He'd continued his therapy through outpatient sessions with Tarina and so far, his recovery had been easy. Until that morning.

He'd sweated through it and had made it to the office without Mikey or Trick suspecting his true problem. The coffee and donut had helped but his mind had drifted, and he'd continued to want a pill. It had disgusted and confused him.

"It's better now that I'm here," said Mason. "But it's still on my mind."

"Why do you think it hit you today?"

Mason scoffed. "It's not a big stretch to realize this correlates with my father's visit."

She studied him. "Have you ever considered how much your father has to do with your addiction?"

Annoyed again, Mason gripped the armrest. "I'm not much for blaming other people for my problems. I took the drugs, not him."

"That's very noble of you. But addiction is very much a mental disease. You were avoiding something by taking the pills. Think about it. What did the pills protect you from? What do you think taking the pill this morning would have helped with?"

Mason shifted again, wishing he was somewhere else. "I took the pills because I was weak. I couldn't face things in my life, and I got hooked."

She didn't back down. "That's a simplified answer, Mason. But you're not a simple man and I think you know what I'm asking." She paused. "What are you trying to avoid or protect yourself from?"

Mason groaned. He clenched his hands together and studied them. He thought of his youth and growing up with his father, mother, and siblings, and how he'd hated Dad and loved Mom. He remembered wanting to be like Max so his father would love him but at the same time, hating Max for his weakness and inability to stand up for himself. And worst of all, he thought of Mikey and how much he'd tried to protect her and how he'd failed when Margaret had swayed her to join Victor's cult, but eventually redeemed himself by helping Mikey to find herself again. Suddenly sad, he recalled hating his abilities for a time and blaming them for his problems. If he hadn't been able to speak to spirits, maybe he would have had a normal life.

An answer popped up in his brain and his chest tightened. "I think I'm protecting myself from the pain of disappointing not just my father but my family." He paused to collect himself. "Seeing Dad again brought up all my insecurities and guilt over my failures." His emotions surfaced and he blinked back tears. "I failed Margaret. Maybe if I'd been a better brother, she wouldn't be so messed up. And I failed Max by not supporting him more. I failed Mikey, too, but worst of all," he struggled to speak, "I failed my mother when she needed me the most." His voice caught and a tear escaped and slid down his cheek.

Tarina didn't say anything, and Mason reached for a tissue and blotted his face.

"Feel better?" asked Tarina.

Mason found it difficult to answer but managed to nod.

"Do you still want a pill?"

Mason wiped his eyes. "No. Not anymore." He sniffed. "But I'm scared that it will happen again."

She pursed her lips. "I'm sure it will. You're an addict, Mason. You'll deal with this for the rest of your life, but it will get easier, with time, patience...and acceptance."

Still emotional, he fiddled with the tissue.

"May I also suggest that you be careful with the alcohol?"

He frowned at her. "I've never had an issue with drinking."

"I didn't say you did, but alcohol weakens inhibitions, affects your judgement and is a depressant. Any one of those makes you susceptible to lowering your guard, but combine all three, and you have a recipe for disaster. It's like taking a muscle relaxant and trying to stay awake all night. It could be done, but you've made it a lot harder on yourself."

Mason sighed and swiped at another tear. "You make a good point. I'll be more careful."

Tarina put her hand on her knee. "And may I suggest something else?"

"What's that?" whispered Mason.

"That your recovery has far more to do with you and your hard work, and not from some drug given to you while you were at Windhaven. Can you at least give yourself some credit for that?"

Mason wiped his nose with the tissue. "That might be hard." His whole body was tense, and he tried to relax. "I tend to give credit to other things."

Tarina smiled. "Then may I also suggest that it's time to get over that? That you have a lot to be proud of? And that your father's issues and your sister's psychopathy have nothing to do with you?"

Mason's tears had slowed, and he felt calmer. "I can try."

Tarina leaned forward. "To paraphrase the magnificent Master Yoda," she said, "Do, Mason. There is no try." She raised a brow at him. "Got it?"

Mason sniffed again but he understood and smiled softly. "Got it."

• • • • • • • • •

Trick walked into the small bar called Bullard's. Kyle followed him in. "It's not that big," said Kyle.

Trick looked around. Kyle was right. It was a narrow space with the bar taking up the right side and a few tables and booths taking up the left. A country tune played from a jukebox that sat against the opposite wall, and a

TV behind the bar had a basketball game on. "Looks like my kind of place," said Trick.

"I'm not in bars often," said Kyle. "I don't like to drink alone."

"Who said anything about being alone?" asked Trick. "It's a great place to meet people."

Kyle smiled. "You mean it's a great place to meet women."

"It can be." Trick spotted an older man behind the bar with a towel resting on his shoulder. "Let's talk to him." Trick glanced at Kyle. "Be friendly and open, but not pushy."

Kyle nodded. "I got it. I'll follow your lead."

"Let's go." Trick walked up to the bar and sat on a stool. Kyle sat on another beside him.

The man saw them and came over. "Can I get you two something?" He pulled the towel from his shoulder and wiped his hands.

"We'd like to ask about—" started Trick. The door opened and a woman entered. Her short blonde wavy hair reached the tips of her ears and flattered her wide eyes and full lips. She wore snug jeans, a snugger T-shirt, and a leather jacket. He forgot his question when she approached the bar.

"Excuse me, sir," she said to the bartender. "I'm meeting someone here. You mind if I wait at the bar?"

The bartender shrugged. "It's a free country."

The woman glanced at Trick and Kyle. "Thanks." She sat on a stool a few down from Trick and pulled out her phone.

The bartender tossed his towel back over his shoulder. "You want some water?" he asked the woman.

She looked up. "Sure. Thanks." She went back to her phone.

Trick made a mental note to visit this bar in the future when Kyle nudged him. "The questions?"

Reminding himself why he was there, Trick focused back on the bartender. "We're here to ask about Jag Trammel. He worked here, didn't he?"

Grabbing a glass, the bartender frowned at them. "Who's asking?" He opened up a bin and scooped some ice into the glass.

Trick pulled out his identification and introduced himself as a private investigator. He introduced Kyle, as well. "Jag's mother hired us." He paused as the bartender filled the glass with water. "Did you know Jag?"

The glass full, the bartender placed it in front of the woman who glanced up, thanked him again, and took a sip.

"I hired him." The bartender walked back toward Trick and Kyle. "I'm Bart Bullard. I own the place. But everybody calls me Bull."

"Nice to meet you, Bull." Trick helped himself to a peanut from a bowl and popped it in his mouth. "I hope you can help us."

"You just missed the cops," said Bull. "Two detectives who I'm pretty sure have sticks up their ass."

"Oh, it's more than sticks," said Trick. "More like two by fours, especially the big guy."

Bull smirked. "You obviously know them."

"Unfortunately, yes." Trick shook his head. "Did they ask you about drugs? And if Jag had a drug problem?"

Bull furrowed his forehead. "Those assholes wouldn't know cocaine from flour."

Trick nodded. "That sounds like an accurate description."

Bull put his hands on the bar. "How is Jag's mom doing?"

"Not good," said Trick. "She wants to know what happened to her son and knows it's got nothing to do with drugs."

Bull straightened. "Jag was a good kid and a hard worker. It's hard to find in this business."

"What can you tell us about him?" asked Trick. "Did he hang out with anyone? Any friends or girlfriends?"

"He kept to himself a lot, but he was good with the customers." Bull grabbed the towel and wiped down the bar. "He sold a lot of drinks to the ladies. He was handsome and talkative and collected a lot of numbers. I know he had a girlfriend in L.A. but I'm pretty sure they broke up not long after Jag moved to San Diego."

Trick helped himself to another peanut. "Did he use any of those numbers?"

"Not that I'm aware of," said Bull. "At least not that he told me." He paused. "That last night though, he was talking to a pretty lady. It seemed like they hit it off. It was my early night, but I saw her before I left."

Trick raised his eyebrow. "Any idea who she was?"

Bull shook his head. "Never seen her in here before."

Trick looked around. "Any cameras?"

Bull stopped wiping the counter. "You mean the footage the police wanted to confiscate?"

Trick wasn't surprised. "Yes. That footage." He hoped they weren't too late. "Did you give it to our two favorite detectives?"

Bull stared before raising the side of his lip. "Not before I made a copy."

Trick breathed a sigh of relief. "I like you, Bull. I think this is my new favorite place." He glanced at the woman who still studied her phone. "For a lot of reasons."

Bull chuckled and followed Trick's gaze. "I can see that." He looked back. "Give me a second and I'll show you the footage."

"Take your time," said Trick, grabbing the edge of the peanut bowl. He shot another glance at the woman. "I'm going to say 'hi.'"

Bull dropped his towel on the bar. "Good luck. Something tells me you're going to need it."

"I'll bet you a beer I won't," replied Trick.

Bull pointed. "You're on." He turned, walked toward the door behind the bar and disappeared behind it.

Trick stood and Kyle leaned over. "Are you sure this is a good time?" asked Kyle.

"No time like the present." Trick picked up the bowl. "Watch and learn."

Kyle made a face, and Trick turned toward the woman on her phone and approached her. "You hungry?" He set the bowl in front of her.

She looked up and glanced at the bowl of peanuts. "I'm good, thanks." She typed on her phone.

"My name is Trick Monroe." He tipped his hat at her. "From the great state of Texas." He paused. "You from around here?"

"Yes." She barely looked up from her phone.

Trick sat on the stool beside her. "You're certainly pretty enough to be from Texas."

She had no reaction. "Thank you."

"I haven't lived in California long," said Trick. "If you're from around here, maybe you can show me the sights."

She sighed and looked up at him. "What would you like to see?"

Pleased he'd gotten her attention, he aimed a charming grin at her. "Anything you'd like to show me."

She put her elbow on the bar and rested her chin in it. "Can I ask you something?"

"Shoot. Anything you want."

She narrowed her eyes. "Does this whole cowboy thing actually work with women?"

Trick chuckled. "You'd be surprised how often."

Her face fell. "I'm sorry, Mr. Cowboy, but I'm not one of them. So take your cute Texas rear end back to the stool from where you came."

Not ready to give in, Trick rested his own elbow on the bar. "You think my rear end is cute?"

She smiled smugly. "It's not bad. I admit, you're not hard to look at, but I know boys like you. Love 'em and leave 'em. So let's get straight to the leave part and bypass all the rest."

Trick leaned in. "But you're skipping the best part."

She sighed. "From your perspective, but not from mine, I'd get more pleasure from a men's fashion magazine. It doesn't cost me much, the guys are hot, nobody expects anything in return, and it won't hurt my feelings."

Trick held her gaze. "How do you know I'll hurt your feelings?"

She studied him. "It's a look you all have, and it's written all over your face." She waved a finger. "Now move along, Cowboy. This cowgirl has other things to do." She went back to studying her phone.

Realizing he'd failed to charm her and feeling oddly sad, Trick nodded at her. "Sorry I bothered you. I hope you and *Gentleman's Quarterly* are very happy together."

She glanced up but then returned to her phone.

He stood. "If you change your mind, I'm just two stools down."

She scrolled. "Believe me, I'm aware."

Trick tipped his hat again and returned to his stool. Kyle smiled at him. "I learned a lot. Thanks."

"Granted, it's not the lesson I was hoping for, but even rejection will teach you something," said Trick.

"What's that?"

"When I know, I'll tell you."

Bull returned to the bar, holding a tablet. He glanced between Trick and the woman. "I believe you owe me a beer." He chuckled.

Trick grabbed another bowl of peanuts near Kyle. "I guess it's just not my day." He popped another peanut in his mouth, and eyeing the woman, felt a flicker of regret. There was something about her he found intriguing. Telling himself to move on, he gestured toward the tablet. "Is that the footage?"

"It is," said Bull. He set the tablet down on the bar and Trick could see a grainy image of the seats they were sitting in plus the other stools and the tables behind them. A man stood behind the counter and Trick recognized Jag.

Bull hit a button and the footage began to play. Jag served a customer and spoke with them. Another bartender helped another customer and then disappeared into the back. Trick checked the timestamp and saw it was close to midnight. A few seconds later, a woman entered the bar. Her dark hair was pulled up in a bun and she wore a dress. She sat at the same stool as Kyle, put her elbows on the counter and waited. Jag came over, spoke to her, and began to make a drink. He served her, and they started talking. The other bartender reappeared and served new customers while Jag and the lady continued to talk. Several minutes passed and Trick could tell from the conversation and their body language that the two of them liked each other. Bull came and went from the office, before talking to Jag, and then left.

"It goes on like that until just before closing," said Bull. He hit another button and the footage sped up until he slowed it down. Trick checked the time stamp again and it was one fifty a.m. Jag came around the bar, spoke to the woman and they left together.

"Any footage outside the bar? asked Trick. He wondered where they had gone after leaving.

"Nope. That's it," said Bull. "Whatever happened after that is between Jag and the mystery woman."

Kyle spoke up. "What about the other bartender?"

The door opened and another man walked in who looked familiar. He held an apron and waved at Bull.

"Hey, Charlie," said Bull. "You're ten minutes late."

Charlie entered the bar and put on his apron. "Sorry. I got stuck at the gym."

Bull shot him a hard look. "Then remind them you have another job." He looked back at Trick and Kyle. "This is Charlie. He was the other guy behind the bar with Jag." He picked up the tablet, scrolled back to where the woman entered the bar, and showed the footage to Charlie. "You have any idea who she is?"

Charlie's shoulders slumped and he looked at Trick and Kyle. "Is this about what happened to Jag?" His voice rose. "I'll tell you right now it had nothing to do with drugs. Jag never touched them. I should know. I offered—" He stopped and looked at Bull. "Well, never mind."

Bull scowled at him and held the tablet out. "Do you know her or not?"

"Yeah. I do." Charlie glanced at the footage again. "Her name is Eleanor."

· · • · • · • · · ·

Kyle spoke to Charlie. His long braid slid over his shoulder, and he brushed it back. "Do you know her last name?" Excited to be doing real investigative work, his heart was thumping. While he enjoyed the paranormal side of the business, it was almost too easy, and he welcomed a new challenge.

Trick looked at Kyle before returning his gaze to Charlie.

"No. She never told me. And I only met her once," said Charlie. "She came here the night before she met Jag, on Jag's night off. I was working the bar and you were out, too." He looked at Bull.

"I had my poker game," said Bull, "but I was back here by midnight. I didn't see her."

Charlie shook his head. "She'd left by then."

"Did you two talk?" asked Trick.

"We did." Charlie adjusted his apron. "But it was weird. I'm used to talking to customers, but she asked a lot of questions."

Kyle noted Charlie's bright blue aura and sensed his honesty. "What did she ask about?"

Charlie put a hand on the bar. "At first, it was the usual stuff. How's your day going? We talked about the weather. She told me her name and we kept chatting. I learned she's from Ohio and she moved here because she got a job as a singer in a night club. She'd broken up with her boyfriend in Ohio and was trying to adapt to a big city. Said she'd considered going to L.A., but it was so huge, it scared her." His face fell. "I told her she had a lot in common with Jag. He had a similar story." He paused. "I wonder if that's why she came back."

"How long did she stay?" asked Trick.

"That's where it got strange. She asked about me and my life. I told her I had a girlfriend who'd just given birth to our child, and how I'm working two jobs to pay for everything, and how we hope to get married. That's when her demeanor changed. She finished her drink, paid, and left, not long before Bull returned."

Trick nodded. "She may have been looking to hook up, and you obviously weren't available."

"But she hoped Jag was, and she came back the next night to meet him," said Kyle. "Seems strange."

"Nothing's strange when it comes to loneliness," said Trick. He spoke to Charlie. "Did she say where she sings?"

"No," said Charlie. "She didn't."

"Figures," said Trick. "Thanks for your help, Charlie." He pulled a card from his pocket. "You remember anything else, please call me. Even if it's the smallest thing."

Charlie took the card. "I will."

"And you should tell the cops what you told me," added Trick. "They need to know." He slid off the stool. "We need to find this Eleanor."

"I've got the detectives' contact information," said Bull. "I'll make sure he calls."

Trick nodded. "Thanks, Bull. I'll be back to buy you that beer." He glanced at the woman at the bar. "And maybe meet a pretty lady while I'm at it."

"You find out what happened to Jag and the beer's on me," said Bull. "You, too." He pointed at Kyle.

Kyle admired Bull's deep pink aura. "I appreciate it, but I'm not much of a drinker."

"Then I'll buy you a soda," replied Bull.

Kyle grinned, choosing not to tell Bull he didn't drink sodas either. "Thank you." He slid off his stool and followed Trick toward the exit.

Trick stopped and spoke to the woman who still studied her phone. He tipped his hat at her. "You take care, GQ."

She looked up. "You, too, Texas." She smiled and went back to her phone.

Trick left, and Kyle followed him back to the truck. They got in, and Trick sat behind the wheel. "What do you think?" he asked Kyle.

Kyle considered everything they'd learned. "If what you say is true about there being two victims, you think Eleanor's the other one?"

"I think it's possible, but we can't assume anything." Trick set his wrist on the steering wheel. "If she is, though, why would the police not tell the press?"

"Maybe there's something they don't want us to know."

"Oh, I'm sure of that. The question is what?" Trick started the ignition and pulled out onto the street.

"Maybe she's somebody important?"

"Even more reason to tell the press."

Kyle rested an ankle on his knee. "Maybe she's not dead, but injured, and they want to keep her safe."

"I doubt it. There was a lot of blood loss and if she's alive, she's hanging on by a thread." He paused. "We need to find out who she is. If she's still breathing, she's our best lead as to what happened to Jag." He rubbed his jaw. "What did you think of Charlie? You think he was telling the truth?"

Kyle nodded. "I think so. His aura stayed pretty consistent while he talked."

Trick glanced over at him. "His what?"

"His aura," said Kyle. "It was a deep blue. In my experience, an aura fluctuates colors when someone is lying, at least most of the time. Bull's was a dark pink."

Trick stared before looking back at the road. "What's mine?"

"Usually yellow, but it gets a little muddled if you're hungover."

Trick frowned. "Good to know. What about the lovely lady at the bar?"

Kyle smiled. "She was green, until you spoke to her. Then it turned red."

Trick smirked. "I bet it did."

"So did yours. But for a different reason, I think."

Trick sighed and tapped the steering wheel. "You're going to do just fine at this job, Kyle." He stopped at a stop sign and kept driving. "Just fine."

Chapter Nine

MIKEY SAT AT HER desk at SCOPE, scrolling through various social media, trying to fill her time. The office was quiet, and she tried to enjoy the silence, but her thoughts drifted to both Dad and Rem, and that annoyed her, so she'd gone online to distract herself.

The previous day had stayed busy as she followed up on clients and called potential new ones. Mason had gone to his appointment with Tarina, and Trick and Kyle had gone to the bar where Jackson Trammel had worked. Max had called after his lunch with Dad with the appropriate amount of shock and horror. Mikey had talked to him long enough to calm him down and was pleased when Max gave her the name of the hotel where Dad and Vicki were staying. After hanging up with Max, she'd called Daniels to let him know. He'd told her he'd inform Lozano and had thanked her for the heads-up.

Mason had gone home after his therapy appointment and Mikey was glad he had. They'd both needed a little time and distance from Dad's visit.

That morning, though, Mason hadn't mentioned Dad or his talk with Tarina and he'd jumped back into work as if nothing had happened. Mikey hadn't said anything other than suggested he take it easy and not push himself, but he'd told her he was fine and had left to do a reading for a grieving family who'd lost a son.

Mikey hoped Mason was okay. Readings were difficult enough, but when it involved a tragedy and occurred right after an ugly altercation with a parent, Mikey couldn't help but worry about her brother. She'd tossed and turned herself the last two nights, and she'd come to a decision about Dad and Vicki, which she knew would displease Mason, but she wanted to do it anyway.

Bored with her scrolling, she wondered what to do about lunch when she heard the door open and saw Mason enter SCOPE on her monitor. She swiveled in her seat, and he entered the office. He was dressed in his typical pressed jeans, boots and ironed long-sleeve shirt. His trimmed handlebar mustache was neatly combed, but his eyes looked tired and there were shadows beneath them.

"Hey," she said. "How'd it go?"

Mason hung his hat on the rack beside the door. "It was rough." He put his hands on his hips and stared off. "Their child drowned in their pool."

Mikey sat up. "That's horrible."

Mason nodded. "The parents are a mess, but I managed to stay detached, and their son came through and spoke to them." He rubbed his eyes. "It was hard, but by the end, I think it helped."

Mikey stood. "Go sit and rest." She walked over and put a hand on Mason's shoulder. "You want some coffee? I just made a pot."

Mason groaned with fatigue. "I'd love one." He went to sit on the couch. "Where's Trick?"

Mikey knew Mason was tired because she'd told him Trick's plans earlier. "He and Kyle went to meet Jag's mother at Jag's apartment, remember?"

"That's right." Mason laid his head back. "I forgot."

Mikey filled a cup with coffee and added some of the cream they kept in a small fridge in the closet. She stirred it and brought it to Mason. "Here. Have you had lunch?"

Mason raised his head. "No." He took the coffee. "Thanks."

"I'll order something."

"I'm not that hungry." He sipped his drink.

"You aren't now, but you will be. These readings take the stuffing out of you. I still think you should have postponed this one until next week."

Mason shook his head. "I'm not going to let Dad dictate my schedule."

"Don't be ridiculous, Mason. In case you've forgotten, you haven't been out of rehab that long. Tarina told you to take it easy. You're pushing yourself too hard."

"I'll be okay."

"I know you will." Mikey braced herself. "I moved all your remaining appointments this week to next week. You're officially on a staycation."

He lowered his coffee. "You did what? What for?"

"You know what for." Mikey turned to face him. "And don't be mad. You worry about me enough. Now it's time for me to worry about you. You need a break. Dad rattled us both."

"Sitting around, doing nothing, is not going to help my mental state. I need to keep busy."

"Who said you were going to be sitting around? I've got stuff for you to do. Just not work stuff."

He narrowed his eyes. "Like what?"

Mikey shifted and settled back on the cushions. "How'd you like to accompany me to the zoo?"

His face lost some of its tension. "I see."

"Like you said, we haven't been in a while. I figure we can go and walk around, see some animals..."

"And if we just happen to bump into Remalla..."

She fiddled with a loose thread on a cushion. "You can go check out the pandas while he and I talk."

He stared and then nodded. "I suppose we could do that." He set his coffee cup down. "Anything else you have planned for this staycation?"

Mikey pulled harder on the thread. "I thought it would be nice to make lunch or dinner plans with Vicki." She prepped for the outburst.

Mason stilled and stared at her, then started to laugh. "That's funny." He pointed. "That's a good one, Mikey. You almost had me."

"I'm not kidding."

His face fell. "We are not having lunch or dinner with Dad and Vicki."

"I didn't say Dad. I meant just the three of us. Don't you think we should get to know her? She is going to be our stepmother."

Mason dropped his jaw and raised his voice. "She is not going to be our stepmother. If they get married, I'll...I'll..."

"What? Shave your mustache?"

He scrunched his face. "Yes. I'll shave my mustache."

"I'll remember you said that."

"Go right ahead." He rested his elbows on his thighs. "And what for? We're not going to have any sort of relationship with them."

"Mason, listen." Mikey sat up. "Dad's not getting any younger. One of these days he's going to die. You want our last words to him to be what was said the other day?"

"That's on him. Not us."

"I know that, but it still doesn't make it right. I think we should at least talk to Vicki. She obviously sees another side to him. Maybe we should find out what that is."

Mason sighed and held his head. "Mikey—"

"I'm not saying this will solve anything, but at least we'll know we tried. Have you stopped to think that she may be able to help?"

"Unless she's a saint sent down from heaven, I doubt she can do anything when it comes to Dad."

"How will we know unless we make the effort? You know how Dad likes his happy hour. We'll just call and see if she wants to meet while he's occupied. The worst that can happen is she says no."

Mason turned his head toward her. "That's not the worst that can happen. If Dad shows up..."

"We'll tell Vicki we want to meet with just her. Dad can at least appreciate that we want to get to know her. I doubt he'd want to be there anyway."

Mason held his head again.

"I'll call her," said Mikey. "See if we can set something up before they leave."

Mason didn't answer.

"I can't force you to go, but I'm going either way."

Mason blew out a breath. "Fine. I'll go. But if this backfires, I'll sit nearby while you and Rem are talking at the zoo and sing 'Rem and Mikey, sitting in a tree, K.I.S.S.I.N.G...'"

Mikey smacked him in the shoulder. "You wouldn't dare."

He smirked at her. "Try me."

. . . .

Trick held his hat and looked out the window of Jag's apartment onto a grassy courtyard below. Mrs. Trammel stood in the living room, her eyes red and swollen and she sniffed.

"Jag never mentioned a woman named Eleanor to me," said Mrs. Trammel. "You think she has something to do with this?" She dabbed her eye with a tissue.

Kyle grabbed another tissue from a box on an end table and handed it to her. "You sure you want to stay here, ma'am?" asked Kyle. "We can talk somewhere else."

She shook her head. "No. I don't want to go somewhere else. And, please, I keep telling you. Call me Sheila."

Kyle nodded. "Can I get you some water, then?"

Sheila sighed. "Sure. Thank you."

Kyle headed into the kitchen.

Sheila walked over to Trick. "He's nice."

"That he is," said Trick. He glanced back toward the interior of the apartment. "There's nothing I see here that will help with figuring out what happened to Jag." The police had searched the apartment earlier and although Jag's place was sparse, they'd left a mess behind. "Unless the police found something of interest."

"I was outside while they searched. They looked rather bored. They certainly didn't act like they'd found a smoking gun, and certainly not drugs."

Trick nodded. "That's good. From what I've learned, there's been nothing to indicate this is drug related, other than where the crime occurred."

"You think this Eleanor can be found?" asked Sheila.

Trick had not mentioned to Jag's mother his perusal of the crime scene and his suspicion that two people had been killed. "We're going to try. We know she's a singer in a nightclub, so Kyle and I are going to start waving her picture around the downtown club scene. Surely someone has seen her."

She dabbed her nose. "Money is not an issue. If you need to hire additional people to help search for her, let me know."

Trick sympathized with her. "Let's just stick with us first. We'll see if we make any progress. If we need help, I'll let you know."

Kyle returned with a glass of water. "Here you go, Ma'am....I mean Sheila."

"Thank you," said Sheila. She took a sip and smiled at Kyle. "You know, if you lived closer, I'd introduce you to my daughter. She'd be absolutely smitten with you."

Kyle blushed. "That's kind of you to say."

"Did I embarrass you?" asked Sheila. "I rarely see a man blush."

Kyle chuckled softly. "I don't often get noticed by parents wanting to set me up with their children. It took me by surprise."

"My dear," said Sheila. "I assure you. You get noticed. Most just don't have the courage to speak up." She blotted her cheek with the tissue. "My daughter would be mortified by my assertiveness until she met you, but then I suspect she'd change her tune."

Trick watched Kyle smile and then glance back at Trick, looking uncomfortable. "Kyle's getting over someone, Sheila. I think he'll need some time before jumping into the shark den again."

"I appreciate the thought, though," said Kyle.

Sheila smiled softly. "Well, if you ever change your mind and find yourself up in L.A., let me know."

"I will," said Kyle.

Sheila drank some water and set the glass on the coffee table. "I taught my children not to back down when they want something. It's much better to face your fears then dwell on them. Dora, my daughter, she's a little shy, but Jag, he...he..." Her eyes welled with tears. "He was so brave." She put the tissue to her lips and her breath caught.

Kyle took her elbow and Trick walked up to her. "You should sit, Sheila," said Kyle.

"You sure you don't want to leave?" asked Trick. "It can't be easy being in Jag's apartment."

She composed herself. "No, no. I want to be here. I feel close to him. Besides, I've got people coming tomorrow to help me clean out Jag's stuff. I'm going to stay here tonight."

"Are you sure that's a good idea?" asked Kyle.

Sheila nodded and swiped at a fallen tear. "Absolutely. I wouldn't want to be anywhere else." She exhaled. "And you two need to get going. You have things to do. Sitting here, comforting me is not going to help you find out what happened to my son."

Trick glanced at Kyle, who held Sheila's elbow. "You sure you don't want to call someone to be with you tonight?" asked Trick.

"Nonsense. I'll be fine. Tomorrow will be the true test." She sniffed. "Now, you two get going and keep me updated." She stared at them with a steely gaze. "I want to know what happened to my son."

Trick eyed Kyle. "You heard the lady. Let's go."

Kyle let go of Sheila's elbow. "If you need anything, please call us."

"I won't need anything," she said. "Now head out. I'm not paying you to console me."

Trick walked to the door and opened it. "You're a strong lady, Sheila. Jag would be proud."

She dabbed at her eyes. "Thank you. I'd like to think so."

Kyle joined Trick and they left the apartment.

Walking down the sidewalk toward Trick's truck, Kyle sighed deeply. "That was really hard."

"This case is a tough one," said Trick.

"I had to put up some shields to block some of her emotion, otherwise, I would have lost it myself."

Trick glanced back at him. "You have that whole empath thing, like Mikey?"

Kyle nodded. "I do." He shook out his hands. "It can be overwhelming at times."

They got to the truck and Trick unlocked the doors. "I've seen Mikey struggle with it." He slid in behind the wheel.

Kyle opened his door and sat in the passenger seat. "She may have it worse than I do." He closed his door. "And thanks for helping me out in there. I wasn't sure what to say when Sheila brought up her daughter."

"You kinda had the deer in the headlights look."

Kyle chuckled. "I suppose." He looked out the window. "I mean, I'm not opposed to meeting someone new, but when she mentioned meeting her daughter, I just sort of shrunk." He hesitated. "I guess I'm more upset by Mikey's choice than I thought."

Trick put his hand on the wheel, debating how much to say. He'd had plenty of conversations with Mikey about Kyle and Rem, but he and Kyle had never spent enough time together to delve into personal matters. "You want to talk about it?" He knew Kyle was close to his mother and grandmother and figured Kyle might need a male perspective.

Kyle shrugged. "Not much to talk about. She wants someone else. It hurts but I can accept it." He rested his elbow on the armrest. "I've just liked her since the moment I met her."

Trick understood Kyle's pain. He'd had a few painful rejections himself over the years and they were never easy. "Listen, Kyle. This isn't about you. Mikey cares about you a great deal, and if Remalla hadn't been in the picture when you and Mikey met, then it may have gone in a different direction. But that's not what happened, and unfortunately, you've been rowing upstream since you met her."

"I get it. Remalla seems like a nice guy."

"It's not just that. She and Rem have both been through some hard times, and they've been there for each other. That forges a bond that's hard to break. Plus, they just have that thing between them."

Kyle raised a brow. "What thing?"

"You know. That thing that certain couples have that either makes them or breaks them. The kind of connection that if they can stay the course through some muddy waters, they'll be together forever, but if they can't, they'll end up hating each other. Kind of like Liz Taylor and Richard Burton."

"Who are they?"

Trick slumped in his seat. "Don't piss me off, Kyle. I'm trying to help you here."

Kyle looked away. "So I guess I shouldn't wait and see if they end up hating each other?"

"That's a lousy waste of your time. And even if they do, they'll still want one another. It'll be confusing and detrimental to anyone else who's attracted to them. My advice is to move on."

Kyle rubbed his forehead. "Easy to say. Harder to do."

Trick tapped the steering wheel. "If there's one thing I've learned, Kyle, in my wacky path of love and relationships, is that you never know what's around the corner. You think you're in love with someone, and then you meet someone else who takes your breath away." He reached over and patted Kyle on the shoulder. "Just hang in there. Mikey isn't the only star in the sky. There's a lot of them. It's like looking up at night in a big city. You can't see them, but you know they're there."

Kyle didn't look convinced. "You think?"

Trick started up the truck. "I don't think. I know."

"Okay. I told myself to stay positive and I will." He sighed. "Thanks for the pep talk. I needed it."

"You got it. You ever need to talk again, Mason and I are always happy to help." He put the car in drive.

Kyle looked over. "Thanks." He stared for a second, then frowned and pointed. "Do you see that car? Across the street?" He leaned forward. "Isn't that...?"

Trick turned to see a white four-door car parked at the curb opposite his truck. A woman sat behind the wheel. He narrowed his eyes and sucked in a breath. "That's GQ." The woman from Bull's bar was in the driver's seat.

She glanced in his direction, and he started to open his door when she abruptly peeled away from the curb and shot off down the street.

"Oh, hell to the no," said Trick. He shut his door and hit the accelerator. The truck's tires squealed, and he shot off after her.

Kyle grabbed the armrest. "What are you doing?"

"That woman is following us." He got close enough to read her plates. He repeated the numbers and letters to Kyle. "Memorize it."

The woman picked up speed, weaving through traffic and running stop signs. Trick followed as closely as he could but was acutely aware of the surrounding vehicles. He zoomed through a light and a car honked at him.

"You should slow down," said Kyle.

"She's good, whoever she is." Trick drove faster. He darted around another car and hit the brakes when a delivery van pulled in front of him. "Damn it." He sped around and flew past it, looking for the white car. He spotted it ahead at a light. It zipped through just as the light changed. Trick tried to get across just as a truck started to cross the intersection.

"You're not going to make it," yelled Kyle, clutching the seatbelt.

Trick hit the brakes and squealed to a stop, narrowly missing the truck, which blared its horn at Trick. Trick had no choice but to wait for the light to change, and when it did, he took off again, but as he zoomed down the road, the white car was gone. It, and the woman, had disappeared.

Chapter Ten

"Soup's ready," said Mason, stirring the chicken tortilla soup in a pot on the stove.

Mikey checked her phone. "Daniels says to go ahead and start. He got caught up at the station, but he'll be here soon."

Trick grabbed some bowls and spoons. "You don't have to tell me twice." He set them on the table and took a bowl to the stove.

Mikey added a bowl of chips and put the guacamole on the table. "Did you talk to Valerie, Mason?"

"I did," said Mason. "She's caught up in a case of her own. She'll be here, but probably not for another hour. I told her I'd save her a bowl. What about Kyle?"

"He's got a birthday party to go to, so he won't make it," said Mikey, hoping Kyle wasn't avoiding her. Mason and Trick already had their beers and Mikey grabbed one for herself from the fridge.

Trick helped himself to a bowl of soup. "Looks fantastic, Red." He set the ladle down and went to the table.

Mikey grabbed a bowl and handed it to Mason. The whole house smelled delicious, and her mouth watered. "I'm glad you made extra," she told Mason.

"It's been a while," said Mason, "plus I know Trick and I will come back for seconds."

"Probably Daniels, too." She scooped some into a bowl and offered the ladle to Mason. She went to the table and set the bowl down when there was a knock on the door. Mikey went over and opened it. "Hey," she said to Daniels. She noted his weary features and slimmer face. His blonde hair was longer, and he brushed it off his face. Normally a big guy with broad shoulders and a muscled frame, he seemed smaller, and she could tell he'd lost some weight. "Come on in." She held the door open.

"Thanks, Mikey." He entered holding his jacket.

"I'll take that." She hung the jacket on a hook in the front closet. "Glad you could make it."

"I appreciate the invite. I've been hearing about Mason's famous tortilla soup for a while now. I'm glad I finally get to try it."

"Well, it's the least we could do," she said. "I figured if I'm going to keep bugging you for information, we should feed you."

"C'mon in," said Mason, holding his bowl. "Help yourself." He put his bowl on the table and handed one to Daniels as he entered the kitchen. "There's beer in the fridge."

"Great," said Daniels, taking the bowl. "It smells incredible."

Trick sat and picked up his beer, and Mikey sat beside him. "Once you have some of Red's tortilla soup, you won't eat it anywhere else," said Trick. He picked up a chip, dunked it in some guacamole and ate it.

Daniels filled his bowl from the pot on the stove, grabbed a beer on the way to the table and sat between Mason and Mikey.

"I texted Rem and invited him," said Mikey, "but he said he's taken somebody's shift tonight." She halfway wondered if Rem had told her the truth.

Daniels set his napkin in his lap. "I asked, too. He told me the same."

Trick slurped from a spoonful of soup. "His loss. He doesn't know what he's missing." He ate the spoonful and moaned. "You've outdone yourself, Red."

"I added a little extra kick to this one," said Mason. "If you want some sour cream, let me know."

Mikey ate some. "It's perfect." She helped herself to a chip and some guacamole. "The guac is great, Trick."

"I aim to please," said Trick, smiling.

Daniels twisted off his beer cap and took a sip. He ate some soup and moaned. "They're not lying, Mason. It's delicious." He scooped up another spoonful. "Rem's going to regret not making it."

Mason lowered his spoon. "I heard he's working at the zoo."

Daniels nodded. "For the moment, at least. Says he likes it, and it keeps him busy."

"Likes it?" asked Mikey. "I wonder how long that will last."

Daniels lowered his spoon. "There's no telling."

"How's your new temporary partner?" asked Mikey. "And I use temporary intentionally."

"I appreciate that," said Daniels. "I prefer to say temporary myself." He set his spoon down and picked up his beer. "I'm training him. He's been a cop for six years, but you know how it is when you're new at something. Everything is by the book. If I do anything outside of the rules, he questions me on it. Add to that, the guy's a health nut."

Mikey stopped chewing and eyed Daniels.

Daniels raised a hand. "I know. I'm a health nut, too, but not compared to Manetti. He counts his macros, warns me against anything that isn't organic, drinks eight, eight-ounce glasses of water a day religiously and works out five times a week. It's like I'm Rem compared to this guy."

Trick looked up from his soup. "That's a strange twist." He grabbed a chip. "Does he at least have some brains? I could deal with all that if he at least knows what he's doing."

Daniels picked up his spoon again. "There have been a few moments where I've wondered, but then he redeems himself. I think it's going to be a 'wait and see' situation." He scooped up some soup. "We're currently working a murder case where a man was shot in his office. The business partner took off and we're trying to locate him, and the wife of the vic has had multiple affairs and planned to leave him. They both benefited financially from his death and we're trying to figure out who did it." He took a bite of soup.

"Sounds like an interesting first case for a new detective," said Mason.

"Too bad you didn't get the Jackson Trammel case," said Trick, through a mouthful of guacamole.

"I asked Lozano about that," said Daniels. "Bevins and Winkler were brought into help, like you thought. If Rem and I were together, we could have handled it, but Lozano wants me to focus on getting Manetti trained and our murder case. Plus, we've been looking into a series of convenience store robberies, so that doesn't help."

Mikey swallowed some soup. "Did you learn anything about the car following Trick?"

Daniels helped himself to a chip. "I ran the plates. It's registered to a seventy-three-year-old man whose car was stolen last month."

Trick sighed. "It's a stolen plate. So much for that lead."

"You're sure she was following you?" asked Mikey.

"Definitely," said Trick. "I suspect she wasn't meeting anyone in that bar. She was there to listen to our conversation."

"But why?" asked Mikey.

"Maybe she's looking into Jag's death," said Mason. "Maybe she's been hired by someone just like you have."

"So she follows me to get her information?" asked Trick. "That's an unorthodox way to investigate. How does she know I'm any good? I could be leading her on a wild goose chase." He drank some beer.

Daniels wiped his mouth with a napkin. "I did some digging into the case. It's possible she's working for someone else. Jackson wasn't the only victim."

Trick stilled and held his beer. "I knew it. There's a second body?"

Daniels put his napkin back in his lap. "There's a second crime scene. But no body."

Mikey frowned, wondering what Daniels meant. "There's evidence that someone else was murdered, but the body is gone?" she asked.

"Exactly," said Daniels. "Bevins and Winkler won't be happy if they discover I snooped, but I'll take the risk." He ate another chip. "Jackson Trammel's neck was slashed open, and he had numerous cuts and scrapes. The working theory is he was trying to get to his car but was attacked and dragged into the brush." He took a mouthful of soup and swallowed. "The second scene is much like the first except no victim. Forensics indicates the blood is from a male, but not Jackson Trammel."

Trick sat back. "That rules out Eleanor."

"Eleanor may have nothing to do with this," said Mikey. "All you know is that Jag met her his last night at the bar. Nobody knows what happened after that."

"She went there the previous night, too," said Trick. "That makes me think she was looking to meet someone. The question is for what? Is she our murderer?"

Daniels glanced over. "You think this woman slashed two men to death in the brush and then dragged one of them away?"

"Maybe drugs were involved," said Mason. "She'd have to be on them to do that." He scooped out some guacamole from the bowl and added it to his soup. "And who was the second man and why was he there?"

"No one knows," said Daniels. "They've checked missing person reports with no luck and the DNA isn't in CODIS."

Trick dug out a piece of chicken with his spoon. "Eleanor is the key. We find her and we'll get some answers."

"That's not going to be easy," said Mikey. "You said Eleanor left a boyfriend behind in Ohio. Maybe he's involved?"

"It's possible. We won't know anything until we locate her. It'll take some time, but if we show her picture around in the right places, someone's bound to have seen her, especially if she's picking up men in bars." Trick chewed the chicken.

"If she'd been to Bullards a couple of times," said Mason, "she might live in the area."

"I checked missing persons for anyone named Eleanor, but no luck," said Daniels.

"I appreciate that," said Trick. "We owe you." He stood. "Anyone want another beer?" He went to the fridge and opened it.

"Not for me," said Mikey.

Mason shook his head. "I'm limiting myself to one tonight. Tarina suggested I hold off on the booze."

Trick grabbed a bottle and closed the fridge. "Really? Is drinking an issue?" He returned to his seat. "Or does this have something to do with your dad?"

Mason stirred his guacamole into his soup. "Both, if I'm honest. Drinking can, well...make recovery challenging." He paused and played with his soup with his spoon. "Dad's visit brought out some cravings I hadn't felt in a while."

Mikey sensed his discomfort and was relieved he'd gone to Tarina for help. "You didn't mention that." She faced him. "I knew you were pushing yourself too hard."

Trick eyed him. "You doing better now?"

Mason nodded. "I am, but it scared me. That's why I called Tarina."

"I'm glad you did," said Mikey.

"Your dad visited?" asked Daniels. "I didn't think you guys were close."

"We aren't," said Mason. "It was a surprise for all of us. He showed up with a fiancée half his age who he's known for three months. And that was the best part of the visit."

Mikey told Daniels more about their conversation with their father. "It rattled all of us."

"I can see why," said Daniels. "I'm not close with my father either and I know how I would have felt. It's good you've got someone to go to for help." He paused. "Marjorie and I, we've been going to a counselor." He stared at his soup. "It's hard."

"Family stuff always is," said Trick. "But you and Marjorie have a good foundation. That will help."

Daniels nodded. "It does, but man, it's tough going home to an empty house. I hate it. I guess I'm used to the chaos."

Mikey empathized with him. "You and Marjorie are meant for each other. Good marriages have rough patches. You guys will get through this one. I believe that."

Mason set his spoon down. "You mind if I ask, do you have a counselor for yourself?" he asked Daniels.

Daniels picked up his beer. "Our therapist suggested that, but I haven't looked into it."

"I can give you Tarina's information," said Mason. "She's excellent and it might keep you sane through all of this. Especially since you're not just dealing with a separation from your wife, but also from your partner."

Daniels took a long pull from his beer and set his bottle down. "I can't say it's been a month I'd like to repeat."

"You should consider Tarina," said Mikey. "Maybe Rem should see her, too." She played with her napkin. "Is he getting counseling?"

"I asked, but he brushed me off," said Daniels. "He's still in retreat mode, and I'm wondering how to pull him out of it."

"I've tried to talk to him, too," said Mikey, "but he won't go there. He's pulled away. I've stopped by his house a couple times and he's either not there or he's not answering." Her appetite fading, she set her spoon in the bowl. "It's so frustrating."

"He's good at disappearing when he wants to, but he's always found his way back before," said Daniels. "He's waiting for that lab report. He wants confirmation on Chloe's paternity. Until he knows that, he's going to hunker down. My hope is once he knows, he'll start to deal with it."

Mikey sighed. "I want to go to the zoo and see him."

Daniels glanced at her. "You should go. Despite his efforts to keep to himself, I think he'd like that. Maybe seeing you will help jolt him back to reality."

"Or drive him back into the shadows," said Mikey.

"I don't think so," said Daniels. "If he's difficult, then get in his face. It may be time for a little confrontation."

Mikey hated that possibility. "I'll do it if I have to. I just don't want to make things worse." She shook her head. "How do I make him see that he's turning away from all the good in his life? He's got people who love and care for him and a job he's devoted to. They're all there, just waiting for him."

"He's been through trauma, Mikey," said Mason. "You know how that goes. It takes time. Think of all he's endured the last six months. Chloe was the last straw." He dabbed his mustache with his napkin. "I had to be patient and give you time to see the light. Rem is going to need the same thing. But once he figures it out, he'll race back. To both of you."

Mikey prayed Mason was right. "Were you this frustrated with me?" she asked Mason.

Mason half-smiled. "It was a good thing I was on the wagon at the time or else I would have taken a lot of drugs." He chuckled when Mikey dropped her jaw at him. "I'm just kidding. It's just a little humor to lighten the mood."

Trick chuckled, too. "Something tells me, Red, that you considered jumping off that wagon a few times."

Mason smirked at him. "Maybe a couple."

Mikey frowned at him. "Was I that bad?"

Mason softened his gaze. "You were under a cult leader's influence who was manipulating you with drugs and convincing you that I was a liar and a fraud. And our sister was helping him. To say you were a little resistant is an understatement. But once you started to realize the truth, you came around quickly." Mason reached over and put his hand on her wrist. "You found your way and so will Rem. But it's going to take a little help from all his people. You're a pivotal person in his life, just like Daniels. Between the two of you, you'll get through his armor and guide him back." He squeezed her wrist. "Just be honest with him. He may not like it at first, and his defense mechanisms will be triggered, but that's normal."

Mikey groaned and held her head. "This sucks."

"I told you this would take time and to prepare to ride it out," said Mason.

"I was hoping you were wrong," said Mikey.

"I wish you were wrong, too," said Daniels. "This business of losing Rem and Marjorie at the same time is brutal." He let go of a long breath.

Mikey told herself to stop complaining. As tough as it was for her, she knew it had to be ten times worse for Daniels. "I can imagine," she said.

Mason set his elbows on the table. "You know you're not alone."

Daniels took another swig of beer. "It doesn't feel like that."

Mason went quiet, narrowed his eyes and stared off. Then he looked back at Daniels. "Have you had a toy, or some sort of game, go off in your house?"

Mikey eyed her brother and felt the energy in the room. She realized he was communicating with someone, and they weren't physical.

Daniels stilled and he furrowed his brow. "One of J.P.'s trucks. Its siren goes off every night when I go to bed. I can't figure out what's wrong with it."

"There's nothing wrong with it," said Mason, interlacing his fingers. "You're getting a message, Detective." He stared off again.

"A message?" asked Daniels. "From who?"

Mason smiled. "Your sister. Melinda, is it?"

Daniels gripped his beer. Mikey recalled learning that Daniels' older sister, whom he'd been close to, had died when he was a teenager.

Mason continued. "She's telling you that she's there, and that she's working on things from her end."

Daniels swallowed. "Melinda's been sounding the siren on J.P.'s truck?"

"She has," said Mason. "She's with you often." He paused. "Is there a smell you associate with her?"

Daniels set his jaw. "Peppermint," he said softly. "She and I would sneak peppermint candies from a stash in the kitchen, then go outside and eat them." He stopped and his eyes widened. "I smelled peppermints on the drive over here."

"Probably because she's standing over your right shoulder." Mason picked up his spoon and stirred his soup. "She says she's glad you got out tonight. You've been too morose lately. And she says you should eat more."

Daniels didn't move and cleared his throat. "That's good advice." He paused and Mikey wondered if he could use a hug. He sighed. "You think she could maybe ruffle my hair or something, instead of setting off that siren? It scares the hell out of me."

"While she's here," said Trick, "can she tell you or Daniels who killed Jag Trammel, because I'd really like to know."

Mason stared again, and then his face paled. "Huh."

"What is it?" asked Mikey.

Mason frowned and looked at Trick. "She said to drop the case." He knitted his brow. "What in the...?"

"Red?" asked Trick.

Mason straightened, his face strained. "She said what killed Jag should never be found."

"What does that mean?" asked Mikey, her skin prickling.

"Damn. Now I'm curious." Trick raised a brow and then reached for a chip. He eyed Mikey. "It means that we keep going because I want to know what shouldn't be found." He dunked the chip in guacamole and ate it.

Chapter Eleven

Aaron Remalla picked up a bag of dirt and dropped it on the rocky surface beside the new flowerbeds. The day was warm, and he wiped the sweat from his brow with his sleeve. He'd already moved two other bags, spread the contents over the ground and was prepared to do the same with the third. His supervisor, Rocky, had told him they had re-landscaped outside the Reptile House, but an area had not been finished and the space needed fresh dirt. Once he finished, Rem would wheel out some flowers and start planting.

He picked up his water bottle and took a swig. He'd finished his coffee an hour earlier and wished he had more. Groups of visitors walked by, reading their maps and drinking their drinks. Checking the time, he saw he had two hours remaining on his shift. After wiping more sweat from his brow, he squatted to open the bag.

"Excuse me, can you tell me where the giraffes are?"

Rem turned to see a middle-aged woman with a young girl beside her licking a lollipop. He pointed behind him. "Straight down this path. You come to a left turn. There will be a sign to the Urban Jungle. Follow the sign." He went back to his bag of dirt.

"But we just came from there. Are you sure?" asked the woman.

"We didn't see any giraffes," said the girl.

Rem glanced back at them. "I'm pretty sure. I was working near the giraffes yesterday. They're hard to miss."

The woman narrowed her eyes. "Are you saying I missed them?"

Rem bit back his impatience. He wasn't in customer service for a reason. "Well, if you were there and didn't see them, then you missed them."

The woman scowled at him. "You don't have to be rude. I just asked you a question."

The girl licked her lollipop, and Rem thought most of the sticky treat was on her face rather than in her mouth. "And I just answered it. The giraffes are that way." He pointed. "If you want to go the other way, that's up to you. But you won't see any giraffes."

"Where are the dinosaurs?" asked the girl.

Rem almost groaned. "You're in the wrong place if you want to see dinosaurs, kid. Only live animals here." Rem sliced open the bag.

"What is your supervisor's name?" asked the woman, looking indignant. "Now you are being rude to my child." She put a hand on her little girl's shoulder. The girl stuck her tongue out at him.

Rem shot a thumb toward the reptile exhibit. "His name is Rocky. Last I saw, he was headed in that direction to take care of the snakes. You can talk to him if you want, just be careful." He leaned in. "He likes to let the snakes out while they clean the tanks. Just watch where you're stepping."

The woman gasped and took her child's hand. "What is your name?"

"Aaron Remalla. One M and two Ls. Nice to meet you." He waved his fingers.

"Expect a complaint, Mr. Remalla." The woman pulled her child away. The child stuck her tongue out again, and Rem did the same back to her. The child widened her eyes.

"I've dealt with worse, ma'am," he said. "You two have a nice day." He frowned, wondering about some people, and went back to his dirt. He'd been at the zoo for three weeks and if the woman followed through, it would be the third complaint against him. Rocky had suggested Rem try to be nicer but hadn't seemed too concerned. Not worrying about it, he dug his hands into the bag and started to spread the dirt over the ground.

"Excuse me, sir. Can you tell me where the bathrooms are?" said a female voice from behind him.

Rem bit back a curse. There was a sign indicating the location of the bathrooms literally right behind him. He sighed but his impatience got the better of him. "There's a sign right—" He turned and saw Mikey.

She smiled at him. "You know, you really should try and be nicer."

Seeing her, his heart thumped. Her purple-tipped brown hair blew in the breeze, the diamond stud in her nostril sparkled, and she wore her typical snug black jeans and t-shirt. "It's not my strong suit." He wiped his hands on his jeans. "What are you doing here?"

Her face tightened. "Mason wanted to see the pandas."

He chastised himself for sounding abrupt and softened his tone. "And you?"

"I heard a rumor you were working here. Mason and I decided to take the day and visit the zoo. He's in the panda line. I asked around and heard you were near the reptiles." She eyed the ground. "Looks like you're keeping busy."

Rem stood and brushed the dirt off his pants. "It's not fancy, and it doesn't pay much, but it won't get me, or anybody else, killed."

"That's always a plus."

"I thought so." A long tendril of hair escaped his ponytail, and he tucked it behind his ear. Anxious, he wondered what to say. They'd spoken only a few times in the past month and had seen each other only once. Not wanting to talk about his job, Allison, or Chloe, he'd avoided seeing people as much as possible. Daniels had been the one he'd opened up to the most, but Rem had even kept that conversation to a minimum. Daniels was still reeling from Marjorie's separation, and Rem figured his former partner didn't need to hear more about Rem's problems. He shifted on his feet. "I wish I had more time to talk." Even though he'd taken a short lunch and had missed his fifteen-minute break, he didn't want to tell Mikey that. The more time he spent with her, the more difficult it was for him. She made him feel things he didn't want to feel.

Mikey crossed her arms. "I spoke to your supervisor, Rocky. He said to encourage you to take a break. To buy you a coffee or something."

Rem cursed inwardly. "That's Rocky. Always telling me to take it easy."

Mikey's face fell. "Since you're so short on time, let's get this over with. Why are you avoiding me? Why do I have to hear from Daniels you're working at the zoo?"

"I didn't think it was that big of a deal."

"You don't seem to think anything is a big deal. I call you and you're in a hurry to get off the phone. I go to your house, and you don't answer the door. That's why I came here. I don't know what is going on with you."

Zoo visitors walked past, and Rem wished he could join them. "I don't know what you want me to say."

"You know exactly what I want you to say. I want to know how you are. I want to know what you're thinking. You and I expressed some things to each other about how we feel, and now suddenly you act like I'm some old buddy who lives across the country that you see once or twice a year." She stopped, looked at the ground, and then looked back up. "Why won't you talk to me?"

Rem's frustration grew. Ever since losing Chloe, he'd been struggling with what to do and where to go next. Getting involved in a relationship with Mikey was the last thing he needed. "I don't know what you want from me."

"I just told you." She took a step closer. "You and I used to talk to each other."

Rem put his hands on his hips and stared at the sky. He tried to compose his thoughts and figure out how to explain it to her. "Mikey, I know you want more, and I know I've been keeping to myself. I've spent the last few weeks just trying not to spin out of control. I thought I had it together, but then Allison and Chloe happened. I was already a leaky ship but that pulled the last plug. I was going under, and I needed to clear my head. I can't be the partner Daniels needs or the man you deserve right now. I don't know if I ever will."

"You're being way too hard on yourself." She brushed back a piece of purple-tipped hair. "You just need time."

Rem shot out a hand. "Everyone keeps telling me that. But no one wants to give it to me. It's been a month, Mikey. And only seven months since Victor. And every time I turn the corner around here, I think I see Margaret." He put a hand on his head. "I appreciate the thought, but I can't be fixed with just time. And if I can, it's going to take a lot longer than a month, or even seven."

"I'm only trying to help. I want to be there for you."

"I appreciate that, but I'm not ready to accept your help or anyone else's."

Her face tightened again, and he wondered if he'd said too much. He'd spent a lot of time thinking about Mikey, wishing they could be together one minute and then glad they weren't the next. She'd dealt enough with Victor's mind games, and she didn't need another man with more problems. As much as she'd helped him in the past, Rem believed that she'd eventually come to realize she'd prefer someone else who didn't carry a ton of baggage. "I'm sorry. I don't mean to hurt your feelings."

She swallowed and he sensed she was composing herself. After a few seconds, she met his gaze. "I know what you're doing. I've been there myself. Mason fought like hell for me when I didn't think I deserved it. I'd put him through so much and I didn't want to put him through more. I've even felt guilty about his addiction, thinking in some way I contributed to it. I've had to work through that, but I didn't do it alone. I've learned the best way to get past something is to trust the people you love. You and I have both trusted each other with some difficult stuff. You can still do that. If the relationship thing is getting in the way, we can hold off on that. I just want you to be well." She took another step. "Just don't pull away from the people who care for you. Daniels is struggling enough as it is. He needs you too, you know?"

Rem wished he could return to the dirt and forget this whole conversation, but Mikey's words pierced him. "I don't want to push you and Daniels away. But I don't want to talk about it either."

She nodded. "Okay. What do you want to talk about?"

Rem sighed. "Anything but me." Since Mikey wasn't going anywhere, he figured he should try to have a conversation. "How have you been?"

"Just great." She rolled her eyes. "Our dad visited, and Trick and Kyle are trying to find a murderer who shouldn't be found, whatever that means."

"Your dad visited? Were you expecting him?" He knew Mikey and her father were not close.

"No. Far from it." She went on to tell him about her father and his new fiancée.

"I bet that was a shock," said Rem. "How are you and Mason handling it?"

"That's one of the reasons we're at the zoo. I'm making Mason take a few days off. He needs them." She paused. "And since you were here, I thought I'd kill two birds with one stone."

Rem nodded. His shock at seeing her had abated and now he was glad she'd come to see him. "You talked to Daniels?"

"We saw him at dinner. You missed a great tortilla soup, by the way."

"I bet." He'd wanted to go but had dreaded the thought of talking and had found a reason to decline.

Mikey put her hands in her jacket pockets. "He's sad. He's got a new partner he's trying to adjust to, and he misses his wife and child. I think he needs a friend." She studied him. "I realize in that head of yours you're telling yourself you are doing him a favor by staying away, but you're not easing his burden by avoiding him. You're only contributing to it."

Rem didn't want to hear that. "How's it going with his new partner?"

"You should ask him that, not me."

Rem had purposely avoided the topic, assuming it might make Daniels uncomfortable. Now he realized he might've made a mistake. "I'll call him."

"This may come as a shock to you, but you're not the only one with problems. If you don't want to talk about yours, maybe Daniels would like to talk about his."

Suspecting she was right, he nodded. "I hear you."

"Good."

"Anything else?"

She kicked at a pebble. "Just that I miss you."

His chest constricted and he wished he was in a better head space. "I miss you, too."

She looked up. "If you want to get a coffee or something, let me know. We don't have to talk about anything you don't want to. But sitting in that house all by yourself and coming here and burying yourself in your work is only going to last so long. So, if you want to go to a movie or just get out of the house and take a walk, call me."

Rem felt a small measure of relief that she didn't expect more than he was ready to give. "Even with Margaret running around? Especially since we know she's seen your dad."

"Mason has been pretty vigilant since what happened with Oswald, but I think an impromptu walk, movie, or coffee isn't going to risk any more than we're already risking."

Rem wasn't convinced but he didn't want to argue either. "Okay. I'll let you know, but don't take it personally if I'm not ready just yet."

She hesitated but then took her hands out of her pockets and walked up to him. He almost stepped back but held his ground. Her closeness unnerved him but also felt good. "I'm not going anywhere, Remalla. You got that?" she said. "You can be as tough and argumentative as you want to be, but you forget, I've put up with Victor and Margaret, and a few other nasty people. You don't scare me at all." She leaned in, patted him on the shoulder, raised up on her toes, and kissed him on the cheek. "You got two weeks. I don't hear from you, and I'll be back, just like Arnold Schwarzenegger. Only cuter."

He couldn't help but smile and his heart fluttered from her kiss and her nearness. "Two weeks, huh?" He paused. "Okay, Arnold. I'll see what I can do."

She stepped back. "You better. And call Daniels."

"I will."

Mikey checked her watch. "I better go find Mason before he frightens the pandas."

"They are pretty jumpy," said Rem. "If I'm lucky, Rocky might trust me with cleaning their enclosure." He raised a hand and crossed his fingers.

"If Rocky asks, I'll put in a good word for you."

"I'd appreciate that. The monkeys don't like me very much. I helped clean one of their pens the other day and Bart the baboon threw his shit at me."

"I like Bart the baboon already," said Mikey, smiling. She held Rem's gaze. "I'll see you. Have fun with that bag of dirt."

Rem nodded. "Me and the dirt will be hanging out all afternoon." He waved. "Tell Mason I said hi."

"I will."

Feeling wistful, but happy to have talked, Rem watched Mikey walk away.

• • • • • • • • • •

Trick left the nightclub and stood on the street, wondering where to go next. He and Kyle had come up with a list of bars and clubs that featured singers in the downtown area and had divided it in half. Using a picture of Eleanor from the footage at Bullards, they'd started looking for her. It was their second day of searching with no luck. No one had seen her. Trick eyed his list; the number of bars with singers had been ordered from most likely to least likely. He'd put the higher end bars at the top and the seedier spots at the bottom. Trick was beginning to think that Eleanor worked somewhere seedier than he'd hoped. By the look of her, she hadn't struck him as a woman who'd work somewhere sketchy, but there was no way to be sure. He'd left his card everywhere he'd stopped, so he hoped he might get lucky, and someone would contact him if they saw her in the future or someone remembered her.

Checking the time, he wondered how Kyle was doing when he heard his name called. He looked up to see Kyle crossing the street and heading in his direction. Trick waited and Kyle jogged up to him.

"Any luck?" asked Trick.

Kyle shook his head. "None. Nobody recognized her."

Trick checked his list. "Then we start with the second half. Those places are a little more questionable, but maybe we'll get lucky."

"Maybe we should call and ask if Eleanor works there. We could reach more places faster."

"We could, but then we couldn't show her picture. And we reach more people this way. We could get someone on the phone who doesn't know her but the guy working next to him does. This way is slower but more reliable."

Kyle nodded. "What happens if we don't find her? She could have lied about being a singer."

Trick hoped that wasn't true. "We'll cross that bridge when we come to it. Right now, though, we keep looking."

"Okay. Where to next?"

Trick checked the time and wondered where to start. "Let's head back to the truck. There's another street we can check not far from here."

They started walking, and Trick kept his eye out for GQ, the woman from the bar who'd followed them. He figured if she'd tried to keep tabs on them before, she might try again, but so far, he hadn't seen her.

He and Kyle made it to the truck and headed to the next location. After parking in front of one of the clubs on his list, Trick got out and joined Kyle on the sidewalk. "I'll go here," said Trick. "See that place down there?" He pointed and Kyle looked.

"The Parakeet?" asked Kyle.

"Go ask there."

Kyle nodded and started to leave when Trick heard a voice from behind him. "Well, well, well. Look who we have here. It's the cowboy and his new sidekick."

Recognizing the voice, Trick grimaced. He turned to see Detective Bevins and slapped a smirk on his face. "And if it isn't Detective Doolittle." He could have said worse but refrained. Not seeing Detective Winkler, Bevins' partner, he wondered if she was inside the bar, asking about Eleanor.

Kyle had stopped to see who was talking and he glanced at Trick.

"Kyle," said Trick, "this is Detective Bevins. You ever need help, do yourself a favor and don't call him."

"Nice to meet you," said Kyle.

Bevins didn't respond to Kyle but chuckled at Trick. "Still an asshole."

"I could say the same," answered Trick.

Bevins yanked on his adequate belt that circled his adequate middle. "Quite the coincidence, us bumping into each other. I'd almost think we were working the same case."

Trick knew once Charlie from Bullards contacted the detectives and told them about Eleanor, they'd be looking for her, too. "Could be. Not that it's any of your business."

"I wondered why Detective Daniels was snooping around this case. Now it makes sense." Bevins spoke to Kyle. "You working with him?"

Before Trick could stop him, Kyle answered. "We're looking for a woman named Eleanor."

Trick sighed.

Bevins shook his head. "I figured. Somebody hired you?"

Trick put his hand up to stop Kyle from speaking. "That's confidential."

"You realize if you find her, you need to tell us," said Bevins. "She may have crucial information in a murder case."

"Once we find and question her, we'll be happy to point her in your direction," said Trick.

Bevins scowled. "You interfere in this case, and I'll report you."

Trick raised a brow. "To who? The P.I. police?"

Kyle smiled.

Bevins' irritation spiked. "I'll get your license pulled. Then you and your woo-woo friend can go speak to your ghosts for a living and leave the police work to the real cops."

Trick chuckled. "Are you referring to yourself as the real cop in this scenario?" He pointed. "Because I picture you more as a clown at a kid's birthday party. My guess is you'd get more information out of them than any witness you find." He adjusted his hat. "Probably steal some of the birthday cake, too."

"And speaking to ghosts is actually quite lucrative," said Kyle. "I do it all the time."

Bevins looked at Kyle and rolled his eyes. "Not another one."

"I'm surrounded by them," said Trick. "Maybe you should move along in case it's catching." He leaned in. "I'd hate for you to get a whiff of insight. It might give you hives."

Bevins glared. "Listen, you smart ass hillbilly, I'll—"

Winkler walked up and put her hand on Bevins' arm. "Looks like you two are getting reacquainted. How wonderful."

"Your partner is just as charming as ever," said Trick.

Bevins set his jaw and Winkler squeezed his elbow. "He's on edge," she said. "We've got a double murder to solve and no suspects." She glanced at Kyle. "We heard you two were at Bullards. You looking for this Eleanor?"

Trick appreciated her honesty. He wondered how this woman put up with her hot-aired partner. "We are. We've been hired to investigate Jackson Trammel's death. We didn't realize we were looking at a second murder, though."

She smirked. "Something tells me you aren't surprised at all." She tipped her head. "Did Detective Daniels give you a heads up?"

"I can't reveal my sources," said Trick.

Bevins scoffed.

"We'd appreciate it if you could let us know what you find," said Winkler. "It can't hurt to help each other out."

Trick tipped his head. "I'm assuming that goes both ways?"

Bevins shot a look at Winkler. "We don't have to do shit. You want information?" he asked Trick. "Then go find it yourself. We've got better things to do than to keep stringing you along like some damn lost puppy."

"Bevins—" said Winkler.

"Besides," said Bevins, "everybody knows this is a drug deal gone bad. That overlook is known for that. Jag and his girlfriend went up there to score meth or cocaine and the dealers probably went after the woman. This Jag kid fought back and probably killed someone in the process before he got killed himself. Our dealers took their dead guy, and this Eleanor is dead in a ditch somewhere or has been sold to the highest bidder."

Trick stared in disbelief.

Kyle frowned. "Maybe you should come work for SCOPE."

Bevins glared. "What the hell are you talking about?"

Kyle shrugged. "We could use a good psychic. Do you read crystal balls, too? Because that would come in handy."

Bevins dropped his jaw, and Trick caught Winkler's almost imperceptible smile. Trick almost patted Kyle on the back. "I think that adequately communicates our opinion on your theory," said Trick. "Any other ridiculous scenarios you'd like to add?"

"I think we've all said enough," said Winkler. "C'mon, Bevins." She pulled on his arm. "Let's keep looking." She spoke to Trick. "And if you do find Eleanor, we need to talk to her."

"You scare her off and we lose her," said Bevins with a sneer, "there'll be hell to pay. I'll arrest you myself for interfering in an investigation."

"We now consider ourselves warned," said Trick, tipping his hat. "You have a nice day, Detective."

Bevins sneered again as Winkler pulled him away. Trick watched them head down the street and disappear into another club. "Kyle," he said. "You've outdone yourself. I owe you a giant...well...whatever you want."

"How about a coffee?"

Trick nodded. "You bet. I'll get you the biggest size they got because you're going to need it."

"I am?"

Trick glanced down the street, determining what to do next. "Yes. Now that those two know we're looking for Eleanor, our goal is to find her before they do, because if we don't..."

Kyle finished his sentence. "We may never get a chance to question her?"

Trick feared Bevins would do everything possible to keep him and Kyle out of the loop. "Exactly." He smacked Kyle's shoulder. "Let's go."

Chapter Twelve

Uncomfortable, Mason squirmed in his chair. He eyed the other patrons at their tables and envied their relaxed demeanor. Mikey sat beside him and shook her head. "Would you take it easy?"

"I told you I didn't want to do this."

"You didn't have to come."

He fiddled with his place setting. "I wasn't going to let you do this alone." After their conversation following Mason's difficult reading with the grieving parents, Mikey had contacted Vicki and had arranged to have an early dinner with her in the lobby of the hotel where Vicki and their dad were staying. The hotel's in-house restaurant had decent reviews and Vicki had agreed to meet them while Martin went to the hotel bar's happy hour. Mason couldn't help but doubt that his dad would stay put and would join them instead. "It better just be her, though."

"I told you. I explained that it would be more productive if we met with her alone. She understood and agreed. Stop worrying so much. If dad shows, we can leave."

Mason opened his mouth to argue.

"There she is," said Mikey.

Mason looked to see Vicki getting off the elevator. Since Mikey had requested a table that looked over the lobby, Vicki was easy to spot. Mikey waved, Mason told himself to be nice and Vicki approached.

She wore a peach-colored dress with a high neck and her hair spilled over her shoulders. Mason again wondered why this woman wanted to marry his father. "Hello," she said.

Mason stood as she sat with them. "Hi," he said.

"Hi, Vicki," said Mikey. "I'm glad you could join us."

Vicki pulled her chair closer. "I'm happy you called. I was hoping we could get a chance to know each other better before Martin and I left." She hooked her purse strap over the edge of the chair.

"Does Dad know you're here?" Mason half-expected her to say she had to sneak out to meet them to prevent his father's wrath.

"Of course, he does," said Vicki. "We don't have any secrets. He's up at the second-floor bar. He likes to have a couple of beers and watch whatever sports game is on. It's his way of relaxing."

"It doesn't bother you that he's got to disappear every day to drink just to relax?" asked Mason. He felt Mikey nudge him below the table.

Vicki smiled. "No, actually. He can hang out in the bar while I have a little time to myself. Neither one of us is very good at being together all the time. I'm used to having my space. It may be unconventional, but it works for us." She took her napkin off the table and laid it in her lap.

"Don't mind, Mason," said Mikey. "This get-together isn't easy for him." She paused. "Me neither, if I'm honest."

"I understand." Vicki smoothed her napkin and Mason wondered if she was just as nervous. "I'm sure you two have a lot of questions."

"You're damn right we do," said Mason.

"Mason," said Mikey, softly. "Please try to be civil. She hasn't done anything to us."

Mason set his jaw, knowing Mikey was right. "I'm sorry, Vicki. I guess this is just hitting all my trigger points."

"I can understand," said Vicki,

Not planning it, Mason spoke what was on his mind. "We hadn't seen Dad in years, and he shows up out of nowhere with you and his big mouth.

You were a surprise, but his mouth wasn't. As far as I'm concerned, he hasn't changed a bit. And here you're willing to marry him after knowing him only three months. Pardon me, but I can't figure out why. Do you have some sort of cognitive disorder?"

Mikey shoved him. "Mason…"

Vicki raised a brow. "Not that I'm aware of, but I guess I can see why you would think I'm crazy. Martin can be a handful."

"A handful?" Mason bit back another retort when the waitress stopped and gave them menus.

They asked for waters, and Mikey put a hand on Mason's arm. "Before my brother says something stupid again, I think the whole reason I wanted to talk to you was to learn more about you. We don't know anything. How did you and Dad meet? How do you know Margaret?"

A busboy showed and set water glasses and straws down for each of them. Vicki picked up her straw. "I know. I don't know much about you either. Martin has told me a few things, but not a lot."

"I can imagine," said Mason.

"He told me about his marriage to your mother and raising his family, but that you all had moved away," said Vicki.

"Did he tell you how he cheated on our mother with her best friend?" asked Mason. "I'd think that would be good for you to know."

Vicki nodded. "He told me he's made some mistakes." She ripped the wrapper off her straw and added it to her water.

"Mistakes?" asked Mason, annoyed. "That's an understatement."

"Mason," said Mikey, with a glare. "Would you let her get through more than two sentences?"

Mason forced himself to shut up. "Fine. The floor's yours, Vicki."

Mason and Mikey waited, and Vicki seemed to gather herself under their appraisal. "I'm an ER nurse. After I graduated nursing school, I moved here for my first job. I was young and having fun and I met a man at the hospital. I thought I was in love but was in no hurry to marry. We were together a few years, and one night we went to a party. My boyfriend had been hanging out with this guy he thought was cool. Looking back, I'm sure it had more to do with the free-flowing drugs and the women this man hung out with. By then, it was clear to me that Barry, my boyfriend, wasn't everything I expected him to be, but I hadn't found the courage to confront him yet." She stirred her water with her straw. "Anyway, I agreed to go to the party. It was a bonfire on a beach in front of a nice cottage. There were several people, most of whom were smoking or drinking something. I've never been much for drugs, so I declined, but Barry didn't hesitate. Before I knew it, Barry was high and drunk, and I was trying to figure out how to get home." She ran a finger down the side of her water glass. "That's when a woman came up to me. She appeared to be as sober as I was, and we started talking. She knew I was with Barry, and she empathized. We spent the rest of the evening and night talking. By the time the party broke up, we'd gotten to know each other. I'd opened up to her about a lot of things and told her some secrets I'd never told anyone else. She was easy to talk to and encouraged me to break up with Barry and find someone better. We exchanged information and, after that party, I took her advice and left Barry. She and I would occasionally get together and hang out and we became good friends." She eyed Mikey and Mason. "It was your sister, Margaret."

Mason fought to hold his tongue. "What happened after that?"

Vicki sipped some water. "I got a lucrative job offer in Dallas and decided to accept it. I moved away and Margaret and I talked every now and then, but we eventually drifted apart. I did marry, but then quickly divorced." She paused. "A long story not worth mentioning." She fiddled with the wrapper from her straw. "Then, out of the blue, Margaret called me a few months ago. Said she was in town visiting her father and would I like to come over and have dinner. It was good to hear her voice and I accepted. I went and met your dad. He was nice and we got along well. Margaret and I caught up. She told me she'd had some issues in California and was in town for a few days. After that night, your father called me and asked me to dinner. I accepted. Margaret left, and the rest, as they say, is history."

"Issues?" Mason snorted. He sat back in disbelief. "That's one word for it. You had no idea that our sister escaped from a psychiatric ward and is wanted by the law?"

Vicki dropped her crumpled straw wrapper. "No idea. I didn't know she was in any trouble at all. She just told me that her friend, whose house we'd gone to that night she and I met, had been murdered and one of her other friends was in jail awaiting trial for killing him. That's all I knew."

Mikey set her menu aside. "I hope you know now what our sister has been accused of. She's a fugitive."

"I know everything, but I find it so hard to believe." Vicki sighed. "I mean, I never saw that side of her."

"Just like you've never seen the ugly side of Dad," added Mason, not bothering to hide his irritation. "You definitely wear the biggest rose-colored glasses I've ever seen." He set his elbow on the table. "I just hope you don't come to regret it."

Vicki's face fell. "I haven't seen Margaret since the day we arrived here."

"And if you were to see her now, would you turn her in?" asked Mikey.

Vicki hesitated. "I won't lie. It would be hard to do. Especially since she and her dad have become so close."

Mason couldn't help but laugh. "Those two close? That's like a starving lion and an antelope hanging out together. I'll believe it when I see it."

"But it's true," said Vicki.

They sat in silence when the waitress returned to take their food orders. None of them had looked at the menus and they asked for coffees instead. Mason wondered if he could stomach any food at all after this conversation.

"I heard about your lunch with Max," said Mikey.

"He didn't take the news much better than you two did," said Vicki. "But it doesn't surprise me. I told Martin to call before we left Texas, but he wouldn't. He can be so stubborn sometimes."

"You saw how it went when he showed up at SCOPE," said Mikey. "Surely you can see why we've been estranged." She eyed Mason. "He wasn't an easy man to grow up with."

"I can see that," said Vicki. "But I can also see a side of him you don't."

"And what's that?" asked Mason, prepared to laugh at whatever lies Dad had implanted in Vicki's head.

Vicki studied her hands. "He's a lonely man. His whole family has moved away, and his only company is a cat and his vegetable garden."

"Vegetable garden?" asked Mikey.

"Since when does Dad eat vegetables?" asked Mason.

"He's got a big garden in his back yard. Takes good care of it, too." Vicki shrugged. "Of course, you're correct about the vegetables. He sells most of what he grows at the local market, and his eating habits are, or were, atrocious. I've been helping with that, getting him to eat healthier and work out more."

"Good for him. He's getting his greens." Mason wasn't convinced his father was lonely at all. "Dad hits the bars with his buddies every night. He can't be that lonely."

Vicki played with the edge of her sleeve. "His best friend Bill died last year and his other buddy, Tom, has cancer. He's been in and out of treatment for months and certainly hasn't been in any bar." She looked up at them. "Your father goes alone."

"What about his poker games?" asked Mason, "And, no offense, but he's always been a ladies' man."

Vicki interlaced her fingers. "George hosted the poker games, but he started showing signs of dementia, and his family moved him into a home. There hasn't been a game since. And your father dated a woman named

Selena for a while, but she broke up with him when she started hanging out with the bartender from the place your father used to hang out."

"What goes around, comes around," said Mason. He felt a twinge of sadness over his dad's circumstances, but then quickly got over it.

"Vicki," said Mikey. "Can I ask you a personal question?"

"I suppose," said Vicki.

Mikey wrapped her fingers around her water glass. "What do you see in Dad? I mean you're a pretty woman half his age. You could find any number of men who are...well..."

"Better looking and younger?" finished Mason.

Mikey nodded. "What Mason said."

Vicki sat back. "I've met plenty of men younger and cuter. And richer. Believe me. But your father had one thing none of them had." She stared off. "He was nice to me." She looked back. "I needed that. Still do. And I think he needs it from me. Somebody who's nice to him."

Mason's anger bubbled up. "Are you saying we should be nice to him?"

Vicki bit her bottom lip. "I can't tell you what to do. He's your dad and your history with him is obviously unknown to me. I saw what happened at your office. There's hurt feelings on both sides."

"Both sides?" asked Mason. "Did I miss where we did something to him we shouldn't have?"

"Mason, don't get upset," said Mikey. "She's just being honest."

Mason couldn't fathom making excuses for his dad. "No, Mikey. I can't speak for Margaret or Max, but you and I suffered the worst of Dad's behavior. He belittled us and was emotionally abusive. Am I supposed to sit here and feel sorry for the man because he's now sleeping in the bed he made for himself? If he wanted to make amends, he's had a million opportunities to do it." He set his jaw when the waitress brought coffee cups and set a thermos in front of them along with some cream. She left and Mason tried to keep his voice down but failed. "You've known him for three months, and you think you know enough about any of this to even try to explain how we should all be a family again? Because he's lonely?"

A woman from another table glanced over and Mason went quiet. Mikey put a hand on his arm. "Just be cool."

Mason shot a look at her. "I've left cool in the dust. Now I'm pissed."

"I'm sorry," said Vicki. "I realize I don't know you and I may have overstepped, but you wanted to know more about me and why I'm with your dad. Now you know." She reached for the thermos and poured herself some coffee.

Mikey held out her cup. "I'll take some, too, please."

Vicki poured coffee into Mikey's cup. "Mason?" asked Vicki, holding the thermos.

Mason's stomach twisted and for a moment, the look on Vicki's face sparked a kernel of anger that flared, and he had an ugly urge to tell Vicki what to do with her coffee. He stifled it, though, and for Mikey's sake, he held out his cup.

Vicki poured and set the thermos down. "I have to admit, when Margaret picked us up, she told us she'd been in touch with you. That's when she mentioned the...well..."

"Let me take a wild guess. My addiction and Mikey's unrequited love for a man who loves Margaret?" asked Mason with a scoff. "That's a lie by the way. Not my addiction, but Mikey's love interest. He's very much in love with Mikey."

Vicki added cream and stirred her coffee. "I have no idea why Margaret said what she said," she spoke to Mikey, "but I hope one day I get to meet this man. Your father would welcome it, too."

Mikey stiffened. "I doubt that will ever happen."

Vicki set her spoon down. "Contrary to what you may believe, he wants you to be happy. Both of you."

Mason snickered.

Vicki ignored the snicker. "My point was that since Margaret mentioned these things about you, I thought she'd also mentioned to you that we would be in town. I assumed your father thought the same."

"Are you saying he was expecting a warm welcome?" asked Mason, narrowing his eyes. A siren wailed in the distance. "He didn't call ahead and make plans to see us because he knew exactly what he was doing. He knew if he'd have reached out, we would have told him to stay away."

Vicki held her coffee cup. "I think he hoped it would have gone better."

Mason could barely contain his frustration. "Why do you keep defending him? He walked into SCOPE with his surly attitude, insulting me and Mikey and Trick, and you expect us to fawn all over him?"

"Mason—" said Mikey.

Mason heard the siren from outside grow louder. "No, Mikey. I can only take so much." He faced Vicki. "If you have truly found happiness with Martin Redstone, then good for you. I wish you well." Blaring, the sirens seemed to stop in front of the building. Mikey glanced behind her, but Mason continued. "But please don't expect that just because the two of you have found happiness, that it magically solves the Redstone family's problems. Dad has some work to do before we can even start to bridge the divide between us."

There was a commotion at the entrance to the hotel as people stepped aside and two EMT's ran through the lobby with their equipment and a stretcher.

"What's going on?" asked Mikey.

"I hope everything's okay," said Vicki, watching them go to the elevator and enter it. The doors closed and they disappeared from view.

"I guess we're not the only ones having a rough afternoon," said Mikey. She sipped some coffee and looked between Mason and Vicki. "I'm sorry, Vicki," she said, "but I have to agree with my brother. Our dad has said and done too much for us to forget. I'm happy if you two have found love. Dad won't be lonely anymore and you can have a nice man in your life. You've obviously been a good influence. He looks better than I've ever seen him. If you make him happy, then that's great. But that doesn't mean our feelings have changed at all." She set her cup down. "Mason has worked super hard to deal with his addiction. He's opened a business I'm proud to be a part of. We work well together and our relationship with Max has never been better. Margaret may have some lingering bright spots remaining, but if she does, she's buried them so deep I doubt there's a bulldozer capable of digging that far." She sighed. "She'll be caught eventually, but until then, she's all we can handle. If Dad can't be civil to us, then it's better we stay apart. And if he wants a relationship, then he needs to figure out how to communicate that, because right now, he sucks at it."

Mason leaned back in his chair. Mikey had adequately expressed what he could not without wanting to punch something. "I think that pretty much says it all."

Vicki lowered her cup. "I'm sorry to hear that. I guess I expected it, but I still wanted to try."

"Personally," said Mikey, "I think you're too good for him. How he found and attracted you is a mystery to me."

"I have to give Margaret the credit for that," said Vicki.

"Speaking of her," said Mason, "we're serious when we say she's dangerous. Has she tried to contact you?"

"No," said Vicki.

"Have you tried to contact her?" asked Mikey.

Vicki shifted in her seat. "The police reached out and asked us that very thing. I gave them the information I had for Margaret. They also asked me to get in touch with her to see if she'd meet with us. I tried the number I had. It did ring, but she never answered."

"Not surprising," said Mason. "She likely dumped that phone the minute you showed up at SCOPE."

Vicki sighed. "If I could do more, I would. I told the police the same. Your father, though, was a little less cooperative."

"There's a shock," said Mason.

"He's protecting his daughter," said Vicki.

"Who's a psychopath," argued Mason, his voice rising again. "She tried to kill Mikey, and if you get in her way, she wouldn't hesitate to kill you either."

Vicki rubbed her head. "I just don't know what to think."

Mason glanced at Mikey with wide eyes. "Vicki," he said, looking back at her. "Please take this seriously."

Vicki still looked dubious. "Maybe we should just enjoy our coffee for a few minutes. Talk about something else."

Mikey sipped her coffee and Mason wanted to leave. As far as he was concerned, there was nothing more to say.

"How long have you been a nurse?" asked Mikey.

Mason almost groaned. He doctored his coffee and felt an uncomfortable twinge run up his back. While Vicki answered Mikey, he squirmed, concerned his need for a pill had returned. He took a big sip of his coffee, trying to nail down what was needling him. The feeling grew and Mason's body warmed. Some part of him wanted a pill but another part felt something else. Was it a spirit? Was one lingering nearby that wanted to communicate? That happened occasionally when he was out in public. He looked around but didn't sense anything non-physical. Sweat broke out on his skin and for a second, he thought he was going to have to find a restroom. His stomach churned and he gripped his coffee.

"You okay, Mason?" asked Mikey. "You look a little pale."

Mason couldn't figure out what was bugging him when a frightening memory hit. He thought of Mr. Dark, the evil spirit that had attached itself to him before he had gone into recovery. Had Mr. Dark returned? He shook his head, not sure what to think. Whatever he was sensing felt ominous, but he didn't think it was Mr. Dark. He held his stomach. "Sorry. I guess this conversation is not agreeing with me."

"You want to go?" asked Mikey.

Vicki furrowed her brow. "Do you need to lie down? You can go upstairs if you need to."

Mason had no intention of going up to Vicki and his dad's room. "No. I'm sure I'm fine. It will pass."

Mikey studied him and he sensed her worry. "You sure?" asked Mikey.

Mason wiped some sweat from his forehead, still trying to figure out what the problem was. It almost felt like a warning. He probed mentally to see what was trying to communicate with him.

The elevator doors opened and the EMTs emerged from the elevator, pushing the stretcher into the lobby. A man with an oxygen mask on his face was lying on it. "I'm okay," said Mason. "I just think—" He got a better look at the man as the EMTs approached.

Mikey and Vicki turned to see the EMTs. Mikey widened her eyes. Vicki frowned and stood. "Is that...?"

Mikey gripped the edge of the table. "That's Dad."

The EMTs rushed out of the lobby and out onto the street.

"Oh my God," said Vicki. She grabbed her purse and ran out of the restaurant.

Chapter Thirteen

KYLE HELD OUT THE picture of Eleanor to a bartender with dirty finger-nails and dirtier hair. "Never seen her," he said. He grabbed a towel from the counter and wiped it down a glass. Kyle didn't want to think about how dirty the towel was. He looked around the small bar. The sun was going down and the counter and few tables were beginning to fill with customers getting off work. A woman with frizzy hair wearing a wrinkled dress stood at a microphone in the corner with a guitar and tried to sing. Tried being the operative word.

He and Trick were on their third day of looking for Eleanor and they were at the end of their list. The establishments had definitely tanked in terms of quality and customer service and Kyle was frustrated. They were running out of places to check.

Kyle pointed toward the singer. "Can I ask her?"

The bartender scowled. "She's busy. Bother her later. And she just got hired, so she wouldn't know anyway."

Kyle put his picture away with a sigh. "Thanks." He slid off the stool.

"Hey, handsome." A woman approached him wearing a very short skirt and a cleavage-revealing top. She put a hand on his shoulder. "Care to buy a lady a drink?"

Smelling the alcohol on her breath, Kyle stepped back. "Sorry. I'm on my way out."

Her face fell and she reached for him. "I could make it worth your while." Her smile revealed yellow teeth.

Kyle shook his head. "Thanks, but no. I've got to go." He eyed the people around him and almost felt sorry for her. "You have a nice night."

Her friendliness evaporated. "Loser." She turned and walked up to the bar.

Kyle left and walked out onto the street. Cars drove past, and he took a deep breath, glad to be out of the smoke-filled bar. He checked his list. There was only one place left. Trick was somewhere nearby, and Kyle hoped he was having better luck. If they didn't find Eleanor today, they were out of leads. He looked around to see where to head next when he felt a tap on his shoulder. He looked to see a short man with a balding head.

"Excuse me," said the man. He held out a piece of paper. "Some woman just paid me twenty bucks to give this to you."

"Some woman?" Kyle took the paper and opened it. It was an address.

"Said she's down the street. You've got five minutes and then she's leaving." He turned away.

"Wait a minute." Kyle pulled out his photo. "Was it her?"

The man stopped long enough to glance at the picture. "Yeah. Maybe. Hard to say." He resumed walking.

Kyle's heart thumped. Excited, he rechecked the address on the paper and realized he wasn't far from it. With only five minutes, though, he had to hurry. He started walking and texted Trick at the same time. He told Trick what had happened, gave him the address and told him he was heading there.

Picking up his pace, he crossed the street. Pedestrians moved along with him, and he dodged those that were moving at a slower pace. Checking the numbers on the street, he realized he was close and stopped when he saw the correct number. It was an older building that had *Closed* and *For Sale* signs on it. A dark neon sign at the front indicated it had once been a bar. A window was broken and there were no lights on inside. He approached the door when his phone buzzed. Trick had texted back, telling him to wait and not to go in alone. He would be there in a few minutes.

Kyle checked the time, seeing it had already passed the initial five minutes. Concerned he'd miss Eleanor and knowing Trick would be there soon, he entered the building. The door closed behind him. The street sounds were muffled, and it was quiet and dark. Kyle turned on the flashlight from his phone. Minimal light entered from the murky windows and he walked further in. "Hello?" he asked. "Eleanor?"

Trash littered the floor, and broken tables and chairs were discarded in a corner. A long, nicked countertop and a broken mirror behind it were the last remains of whatever business had occupied the space. A dirty mattress on the floor indicated that perhaps a few homeless people may have camped out here. A set of stairs in front of him led up into a shadowed space. He walked over to them and yelled. "Hello? Anyone up there?"

There was no response, and Kyle hoped he hadn't been too late. "Eleanor?" He was about to go upstairs when he heard footsteps. Kyle stepped back from the stairs and looked back into the other room. A shadow moved across the floor and his heart raced.

"Eleanor? Is that you?"

He heard a whispered female voice. "You've been looking for me?"

Squinting, he followed the sound of her voice, and saw a silhouette in the back of the room. He shined his light and caught a glimpse of a woman with dark disheveled hair raising her hand and looking away.

"Please. Put that away."

Not wanting to frighten her, he lowered it and turned it off. "My name is Kyle. Is that you, Eleanor?" He moved further into the room. "I wanted to ask you about Jackson Trammel." His foot hit a broken piece of glass and it skittered across the floor.

She remained in the shadows, and he couldn't see her face. "Jag." She paused. "He was nice. I liked him."

Kyle moved closer. "Do you know what happened to him?" The sun's descent made it almost impossible to see her.

"Please," she whispered. "Stay where you are."

He stopped. "Are you okay? Are you in hiding?"

There was a shuffling sound. "I'm fine. And yes. I know about Jag."

Kyle waited but she didn't offer more. He wondered when Trick would arrive and what he would do in this situation. "What can you tell me about that night?"

She remained quiet and Kyle felt a chill run up his spine. His skin broke out in goosebumps, and he smelled a faint scent of something foul in the air. He wondered if a rodent had died behind the walls. His heart raced faster, and his stomach clenched.

"You're handsome," she said softly, "like him."

Kyle swallowed. All his senses went on alert, and he heard an urgent voice in his head, telling him to leave. He knew then he'd made a mistake; he should not have entered alone. He stepped back. "I'm going to—"

Before he could finish the sentence, there was a loud-pitched shriek, and she rushed at him.

· · • • • • • · ·

Trick double-checked the address, spotted the building and jogged up to it. He didn't see Kyle and studying the dilapidated exterior, he hoped Kyle hadn't gone inside, but had a sinking feeling he had. Cursing, he reached for the door when he heard a blood-curdling shriek. Startled, he grabbed the gun from his ankle holster, threw the door open, and ran inside. The building was dark, and he squinted to see. There was a moan and another shriek and Trick whirled toward the sound. Before his eyes could adjust, something rushed at him and knocked him backward. He fell to the floor but managed to hold onto his gun. Scrambling to his knees, he aimed but had no idea at what. "Kyle?" he yelled. He had no idea what had charged him, but whatever it was had run out of the building and he hoped it wouldn't return. Breathing fast, he took his phone from his pocket.

Managing to hold his gun and turn on the flashlight with shaky hands, the space illuminated enough for Trick to see a pair of jeans-covered legs on the floor. Trick heard another moan and, moving the light, he saw blood on the jeans and a bloody torso. He sucked in a breath when he realized it was Kyle. "Shit." He jumped up and ran over. Shining the light, he saw Kyle on his back, holding his neck. Blood ran through his fingers, and he blinked heavy lids.

Trick dropped beside him. "Kyle?" He dialed nine-one-one, put it on speaker and set the phone beside him with the flashlight still on. He pulled off his jacket, balled it up, moved Kyle's hand away from the injury, and pressed his jacket against Kyle's neck. Someone answered and he quickly relayed his emergency and to send an ambulance. Kyle grimaced and raised his hand to his neck again. He grabbed Trick's wrist when Trick pressed harder.

"Kyle?" asked Trick. "Hang in there. Help is coming." Sweat popped out on his skin, and he said a prayer. "Don't die. You hear me?" He checked the rest of Kyle's body and saw he had what looked like another wicked slash across his stomach, but his neck needed the most attention.

Kyle whispered. "It was her."

"Shut up. Don't talk."

"I didn't...she isn't..." He grit his teeth.

"Be quiet. Conserve your strength."

Kyle went still and Trick prayed some more. If Kyle died, he'd never forgive himself.

"I screwed up," whispered Kyle.

"Rule one in investigation," said Trick. "Don't go in alone." Seeing blood trickle down Kyle's neck, he increased the pressure against his jacket. "I think you've learned why."

Kyle clenched his eyes shut. "Hard lesson."

"You'll be okay." Trick waited to hear the sound of the sirens. What was taking so long?

Kyle opened his eyes and he studied Trick. "I'm not afraid to die."

Trick froze. "You listen to me. No one is dying. You got that?"

Kyle blinked again. "Tell Mikey..."

Trick shook his head. "Oh, hell no. I'm not telling Mikey anything. You can tell her yourself. You can have all the conversations you want with your mother and grandmother, too, when you're better, because I'm not doing it. So, if you've got something to say, you'll have to live to say it. You understand me?"

Kyle went quiet.

"Do you understand?" asked Trick forcefully.

Kyle fluttered his eyelids. "Yes."

Trick could barely hear him. "Good." Kyle flinched and his other hand gripped his stomach. "Just focus on my voice," said Trick. "Stay with me."

Kyle smiled softly at Trick, but his hand at his neck went limp, and he drifted into unconsciousness.

Chapter Fourteen

MIKEY RETURNED TO THE waiting area, handed Mason a Styrofoam cup of coffee and sat beside him. "Anything?" she asked.

Mason shook his head. "No. Vicki's still back there. I haven't heard a thing."

Mikey held her own coffee and took a sip. After their dad had been rushed away in the ambulance, she and Mason had driven Vicki to the hospital. They'd gone to the emergency room and Vicki had filled out the required information while Mikey and Mason waited. Mikey had called Max and had been told he'd just stepped onto a flight to the east coast. She'd left a message for him to call her back asap.

All they'd learned since arriving is that their dad had collapsed at the bar and the staff had called for help. The nurse had told them they'd keep them updated but two hours had passed before she'd returned and had told Vicki that Martin was asking for her and that she could come back. Vicki had followed her, and Mikey and Mason had continued to wait.

"It's been a while since they took Vicki. What the hell is going on?" Mason stood and stretched.

"Let's wait a few more minutes," said Mikey. "Then we'll go ask."

Mason twisted at his waist and touched his toes. "I bet he's just fine. He's probably making us sweat it out as some sort of payback. I don't even know why we're here." He put his hands on his hips and paced.

Mikey watched her brother, understanding and feeling his irritation. "He's our dad. And if this is a joke, it's an expensive one." She sipped some coffee and grimaced at the bitter taste. Ever since they'd arrived at the hospital, she'd had an uncomfortable feeling in the pit of her stomach, and she sensed her father was not well. "What if it's serious? What if he's dying?"

Mason stopped. "He's too mean to die. He probably had a heart attack. No matter what Vicki's been feeding him, I suspect the bad years of booze and fast food have caught up to him."

"What if it's a stroke?" Mikey eyed her coffee, imagining her father unable to speak or move.

"Stop thinking the worst. They're probably running tests." He sat beside her. "The more likely scenario is that he just doesn't want to see us."

"Vicki wouldn't go for that. She knows we're out here, worrying."

"I'm not buying it. He's stalling."

Tired, Mikey pinched the bridge of her nose. "Fake it all you want, but I can tell you're concerned."

"I'm concerned about what happens next. If he thinks he's getting sympathy, he's wrong."

Mikey's fatigue got the best of her, and she glared at Mason. "Would you stop it? How can you be so cavalier about this? This could be it. Our father could be really sick and you're being an ass."

Mason set his jaw and looked away. "I'm sorry. I don't mean to minimize your feelings, but I can't summon much of my own." He looked back at her. "Where was Dad when you were reemerging from Victor's cult? Where was he when I got shot or went into rehab? He knew about both from Max, but did we even get a flower or a card or a phone call?" Mason hung his head. "To be honest, I'd leave right now if it weren't for you and Vicki."

Mikey swallowed. "I get it. But if this is Dad's last moments, I don't want to leave things as they are. Even if he's a jerk about it, I'd still want to talk to him."

Mason sighed. "You've always been a better person than me."

"So if he died, you'd have no regrets?"

He interlaced his fingers. "Regrets about what? What have we done wrong?"

Mikey bit her lip. "It's not about that. It's about having the courage to tell him..." Her emotions bubbled up.

"Tell him what?"

She swallowed. "That no matter what he's done, I still love him, and I...I...forgive him." Tears surfaced and she blinked them back.

Mason put his hand on her arm. "Oh, Mikey." He squeezed her wrist. "I think all the goodness Margaret somehow missed found its way to you." He pulled a tissue from a box and handed it to her.

Mikey took it and composed herself. "You think Marge knows Dad's here?"

"Knowing Margaret," said Mason. "I'm sure she does." He raised a brow. "Maybe we should tell the police. They can watch the hospital in case she shows."

"There's no way she'd come here. Too risky."

"We're talking about our sister. Risk is her middle name. She'd probably like the challenge."

Mikey nodded, wondering if her sister would actually come to the hospital. "I'm going to ask about Dad." She stood just as Vicki emerged from the ER and joined them. Her face was pale, and her eyes were red.

"What happened?" asked Mikey. "How is he?"

"I'm sorry it took so long." Vicki swiped at a watery eye. "They took him back to do tests and I went with him because he was being belligerent. They're going to admit him and they're looking for a room. They think it's his heart, but they can't be sure yet."

"Belligerent?" asked Mason. "That's Dad for you."

"Where is he now?" asked Mikey.

Vicki spotted the tissue box and pulled one out. "He had another episode. I was just sitting and talking to him. I wanted you two to come back, but he...well..."

"Wasn't going for it, was he?" asked Mason, his face taut.

Vicki dabbed her eyes with the tissue. "He doesn't want you to see him like this. He thinks he looks weak in that gown."

Mikey scoffed. "What the hell do we care about his gown?"

"Anyway, we were discussing it and he just clutched his chest. The nurses ran over, and they asked me to leave." She sniffed. "I stuck around though, and they seemed to get the pain under control, but then they saw me and insisted I go." She pushed her hair off her face.

Mikey took her hand. "It'll be okay. The doctors will take good care of him." Mason gave her a look and Mikey ignored it. "Mason already said Dad's too mean to die, and he's right."

Vicki sniffed and smiled. "You're probably right. He is ornery." She wiped her nose and seemed to pull it together. "It's going to be a long night. There's no point in all of us waiting and getting no sleep. Why don't you two go home? I can call you when I know something."

"That's a good idea," said Mason.

"I don't mind waiting," said Mikey at the same time.

Vicki looked between the two of them. "It's okay, you know? To be mad, confused and concerned at the same time. This has to be hard for both of you."

Mason huffed. "I think we should go," he said. "Vicki's right. It's going to be a while before we know anything and sitting here is only going to make us crankier than we already are. We can come back tomorrow when he's settled in his room and the doctors know more."

Mikey debated whether she'd actually get Mason to return. "Are you sure?" she asked Vicki. "I don't want you to wait by yourself."

"Actually, I think I could use some time alone," said Vicki. "I'm sort of a mess. And I suspect they'll come and get me again when he's better so

I can wait with him until they take him to his room. But he's tired, too. Tomorrow might be a better time for a visit for all of us."

"You're sure?" asked Mikey. "How will you get back to the hotel?"

"I'll manage. I may not go back tonight, but if I do, I can call a rideshare," said Vicki. "I'll tell your dad you waited but you'll be back tomorrow."

"I'm sure he'll be thrilled," said Mason. He stepped away. "You ready, Mikey?"

Mikey sighed, hoping she was doing the right thing. She wanted to see her father, but sensing he wouldn't die that night, she gave in. She spoke to Mason. "Okay. You win. We can go. Maybe we can sit with Dad in the morning while Vicki gets some rest."

"That would be nice," said Vicki.

Mason narrowed his eyes but didn't say anything. Mikey gestured toward Vicki. "Call if you need anything or if something happens."

"I will, but I hope the worst is over." Vicki tossed her tissue in a nearby trash can.

Mikey prayed she was right. "Me, too." She eyed Mason. "Let's go."

Mason rubbed his neck. "Finally." He turned and Mikey followed. As they neared the ER doors, they flew open and two EMTs pulled a stretcher with a man on it. He had an oxygen mask over his mouth, was covered in blood, and they raced him back into the ER.

Despite the blood, Mikey recognized the high cheekbones and the dark hair and long braid. Her heart plunged. "Is that—"

Trick raced inside, his face white, his hands covered in blood and gasping. He saw them and stopped cold. "What the hell are you two doing here?"

• • • ● • ● • • •

Rem knocked on Daniels' front door. After getting off work, he'd called his former partner, but he hadn't answered. Rem had stopped on his way home from the zoo to eat a taco and drink a beer, and when Daniels didn't call him back, he decided to stop by. The conversation he'd had with Mikey weighed on him, and he needed to check in on his friend.

He waited, but no one came to the door. Daniels' car was in the driveway, so Rem assumed he was home. He knocked again and was about to look for his copy of Daniels' key when the door opened. Daniels stood there, his hair askew, his jaw unshaved, and his eyes puffy.

Rem put a hand on the door frame. "Hey."

Daniels stared for a second. "Hey."

Rem got a whiff of alcohol. "Thought I'd drop by."

"I see." He blinked his dull eyes.

Rem waited but Daniels didn't say anything else. "You mind if I come in," Rem asked, "or should I stand here while we stare at each other?"

Daniels ran a hand through his longer hair and shrugged. "Come on in." He widened the door.

Rem stepped inside and looked around. There were dirty dishes in the sink and empty beer bottles on the counter. "How are you?"

Daniels closed the door but stumbled and grabbed onto the wall.

"Whoa," said Rem, grabbing Daniels' arm. "Careful, there." It was obvious Daniels was drunk.

"I'm fine. Just a little…" he waved a hand, "…off-balance."

"That's one way of putting it." Rem let go and Daniels wobbled into his living room. Rem followed, ready to catch Daniels if he fell. The TV was on and there was a large, three-quarter filled tequila bottle with a shot glass beside it on the coffee table. Rem picked it up. "Please tell me this isn't a new bottle."

Daniels dropped onto the sofa. "Brought it on the way home." He smiled. "I mean bought it. Hep yourself," said Daniels, slurring his words. "It's a free country." He waved.

Rem didn't know what that had to do with drinking, but he set the bottle down. "Did you eat dinner?"

"Dinner?"

"Yeah. You know. It comes after lunch."

Daniels dropped his jaw, stared and pointed. "Did you know how many carbs there are in a banana?"

Rem had no idea what Daniels was talking about. "A banana? I don't know. How many?"

Daniels waved again. "A lot." He chuckled. "But I had one anyway." He made a snorting sound. "Screw carbs."

Rem squinted at him. "Should I infer that you ate a banana for dinner?"

Daniels eyed the TV and waved at it. "These stupid people can never find Bigfoot. How hard is it? I mean, he's like huge."

Rem eyed the TV, seeing a program he occasionally watched about a team of scientists searching for Bigfoot using the latest technology. "He's pretty sly."

"Please," Daniels scoffed. "You put me out there and I could find him. In a heartbeat."

Rem sat in the chair across from the couch. "You could, huh?"

"Absoutlee. No problem." He rolled his eyes. "I bet he eats bananas."

"Well, he is a primate," said Rem.

"See," said Daniels. "Even Bigfoot likes carbs."

Rem studied his friend. While Rem had had plenty of occasions where Daniels had found him drunk, or had gotten drunk with him, Daniels rarely drank alone. "I tried to call earlier."

Daniels glanced at him. "I saw."

Figuring that was all he was going to get, Rem tried again. "You have a busy day?"

Daniels reached for the shot glass. "Routine."

"How's Marjorie?"

Daniels stilled and held the shot glass. "Fine." He grabbed the bottle and poured some liquor into the glass. "We had another seshion today."

Rem nodded, wondering if that was the reason for the alcohol. "How'd it go?"

Daniels put the bottle back on the table. "It sucked." He downed the tequila.

Rem sighed and sat back. "I guess I'm glad this isn't your reaction to a good session."

Daniels grimaced. "And what, exactly, would that be?" He plopped the glass on the table next to the tequila.

Rem rested his elbow on the armrest. "I'm guessing you haven't had many good ones?"

Daniels fell back against the cushions. "They're ganging up on me."

"Who?"

"Marjorie and Erica, the doctor, or therapist, or whatever she is." He waved a hand. "They both seem to think that I'm a bad husband."

Rem suspected Marjorie would disagree. "Why do you say that?"

Daniels tensed. "Because I'm a cop, that's why." He eyed the TV. "I'm either home too late, or spending too much time with you, or inviting bad guys into our home. It's ridiculous."

Rem picked at the armrest. "Maybe that's just how Marjorie feels. Doesn't mean it's true."

Daniels glared. "Please don't tell me you're taking her side."

"I'm not taking anyone's side. I want both of you to work this out."

Daniels rubbed his face, blinked, and stared at the TV. "I'm just tired, and I miss J.P., and this house is too quiet."

Rem empathized, remembering how badly he'd felt after Jennie's death. It had taken him a long time to get used to her not being around. "It'll get better. You two just need some time."

Daniels scoffed again. "Time. What a stupid word." He paused. "I hate that word."

Rem pursed his lips. "It's just a word, but I guess it sounds a little abrasive."

"I mean," Daniels sat up, looking annoyed, "don't you get tired of people telling you *it takes time*." He drew out the words. "Over and over again. I want to throw up."

Rem figured with the amount of alcohol Daniels was drinking, he probably would. "I absolutely get that. It's all I've heard for the last three years."

"Well," Daniels scooted to the edge of the couch, "let me be the first to apologize." He almost fell off the sofa before righting himself. "I will never say those words to you again." He pointed and came close to knocking over the tequila bottle.

"Thanks, I think," said Rem. "But what else would you say?"

Daniels opened his mouth but then hesitated. "That's a hell of a question, partner."

Rem was happy to hear Daniels still call him partner.

"Here's what I will say to anyone," Daniels weaved and grabbed at a couch cushion. "What's taking so damn long? Get over it all ready." He burped. "Time's a wastin'."

Rem nodded. "Would you say that to Marjorie?"

Daniels' face fell. "Hell, no. What am I, stupid?"

Rem smiled. "She might feed you to Bigfoot."

Daniels grunted and then chuckled. "She probably would." He pushed back on the couch and glared at the TV. "I bet you she could find Bigfoot."

Rem glanced at the TV show. "I bet. She's intense when she sets her mind to something."

Daniels looked back at Rem. "We should start our own show. Teach these people a few things." He watched the TV for a second and then shouted. "Those trail cameras don't work, you morons."

Rem couldn't help but grin. "You're taking this show pretty seriously. What happened to your documentaries?"

Daniels furrowed his brow. "This is a documentary. Was the matter with you?"

Rem shook his head. "I hate to tell you this, partner, but I think you've confused your channels."

Daniels threw out a hand. "You don't know what you're talking about." He patted his chest. "I know my documentaries." He shot a thumb at the TV. "Jane Good something. Goodboy…Goodman…"

"I think you mean Jane Goodall," said Rem.

Daniels nodded. "That one. She does these all the time."

"I think you mean chimpanzees."

"Exactly." He sat back, looking pleased with himself.

Rem figured it was pointless to argue. "How about I get you something to eat." He stood. "You got any food in this house?"

Daniels held his stomach. "I got carbs. Lots and lots of carbs. Manetti hates them." He raised up and lowered his voice. "So I intend to eat them all the time."

Hearing the name of Daniels' new partner, Rem's stomach tightened. As much as he realized it was necessary, he didn't like that he'd been replaced. He and Daniels had worked together for so long, it didn't seem natural. "Why doesn't he like carbs?"

"He's anti-carb, dairy, sugar, gluten, alcohol—"

"Bananas?" asked Rem.

Daniels bobbed his head. "That too."

"And he has a problem with the way you eat?"

"He's a food…food…" He waved his fingers. "…bigot." He widened his eyes. "All fruit matters. That's what I think." He smiled.

Rem shook his head. "Then my eating habits would definitely send him into shock."

Daniels paused. "I think he'd arrest you if you ate a Taco del Fueno in front of him."

"Fuego," corrected Rem.

"Whatever," said Daniels. He reached for the shot glass again.

"How about we hold off on that until we get you something to eat?" Rem picked up the glass and the bottle.

"No way," complained Daniels. "I'm just getting started."

Ignoring Daniels' protests, Rem carried the bottle and glass into the kitchen, set them on the counter and dug through the pantry. Daniels was right about the carbs. He had pasta, but not much else. He stuck his head out and yelled. "How about some spaghetti?"

He heard a grumble from the living room. "Great," said Rem. "It won't take long. Watch Bigfoot and let me know if they find him." He found a pot, filled it with water and put it on the stove to boil. He glanced into the other room and saw Daniels fiddling with the remote, looking like he was trying to change the channel, but failing. "You want some water?" He pulled out the pasta and a bottle of sauce and filled a glass with water. He brought the glass to Daniels. "Here. Drink this."

Daniels stared at it. "Does Manetti drink water?"

"I believe so, if he intends to remain alive."

"Then I don't want it."

Rem set it on the coffee table. "It's our secret. I won't tell if you won't."

Daniels eyed him and sighed. "Fine." He sat up, grabbed the water and drank some.

"Good." Keeping an eye on Daniels, Rem returned to the kitchen. Daniels gave up on trying to change the channel and complained about Bigfoot while Rem finished the spaghetti. Once it was ready, he made a bowl for each of them and brought them into the living room. "Here," he said to Daniels. "Eat."

"I'm not hungry," said Daniels. "You want some tequila?"

"How about this?" Rem held out the bowl. "You eat all of it, and I'll get you something else to drink. Sound good?" He hoped Daniels wouldn't challenge him on what that drink would be, because it wouldn't be liquor.

Daniels hesitated.

"You'll thank me later," said Rem. "I promise."

Sitting up, Daniels reached for the bowl. "Maybe I'll eat a little."

"Great." Rem sat and they both ate while a new Bigfoot program came on.

"How many of these are there?" asked Daniels.

"A lot," said Rem, chewing his noodles.

Daniels drooped. "They're never going to find him, are they?"

"It's not easy. It takes time." Rem smiled and Daniels stopped chewing and scowled. "Sorry," said Rem. "I couldn't resist."

He and Daniels continued to eat until Daniels took a final bite, wiped his face and put his empty bowl down. "Thanks for the food."

"Feel better?"

"I feel fine. Never felt better." He belched again. "Where's that tequila?"

"You need to finish your water."

Daniels aimed another glare at him.

Rem set his bowl down, determined to hold his ground. "Listen. I've had a few drinking binges myself where you held back on the liquor. Now I get to return the favor."

Daniels waved. "I was wrong, and you were right. I can admit that."

"Now I know you're drunk."

Daniels narrowed his eyes. "I can handle my liquor."

"Don't you have to work tomorrow?"

Daniels fell back onto the sofa. "What are you? My mother?"

Rem sighed. "Your mother wouldn't give a shit. I do."

Daniels stared at the ceiling. "You do?"

"Of course I do." Rem tossed his napkin on the coffee table. "I admit. I haven't been around much, but I'll do better."

"You've had a lot on your mind." Daniels stifled a yawn and his eyes sparkled when his eyes watered.

Rem nodded, feeling guilty. "I'm still dealing with it, but that doesn't mean we can't talk."

"You haven't acted like you wanted to."

"I know. I'll work on that. I can't promise I won't have some setbacks, though." He thought about the impending lab results and what he would do if he learned Allison's baby had been his.

"It's okay."

"No, it isn't."

Daniels yawned again, leaned to his side and laid his head against a cushion. "I could go for a brownie right now. I'd take a pitchure of it and send it to Manetti."

"If you had a mix, I'd make you some."

Daniels pulled the cushion closer. "You want a banana?"

Rem chuckled.

"Because I'd share one with you, Manetti be damned." He blinked his tired eyes.

Rem's heart fell. "I appreciate that." He watched his partner's eyes grow heavier. "You're a good partner, Daniels. And I'm sorry about what I've put you through."

Daniels tucked his legs up and sighed. "Don't apologize. You need time." He snorted. "I just broke my promise."

Rem smiled softly. "You're forgiven." He paused. "Get some rest. I'll be here. You won't be in the house alone."

Daniels closed his eyes. "Just gonna take a little nap."

He went still and within seconds, his breathing deepened. Rem stood, went into a downstairs closet, and pulled out two blankets. He returned to the living room, covered Daniels with one, and settled back into his seat with the other. He grabbed the remote and getting comfortable, he flipped through the channels before returning to the Bigfoot program, hopeful the researchers might find him.

His eyes still closed, Daniels stirred, pulled the blanket up and spoke so softly, Rem almost didn't hear him over the TV. "I miss you, partner," he said.

His chest tightening, Rem watched his partner drift back to sleep and answered. "I miss you, too."

Chapter Fifteen

MASON STARED OUT THE window of the surgical waiting area. Not long after Kyle had been brought in, they'd rushed him upstairs for emergency surgery. He, Mikey and Trick had followed and were now trying to fill the time until someone came out and told them something. He glanced behind him, seeing Trick pace and Mikey sit in her chair, her arms crossed and clenching her elbows. All of them were scared. Based on what Trick had told them, it didn't look good.

The elevator dinged and the doors opened. An older woman stepped off and Mason recognized Lena, Kyle's grandmother and the shaman who'd helped banish Mr. Dark from Mason's home.

Mikey saw her and ran over, giving her a hug. Lena hugged her back. "How is he?" asked Lena.

"We don't know," said Mikey. "We're still waiting."

Mason walked over along with Trick. They both welcomed her and gave her a hug. "It's good to see you," said Mason.

She smiled softly and the wrinkles around her eyes deepened. "It is good to see you, too."

"Too bad it has to be like this," said Trick. He eyed the doors to Surgery as if willing them to open.

"Where's Kyle's Mom?" asked Mason.

"She's in Arizona but on her way back. She should be here in the morning," said Lena.

"She must be so worried," said Mikey.

Lena nodded. "We are all worried, but Kyle has a strong physical connection to this earth. If he's not ready, he won't leave it."

"He also has a strong spiritual connection," said Mikey. "I don't want any of those ancestors to sway him to the other side."

Lena smiled. "They only want what is best for him, as do we. Kyle must decide for himself what he wants to do."

Trick ran a hand through his hair. "Well, Kyle better choose here, or I'm going to kick his butt to Kansas." He'd cleaned the blood from his hands, but his bloody shirt and sleeves remained.

Serene despite the circumstances, Lena took his hand. "Come. Sit with me."

Trick hesitated, but when Lena tugged on him, he went with her. Mason and Mikey watched as she sat with Trick.

After arriving at the ER, Trick had told them what had happened, and Mason knew Trick was blaming himself. None of them would do well if Kyle died, but Trick would take the brunt of it.

"Lena knows what happened?" Mason asked Mikey.

"I told her what Trick said." Mikey leaned back against the wall and stared at the ceiling. "He can't die, Mason. He just can't."

Mason figured Mikey was feeling some guilt of her own whether it was deserved or not. "Lena's right. He's strong. He'll survive."

Mikey ran her hands through her hair. "This whole thing is crazy. Who could have done this to him, and why?"

"Trick said he went to meet Eleanor."

"You think Eleanor did this?"

"I don't know. Only Kyle can tell us that."

The elevator doors dinged again, and Mason deflated when Detectives Bevins and Winkler stepped off. "Hell."

Mikey looked over and sighed.

"We need to keep Trick away from Bevins." Mason stepped toward them. "Detectives."

They approached. "How is Mr. Willow?" asked Winkler. Bevins eyed all of them but didn't say anything.

"In surgery," said Mason.

"It's serious," said Mikey, who'd joined them. "He may not make it." Her face was pale, and she struggled to say the words, but to her credit, she held it together.

"I'm sorry to hear that," said Winkler. "I hope he pulls through."

Trick spoke from behind Mason. "What do you two want?"

Winkler glanced behind Mason and Trick stood and came over, his face stony. "You have anything bad to say about Kyle and I'll kick you out of here myself."

Bevins opened his mouth, but Winkler spoke first. "We came to see how he is, but also to ask some questions. We need to find out who did this to him."

"He went to meet Eleanor," said Trick. "And he was attacked."

Bevins snickered. "You think she did it?"

Trick set his jaw. "Let me guess, Doolittle. This is a drug deal gone bad."

"If the shoe fits," said Bevins.

Trick erupted. "You son-of-a—" He reached for Bevins. Mason jumped between them and caught Trick's arm.

Trick cursed but Mason held him back. "Take it easy. You can't beat up a detective."

"Watch me," said Trick, breathing hard.

Winkler turned, took Bevins' elbow and spoke softly to him.

Lena came over and stood beside Trick. Bevins frowned and said something to Winkler.

"You are angry," said Lena to Trick. "But Kyle wouldn't want this. Don't let this man's words control you."

Bevins straightened, still frowning. He yanked on his belt buckle. "I'm going to use the john." He turned and headed down the hall.

Trick calmed at Lena's advice. "The guy's an asshole."

"He may be," said Lena, "but that's his cross to bear. Don't match his energy. That only makes you an asshole, too."

Trick put his hands on his hips and hung his head.

Winkler tried again. "We just need to know what happened." She paused and eyed Trick. "Do you think Eleanor did this?"

Trick raised his head and sighed. "I don't know. He told me someone gave him a note with an address. Said Eleanor wanted to meet him. Whoever sent it supposedly matched Eleanor's description. Kyle went and didn't wait for me. When I got there, I heard a shriek, and I entered. But it was dark." He shook his head. "Something rushed at me and knocked me down. Whoever it was took off and that's when I saw Kyle."

Winkler took out a notepad and scribbled on it. "You said something rushed at you. Can you give me any kind of description?"

Trick groaned. "It happened so fast."

Lena took his wrist. "Close your eyes and relax. You're trying too hard."

Trick scoffed. "Miss Lena, I appreciate—"

"Come sit," said Lena. "I'll help you."

Trick hesitated.

"Let her help," said Mikey. "She knows what she's doing."

Trick huffed. "I don't see—"

"Shut up, Trick," said Mason. "Just try it. You want to find this person, don't you?"

Trick slumped. "Fine." He walked to a chair and sat. "What do I do?"

Lena sat beside him. "Close your eyes."

Trick shot a look at her, but then settled back and shut his eyes.

"Take deep breaths," said Lena, touching his arm.

Mason watched as Lena guided Trick to relax. Trick's shoulders dropped and his body lost some of its tension.

"When you're ready," said Lena. "Go back to the building where Kyle is. You're outside of it. What do you see?"

Trick described the area.

"What do you hear?" asked Lena.

Trick mentioned the street noise and then the scream.

Lena nodded. "Is the scream male or female?"

Trick's face scrunched. "Female."

"Go into the building. What do you see and hear?"

Trick squirmed. "I hear shuffling. And moaning, but it's dark. Hard to see." He jolted. "Something's there."

"What's there?" asked Lena.

Mason, Mikey and Winkler had moved closer, and Mason leaned in to listen.

Trick's face lost some color. "It...It's there." His face tightened. "I can't see it."

"Slow it all down," said Lena. "Like a movie projector."

Trick clenched his eyes. "I see a flash. It's white." He paused. "No, red." He flinched. "She had blood on her. Her face." He gasped and opened his eyes.

Lena pulled back, her own eyes wide.

"What did you see?" asked Winkler.

Trick caught his breath. "I...I...think it was Eleanor. She had Kyle's blood on her face."

"Eleanor attacked Kyle?" asked Mikey. "But why?"

Lena held her stomach. She held a faraway look and appeared almost as pale as Trick.

"Lena?" asked Mason. "You okay?" He squatted next to her.

Lena blinked and then looked at them. "I saw it, too, through Trick's eyes." She stilled and her posture stiffened. "It's not Eleanor," she paused. "at least not anymore."

• • • • • • • • • •

Margaret Redstone stood at the end of the hall, watching the group in the waiting area. Seeing them gathered around an older woman, she wondered what they were discussing. The detective wrote in her notebook and the older woman spoke. Then the older woman shook her head, blinked and looked in Margaret's direction. Turning away, Margaret entered an adjacent supply closet but left the door slightly ajar. A minute passed before she widened the door and looked down the hall. The group was talking and paid no attention as she left the closet and entered the restroom across the corridor.

Smiling, she stopped at the mirror and studied her reflection. Her blue eyes sparkled, and she ran her hands down her nurse's uniform. She'd found it in a staff locker room, and it had fit her perfectly. She'd pulled her long hair into a bun at her neck and had found a nametag in another locker. It was for a woman named Veronica who was a pediatric nurse.

Avoiding pediatrics, she'd found her way to her father's room. She'd poked her head in and had spoken briefly to Vicki, explaining her disguise and the need for it. Her father was sleeping, and she didn't speak to him, but Vicki had told her all she'd needed to know. Vicki had said the police were looking for her and were expecting Vicki to turn her in. Margaret assured her that everything she'd been told was a lie, that she loved her family, and that she would one day prove her innocence.

Vicki had hesitated but agreed to keep Margaret's visit a secret. Margaret had kissed her dad's cheek with a smirk and then left to find the surgical wing where her brother and sister had gathered, waiting to hear about Kyle's condition.

She'd watched briefly, much as she had the other day at the zoo, while Remalla had spoken to Mikey. The encounter still annoyed her, but she reminded herself it was only temporary. Mikey would be dead soon and Remalla would be hers. And when she was done with him, he would be dead, too.

Smoothing her hair, she reviewed her plan again. The risks were high, the room for error minimal, and the danger grew with each passing day, but if she could pull it off, it would cement her role as a woman not to be messed with. Her power would be absolute, her followers would worship her, her brother and sister would be dead, and her father wouldn't be far behind. Max would stay alive, at least for now.

Anticipating her victory, she smiled. If she could keep Vicki on board, everything would fall into place. The bigger issue would be Eleanor, who posed a much greater threat. But Margaret liked a challenge, and she would handle this one as she'd done others–with determination, fearlessness, and an unbending will.

Satisfied with her progress, she tucked a loose strand of hair behind her ear and left the bathroom. The portly Detective Bevins left the men's restroom at the same time; the two almost collided. She excused herself, Bevins grunted, and she went one way, and he went the other.

Chapter Sixteen

MIKEY STOOD OUTSIDE HER dad's hospital door. "You ready?" she asked Mason, who stood next to her.

It had been two days since her dad's and Kyle's attacks. Kyle had made it through surgery, had spent a day in ICU and had been settled into a private room that morning two stories above. Her dad remained in the hospital, still suffering from bouts of chest pain, nausea and dizziness while the doctors tried to figure out the cause. Mikey had waited a day to give her dad some time to rest but Vicki had told her today would be fine to visit.

Mason groaned. "You sure you want to do this?"

Mikey sighed. "This is our dad. He's in the hospital. You don't want to at least check in with him, tell him you hope he's okay?"

"Mikey, you seem to think he'll care."

"This health scare has to be a big wake up call for him. That can change people."

Mason raised his brow. "This is Dad we're talking about. The only thing changing him is too much, or too little, booze."

"Mason—"

"I appreciate what you're trying to do, but I don't think Dad's changing anything. If you want to try and talk, then go for it, but don't expect much. If you do, you're only going to get your feelings hurt."

"I know what I'm doing, and I'm under no illusions when it comes to Dad. But I have to do this."

Mason eyed the door with wariness. "Fine. I'll go in with you, but I reserve the right to leave the minute he starts in on us. I'll go find Kyle's room and Trick."

"That's fair." Mikey put her hand on the door and took a big breath. She knocked softly and heard someone say, "Come in." She pushed the door open.

Her father was lying in bed, an IV pole beside him and an oxygen tube at his nose. He looked pale, and the covers were up to his shoulders. Vicki sat beside him, holding a book. Seeing them, she set the book down and stood. "Hi."

"Hi," said Mikey. She'd brought her dad some flowers in a small vase, and she carried them in. "Hey, Dad," she said. Mason walked in behind her.

Her father blinked at them, then widened his eyes. "Well, look who's here."

Mikey set the vase on a table against the wall. "I brought you some flowers."

"They're lovely," said Vicki. "Aren't they, Martin?"

Her dad looked at them but didn't show much interest. He glanced at Mason.

"How are you feeling?" asked Mason.

Martin attempted to sit up, but Vicki put her arm on his shoulder. "Take it easy. I'll get it." She found the remote and hit a button. The head of the bed began to rise.

"I keep telling these doctors I'm fine," said Martin. "But they keep insisting something's wrong."

"Their tests haven't found anything?" asked Mikey.

"Screw their stupid tests," said Martin. "I got some kind of low counts that should be higher and maybe some heart damage, but at my age, that's normal." Martin adjusted his position in the bed, but grimaced. "But if you're here because you think I'm dying and hoping for some kind of inheritance, you're out of luck."

Mikey approached the bed. "That's ridiculous. We're not here for any inheritance."

"Good," he said. "Because I don't have any." He pulled his arms out from under the blankets and rested them on the covers.

Mikey saw the IV and the bruises on his forearms. "Dad, what happened?"

Martin glanced at his injuries. "Damn nurses keep poking and prodding at me like I'm some damned pin cushion. I'm amazed my whole body isn't bruised."

"That's the hospital for you," said Mason.

Martin ticked up an eyebrow. "That's right. You've had some experience with hospitals."

Mikey glanced at Mason, not sure if her dad's comment was a dig or not.

"We're hoping he can leave soon," said Vicki. "He's got doctors in Texas who can treat him."

"Better they find out what's wrong first," said Mason.

"You don't want to be on a plane and collapse again," added Mikey.

Martin sneered. "I'm fine. Everybody's too damn worried. I talked to your brother on the phone this morning. He was gonna hop on a plane and come home a day early just to see me. I told him not to bother. He's got some deal he's working on and that's way more important. You two on the other hand, don't have those issues."

Mikey sensed Mason's mood swing. "On the contrary, Dad," said Mason. "We have a business to run, too."

"Not like your brother. At least he's got some money coming in." Martin scoffed.

Mikey touched Mason's arm. "We do too, Dad," said Mikey. "We're not destitute."

"Not yet," said Martin.

"Martin, maybe you should rest," said Vicki.

"I've rested enough," said Martin. He eyed Mason. "You know, your brother would be happy to employ you both. He's told me as much."

"All right. That's it." Mason headed for the door.

Martin raised his voice. "And if you weren't so damn stubborn and pig-headed, Mason, you'd see I'm right. You can't keep doing this paranormal crap forever."

Mason yanked the door open. "You know where I'll be, Mikey." He walked out and the door closed behind him.

Mikey squeezed her temples. "Why do you do that, Dad?"

"Martin, please. Try and relax." Vicki put a hand on his shoulder. "The doctor says not to get too excited."

Martin ignored her and spoke to Mikey. "Listen to me, Michaela. You need to get out while you still can. All this nonsense of helping your brother is going to hurt you in the end. I've heard about all the shenanigans. Mason and you almost getting killed, Monroe getting stabbed. Some dark man going after Mason and now this coworker and boyfriend of yours almost dying the same time as me. It's no wonder your brother got hooked on pills."

"He's not my boyfriend," said Mikey.

"Probably because you're drooling over some other man who doesn't want you." Martin rolled his eyes.

"Martin...," said Vicki.

"You can come back to Texas," said Martin. "Stay with me if you want. I can probably get you a job at the plant—"

"Dad, stop," said Mikey, raising her hand.

"You could make decent wages and you wouldn't have to worry about Mason's weird friends and getting caught up in some damn cult again. Maybe you and your sister can make peace—"

"I said stop it," yelled Mikey. She hadn't meant to raise her voice, but she couldn't take it anymore.

Her father closed his mouth but scowled at her.

"I'm not going back to Texas and I'm not leaving Mason." Mikey tried to breathe evenly. "I didn't come here to argue about my future nor discuss my love life. None of it is your business. I'm here because you're sick and I want to be sure you're okay." She crossed her arms. "And I'll tell you again. Margaret is dangerous. She and I will never be close. She needs treatment."

"Don't talk about your sister like that," said Martin.

"How can you protect Margaret and constantly malign me and Mason?" asked Mikey with surprise. "I don't get it."

Martin frowned. "There's hope for you, Michaela. Mason is a lost cause, but you—"

"Don't say that," said Mikey, her tone serious. "Mason has been better to me than you ever have." Her anger rose to the surface. "Mason was there when you were out with your women and your liquor, leaving Mom to raise all of us. And when Max left the house and Margaret followed, it was just me and Mason. And Mom. We took care of each other while you took care of yourself."

"Watch your mouth, Michaela." He sneered.

"You watch yours," said Mikey. "You can't question someone's character without questioning your own. Maybe you should try a little self-reflection before you start judging me and Mason."

Martin set his jaw but then grimaced and gripped the sheets.

"That's enough," said Vicki. "You're upsetting him. Martin, lie back. I'll get the nurse." She grabbed the remote and started to lower the bed.

"*I'm* upsetting *him*?" asked Mikey.

"I don't need a damn nurse," said Martin, but his face paled more, and he held his chest.

Vicki got him level and she hit the call button. "I think you should go," she said to Mikey.

Mikey, disappointed in herself for letting her father get to her, agreed. "Mason was right," she said. "We should have never come." She walked to the door and opened it. "Have a nice life, Dad."

He narrowed his eyes at her and she walked out.

• • • • •• • • • •

Mason stepped out of the elevator onto Kyle's floor. Trying not to think about his dad because it only pissed him off, he eyed the room numbers, looking for Kyle, when he heard his name called. He turned to see Trick sticking his head out of a doorway and waving at him.

Mason turned and walked over. "What are you doing?" He stopped and saw a small visitors' lounge. It had a round table with four chairs, a refrigerator, vending machine, sink and a coffeemaker on a counter. "I found the free stuff." Trick walked to the counter. "You want some coffee?" He grabbed a Styrofoam cup.

"No thanks." Mason walked in. "I've had more coffee these last two days then I've had all year." He eyed the vending machine. "What are you doing in here? Where's Kyle?"

Trick poured coffee in his cup. "His Mom, Lena and a few other family members are in his room, doing some sort of healing chanting ceremony."

Mason swiveled to face Trick. "Is he okay?"

Trick sipped the coffee and sat at the table. "Better than yesterday. I saw him for a few minutes, and we talked. Winkler even showed and asked him a few questions before he tired out. Then the family arrived."

"You didn't want to join the chanting ceremony?" asked Mason.

"They invited me, but I declined." He eyed his coffee. "I sort of felt like a fifth wheel." He looked up at Mason and Mason could see his friend's fatigue. "It's kind of like you hanging out with your dad," said Trick. "The two don't quite fit."

Mason nodded, guessing why Trick felt uncomfortable with Kyle's family. Guilt. It was all over Trick's face. Mason turned back toward the vending machine. Seeing some bottled water, he fed some money into the machine and punched a button. The bottle fell and Mason retrieved it. "You know," he said, cracking the bottle and sitting next to Trick. "This isn't your fault."

Trick blew out a deep breath. "I should have been there."

"You told him to wait."

"And he's young and was excited about solving Jag's case." He sat up. "You and I? We were trained properly. As Rangers, we knew the pitfalls and understood what we'd signed up for." He shook his head. "I didn't prepare Kyle for anything. I might as well have attacked him myself."

Mason stared in disbelief. "We're private investigators, Trick. We're not Rangers anymore. Most of our business is mundane. You had no reason to believe this would be any different."

"I shouldn't have assumed anything. You gave us that message that night we had dinner with Daniels. That whatever it is we're dealing with shouldn't be found. Did I listen? No. I went off half-cocked, thinking I knew everything, and Kyle almost died because of it."

"None of us argued with you. If you're going to blame yourself, then you might as well include me and Mikey, too." Mason drank some water. "I mean, what if the situation were reversed? What would you tell me if I'd been with Kyle instead of you?"

"I'd be saying the same thing you're saying to me, but you wouldn't be listening, either."

Mason couldn't deny it. "If I've learned anything from Tarina, it's that I can't take on the responsibility for everything. We do our best and learn from our mistakes. But the key is how we judge our mistakes." He paused. "You and I suffer from a similar affliction. We judge ourselves too harshly.

You had no reason to believe Kyle was in danger. It could just as easily have been you in that building." He considered another possibility. "And what if you two had gone in together? You might both be dead because no one would have arrived to scare Eleanor off." He played with the cap of his water. "Instead of blaming yourself, maybe you should give yourself credit for saving his life."

Trick stared off and picked at his cup. "Maybe."

"He's alive," said Mason. "Let's not dwell on what could have happened. You'll only drive yourself crazy. I should know."

Trick paused and swirled his coffee. "When you were on the pills, Red, conversations like this were rare." He held Mason's look. "It's really good to have you back."

Mason smiled. "It's good to be back. And it's good that I can be there for you and Mikey, instead of the other way around."

Trick nodded. "It's been a while since you've given me a pep talk."

"It's way overdue."

Trick chuckled. "I suppose it is." He sipped some coffee. "Where's Mikey?"

Mason rolled his eyes. "In the lion's den."

Trick furrowed his brow.

"She's with Dad, God help her. Thinks she needs to tell him she loves him and forgives him. She's afraid he's going to die."

"Is she sick?" asked Trick. "Feverish?"

"No. She's quite well."

"I wish her luck." Trick checked her watch. "How long do you want to give her before she realizes her mistake and finds us?"

Mason shrugged. "Ten minutes?"

"Such the optimist," said Trick. "I give her five."

"You're on," said Mason. He took a swig of water. "What happened with Winkler? Was Bevins with her?"

"No, thank God because I never would have let him in Kyle's room." Trick smirked. "I think Winkler suspected as much."

"Smart move on her part."

"I agree." Looking more relaxed, Trick leaned back in his seat. "Kyle was able to tell her that he went into the building, but it was dark. Said there was a woman in the shadows. He spoke to her, and she told him he was handsome. He said he smelled something funny and had a horrible feeling. He wanted to leave. The next thing he remembers is waking up in the hospital."

"The woman never identified herself as Eleanor?" asked Mason.

"Not that Kyle recalls."

Mason set his bottle down. "None of this makes sense. Why would she go after Kyle? Do you think Eleanor killed Jag and the mystery man?"

"You've seen her picture. She's a petite woman. How could she overpower two men and Kyle?"

"And you. She knocked you down, remember?"

"If that was her, she was strong. And fast." Trick shook his head. "Hell. Maybe Bevins is right. What if this is about drugs? Did she take some and lose her mind? That's the only explanation."

"Lena said it wasn't Eleanor anymore," said Mason. "Maybe that's why. Some hallucinogenic could do that to you."

"The question is, where is she now?" asked Trick. "Where did she go? Will she attack again? And where is she getting these drugs?"

Mason picked at the label on his water bottle. "Maybe we should consider dropping this case."

Trick straightened. "Are you serious?"

"I am. You and Kyle almost got killed by some crazed woman who has the strength of both of you combined, the speed of a cat, and wicked sharp dagger skills. There's no shame in cutting our losses. Let the cops find her."

"There's no way I'm dropping this. This woman injured Kyle, and Jag's mom wants to know what happened to her son. Do you honestly think Bevins and Winkler are going to get to the bottom of this?"

Mason narrowed his eyes. "You want to risk your life for a woman you barely know? I realize she's paying us, but it's not worth your life."

Trick set his jaw. "There is more going on here than just a lady on drugs. I don't know what it is, but I want to find out. Plus, there's GQ to consider."

"GQ?"

"The woman who followed us. She's in this mess too and I bet if I find her, she can give me some answers."

Hearing his friend's tone, Mason held his head. "Now you want to look for someone whose name you don't know and that you've only seen once..."

"Twice."

Mason rolled his eyes. "How do you propose to do that?"

Trick shrugged. "Use my considerable charm and skills." He smiled. "She followed us once. Odds are, she's still following. I just need to lure her out."

Mason hesitated. "This doesn't bode well at all."

Trick smacked Mason on the arm and grinned. "Trust me, partner."

Mason was about to offer a colorful response when Mikey stuck her head in the room. "What are you two doing in here? Where's Kyle?"

Mason sighed. "Kyle's in a chanting ceremony. How'd it go with Dad?"

Mikey cursed and sat in a chair beside Mason. "I don't want to talk about it."

Trick eyed his watch. "Six minutes, Red." He sat back with a grin. "I win."

Chapter Seventeen

MIKEY POINTED AT THE laptop screen. "We could move Mrs. Lindler to next Tuesday and then you could see the Jeromes that morning."

Mason eyed the calendar. "That would work."

Mikey typed on her laptop. "I'll call them." She added another task to her to-do list.

Another day had passed since visiting their father in the hospital and checking in on Kyle. Kyle was sleeping a lot but was getting stronger and Mikey planned to visit him again later that afternoon. She hadn't spoken to Vicki or her dad since leaving the hospital the previous day.

She and Mason had come into SCOPE that morning ready to figure out how to handle their upcoming cases without Kyle's help. It would take some juggling, but Mikey had figured most of it out. "Be glad you had a few days off," she said to Mason, "because you're going to be busy until Kyle gets back on his feet."

Mason eyed his schedule and nodded. "We'll make it work."

"I don't want you to overdo it. If it gets to be too much, tell me. We'll just have to push a few other appointments back."

"I won't have to tell you a thing. You pick up on my fatigue just fine."

"That's true. Just don't try to hide it because that will piss me off." She set the laptop down on the coffee table.

"You heard from Vicki?" asked Mason.

"No. And I don't expect to." She picked up her cup of coffee. "She knew I was mad when I left and she defended Dad, so I think her attempts to calm the waters may be over." She sipped her drink but couldn't help but worry. "I suspect if Dad gets worse, she'll contact us, but other than that, they could be back in Texas for all I know."

"They'd tell Max."

Mikey shrugged. "I guess." She played with the seam on a couch cushion.

"You tried, Mikey. What did you expect?"

Mikey's dashed hope resurfaced. "I had this vision in my head where I told Dad how I felt, and he accepted it. Then we hugged and apologized, both said sorry, and that we loved each other."

Mason sighed. "I wish it could be that easy."

"I know." Tired of being sad, Mikey told herself to move on. "Where is Trick? Isn't he supposed to be here?"

"He's still on the Jag Trammel case."

Mikey frowned. "After what happened to Kyle?"

"He wants to find who did this."

"Isn't he just running around in circles?"

"He is, but he'll figure it out eventually."

Mikey heard the outer door to SCOPE open. "Speak of the devil."

"I can't wait to hear what he's been up to," said Mason.

"If it's dumb, I reserve the right to tell him."

"Feel free. It's your turn."

The inner door opened, and Trick entered, holding a folder. He took his hat off and hung it on a hook on the wall. "Where have you two been?"

Mikey stared at him. "Uhm...well...after a busy morning of crime fight-ing–I caught two bad guys and Mason caught one– we came to SCOPE. Now we're figuring out how to handle our cases with Kyle's absence. Where have you been?"

Trick smiled and sat beside Mason. "Having my next epiphany."

"Did it hurt?" asked Mason.

Trick opened the folder. "Check this out." He removed a piece of paper. Mason took it and Mikey leaned to look.

"Who's that?" asked Mikey. It was a sketch of a woman with a round face, short hair, wide eyes and full lips.

"That's GQ," said Trick. "The woman who followed me and Kyle." Looking satisfied, he leaned back.

Mason studied the photo. "Attractive woman."

"She is," said Trick.

"Who drew it?" asked Mikey.

Trick placed an ankle on his knee. "A lovely lady I met not too long ago. She's an artist." He smiled. "She and I...we met at the grocery store. We went for drinks and then, well, we spent a few hours...painting."

"Painting, huh?" asked Mikey. "I suspect we're not talking landscapes?"

Trick ticked up a brow. "No. We are not. More like nudes."

Mikey raised a hand. "I get the picture, so to speak." She eyed the sketch. "She drew this?"

"I told her what GQ looks like and she did a damn good job. Captured her likeness well." Trick took the sketch back from Mason.

"What exactly do you plan to do with it?" asked Mason.

Trick returned the picture to the folder. "Look for her."

"Why?" asked Mikey.

"Good question," said Mason.

"This woman watched us for a reason," said Trick. "She was looking for Eleanor, too, but didn't want to do the asking herself. She followed me and Kyle because she hoped we'd find Eleanor for her." He smoothed the cuff of his jeans. "Whoever she is wants to stay hidden as much as Eleanor. I figure if I start showing GQ's picture around and bring some attention to her, she might just come out into the open." He raised a finger. "In fact, I might make some copies and start plastering her picture around town."

"Or she could do exactly the opposite of what you expect," said Mason. "She'll stay out of sight. And then you've wasted more time looking for a ghost."

"Maybe you should let this go," said Mikey. "The police are looking for Eleanor. They even showed her picture on the news last night."

"I know," said Trick. "Which means my window is closing. If I don't find her before the cops do, who knows if we'll ever learn the truth."

"Your window?" asked Mason. He shifted in his seat. "Let me ask you. What does Jag's mother say about all this?"

"She wants me to keep going," said Trick. "She thinks there's something off about what happened to her son, too."

"Are you sure you're not swaying her decision?" asked Mason. "Based on what happened with Kyle, this Eleanor could definitely be on drugs, and she likely killed Jag. And maybe some stranger at that overlook who showed up at the wrong time. What else is there to know?"

"And Eleanor dragged that stranger off and hid him?" asked Trick. "That makes no sense."

Mikey hoped Trick's guilt wasn't pushing him to solve the case. "You're going to show that picture around like you did with Eleanor's?"

"I am," said Trick. "I'll go to the same places I did with Eleanor. And I'll keep showing Eleanor's picture, too. Might as well keep trying to find her."

Mikey dropped her jaw. "Trick. Eleanor is dangerous. You can't go alone."

"And with my schedule, I can't go with you," said Mason. "Plus, I'm not sure it's the best use of our time."

Trick narrowed his eyes. "I'm not dropping this case." Mason started to argue. "Red, listen," said Trick. "I get it, but you have to admit, there's more to Eleanor than meets the eye."

"Yeah," said Mikey. "She's a psychopath."

"What Mikey said," said Mason.

Trick straightened. "I know what you're saying but there's another possible scenario we should consider." He paused. "What if it's Eleanor's boyfriend?"

Mikey put her coffee cup back on the table. "Her ex? Considering what we know, I doubt it."

"Bear with me," said Trick. "What if he followed her? What if he saw Eleanor at the overlook with Jag and attacked Jag and maybe some other poor soul out there? Eleanor took off and the ex hid the stranger's body but wasn't able to hide Jag's. Then, he either catches up to Eleanor or she goes back to him, and Kyle enters the picture. Maybe Eleanor sent the note because she needs help. Kyle went but the ex attacked him, not Eleanor."

"But Kyle said he saw her," said Mason. "And you said you saw her, too. With blood on her face, when she rushed at you."

"But what if Kyle and I misinterpreted what we saw?" asked Trick. "What if the ex came up behind Kyle and Kyle never saw him? What if Eleanor was bloody because her ex hit her and she was only trying to help Kyle? Maybe her ex would have come after me, but she rushed and knocked me over to protect me."

Mason didn't say anything but looked at Mikey. "I believe it's your turn," he said.

Mikey nodded. "It is." She eyed Trick. "That's just dumb."

"You're much nicer than I would have been," said Mason.

"I'm in a decent mood," said Mikey.

Trick glowered. "I know what I'm talking about. You know me, Red. I've had some cockamamie ideas before, but they always lead to something."

"You mean the dumpster where bad ideas go to die?" asked Mason.

Trick waved the folder. "This woman knows something, and I intend to find out what it is."

"And what if you don't find her?" asked Mason. "Or Eleanor?"

Trick rubbed his neck. "Give me forty-eight hours. I come up empty or Bevins and Winkler, God forbid, find Eleanor first, then I'll contact Mrs. Trammel and tell her we've hit a dead end. And I'll..." he waved at the laptop. "I don't know. Help you pick up where Kyle left off."

"You could do some consultations," said Mikey. "That would help."

"Fine. But I get the forty-eight hours first. Deal?" he asked Mason.

"One condition," said Mason. "You find Eleanor, you don't go in by yourself. You could end up as her next victim."

"Red," said Trick. "I need to talk to her. Before the police do."

"This woman may have killed two men and almost killed Kyle," said Mikey. "Remember how you told him not to go in alone? The same applies to you."

"Kyle is new to this," said Trick. "I've got more experience."

"Regardless, you find her, you call me," said Mason. "You don't agree to that, and you can sit your butt down and start practicing how to talk to spirits, because right now, that's what we need the most."

Trick groaned and sat up. "Okay. I locate Eleanor, I'll call you."

"Promise?" asked Mason.

Trick smirked but crossed his heart with his fingers. "Promise."

· · · · ● · ● · · ·

Trick left the bar and stepped out onto the sidewalk. Tired and frustrated, he feared he'd have to call it quits soon. He'd spent the last day and a half showing both women's pictures around with no luck. He'd even plastered GQ's photo on several electricity poles, bulletin boards and lampposts, asking that if anyone saw her, to call his number. So far, he'd had two crank calls, but that was it.

Checking his watch, he had a few hours before he'd have to admit to Red he'd come up short. But he wouldn't give in yet. If he had time, he'd use it. So he kept going. He'd stopped at the same bars and clubs as before and had also tried neighboring drug or grocery stores. Eleanor had to shop somewhere, so it was possible someone might recognize her.

His list of places to check dwindling, he stopped for an espresso and downed it. He went into another bar and, having no luck, he left. Stopping on the sidewalk, he spotted another lamppost and posted GQ's picture again. Watching cars drive by and pedestrians head to their destinations, he slumped against the post, questioning his next move, realizing he'd run out of options. The only good news is that the cops hadn't found Eleanor either despite running her picture on the news. He had to wonder if she'd left town. If she was with her boyfriend, they could be anywhere now. Or even worse, the boyfriend could have killed and hidden Eleanor's body. If that were true, Eleanor might never be found.

Sighing, he walked down the sidewalk. The sun was beginning to go down, the streetlights were coming on, and the bars were getting busier. Heading to his truck, expecting to do a few consultations tomorrow, he turned down a small side street as a short cut, and stopped when he saw a sign for a bar that hadn't made his list. It was called O'Rourke's and a big poster board that read *Live Music* sat in a window of the bar. Trick could hear a guitar playing and a woman singing, and he headed inside.

The space was small but tidy and only about half-full. A man behind the bar with frizzy hair and smoking a cigarette greeted him. Trick sat at the counter and ordered a beer. He figured if this was his last place to stop, he might as well relax. The bartender gave him a beer with a frosted glass and Trick thanked him. He took a sip. "How long you guys been here?" he asked the bartender.

The man cleaned a glass. "Not long. I just opened the place about six months ago."

"You've always had a singer?" Trick listened as the woman with the guitar started a new song.

"Nah," said the man. "That's recent."

Trick figured that was the reason he hadn't pegged this bar as a place to check. He nodded toward the singer. "She's not bad."

The man shrugged. "Not as good as the other one we had."

His interest piqued, Trick gave it one last shot and pulled out the pictures of Eleanor and GQ. "Did she happen to be one of these ladies?"

The man came over, put out his cigarette in an ashtray, and studied them. "Never seen her." He pointed at GQ.

"I figured." Trick folded GQ's picture and put it away.

The man studied the second picture and pursed his lips. "That's Eleanor." He glanced at Trick. "You know her?"

Trick wasn't sure he heard correctly. "Eleanor?" He pointed at the photo. "You recognize her?"

He nodded. "Sure. She's the one I hired to sing. Did great, too. Customers liked her. She was a little shy. She came from a small town or something and was trying to get comfortable out here. She was starting to come out of her shell, though."

Forgetting his beer, he stood. "What's her last name?"

"Clyde," said the man. "Eleanor Clyde."

"You ever seen her with anyone? A boyfriend? Or did anyone come looking for her?"

The man shook his head. "Not that I recall. She kept to herself, until that last night. She did her set, then hung out with some friends at the bar. Seemed to be having a good time. Then they all left. Said they were going home. And I haven't seen her since."

Trick frowned. "Did she act strange or funny? Did she seem uncomfortable or appear threatened?"

"Not at all. Looked relaxed. I tried calling her when she didn't show, but she never picked up. I even went to her place and knocked a few times, but she didn't answer. I figured she just didn't want to sing anymore and didn't have the courage to quit. Or she'd met some guy and took off, but she'd never struck me as the type."

Trick wasn't sure he'd heard right. "You went to her place? You have her address?"

The man stared at him. "I hired her, didn't I? Of course I have her address. She lives in the small apartment down and across the street at the intersection. Above the dress shop." He pointed. "If you go outside and look left, you can see it from here."

His heart thumping, Trick grabbed his wallet and tossed some cash on the bar. "One more question," he said. "You watch the news?"

"The news?" asked the man. "No time for that while I'm working." He went back to cleaning his glass. "You find her, tell her she still has a job at O'Rourke's if she wants it."

Trick grabbed Eleanor's picture and returned it to his pocket. "Will do," he said and ran out of the bar.

Grateful the bartender hadn't called the police to tell them about Eleanor, Trick jogged down the street to the intersection. Seeing the dress shop, he crossed the road at the light, spotted a door next to the shop and opened it. He saw a staircase and entered far enough for the door to close behind him. Once it shut, he listened to the quiet and wondered what to do next.

Peering up the stairs, he could see a door and he hesitated, recalling his promise to Red. Should he call him? Technically, Trick hadn't yet located Eleanor. He could easily knock, and if she didn't answer, there was no reason for Red to join Trick just to stare at a door.

Deciding to at least go up the stairs and listen, Trick walked up. The stairwell light was on, and he approached the door. He put his ear against it and listened but didn't hear anything. Before he could talk himself out of it, he knocked softly. Not getting a response, he knocked harder. "Eleanor?" he called. "You home?" He knocked once more with no luck.

Telling himself to leave, get in his truck, park on the street and watch the place, he put his hand on the knob and gently turned it. To his surprise, it was unlocked.

Cursing, he debated his next move, but knew he couldn't leave. He opened the door a crack. "Hello?" he said through the crack. "Anyone home?"

It was dark inside and Trick heard nothing. He widened the door. "Hello?"

It remained quiet and Trick poked his head inside. "Eleanor Clyde?"

Nothing.

His heart thumped harder and making up his mind, he reached for the gun in his ankle holster, steeled himself, and opened the door further. "Anybody home?"

He flipped the light switch and the room brightened. The bartender had been correct. It was a small space. The living, dining room and kitchen shared one area and a small hall led to a bedroom and bathroom. Trick closed the door behind him.

He walked down to the bedroom and poked his head in. It was dark and he saw a rumpled bed and a closet. Clothes were strewn on the floor and over a small chair beside the bed. He checked the bathroom, but no one was home. Returning to the kitchen, he looked around, checking for anything that might indicate Eleanor's location.

Seeing a set of drawers against the wall beside a small table, he tucked his gun into the back of his waistband, walked over and opened a top drawer. He rifled through some papers but saw nothing of interest. He closed the drawer and opened the second one.

"Who the hell are you?"

Trick whirled at the voice and froze. Eleanor Clyde stood across the room from him.

Chapter Eighteen

MASON FOLLOWED MIKEY INSIDE his house. He tossed his keys onto the kitchen counter and opened the refrigerator.

Mikey set the to-go food bag on the table, opened it and pulled out the Styrofoam containers.

"You want a beer?" asked Mason.

"Just a water. Thanks." Mikey crumpled the bag and set it aside. "You heard from Trick?"

Mason took out two bottled waters and closed the refrigerator. "He texted earlier. He's still looking for Eleanor and this GQ, but he's had no luck." He brought the waters over to the table.

"He's stubborn, isn't he?" Mikey went to the sink to wash her hands.

"More than me." Mason waited and washed his hands after Mikey. "Plus, he doesn't want to admit failure." He turned off the faucet and dried his hands.

They both sat and opened their food. Mason's stomach grumbled. It had been a busy day at SCOPE and too tired to cook, Mason had suggested they stop for turkey burgers. Mikey had eagerly agreed. "You think he's eaten anything?" She poked the extra container on the table. "Should we tell him we got him a burger?"

Mason chewed a bite and drank some water. "I'll call him. Probably should check in anyway. Make sure he's okay and tell him to admit defeat." He pulled his phone from his pocket and hit a number to call Trick.

• • • • • • • • • •

Trick didn't move but held out his hands. "Eleanor Clyde?"

She stared intently at him. Trick thought she looked thinner than her photo. She had circles under her eyes and her hair was still up, but several pieces of it were falling in her face. He wondered how he'd missed her. She hadn't been in the bed or the closet. It hit him then that she must have been under the bed. But why? If she was hiding from someone, why leave her apartment door unlocked?

"Who are you?" she asked angrily. "What are you doing in my apartment?"

Trick stayed relaxed and projected calm. "Looking for you. You're a hard woman to find."

"Maybe because I don't want to be found."

She wore jeans that were loose on her and a wrinkled brown t-shirt. There were stains on it and Trick couldn't help but wonder if it was blood. "I just want to talk. The police are searching for you, too. We want to ask you about Jackson Trammel."

"Who?" She scrunched her face and swiped the hair off her neck.

"Jag Trammel. You are the last person to see him alive."

"Oh, him." She crossed her arms.

"Yeah. Him." Trick lowered his hands but kept them visible. Aware of the gun in his waist band, he kept his hands near his hips. "You two were talking at Bullard's. He was a bartender. You two left together. Remember?"

Her face fell and she spoke quietly. "He was nice. I liked him."

"What happened after you left the bar?"

"Uhm…" She stared off, then looked at Trick. "You didn't tell me who you are."

Trick slowly moved his hand to his jacket pocket. "My name is Trick Monroe." He slid out his PI identification. "I'm a private investigator hired to find out what happened to Jag." He held it out.

She barely looked at it. "Huh. You've been looking for me?"

Trick studied her and wondered if she was impaired. "Yes. Me and my friend Kyle have both been looking. Do you remember him?"

She narrowed her eyes. "Why would I?"

Trick stayed alert, in case she was on drugs, or her boyfriend was around. "You sent a note, telling Kyle to meet you at an abandoned building. But then he was attacked."

"When was this?" She scratched her head.

Definitely on something thought Trick. "A few days ago. Kyle was hurt, but he survived. He's in the hospital."

"Hospital?" She dropped her hand and rubbed her stomach. "You've been looking for me?"

Trick nodded but his concern grew. "Yes. I want to ask about Jag. What happened after you two left the bar?" He slid his ID back into his pocket, wanting both hands free.

She sighed and looked lost. "I don't know. We...he...invited me somewhere."

"To the overlook?"

She bobbed her head. "It was pretty."

"You went?"

She clutched her shirt. "I liked him." She paused. "We kissed."

Trick wondered if his boyfriend theory was more accurate than he realized. "What happened after that?"

She eyed the floor. "Something...I...don't remember." She shook her head. "Who's Kyle?"

Trick swallowed. "Kyle is my friend."

Eleanor stared off and then smiled. "He was handsome. I liked him, too."

Trick's heart thumped harder. There was definitely something off with this woman. "You okay? Are you sick?"

She didn't answer but her grip on her shirt tightened. "I'm hungry."

Trick used that, hoping it would help. "How about we go get something to eat after we talk? My treat."

Her hand on her stomach began to turn in circles. "Maybe."

Trick tried again. "Tell me about Jag, Eleanor. What happened on that bluff? Did someone attack you? Was there another man?"

She stilled. "Another man?" She exhaled a long breath and her eyes narrowed. "Yes."

Surprised, Trick took a small step toward her. "Who was it? Did he try to hurt you?"

The hand at her stomach moved faster and her face lost color. "He had a knife." Her body went rigid, and she turned angry. "They did this. They did this to me."

Trick froze. "Who did what? Did someone do something to you?"

"He...that man...wanted to kill me." Her voice shook. "And she...she made me. Said I could trust her."

Trick didn't understand. Eleanor seemed to be changing subjects at a rapid rate. "Maybe we should sit down. You want something to drink?"

She shot a hard look at him. "Do you want to kill me, too?"

Anxious, Trick moved his hands closer to his weapon. "No. I'm not here to hurt you. I want to help you."

Eleanor took a step toward him. "You said you'd feed me?"

Sensing her mood shift, Trick stepped back. "Eleanor, take it easy. Just relax."

She tipped her head and her eyes traveled over him. "You're handsome, like your friend."

A cold wet finger of fear slid up his spine and a putrid smell hit his nose. "Eleanor. Just stay where you are. Don't do anything stupid."

Her gaze held his, and Trick stepped back again, and he bumped into the set of drawers. His mind whirled with what to do. He didn't want to shoot her, but he didn't want to die either. "What's wrong, Eleanor?" He slid his hand behind him, grabbed his gun and slid it out of his waistband.

Her eyes darkened and she sneered. "The whole world's gone dark."

His heart raced. "What does that mean?"

She advanced. "I'm so hungry."

Trick's phone rang, she shrieked, and Trick pulled his weapon. But before he could even aim, she tackled him.

• • • • ● • ● • • •

Mason chewed and listened as the call went to voicemail. He waited for Trick's message to end, and left his own message, telling Trick to call it a night and to come to the house and enjoy a hamburger. He promised that he and Mikey would only hold his failure over him for a few minutes before they started teaching him how to contact spirits. Amused at himself, Mason chuckled and hung up the phone.

• • • • ● • ● • • •

Knocked against the wall with the force of Eleanor's assault, Trick slammed into the chest of drawers which tipped over and fell. Trick slid sideways onto a small table which cracked and broke under his weight. His gun flew from his fingers, and he hit the floor hard with Eleanor on top of him. Eleanor, her eyes wild, screamed and swung out at him and he raised a forearm to defend himself. She reached for his neck, and he flailed, trying to get her off of him. Her strength shocked him, and he managed to free a hand and grab her by the throat to push her away. She gnashed her teeth at him, and he twisted his body but couldn't get her off. He pushed harder but she fought him. Gaining leverage, she lunged again, and Trick felt a searing pain on his lower arm. She'd bitten him and blood began to drip from his injury. His phone stopped ringing and he made one last attempt to get free of her, but her strength only increased. She screeched again in his ear, and he fought to get the upper hand by pushing her to the side. If he could get her off, he might be able to run for the door. Her balance wavered and Trick shoved her to the ground. There was a second where he was free and he desperately tried to get away, but then she lunged for him again.

Realizing if she got access to his neck, he was dead, he made one last effort to fight, but she bit down on his arm again. The pain crushed him, and he prepared himself to become her next victim when something swooshed by his head.

Eleanor darted back just as a wicked blade narrowly missed Trick's face. The weight of Eleanor's body against his vanished and he pushed back and bumped into the refrigerator door. Trying to get his bearings, he heard another screech and saw Eleanor lunge at someone else in the room. He blinked, holding his injured arm and gasping for air. A woman holding a long knife swung it at Eleanor, who cackled and dodged it. The woman attacked again, and Trick saw a small dagger in her other hand. He expect-ed her to plunge it into Eleanor but at the last second, Eleanor twisted, brought a hand up, and swiped it across the woman's chest. A red streak of blood appeared, and the woman gasped, but quickly rebounded. She swiped the long knife again, but Eleanor was faster. She jumped up and kicked, landing a direct blow into the woman's midsection.

Trick, finally finding his strength, saw his gun on the kitchen floor. He reached for it as the woman was knocked into the sofa with the force of the kick. Trick stood as Eleanor hissed and raced at the woman.

"Eleanor," he screamed, aiming his gun, his hands shaking.

Eleanor stopped. The woman lay on the couch, blood seeping through her shirt, but she quickly jumped up and it finally hit Trick who she was. GQ.

"Shoot," she yelled.

Trick fired as GQ swung again with the knife. But Eleanor dodged both the bullet and the blade, scampered away with another shriek, and raced out of the apartment.

Chapter Nineteen

Stunned, Trick held his gun toward the empty doorway, expecting at any moment for Eleanor to return. His whole body trembled, and he couldn't stop looking at the door.

He heard a curse and managed to break free from his frozen state. Catching his breath, he lowered his weapon and turned to see GQ, her shirt red and her face sweaty, head toward the door. He could barely bring himself to speak. "Don't," he said. He expected Eleanor to be nearby and when GQ walked out the door, he braced himself. He watched as she went to the stairs and stared down them, before returning to the apartment, and closing and locking the door.

"Damn it," she said. She slid her dagger into a sheath on her belt and set the wicked looking knife on the kitchen counter.

Trick, still trying to comprehend what had happened, shook his head in disbelief. "What the hell?"

GQ finally looked at him. "You should have stopped looking." She walked over to him and tugged on his injured arm. "Let me see."

He winced but carefully loosened his hold on it. Blood soaked his sleeve and dripped onto the floor. She turned his forearm and studied it. "You'll need stitches." She let him go.

"You think?" he asked, gripping his arm again.

She started going through kitchen drawers, seemingly unaffected by her own injury. After finding a dish towel, she pulled it out, returned to Trick and grabbed his arm again.

He gasped. "Easy."

She wrapped his arm with the towel. "Relax, Texas. You'll live." She pulled the towel tightly and he fought not to gasp again. "Keep the pressure on it."

Trick tucked his arm against his stomach. "You're hurt, too."

GQ glanced down at herself. "It's minor. I've had worse." She looked around the apartment. "But we made a hell of a mess." She returned to the drawer, found another towel and held it against her chest. "We need to stop bleeding all over her floor."

"Who the hell are you?" asked Trick. Feeling a little more centered, he returned his gun to his waistband.

"Later," she said, pulling a phone from her pocket. She dialed and held the phone to her ear. Trick listened as someone answered, and she spoke. "I need you," she said and paused. "Negative. She escaped. But we need cleaners. Blood only. Oh, and a bullet. In the wall." She paused again and eyed Trick. "One witness." She sighed. "Yes. I know. I'll handle it." Another second passed and she set her jaw. "I said I'll handle it." She hung up and returned the phone to her pocket. "We need to get out of here. Hopefully no one called the cops from the sound of the gunshot." She went to the window and parted the shades to look outside. "Thankfully, the dress shop is closed and maybe the street noise muffled it."

Trick narrowed his eyes at her. "You going to tell me who you are?"

"It's not important." She turned and dabbed at her bloody shirt with the towel. "I need another shirt."

"It's not important?" asked Trick. "Eleanor almost killed me and if you hadn't showed, I'd be dead."

"You can thank me later." She walked away. Trick followed. His arm throbbed and he bit his lip with the pain. GQ went into Eleanor's room.

"What are you doing?" he asked.

"I told you. I need another shirt. I can't walk out of here like this." She dug through the closet and pulled a sweater from a hangar. "This should do."

"We need to go to the hospital," said Trick. "And call the police."

Regardless of Trick's presence, she pulled her bloody shirt off. Her bra was stained red, and her toned shoulders and midriff were smeared with blood. Her wound still oozed, and she pressed the towel against it. For the first time, she grimaced and, holding the towel against her wound, she tucked it into her bra straps and slid the sweater over it. "You can go to the hospital."

"What about you?" he asked.

She checked herself in the mirror. "I'm leaving."

Trick dropped his jaw. "Where are you going?"

Appearing satisfied with her appearance, she turned toward him. "That's not for you to know, Texas."

"You're not going to tell me your name?"

She left the bedroom and passed him. "Nope. You don't know me, and I was never here."

Trick, staring in disbelief, followed her. "I'll tell the police you were here."

"Go ahead." She picked up her knife from the counter, pulled a paper towel off a roll by the sink and wiped blood off of it. "I injured her, at least." She tossed the towel on the floor and slid the knife into a belt loop next to her dagger. The sweater effectively covered both the dagger and knife.

"You're just going to walk out of here as if nothing happened?" asked Trick.

"So are you." She walked to the door. "Let's go. I'll drop you at the hospital, but you can't tell them what happened here. Tell them you were attacked on the street. Say you were mugged.

"Why would I say that?"

GQ put her hand on the knob. "Because if you don't, you're risking the life of anyone who comes here. The fewer who know about this the better."

"The police have to know."

"The police can't do shit against Eleanor. You tell them this, they'll think you're crazy and they could end up dead. I have to find and kill her first. Then you can say whatever you want."

"If I found this place, then so will they."

"They stopped looking two days ago. They're hoping the picture on the news will work."

"And it might."

"It hasn't worked so far. It took your feet on the ground."

Trick finally understood. "You've been following me, hoping I'd lead you to her?"

She shrugged. "You're way more tenacious than those two detectives."

"They have to know. Eleanor killed Jag."

She tipped her head. "You barely survived this attack. How do you think they would fare if they locate her?"

Trick imagined Bevins fighting off Eleanor and almost laughed. "I can't sit on this information. Jag's mother wants to know what happened to her son. I have to do something."

"You did. You found Eleanor. Now let us do the rest. She'll come back and we'll be ready."

"Us? Who's us?"

GQ sighed. "I've said enough already."

She started to open the door when Trick walked over and closed it. "If you expect me to go to the hospital, pretend I was mugged and not say a word to anyone about this, you're as crazy as Eleanor."

She stared at him and nodded at the door. "I've got to go."

Trick shook his head. "I want to know your name."

"Not going to happen, although I appreciate all the flyers of my face you've been posting. I took them all down, by the way."

Trick kept his hand on the door. "I'm just getting started. You think I've posted flyers today? Just wait until I'm out of the hospital. I'll post them from here to L.A." Her face tensed and he knew he'd hit a nerve. "If I have to, I'll go to the police. Tell them that the woman in the flyer has knowledge of Jag's death and is on the run."

She tensed. "They won't believe you."

"I can be very convincing. I'll tell them you're a drug dealer. They're into that whole drug scenario thing. And I'm sure I can get footage of you in Bullard's with me and Kyle. It would at least prove you exist. From there, it's just a short hop to the press. They've already showed Eleanor's picture. I'm sure they'd be happy to show yours."

She aimed a steely glare at him. "You're a pain in the ass, Texas."

"I'm just getting started, GQ."

"You have to back off this thing. For your own safety."

"Eleanor slaughtered Jag, and almost Kyle, and someone else on that overlook."

She shifted and looked away.

Trick straightened. "You know who it is, don't you? The mystery man in the woods whose body is missing?"

She glared more. "Leave it alone."

Trick shook his head. "I won't leave it alone. Who was it?" She didn't answer. "Did you know him?" She narrowed her eyes and Trick held his breath. "Did you move his body?"

GQ stepped up close, her gaze hard. "I said, leave it alone."

Trick's arm throbbed and he held it against him. "I won't."

She didn't back down. "You don't know what you're asking."

"So tell me."

She hesitated. "You go down this rabbit hole, there's no going back."

He raised the side of his lip. "I'm intrigued."

GQ studied him. "You won't like it."

"I don't care."

She took a step back. "It's too dangerous. Just listen to me and do as I say. Go to the hospital. If you insist on telling the cops what happened, then at least make sure they don't show up here for another hour. We have to get this place cleaned up."

"Why? I'm injured. That will explain the blood."

"It won't explain mine."

"I'll tell them you saved me and left."

"I can't allow that. I can't have my blood in their system. For my safety and others. So if you're going to say you were attacked here, you better have a reason as to why there's no blood in the apartment."

Trick didn't like any of this. "I have a better idea. You tell me who you are and why you're here and I'll leave the police out of it."

GQ shook her head. "Just leave Eleanor to me and go back to your life. Trust me. I know what I'm talking about."

"What do you plan to do if someone already called the cops because of the gunshot?"

"I'm not hearing any sirens, so I think that's a non-issue."

"But what would you have done?"

She batted her eyelashes and smiled demurely. "Why officer," she said in a sultry voice. "I didn't hear any gunshot. It must have come from the street." She held her chest. "This area is just so dangerous."

"You think that would have worked?"

"I know it would have."

Trick had to admit she was probably right. "What about me?"

She smirked. "You would have been in the bedroom, resting. Either voluntarily or involuntarily."

Trick debated whether she would have actually knocked him out if he'd argued. Despite his inner conflict, he couldn't let her leave. "Listen to me, GQ. It's become quite clear that Eleanor is not your typical meth head with a mean streak. Women with daggers and knives don't follow P.I.'s to find drug addicts. And they certainly don't call a cleaner and then expect to walk off into the sunset after saving a witness. If you expect me to leave without getting some answers, then you obviously don't know me well."

She chuckled. "I know you very well, Trick Monroe."

He startled. "You know my name?"

"I do." She crossed her arms. "Travis 'Trick' Monroe. Born and raised in Texas. Mother is Pamela Monroe who struggles with addiction issues. Father is unknown but you have five stepfathers. I'd name them but we're pressed for time. Eight years on the Fort Worth P.D. and four as a Texas Ranger. The first two years, you were partnered with Mason Redstone and the other two years, well, that's another deep well we don't have time to jump into. Redstone left to pursue his paranormal exploits and opened SCOPE. His sister Mikey joined the firm after escaping her own difficult past. You, after a year in a drunken haze and sleeping with more women than usual, decide to patch up your difficulties with Mason and move out here to join him at SCOPE." She smiled. "It's the tip of the iceberg, but you get the picture."

Shocked, Trick grit his teeth but held his ground. "I want to know who you are and what your role is with Eleanor, lady." He pointed. "And if you don't tell me, I'm going to raise a stink with every law enforcement agency I can, and I'll plaster your face across this damn state." He stepped closer. "And if you think I won't, then you didn't do enough research." Trick eyed the apartment. "In fact, screw the hospital. I'll call the police from here. Right now. Tell them there's an intruder. Your damsel in distress act won't stop them from checking the apartment and there won't be any time for a cleaner."

She clenched her fingers. "You're threatening a woman with a dagger and a knife who knows how to use them."

"And you're threatening a man who's got just enough information to make a hell of a mess for you. Which do you think is more dangerous?"

She stepped closer to him. "You have no idea what you are dealing with."

Trick had a moment of doubt but let it pass. "A woman who weighs barely a hundred pounds attacked me and almost ripped my throat out. Then you show up with your Black Widow moves and weapons, save me and almost kill Eleanor. I'd say I'm getting a glimpse. I don't know of what, but I'm too far in now for you to ignore me."

She scowled back at him and went quiet. Trick could tell her mind was whirling. He waited, hoping he'd changed her mind. Considering her skills, she could knock him out cold, dump him at the hospital and he'd be screwed trying to explain what happened to him.

She put her hand on the doorknob and glared. "You do exactly as I say, got it? You deviate one step from what I tell you, I'll kick you to the curb so fast, the damage to your arm will feel like a sponge bath. And if you bring any scrutiny my way that endangers me or anyone else, Eleanor will not be the only one I hunt down and kill." She leaned in. "You understand?"

Her intensity almost made him back down, but he dropped his hand from the door instead. "Lead the way."

She hesitated once more, and with another glare, she opened the door. "Remember," she said, "you asked for this."

Trick didn't respond and followed her out.

Chapter Twenty

THEY WALKED DOWN THE stairs and stopped at the door to the street. GQ glanced outside and spoke to Trick. "Hold your arm close. If anyone asks, you slipped and fell and I'm taking you to the hospital."

Trick nodded, wondering where they were going. He looked her over and saw her sweater was still free from blood. He wondered how long that would last.

"My car is down the street," she said. "When we get to it, you get in the back seat."

"Why?" asked Trick.

She stopped and glowered. "Fine," said Trick. "I'll get in the back seat."

GQ opened the door wider and stepped out. Trick followed and they walked down the sidewalk. He held his arm and looked for Eleanor, wondering where she'd gone. "You think she's nearby?" asked Trick.

"No way to know," said GQ. She kept walking, and Trick noted how she kept her eyes on her surroundings, watching for any threat.

They made it to the same white car Trick had chased through the streets before it had eluded him at the stop light. He got in the back, and she got in the drivers' seat. Trick gasped again when his arm flared, and he put more pressure on his injury. "I...we still need a doctor."

"I know." She opened the glove compartment, pulled out a handkerchief, and handed it to him. "I want this over your eyes. Like a blindfold. Then lie down flat."

Trick stared in surprise. "Why do I need a blindfold?"

"I said do exactly as I say, remember?"

Trick didn't like where this was going.

"Listen, Texas. You either do as I ask, or I'll drop you at the nearest hospital. And by nearest, I mean at least an hour from here. You can go your way and I'll go mine." She held out the cloth. "Your choice."

Uncertain, Trick eyed the handkerchief. "You're not going to kill me, are you?"

She studied him, but then sighed. "Tempting, but no. Unless you bleed to death in the back of my car." She glanced into the backseat. "And watch where you're dripping."

Trick took the fabric from her and fashioned it into a blindfold. "That's going to be hard to do if I can't see."

"Then it's a good thing I have access to cleaners. They can get blood out of anything." She waited.

Murmuring and cursing to himself, he put the blindfold on and tied it behind his head as best he could with his injury. A small amount of light got in from around his nose, but he was effectively blind. He felt GQ's hands on his head as she checked his work.

"Good," she said. "Now lie down." She started the car.

Reluctantly, Trick laid flat and did his best to get comfortable. Feeling his gun in its holster, he gave thanks she hadn't taken it from him. "How long? Where are we going?"

The car moved and accelerated. "It'll take thirty to forty-five minutes," she said, "depending on traffic, and none of your business."

Trick closed his eyes and told himself to relax, figuring he'd know their location soon enough, but then remembered he'd received a phone call when Eleanor had attacked. Red had probably tried to reach him. "Can I make a call?"

"As long as it doesn't require you to see, and you keep all of this to yourself, then yes."

He pulled his phone from his pocket and using the sliver of light, managed to access his voicemail despite his minimal vision. He listened to the message and called Red.

· · ● ● ● ● ● ● · ·

Mason dumped his empty food container in the trash along with Mikey's. Wondering where Trick was and why he hadn't called, he began to worry. He reached for his cell just as it rang and smiled when he saw it was Trick. He answered. "You finally give up?" he asked.

Trick was quiet but then responded. "Let's just say it didn't turn out the way I expected."

"No Eleanor or GQ?"

He paused again. "Eleanor may have skipped town and GQ, God knows where she is. I barely know where I am."

"Tired?" asked Mason. "Did you eat? We got a hamburger for you."

"Just hold onto it for me. I'll eat it tomorrow, provided I can."

"Why wouldn't you?" Mason tossed his empty water bottle in the trash. Trick's voice caught and he gasped.

"You okay?" asked Mason.

"Just hit a damn pothole. Jarred something."

"You did do a lot of walking, didn't you? Go home then and get some rest. We'll talk more in the morning and decide what to do next. You still plan on calling Mrs. Trammel?" He walked into the living room where Mikey sat on the couch, watching a TV show and holding the remote.

"Yeah. I'll call her. But I don't think she'll like what I have to say."

"We can't solve every case, Trick."

"You know me, Red. I don't like to give up. If there's more going on, I want to know what it is."

"I understand. But cheer up. Eleanor may still show. At some point, she may come out of hiding, if she isn't dead."

Trick sighed over the phone. "I don't think she's dead, and when she comes out of hiding, well, let's just hope I'm prepared."

"Since when are you not prepared?"

Trick paused. "That's a discussion for another day."

Mason didn't know what that meant but figured Trick was exhausted. "Go home. Sleep and we'll see you tomorrow."

"That's the plan."

"Okay. Goodnight." Mason started to hang up.

"Hey, Red."

Mason returned the phone to his ear. "Yes?"

"Do me a favor. You happen to see Eleanor, don't approach her. You hear me?"

Mason frowned. "Why would we see Eleanor?"

"You probably won't, but just in case. Keep your distance and call the cops. Okay? You and Mikey both."

"What's going on?" asked Mason. "You know something?"

"Nothing at the moment, but I don't like the way things are adding up. Just promise me you'll stay away from her."

Mason nodded. "I promise. Mikey, too."

Mikey glanced at him.

"Thanks, Red," said Trick. "I'll see you later."

Mason knew his friend well enough to realize something was on his mind but decided to bring it up after Trick had some rest. "See you." He hesitated, feeling a flutter in his gut, but told himself he was overthinking and hung up the phone.

• • • • • • • • •

Trick hung up and lay quietly in the back seat for the rest of the drive. GQ said nothing and although he had numerous questions, he guessed she wouldn't say a word until they arrived at their destination. He held his injured arm and breathed through the pain, hoping he'd get some medical attention eventually.

He couldn't be sure how much time had passed when the car slowed and stopped. The sun had gone down, and his sliver of light was gone.

"You alive back there?" asked GQ.

"I am."

"You're quiet. I suspect that's rare for you."

"It's not something I'm known for, but I don't take you for the talking sort."

"Not when you have questions I can't answer...yet."

Trick cradled his arm and winced. "You actually plan to answer my questions?"

"You wouldn't be in this car otherwise."

The car bounced, and Trick grabbed on to the back of the seat. He heard the window open and felt a breeze in the car. "We almost there?" he asked.

The window closed and the car bounced forward. "Just about," she said.

The car drove on and the ride became smoother. Tense, Trick waited to see what would happen next. GQ drove for another minute, then the car stopped, and Trick heard her put the car in park and undo her seatbelt. "We're here," she said. "You can take off the blindfold."

Trick pulled the covering off his eyes and slowly sat up. Despite the darkness, the first thing he saw was trees. Big, tall, majestic trees surrounded them, and Trick looked behind him. A large almost mansion-sized house with a tiled roof, lighted manicured landscaping and illuminated stone stairs that led to the front door sat just beyond the car and driveway.

GQ got out.

"Where are we?" Trick opened the back door and slid from the seat, holding his arm.

GQ didn't answer but headed toward the stairs. "Let's go, Texas." She glanced back at him. "You want answers? Then let's talk."

Trick watched her stop at the front door, punch in some numbers and open the door. He hurried to catch up before she closed the door on him. Getting past the stairs, he walked inside to see an ornate interior. A beautiful marble staircase led to an upstairs and a circular polished wooden table in the foyer sported a majestic and huge flowery centerpiece. To his right was a living room with big furniture and a giant fireplace and to his left was a dining area with a long table and multiple chairs. The kitchen was just beyond the dining room.

He whistled. "Is this your place?"

"You might say that. Follow me."

She walked down a hallway past the stairs and Trick admired a large oil painting on the wall of a regal woman in a ballgown. He followed GQ, and she led him into a library with numerous well-stocked bookshelves. Trick admired the room. "Read much?" he asked.

She walked to a big desk with carved edges and tall legs. "You buy that from Paul Bunyon?" he asked.

"Have a seat," said GQ. She opened a drawer and pulled out a piece of paper.

Trick picked a big, upholstered, overstuffed chair and sat. "You're not worried about getting blood on your furniture, I guess."

GQ walked over and sat in a chair across from him. "I think you've stopped bleeding." She put the paper, along with a pen, on the glass coffee table beside the chairs.

"What's that?" asked Trick, eyeing the paper.

"The rules." GQ sat back in her seat.

"Rules? What rules?"

"The ones you have to follow if you expect me to tell you anything."

"What rules are those?"

She reached under her sweater and pulled out the bloody dishcloth. "Guess I've stopped bleeding, too."

"Maybe some medical attention would be nice."

She tipped her head. "You'll get it but when depends on whether you agree to the rules."

Tired, Trick blinked and told himself to hang in there. "What are they?"

GQ raised a finger. "First. You must never tell anyone about me, this location, what happened today or what happens later. There are secrets on top of secrets in this house and their safety is far more important than your life or mine. Failure to abide by this rule will get you either defamed, defrauded or dead." She sat up. "And if you think I'm joking, I'm not."

Trick set his jaw. "I can't tell Red about any of this?"

"None of it."

"I don't like lying to him."

"Then I suggest you get over it."

Trick hesitated. "If I don't agree?"

She shrugged. "We return to the car, you put the blindfold back on and I drive you to the nearest hospital. You'll never see me again."

"What about Eleanor?"

"That's up to you. My suggestion would be to forget you ever saw her today. Leave her to me. Let the cops do their search and pray they don't find her before I do. Tell Jackson's mother he was the victim of an unfortunate accident. He was in the wrong place at the wrong time. Call it drugs. Call it a serial killer. I don't care. But forget Eleanor."

"And if I don't forget her?"

"I can't stop you from going to the police. You can tell them what happened today if you want. But by the time they get to Eleanor's, the blood will be cleaned, and your story will make no sense. They'll think you're the one on drugs. And if you choose to plaster my picture all over the state, don't be surprised if some incriminating evidence is found in your home. Maybe it will be an illicit substance or some nasty stuff on your computer, but it won't look good. And people tend not to hire P.I.s who break the law."

"Are you threatening me?" asked Trick.

"I'm simply telling you the consequences of your actions. As I said, we take our safety seriously. You threaten it, and we threaten yours." She crossed her legs. "Which is why I suggest you take my advice and forget Eleanor."

"And wake up tomorrow morning like I took the blue pill."

"Exactly."

"But if I take the red pill?"

"You follow rule number one. No exceptions. Everything you learn today cannot be discussed with another living soul, even if your life or the life of someone you love depends on it."

Trick dropped his head and gripped his temples. "Any other rules?"

"Communication between us, if deemed necessary, will be through approved devices only. You can't make any contact using your personal information or phone. You will make no effort to communicate with us unless we make contact first. And you will only know what we tell you and nothing more. You will make no attempt to learn more than what you're given."

"What about names?"

"First ones only. No last."

"Why can't I contact you?"

"You can if it's allowed, otherwise, it's too risky."

Trick sighed. "What else?"

"You choose to go down this path, you take orders from me. You do not stray or question them. You have to trust me implicitly."

"This coming from the woman who just threatened me and told me your cause, whatever it is, is more important than my life?"

"Yes."

"You could lead me to my own death."

"I could."

Trick nodded. "Good to know."

"Third," she continued. "Failure to comply with the rules will result in immediate and harsh punishment which will be determined by the group. This punishment could include anything up to and including death. Our decision is final and extends to anyone you share information with. No exceptions."

"The group? Sounds like a rock band."

She studied him. "Any questions?"

"Those are all of the rules?"

"Other than we reserve the right to change the rules at any point and your agreement is implied."

Trick chuckled. "You don't make this easy."

"It's not designed to be easy. It's designed to be balls to the wall. You either risk it all or you leave."

He stared at the bloody rag on his arm. "Have you ever had a breach of the rules?"

He caught her gripping the armrest of the chair. "Once," she said. "It didn't end well."

"I can imagine."

She relaxed and touched her chest with a wince. "Well?"

Trick studied the paper on the coffee table. He thought of Mason and Mikey, and his encounter with Eleanor. And he thought of Jag and Mrs. Trammel and then of Kyle, lying in a hospital bed. Taking a deep breath, he prayed he was doing the right thing and reached for the pen with his good arm. "Where do I sign?"

Chapter Twenty-One

TRICK SIGNED AND PUT down the pen. GQ took the document, folded it and stood. "Come with me."

"Hold up." Trick stood, too.

She paused. "What?"

"Your first name. What is it?"

Hesitating, she narrowed her eyes. "Lindsey."

"Lindsey," he said. "That's a lot better than GQ."

She pointed at his injury. "You want to fix that?"

Trick cradled his forearm. "I do."

"Then stop talking and follow me." She walked to a bookshelf.

"Whatever you say, Lindsey."

She reached for the first book in a set of Nancy Drews and pulled it out. Behind it was a button which she pushed. There was a click and the bookshelf moved. Lindsey returned the Nancy Drew book and pulled on the case. It swung open and Trick saw a staircase leading down.

"How cloak and dagger," he said.

She stepped onto the top step and waited for Trick to join her before closing the case again. After hitting another button on the wall, Trick heard a corresponding click and the bookcase locked shut. "After you," she said with a wave toward the stairs.

Apprehensive but curious, Trick headed down. The stairs led to another door with a numbered panel beside it. Lindsey punched in a code she prevented Trick from seeing and opened the door. She walked in and

Trick followed but stopped short when he saw the room. "What in the..."
A large windowless bricked space contained numerous desks and tables,
most with a computer monitor on them. Some monitors showed various
black and white footage and others had spreadsheets and other various data
displayed. Trick could hear a hum and wondered if they were piping in air
to get some circulation and to keep the machines cool. A man and a woman
were each sitting at one of the tables with a computer. When Trick and
Lindsey entered, they both swiveled in their chairs and faced them.

The woman smiled and the man frowned. "What in the hell are you
doing, Lin?" asked the man.

Trick guessed he was tall by the length of his legs and strong based on the
breadth of his shoulders.

"Relax," said Lindsey. She eyed the woman who was closer to Lindsey's
size and had similar eyes, although her darker hair was longer. "Any sign of
her?" asked Lindsey.

The woman shook her head. "None. We reviewed the street footage
when she ran out of the building. She headed down an alley and I lost her
from there."

Lindsey nodded. "We'll have a camera up soon so we'll have eyes. Once
it's set up, let me know. Hopefully, she'll return."

"Okay," said the woman who looked at Trick. "You going to introduce
us?"

Before Lindsey could answer, the man stood. "He shouldn't be here."

Trick had guessed accurately that the man was tall and strong. He wondered if the upstairs desk belonged to him.

"He agreed to the rules," said Lindsey.

"He should have never been offered the rules." The man stepped closer.
"You should have left him behind."

Lindsey stepped closer. "I made the call and I stand by it. Pete said we
needed someone like him, and I agree."

"He's a moron." The man glared at Trick.

"Excuse me?" asked Trick.

"He found Eleanor, didn't he?" asked Lindsey. "I can't say the same for you."

The man set his jaw. "If I'd been the one at the apartment, Eleanor would be dead now."

Lindsey straightened. "Maybe if you'd given me the benefit of the doubt and gone with me, instead of telling me that following him," she pointed at Trick, "was stupid, then Eleanor would be dead, he wouldn't be here, and we wouldn't be having this discussion. If anyone is a moron, it's you."

The man started yelling and Lindsey yelled back. Trick had no idea what to do and he watched along with the woman until a loud-pitched whistle echoed through the room.

Lindsey and the man stopped yelling and Trick turned to see an older man who the younger man resembled. He was just as tall and big, but his face bore more creases around his mouth and eyes. "Both of you, shut up," he said.

Lindsey put her hands on her hips and frowned, and the man went quiet but maintained his glare.

The older man looked at Trick. "Who are you?" He looked at Trick's arm with concern.

"Trick Monroe, sir," said Trick. "I'm...uh...a friend of Lindsey's."

The younger man snorted, and Lindsey shook her head.

"It appears you have an injury," said the older man. He walked closer, took Trick's arm and Trick winced.

"You could say that," said Trick.

The older man looked toward Lindsey. "Did Eleanor do this?"

"She's hurt, too," said Trick, nodding toward Lindsey.

Lindsey shot a narrow gaze at him.

"You are?" asked the older man.

"It's not bad," said Lindsey.

"It's not good either," said Trick. "It's under her sweater."

The older man was quiet for a moment before he spoke. "He signed the rules?"

"He wouldn't be here otherwise," said Lindsey.

"He shouldn't be down here at all," said the younger man.

"Your sister made a choice," said the man holding Trick's arm. "If you expect her to trust your decisions then you have to trust hers. And she's right. Pete said this would help. So why not try it? If it fails, we can dump him in the nearest body of water."

Trick stilled, widened his eyes, and considered his escape route.

The man chuckled and smacked Trick's back. "I'm just messing with you."

Trick breathed a sigh of relief and jumped when the man bellowed. "Janice?"

Trick heard a distant answer. "Yes?"

"You have a patient." The man shot a thumb down the narrow hall he'd entered from. "Go see Janice, Lin. She'll patch you up." He glanced at Trick. "And you come with me."

"I'm fine, Dad," said Lindsey.

"Dad?" asked Trick. He eyed the younger man. "And that's your brother?"

"His name's Garret." Lindsey smirked. "And that over there is my sister, Marcy."

The other woman waved at him. "Hi," she said.

Lindsey nodded at the older man. "And my father is Benjamin."

The older man smiled. "Call me Ben."

Trick stared in surprise.

"Welcome to the family," said Lindsey.

• • • • • • • • •

Trick followed Lindsey's father down the hall and into a room that held a desk with a laptop and various folders stacked on the corners. A chair was tucked up beneath the desk. Against the far wall stood a neatly made cot and a stack of drawers beside it. Across from Trick was a large lamp on top of a wide table.

"It's sparse, but it's mine." The man grabbed the chair from the desk and wheeled it toward the table. "Have a seat."

Feeling uncertain and questioning why he'd agreed to the rules, Trick reluctantly sat in the chair.

Ben flipped on the table lamp and bright light filled the room. He opened a curtain beside the cot and Trick saw another chest of drawers and some hanging clothes. Ben opened a large bottom drawer and took out a bag. He closed the drawer and brought the bag to the table where he sat it down.

"Let's take a look at that arm." Ben walked to his desk and picked up a pair of glasses and put them on.

Trick wondered what he'd gotten himself into. "Are you a doctor?"

"Nope." Ben opened the bag and took out a bottle. He squeezed something into his hands and rubbed them together, then removed a pair of gloves from a plastic bag and slid them on. "But don't worry. I'm well-trained. We all are."

Nervous, Trick waited as Ben removed a bundled cloth. He set it down on the table and unrolled it. Several medical instruments were inside the cloth.

"Don't worry. It's all sterilized," he said.

"What are you all trained for?" asked Trick, telling himself he wasn't going to die.

Ben returned to the drawers, opened the top one and pulled out a vial and a packaged syringe. "For medical emergencies," said Ben. "We have to be. Going to the doctor isn't always an option." He set the vial down and opened the package with the syringe. "Janice and I are better at it than the others, though. Be glad Lindsey isn't doing this, or you'd end up with a hell of a scar." He chuckled.

Trick watched with trepidation as Ben took the syringe, plunged it into the vial and sucked out some of the liquid contents.

"I mean, I can't do open heart surgery," said Ben, pulling out the syringe, "but I can manage a hell of a stitch." He set the vial down and held the syringe. "You ready?"

Trick's heart thumped. "For what?" Trick wondered if him ending up in a body of water wasn't an actual joke.

"We have to clean your injury. You want me to numb it first, I hope. Or it's going to hurt like hell." He pointed. "Just rest it on the table under the light."

Trick forced himself to lie his forearm on the table.

"Take the cloth off and pull your sleeve up."

Gritting his teeth, Trick did both. His sleeve stuck to his skin, and he sucked in a breath when he pulled on the fabric. Blood began to ooze from the wound.

Ben leaned in. "She got you good, didn't she?" He turned, grabbed a towel from the drawer, and unfolded it. "Here. Put this beneath your arm."

Trick did as he was asked and rested his arm on the towel. Ben lowered the syringe and Trick clenched his eyes shut when Ben injected him in various spots beside the torn skin.

"That should do it. We'll give it a minute to numb up." He set the syringe aside and pulled out a cloth and another bottle.

Trick tried to think of something else. "I suppose at some point someone is going to tell me what exactly is going on with Eleanor and who you all are?"

Ben peered at Trick over his glasses. "What has my daughter told you?"

"Absolutely nothing. I don't even know where I am right now."

Ben poked at Trick's arm. "Feel that?"

Trick shook his head. "No."

"Good." Ben picked up the cloth and the second bottle and squirted liquid into the cloth. After the cloth absorbed the moisture, Ben began to clean Trick's injury. Trick gave thanks he couldn't feel a thing. "What do you want to know?" asked Ben. He grunted. "Definitely going to need some stitches."

Trick looked away as he started to bleed again. "Let's start with Eleanor. What's wrong with her?"

Ben didn't look up. "Eleanor is a very sick woman."

"Sick? From what? What kind of sickness turns a small woman into a violent rage queen?"

"The kind of sickness you can't recover from."

"Is it drugs?" asked Trick. "Is she on something?"

"I wish it was that simple." He dug deeper into the wound and grabbed another towel to dab at the blood. "But there's no recovery for Eleanor."

"What is she sick from? I hope it isn't catching."

Ben paused and glanced at Trick. "You've just hit on exactly what we do here."

"What is that?"

"Make sure it doesn't spread."

Trick eyed his wounded arm and made some uncomfortable deductions. "She bit me. Does that mean I'm at risk? Could I catch her illness?" His heart rate picked up its pace.

"If that were true, Lindsey would have killed you."

"Killed me?"

Ben moved to clean another area. "Would you want to end up like Eleanor?"

Trick couldn't imagine it. "You haven't told me what's wrong with her. How did she catch this?"

Ben sighed, wet the cloth again and resumed his cleaning. "Eleanor is what we call a Craver."

Trick frowned. "What the hell is a Craver?"

"A person who craves something enough to kill for it."

"What does she crave?"

"Blood."

Trick stilled. "Blood?"

Ben nodded. "Human blood. It drives her. It feeds her. She loves the taste, feel and smell of it. It overrides every other instinct and when she's hungry, she'll do whatever it takes to get it." He dabbed at Trick's arm again with the dry cloth. "Which is why I'm bandaging your arm. You're a lucky man. Most don't survive an encounter with a Craver."

Trick gripped the edge of the table with his good hand. His mind whirled with the implications. "Wait a minute. Are you saying...? You can't be saying..."

"What?" asked Ben.

Trick gaped at him. "Is Eleanor a vampire?"

Ben chuckled. "Blows the mind, doesn't it?"

Chapter Twenty-Two

STUNNED, TRICK DIDN'T KNOW what to say.

"'Course, don't let my kids hear you call her that. It's not PC anymore." Ben shook his head. "Vampire is out. Craver is in." He shrugged. "I guess I can see why though. Vampire brings to mind all sorts of falsehoods based on fictional books and movies." He wet the cloth again and resumed cleaning Trick's injury. Trick sat in stunned silence as Ben double-checked the area and dried and cleaned the wound again.

Finally finding his voice, Trick sputtered. "Vampires aren't real, Ben." He wondered what the hell he'd gotten himself into and hoped he could still get out.

Ben smiled. "No. They're not. But Cravers are. You saw Eleanor. What else would you like to call her?" He set the wet cloth down and dried Trick's arm. "And please don't say it's a mental issue." He set the cloth aside and reached for the thread.

"But it could be."

"It's not." He pulled the thread through a curved needle. "Believe me. It was tough for me at first, but I've seen too much." He grabbed the dry cloth and dabbed at Trick's skin again.

"Who are you people?" asked Trick. "Why do you live in the basement of a big house in the middle of nowhere? Why all the secrecy and the computers and the crazy rules?" He had too many questions to get them all out.

"We have benefactors who support us. They own this house and others. We can stay upstairs if we want but I'm ex-military and these quarters are more my speed."

"What benefactors?"

Ben peered at him again. "That's need-to-know, and you don't need to know."

"But they don't live here?"

"They're here occasionally." Ben lowered the needle to Trick's skin and Trick looked away. "As I said there are other homes. We're not the only ones."

Trick felt a slight tug on his skin. "There are more of you?"

"Of course there are. We can't monitor everything. We also have central and eastern divisions. We're the western. This house and those who own it provide the cover we need to do our job."

"And what exactly is that?"

"Protect you and everyone else."

"From what?" asked Trick. "The Eleanors of the world?"

"Yes. And those who create them."

"Who created Eleanor?" Trick glanced back and regretted it when he saw Ben stick the needle through his skin. His stomach churned and he turned his head.

"Not sure yet. We're trying to figure that out."

Trick clenched his eyes shut, trying to think. Had Lindsey dosed him with some sort of hallucinogenic? Was he going to wake up in some alley wondering if this was all a dream?

"I'm not sure why you find this so hard to believe, considering what your partner does."

Trick opened his eyes. "You know Red?"

"Not personally, but he speaks to ghosts, doesn't he?"

"He does."

"Hell. The name of his firm says everything. SCOPE. The Study of Cryptids and Paranormal Entities. We're not much different than you. He's just focused more on the spirit side of things."

Trick couldn't help but turn back, yet he avoided looking at his forearm. "Should I infer then that you all focus on the cryptid side?"

Ben pulled the thread through and brought the needle down again. "We do."

Trick took a slow breath to calm himself. "Does this have something to do with you being ex-military?"

Ben peered at Trick again. "It might."

"Are you able to explain or is that need-to-know?"

"I'll tell you what I can." Ben pulled the thread again. "Years ago, I was a member of a top-secret unit of the government designed to subvert unconventional and non-terrestrial attacks against the public. The non-terrestrial side got most of the attention, but our side had its share of difficulties."

Transfixed, Trick ignored his arm. "Like what?"

"Mainly outbreaks." Ben checked Trick's arm and dabbed again at the injury with the cloth. "And not the influenza kind. Ebola is a breeze compared to our assignments. We've had some scary moments since I've been involved. Without constant monitoring, an outbreak could lead to eradication of the human race. We told the public what we had to because if they'd known the truth, it would have caused mass hysteria. It was an international effort of course. We've lost people as you do in any war, but for the most part, we successfully eradicated most threats."

Trick stared in disbelief. "We're still talking about vampires?"

"And a few other cryptids. But again, that's need-to-know." Ben smiled. "We were the CU. Still are, actually."

"CU?" asked Trick.

"Cryptid unit."

Trick dropped his head and cursed.

"As time passed, our unit became less and less needed and more obsolete until the military dropped us all together and focused on the non-terrestrial side. But what they didn't understand is that the threat is never over. It's just like any other virus. It can reappear at any time. And if someone doesn't keep an eye on things, more outbreaks are possible. Some higher-ups understood that and realized the danger in abolishing our unit. That's when benefactors stepped in and a select few were chosen to maintain security and keep an eye out for future infection." He made another stitch. "That's what you saw out there." He pointed toward the hall. "We monitor the population for the express purpose of identifying and stopping any outbreaks."

Trick rubbed his head with his free hand. "I don't know what to believe."

"What's so hard about it? Hell. Your partner put cryptid in the name of his firm. It's why we keep an eye on you guys. If he has any encounters, we need to know."

"You keep an eye on us?"

"Sure do. Lindsey wouldn't have brought you in otherwise. Most wouldn't handle or understand what we do. But you're already comfortable with the non-physical side. Cryptids aren't a much bigger jump from that."

"It's a bigger jump than you may think," said Trick.

"You're aware of Bigfoot, aren't you?" Ben perked up a brow.

Trick scoffed. "You investigate them, too?"

Ben smiled again. "Also need-to-know, but let's just say they're friendlier than you may think. They just like to put on a good show." He lowered his voice. "They don't like their privacy disturbed."

Trick blinked but didn't say anything.

Ben dabbed at Trick's stitches and studied them. "Almost done. Just need a few more." He picked up the needle.

Trick sighed with consternation. He figured if he was now part of this delusion, he needed to know more. "How is it that your whole family is involved?"

Ben wiped some blood from Trick's skin. "It's a long story. But the short version is that after I left the military and agreed to continue my work with the CU, I made it clear that family came first. The benefactors were doubtful, and I had to sign my own version of the rules, but basically, I no longer kept secrets from the people I loved. My kids, once they got old enough, new exactly what I did, and all of them have followed in my footsteps."

"I find that hard to believe." Trick couldn't imagine what he would have done if his mother had told him she'd worked for a secret organization that hunted threats against the human population.

"So be it. As I said, that's the short version. We've had our ups and downs, and plenty of crisis to deal with, but we've managed to get through it and now we're a strong team."

Trick imagined the long version of the story was full of twists and turns. "I guess I'll have to take your word for it."

Ben smiled and set the towel aside. "I'd say so, considering."

Trick thought of Eleanor again. "So if Eleanor's bite doesn't make me a vamp...I mean craver, then what does?"

Ben started another stitch. "Hybrids."

"Oh, God. What's a hybrid?"

Ben sighed. "It's complicated, but I'll try and keep it simple."

"I'd appreciate that."

Ben pulled on the thread. "Hybrids are the product of a craver and a human pairing."

Trick narrowed his eyes. "Wait a minute. Cravers are having sex with humans?"

Ben glanced up. "Can you adjust the light? Point it more toward this way?" He tipped his head.

Trick grabbed the light and moved it.

"Thanks." Ben resumed stitching Trick's injury. "You have to under-stand. This virus is like any other. Some get very sick very fast, like Eleanor, but others only experience mild symptoms at first. Those cravers can lead fairly normal lives until the cravings build and can't be ignored. Some make do with finding a blood supply, whether it be from an animal or blood donation sites or even a hospital. Eventually though, the cravings worsen, their rage and violence become uncontrollable, and they'll kill. In the meantime, though, they're living their lives like anyone else."

"A female craver can give birth to a child?"

Ben made another stitch. "No. Not usually. The virus will take over before they make it to term, and they won't survive long enough. They'll either be killed by us or will eventually die from the virus. But a male craver can impregnate a healthy woman. And if she gives birth, the child is considered a hybrid. Half-craver, half-human."

Trick took a deep breath. "How does that work?"

Ben shrugged. "It's not terrible. Most survive and live normal lives. They may crave a lot of red meat though." He chuckled. "And they'll like it bloody."

Trick just stared at him.

"Others, though, have it worse. They'll crave blood. Our unit, once we find them, and we know most of the hybrids that exist, we'll make contact discreetly and suggest ways to satisfy their cravings without breaking any laws."

"What ways are those?"

"Again. That's need-to-know. But I'll tell you a secret. Synthetic blood helps."

"Synthetic blood?" asked Trick. "You have synthetic blood?"

"It's not perfect, but it will do for most hybrids."

"But not all?"

Ben put the needle down and used the cloth to blot Trick's stitches. "Some hybrids insist on the real deal. They're the ones we have to keep an eye on."

"Do they kill?"

"Not usually, but if they're not careful, accidents happen." He glanced at his bag. "Can you pull that over? There's some gauze in there. Can you grab it?" Ben reached for a small jar and opened it. He scooped out some ointment and spread it on Trick's stitches.

Trick snagged the bag, dug through it and found the gauze. He placed it on the table and put the bag back. "What happens if they're not careful?"

"Some hybrids feed off of humans." He closed the jar and set it aside. "Not enough to kill them, but enough to satiate their need."

Trick dropped his jaw. "Doesn't the human protest?"

'They don't know." Ben wiped his gloves with the towel, grabbed the gauze and unrolled it. "Hybrids have a very unique skill set. I suspect their craver parent has the same skill set, but their rage circumvents their ability to use it." He began to wrap Trick's wound with the gauze. "Their saliva is unique. It can numb the host long enough for the hybrid to bite and take blood, and once they're finished, the saliva secretes something that allows the host to heal quickly. I've seen it with my own eyes. A human can sleep right through it and wake up with nothing more than a headache and feeling slightly sluggish."

"How often does the hybrid do this?"

"Not often, but there's always the exception."

"And what happens with the exception?"

Ben finished wrapping the gauze and cut it with some scissors. "Therein lies the problem. If the hybrid goes too far, drinks too much blood, it weakens the host to the point where they cannot recover, and they become a craver." He snipped the end of the gauze and wrapped the ends around Trick's wrist.

Trick tried to keep up. "That's what happened to Eleanor? Some hybrid took enough blood from her to infect her?"

Ben took off his gloves. "Yes. That's the crux of it. It's hard to know exactly what happens during the process, but we assume the hybrid transfers a virus while they feed. In small doses, the host's immune system protects them, but in large doses, they can't fight it off and succumb."

Trick shook his head. "But you said you keep up with the hybrids. Don't you know who did this to her?"

Ben tossed the gauze back into the bag. "We know most but not all. Some stay under our radar. It's why we can never stop what we do here. We have to keep constant surveillance. All it takes is one." He returned his instruments to the cloth.

Trick had numerous questions. "But, if the cravers were eradicated, wouldn't that mean that the hybrids would eventually die out?"

"Over time, yes. But hybrids have children, too. They are hybrids of hybrids. The symptoms decline with each passing generation but there's always an outlier. And if they create a craver who produces a hybrid, then the cycle starts all over again."

Trick began to understand. "How many cravers have you killed?"

"More than I care to admit." He put the bloodied towels in a pile next to the instruments, presumably to be cleaned. He picked up the small jar of ointment. "Keep the bandage on for twenty-four hours and don't get it wet. Then you can use soap and water to clean the wound and replace the bandage. Put this ointment on it to keep it moist." He set the jar on the table and added a fresh roll of gauze beside it.

Trick recalled Eleanor's attack. "Do cravers have an odor? Can you smell them?"

Ben turned off the light above the table. "Did Eleanor have a nasty scent, like the smell of decay?"

"Yes. Just before she attacked."

Ben sighed. "She's deteriorating. As the virus advances, cravers will give off an odor just before they attack, but not at first. It usually takes time." He shook his head. "She's an unusual case."

"Lucky us." Trick grimaced but still had more questions. "How do you find them? The cravers?" He thought of Lindsey following him. "Lindsey followed me for a reason. She must have known what Eleanor was."

"She did." He took his glasses off and pinched the bridge of his nose. "We monitor police bands and hospital admissions. We listen for anything that could fall within the parameters of an attack. We know what to look for." He lowered his glasses and wiped them with the hem of his shirt. "Last week, we heard of a report of a homeless man killed not far from where you and Lindsey were today. The wounds matched the description of a potential attack but there's no way to be sure until you investigate. My brother, Pete, followed up. He watched the scene of the incident for a couple of days." He put his glasses back on. "Cravers will frequently return to the scene of their first kill. They can be confused at the onset of the virus. Depending on how bad their symptoms are, they can be disoriented and not sure what's happening to them. The smell of the blood will draw them in. The scent of a kill never leaves them."

Trick straightened in his seat and set his bandaged arm in his lap. "Did Eleanor return?"

Ben nodded. "She did. Pete saw and tracked her. She went into a bar and met Jackson Trammel. Pete watched, certain she was the craver, but it's not always easy to be sure. When Eleanor left the bar, she and Jackson separated. Pete followed Eleanor and we assumed she would keep to herself for the night. Cravers can go days without blood, and there was no way to confirm if she was one until she attacked again. Pete stayed with her and when he followed her to the overlook to meet Jackson, he sensed she might kill and contacted us. We were on our way when the attack occurred."

Ben set his jaw and stared at the ground. "By the time we got there, we were too late. Jackson and Pete were both dead."

Trick sat in silence. "She killed your brother?"

Ben remained quiet before he looked up. "We had just enough time to remove Pete's body from the scene, but nothing else. The sun was coming up and we couldn't risk discovery."

Trick's stomach churned but for a different reason. "I'm sorry for your loss."

Ben shook off his reverie. "It comes with the territory. We understand the risks."

"You lost your brother, and your kids lost an uncle. It must have been a hell of a shock."

Ben bundled up the dirty instruments and wrapped them in the towel on the table. "Before you leave, I'll give you a shot of antibiotics. Other than that, you should be good to go. We'll check the stitches next week."

Trick moved the fingers on his injured arm. "Thank you."

"It's gonna hurt when the numbness wears off. I can't offer you anything stronger than an aspirin."

"I'll be fine. I've dealt with worse."

"So I've heard," said Ben.

Trick stood and tested his legs. "What happens now?"

"We'll check on Lindsey and then we get busy."

"On finding Eleanor?"

Ben nodded. "She's hungry and she didn't get to feed on you. Which means she'll be looking for someone else and the longer she waits, the worse it will be."

"What can I possibly do? Lindsey said Pete thought you could use someone like me. What did that mean?"

Ben walked to the door. "You're one of the few civilians capable of understanding what we do. Plus, you have a law enforcement background. You can work among the public without arousing suspicion. You found Eleanor through hard work and your ingenuity kept Lindsey on her toes, and you even managed to convince her to bring you into the fold. The hope is that with you being on the outside, we can get access to more information. We try to stay out of sight as much as possible. You don't have to worry about that."

"I still don't know what I can do to find a craver desperate for more blood."

"As Pete always said, we'll figure it out as we go. But you'll have to be careful."

Trick walked to the door. "I'm always careful, but I'll be especially careful now that I know what's out there."

"It's not just that. Eleanor has tasted your blood. She has your scent and taste in her mind and if she smells it again, there's no force I know of that will stop her from coming for you."

Recalling the ferocity of Eleanor's attack. Trick wanted to shrivel up into a ball. He clutched his stomach with his hand. "Then I guess we better find her, huh?"

"For your sake, we better." Ben turned and left the room.

Chapter Twenty-Three

MIKEY STARED AT THE page in her book and for the third time, started it over. After dinner, she'd watched a little TV with Mason and they'd both agreed to turn in early since they would have another busy day tomorrow. Mikey had expected to read a chapter or two. She'd been trying to read the book for a week, but every time she picked it up, other thoughts would intrude about her dad, Rem, Mason, or Margaret and she'd never get far. She found it surprising she ever slept at all.

Determined to get through at least a few pages, she refocused. At the end of the page, she turned to the next one when her phone rang. She reached for it and seeing Rem's name on the display, she sat up and answered. "Hey."

"Hey," he said. "Is this a good time?"

"Of course. I was just trying to read. How are you? How's the zoo?" Her heart thumped. Rem hadn't called her in a while, and she hoped this was a sign of progress.

"The animals are still there," he said.

"I'm glad to hear it." He asked about Mason and SCOPE and Mikey answered, keeping the conversation light.

He sighed over the phone. "I wanted to tell you that you were right about Daniels. I went to see him the other night."

"How is he?"

"He's definitely struggling without Marjorie."

"He is."

"And I haven't been around much." He paused. "Anyway, I'm glad you said something. I should have known myself, but...I don't know..." His voice trailed off.

Mikey sensed Rem's somber mood. "You okay?"

"Yeah...sure...maybe..."

"That didn't sound encouraging."

She heard him expel a deep breath. "It's late. I shouldn't have bugged you."

"Whoa," said Mikey. "Don't do that. You called me when something is obviously on your mind. That's a breakthrough. What is it?"

"It's stupid."

She rolled her eyes, pulled the sheets up, scooted down, and rested her head on the pillow. "I suspect it's not as stupid as you think."

"I...uh...was gonna call Daniels, but he's got J.P. tonight and I don't want to bug him."

Mikey gave thanks Rem had contacted her. Her visit to the zoo must have made a difference. "What is it? Did you have a bad day? Did Bart the baboon throw more poop at you?"

He chuckled. "I've gotten used to Bart but he's still getting used to me. He doesn't like me for some reason."

"Bart? Not like you? I find that hard to believe."

"It may have something to do with me picking his poop up and throwing it back at him."

Mikey sucked in a breath. "You didn't."

"I did."

"What did Bart do?" she asked.

"He screeched at me and threw it back. Then Bertha joined him. Needless to say, I had a lot to clean when that battle was over."

"I suspect you lost."

"It wasn't even competitive. But I got a few good shots in."

Mikey put a hand on her head. "I can't imagine what you smelled like."

"I had to shower and borrow a zoo uniform to go home."

Mikey laughed. "That'll teach you not to pick a fight with a baboon."

"You'd think I'd learn." His animated mood diminished. "On the bright side, though, the chipmunks are cute."

"They have chipmunks at the zoo?"

"No, but there's several of them on the grounds. I'll get lunch and watch them dart around."

"You're at the most popular zoo in the world and you're watching the chipmunks?

"I'm easy to please."

She smiled. "Maybe you should tell that to Bart."

"Maybe. Bart's not my issue though. He quieted and softened his voice. "I...uhm...think I saw Margaret."

Mikey frowned at the abrupt change in subject and lifted her head. "At the zoo?"

"Yeah."

"Are you sure?"

"No."

Mikey turned to her side. "Why do you think you saw her?'

Rem made a muffled groan. "I don't know. I was working and it felt like I was being watched, but when I looked, I never saw anything. Then, I was walking toward the elephants, and feeling that same sensation, I turned to look behind me. I saw a woman about fifty yards away. She was wearing a sunhat and sunglasses. Her hair was pulled back and she stopped too. She just stared and I stared back. I couldn't see her eyes, but for a second, she smiled. Then a group of school kids walked past, and I lost sight of her."

Mikey could hear the strain in his voice. "Did you call anyone?"

"Who am I going to call? By the time anyone got there, it wouldn't matter."

"How certain are you it was her?"

"That's just it. I don't know. Is it my overactive imagination? Or should I contact Lozano?"

"It can't hurt to call him and tell him your concerns. Have someone watch you for a few days. See if this person turns up again."

He blew out a ragged breath. "I guess. I just don't want to waste anyone's time."

"Rem, if there's the slightest possibility it was her, Lozano needs to be told. You know Daniels would tell you the same thing."

Rem took a few seconds before responding. "Have you had any weird feelings that she's been around?"

Mikey thought of her father. "Now that you mention it." She told him about what had happened since her dad's visit, what he'd said about Margaret and how he, and Kyle, were in the hospital.

"Hell," said Rem. "Your Dad and Kyle? How come you didn't tell me?"

"I figured you've been dealing with enough."

"Well, if you want me to do better, then that goes for you too."

"You want me to call you?" She adjusted her head on the pillow. "You've kind of not been answering."

"If you'd left a message and told me what was going on, I would have called back. Are they okay?"

"Kyle's getting better, but Dad, I don't know. I haven't heard anything since I visited and we argued."

"You can still call. Ask how he is."

She sighed. "It's complicated."

"He's your dad, Mikey. Don't leave things unsaid."

"I tried."

"You tried to convince him you were right, and he was wrong. That won't work. Let him say whatever he wants. You don't have to agree. Just nod. Tell him you'll think about what he said, you appreciate his concern and that you love him even if you disagree."

Her throat tightened. "He just pushes my buttons so easily."

"He's a dad. That's his job. Believe me, I wish I had a chance to make amends with my father, and he was a pain in the ass. But once he's gone, he's gone."

She nibbled her lip.

"You should tell Mason the same."

Mikey turned on her back and eyed the ceiling. "Since when did you become so wise?"

She heard him grunt as if he was moving around. "Probably ever since I got my finger slammed in the door of Mrs. Carmichael's eighth grade classroom. I was staring at Ainsley Churchill walking down the hall in her snug shorts and wasn't paying attention. Once I got my thumb back, Mrs. Carmichael told me to start using my brain to focus on what's right in front of me instead of what's out of reach. It was good advice."

"Smart lady."

"My thumb throbbed for a week."

Mikey tugged at the edge of the sheet. "Lessons can be painful."

"That seems to be my motto."

Mikey thought of her dad. "Okay. I'll think about it. Maybe I'll call tomorrow."

"I hope you do."

Mikey heard him yawn. "You tired?" she asked.

"Haven't been sleeping well." He paused. "I keep having nightmares."

"About Margaret? I thought they'd tapered off."

"They had, but when I started thinking I was seeing her around the zoo, the dreams picked up again." He hesitated. "It's part of the reason I called you."

She pursed her lips. "Why?"

"Because...you and Mason are in the dream. Daniels, too. You're all being chased by Margaret. I'm trying to get to you, but I can't. Margaret laughs at me, tells me I can't win, that I'll never win and that she'll do whatever she wants. Then she..."

"She what?"

"She stabs you, and Daniels and Mason. The order changes, but you're all dead, and I'm screaming."

Mikey held her chest. "That's horrible."

"I can't shake it." He made a soft sigh. "And I can't help but think…what if it's a premonition?"

Mikey considered what to say. "You've had bad dreams before, and they've never come true. Why would this dream be any different?"

"Because I keep having it. That hasn't been the case with the others."

Mikey ran a hand through her hair. "Well, maybe you've turned a corner. Maybe this is a good thing."

She could picture him scrunching his face in confusion. "Huh?" he asked. "How is this progress?"

Mikey shrugged. "Maybe as you heal and begin to deal with all that's happened to you, the subconscious fights back and tries to put you in your place, so to speak. Maybe it wants to see how determined you are to be well again. If you keep moving forward, face the nightmares, and realize you're stronger than they are, they'll fade away."

"So this is a test of my fortitude?"

"Maybe."

"Well, this test is pushing my buttons just like your dad pushes yours. I almost fell asleep while driving the van with the animal feed. I came close to landing in the zebra pen."

Mikey smiled softly. "Then maybe take your own advice. The nightmare wants to be right, and you want it to be wrong. Perhaps you should stop arguing with it. Let it play out, ride out the fear and remind it that it's not real but thank it for playing. Then roll over and go back to sleep."

He took another moment to answer. "As you said, it's complicated."

"I get it. But it only has the power you give it."

"Are we talking about me, or you and your dad?"

Mikey fiddled with the edge of her book. "Seems we've both solved each other's problems. Maybe we can work on world peace next."

She heard him yawn again. "Maybe tomorrow. I'm tired."

"Then go get some sleep." She paused. "Call Lozano tomorrow and let him know your suspicions and tell your brain no more nightmares."

"Okay. But I'll be honest. Until your sister is caught, I'll never rest easy. You don't know how close I came to selling this house when I realized she'd walked through it."

"I know." She wanted to ask if that meant he wouldn't return to the force and would continue to prevent any potential romance between them, but he'd asked for some space, so she gave it to him.

"Have you asked about putting an officer in front of your dad's door at the hospital, in case Margaret shows?"

"Mason suggested it but was told they don't have the manpower."

Rem huffed. "Which means until she actually kills someone, they won't do anything. Stupid bureaucrats and red tape. That's one thing I don't miss."

"I can't imagine she'd go there, though. Not with all those people around."

"Don't underestimate your sister, Mikey. Hell. She picked them up from the airport and took them to lunch."

Mikey couldn't deny that. "Yeah."

"Just be careful, okay? Pay attention to your surroundings. If she is watching me, she could be watching you, too. Especially considering what happened with Oswald. If he was crazy enough to befriend your sister and do her dirty work, then God knows who else might be, too."

Mikey closed her eyes, hating to think about that. "I hope not, but I hear you. I'll be careful."

"Good." He paused. "And hey..." he said softly. "I'm glad I called."

Her heart thumped again. "I'm glad you called, too."

"Read your book and think about what I said about your dad and be safe."

"I will. And you sleep easy. No nightmares tonight. Okay?"

"Okay. I'll do my best." She heard a long sigh. "Goodnight, Mikey."

"Goodnight, Rem." She hung up and held the phone to her chest, happy he'd called and hoping she'd helped. Recalling Mason's advice to just be Rem's friend until he was ready for more, Mikey told herself to be patient. Mason had said it wouldn't happen overnight but believed Rem's defenses would eventually crumble.

Margaret's presence wasn't helping, though, and Mikey wondered if her sister had been watching all of them. Thinking of Margaret chasing her and Mason with a knife, she shuddered but just as quickly chastised herself. It was just a dream, and it held no power over her either. But she'd had a few premonitions herself and those dreams were quite different. Telling herself to relax and that Rem was indeed fighting his inner demons, she returned her phone and book to the nightstand and turned off the lamp. Thinking of Rem, she closed her eyes and went to sleep.

Chapter Twenty-Four

TRICK FOLLOWED BEN BACK into the room with the tables and monitors. Lindsey was sitting at one of them wearing a navy tank top with a scoop neck. The edge of a bandage peeked out from the fabric. Another man was in the room who appeared younger than Lindsey. He sat at another table and typed at a keyboard.

"This is Trey," said Ben. "My youngest."

Trey glanced at Trick. "Hey," he said and went back to his typing. He resembled his father but wasn't as big as Garret.

"How's Lindsey's injury?" asked Ben.

Lindsey glanced at her father. "I'm fine."

"Nothing major," said Trey. "Janice said she needed a few stitches."

"Where's Janice?" asked Ben.

"She went upstairs," said Lindsey. "How're you?" she asked Trick.

Trick raised his bandaged arm. "I'll live. Ben did a good job." He didn't see Garret or Marcy. "Is Janice your daughter?" he asked Ben.

Ben shook his head. "No. My niece. She's Pete's daughter. For obvious reasons, she's keeping her distance from Eleanor's case."

Trick nodded. "Understandable." He wondered where Garret and Marcy were when the door opened and they both entered, each carrying a tray. "We brought some food from the kitchen," said Marcy. She set the tray down at an empty table and Trick saw chicken, macaroni and a bowl of salad.

Garret set his tray down and Trick saw paper plates, napkins, plastic silverware, cups and a pitcher of liquid. Garret grumbled at Marcy. "Can I get back to work now?"

"Marcy's right," said Ben. "We need to eat. You're not going to be any good to us, Garret, if we find Eleanor and you're starving. You need all the strength you can get." He waved at Trick. "Help yourself, Trick."

Trick noted how everyone looked at him and knew none of them trusted him. "You first, sir."

Garret snorted and Ben grabbed a plate. "It's Ben. No sirs around here." He grabbed a fork and helped himself to some chicken and macaroni. "Come on, Lindsey. Eat."

Lindsey sighed, lowered her head and rubbed her eyes. "Okay." She stood. "But we need to find Eleanor."

"Trey's got the necessary alerts set up. If something triggers, we'll know it. Right Trey?" asked Ben.

Trey finished typing. "If she returns to her place, we'll know. And if a body turns up, we'll know that too."

Garret grumbled some more. "We should be out there, looking. Not sitting here, eating chicken and talking to strangers." He eyed Trick.

Ben scooped up some salad. "You walking around at night, hoping to find her, is a waste of your time. We need to wait her out. Odds are, she'll return home before daylight."

"After she's killed someone else," said Lindsay, grabbing a plate.

"Maybe not," said Ben, sitting at the table. "She fled after attacking you and Trick. She may go to ground tonight and conserve her energy."

"You didn't see her," said Lindsey, getting some chicken. "I'd say we have twenty-four hours at most before she has to feed again." She added some salad to her plate. "And after that it will only escalate." She picked up a napkin and set her plate next to her dad's, then poured herself a drink from the pitcher.

"It's iced tea," said Marcy to Trick. "Unsweet, but I brought sugar if you want any." She made a plate and sat at the table.

Trick nodded. "Thanks." He watched the group help themselves to dinner, still reeling from all that he'd learned. He wasn't sure he could eat. "How will you know if she returns?"

"The cleaner placed a camera for us," said Trey. "It's discreet and easy to retrieve."

"Did the cleaner finish?" asked Ben.

"He did," said Trey.

"Don't you worry about the cleaner?" asked Trick. "What if Eleanor had returned?"

"The cleaner is well-trained, like us," said Ben. "But it's unlikely she'll be back before sunrise."

Garret and Trey helped themselves and returned to their seats at the monitors.

"You going to eat?" Ben asked Trick.

Trick grabbed a plate. "I guess." He picked up a napkin. "Who do you find to clean something like that?"

"That's need-to-know," said Ben. "But being former military helps."

Trick shook his head and scooped some macaroni onto his plate.

"He looks pale," said Marcy.

"Are you surprised?" asked Lindsey. She looked at Ben. "Did you tell him everything?"

"About Eleanor?" Ben nodded. "I did."

Garret snorted. "He'll never make it through dinner. I bet he'll puke it all up and want out before the end of the night."

Trick couldn't help but wonder the same. It was a lot to absorb. "I'll manage," he said. "Although I'm still not sure what I can do."

"Me, either," said Garret. "I don't care what Pete said, this is a bad idea."

Ben straightened. "Watch what you say about your uncle. He just gave his life for the cause. Be respectful."

Garret slumped. "I meant no disrespect. I just disagree."

"There's no way to know until we try," said Lindsey. "Like Dad said, we can always get rid of him if we need to."

Trick raised a brow.

Ben chuckled. "That joke never gets old."

"I fail to see the humor," said Trick.

"Meaning I'll drive you back and you never have to see or speak to us again, but you remember the rules." Lindsey stabbed at her salad and took a bite.

"How could I forget them?" asked Trick. He put some salad and chicken on his plate, poured himself some iced tea and sat next to Marcy. "If I stick around though, what would I do next? How can I help find Eleanor?"

Ben wiped his face with a napkin. "It's not just Eleanor. We have to find the hybrid that created her too, and make sure he or she doesn't do it again."

Trick wondered how he would keep all of this from Red and Mikey. "How?"

"We start at the end," said Marcy. "Eleanor's last moments before she was turned. Who was she with? Where did she go?"

"She wouldn't kill the hybrid who made her?" asked Trick.

"No," said Ben. "There's an almost parental connection between a new craver and their creator. It's rare for a craver to kill so soon anyway. The cravings can hit at various times depending on the virus, but it will take at least twenty-four hours before the initial urge strikes. Some take much longer, but Eleanor isn't one of those."

"She came out of the gate swinging," said Trey. He ate some chicken and studied the computer screen. "Which is good and bad," he said to Trick. "Good because we find her faster. Bad because that means at least one person is dead."

Trick nodded and picked at his macaroni. "What do you all do in the meantime in between craver attacks? Or when there is no craver to track? You all hangout in this house?"

"We do our best to live a normal life, as far as it's possible, but we have to monitor constantly." Ben cut some chicken. "All of us have false identities in the event they're needed."

Marcy grinned. "Lindsey's is Lindsey Eilish. I made it myself. She's a fan of Billie."

"Marce," said Lindsey, shooting Marcy a look.

"Really?" asked Trick, glancing at Lindsey. "Good to know."

"Garret is Garret Cobain, I'm Marcy Spears and Dad is Ben Sinatra." Marcy scooped a forkful of macaroni. "And Trey is Trey Petty."

"Hell, Marcy," said Garret with a glare. "Why don't you give him the downtown address, too?"

"She'll have to," said Ben. "He'll need to know it."

Garret scoffed. "Great."

"Downtown address?" asked Trick.

"We can't provide this one," said Ben. "We have a townhome in the city. It's the address on our IDs. It's a safe house, so to speak. We're not there often, but it provides the cover we need if anyone asks." He sipped some tea. "You should know it in case you need it." He glanced at Marcy. "Maybe get him a false ID, in case there's an emergency."

Trick raised a hand. "I'm sure I'll be fine. As you said, that's the whole point of having me. I'm already on the outside and don't have to hide."

"You never know," said Ben. "You may never use it, but in this line of work, it's better to be prepared."

"Who's your favorite singer?" asked Marcy, with a smile.

"How about Trick Buble'?" asked Garret.

Trey chuckled.

Trick caught Lindsey's smile. "How about Trick Swift?" said Trick.

Everyone went quiet.

"As in Taylor Swift?" asked Marcy, her face somber.

"Something wrong with that?" asked Trick, wondering why the mood had shifted in the room.

"I pegged you for a country guy," said Marcy, fiddling with her napkin.

"Swift's been taken," said Lindsey, poking at her salad.

"It was Pete's,' said Ben. "Guy could belt out *Shake it Up* like no one else."

Trick sunk in his seat. "Hell. I'm sorry." He looked at Marcy. "Then let's go with Trick Brooks. I'm partial to country, too."

Marcy perked up. "That's perfect."

"I still doubt I'll need it though," said Trick. He eyed the room, sensing the distress and figured he should change the subject. "So, we find the hybrid that created Eleanor. How does that help us find Eleanor?"

Ben returned his napkin to his lap. "Eleanor is still new. That serves as an advantage. She'll stick to what she knows which is her apartment and the person who made her, if that person is still around. They're touchstones to her old world and help with her stability. It won't last forever though, so the sooner we can find her, the better."

"You think she'll return to her apartment?" asked Trick. "Why? When she knows we're aware of it."

"Her newness doesn't make her smart. Right now, she still connects to her old self, but she knows enough to stay hidden. She prefers the dark and will avoid the daylight." Ben chewed and swallowed some macaroni.

"Can they be in the sun?" asked Trick, recalling the Dracula movies.

Garret scoffed again.

"They can," said Ben, "but they prefer not to. Their skin and eyes are sensitive, and the sun irritates both. Those who survive long enough adapt. They'll wear long sleeves, hats and sunglasses, and even carry umbrellas, but only for brief periods. But most don't survive long enough to get to that point. We usually find them by then, and if we don't, they'll eventually succumb to the virus."

"They venture out at night," said Lindsey. "And prefer solitude. Which is why it would be hard to find Eleanor right now. She'll stay out until the sun comes up. And then we pray she comes home."

"And then we'll have her," said Garret. He ate a big bite of macaroni.

Trick couldn't help but ask the obvious. "How do you kill her? I don't see any of you carrying guns. Knives seem damn risky."

"Guns are the risky weapons," said Trey. He'd slid his plate to the side of the keyboard and was typing again.

"You saw how fast she moved," said Lindsey. "You didn't come close to hitting her."

"You fire and miss, or only wound her," said Ben, "you won't get a second shot. Close combat works better. And with two people. One person can succeed but it's hard and you're likely to be injured." He shook his head. "Pete didn't wait for us because he was trying to save Jackson."

"But if he'd had a gun, he could have shot her," said Trick.

"Maybe. Maybe not. Cravers have an uncanny sense of their surroundings. If she'd moved, Pete could have just as easily shot Jackson. It's why guns are not preferred. You're more likely to shoot an innocent bystander instead." Ben raised a hand. "The CU is well trained in hand-to-hand combat. If we can get close enough, a craver's rage and aggression, while terrifying, makes them sloppy, and it gives us the advantage. You still have to mortally wound them, though. They're fast healers and injuries will slow them down, but not for long."

Trick tried to keep up. "And once you kill them, what happens to the body?"

"Depends on the situation," said Lindsey. "We either dispose of it or leave it behind."

"Leave it behind?" asked Trick. "Won't an autopsy reveal their illness?"

"No," said Ben. "It will reveal a viral infection that strangely enough, most doctors attribute to the flu. But the wounds on the body are pretty indicative of cause of death."

"And if you don't leave it behind, how the hell do you dispose of it?" asked Trick in disbelief.

Nobody answered.

"That is need-to-know," said Ben.

"Of course it is," said Trick. His mind whirled and he told himself to think like an investigator. If they could find Eleanor, then maybe he could get back to his normal life. He held his temples. "What about Eleanor's car?" he asked, looking up. "She had to have driven to that overlook. Could that help us find her?"

"Been there, done that," said Trey. "Pete gave us her plate number, but the car isn't hers. It was registered to a female patient at an old folks' home. We couldn't determine whether or not she was any relation to Eleanor, so Eleanor either borrowed or stole it."

"Did you talk to the owner?" asked Trick.

"The owner didn't or couldn't remember who Eleanor was," said Lindsey. "I snuck into the nursing home and spoke to her."

Trick considered something else. "What about a purse? Did Eleanor leave one behind at the scene? It would have had her ID, or other info that could help."

Ben stabbed some macaroni. "By the time we arrived, she and her car were gone. We barely had enough time to find Pete's body and remove it. But we should have done a better job of searching the scene." His face fell. "That should have been done first."

"We were reeling with what happened to Pete," said Lindsey. "Nobody was thinking straight." She picked at her food with her fork.

The room went quite again, and Trick glanced at Lindsey. "How did you know to follow me?"

Ben answered. "Once we learned Jackson's name, we surveilled his mother. We saw you talking with her."

Lindsey looked up from her food. "I got your name and did some research. Found out you worked for SCOPE."

"We've been aware of SCOPE for a while now," said Marcy, "considering your clientele and areas of interest."

Garret huffed. "Waste of time as far as we're concerned. Ghosts aren't going to kill you."

Trick thought of Mr. Dark. "You'd be surprised what can kill you, Garret."

Garret stopped chewing and narrowed his eyes at Trick.

"Anyway," said Lindsey, looking between Trick and Garret, "After getting your background, I decided to follow you. Figured why do all the work if you're going to do it instead."

"Plus," said Marcy with a grin, "she said you were cute."

Surprised, Trick ticked up a brow at Lindsey. "Is that so?"

"There's no accounting for taste," said Garret with a scowl.

Lindsey glared at Marcy. "Shut up, Marcy."

Ben smiled and ate a bite of salad.

Lindsey returned her attention to her food, but Trick noticed the hint of red in her cheeks. She poked at her chicken. "Too bad you have the social graces of a caveman."

Trick almost chuckled. "You met many cavemen?"

Nobody answered and Lindsey gripped her fork.

Trick thought of the obvious. "Oh, hell. Don't tell me you investigate them too?" He crumpled his napkin. "What? Do they hang out with Bigfoot?"

Ben shook his head. "Not that we've seen."

Not knowing how to respond, Trick just stared.

Marcy broke the silence. "Getting back to Eleanor, did you learn anything else while you were searching for her?" she asked Trick. "Anything that might help track her or her hybrid down?"

Trick eyed his food, which he'd barely touched, and recalled the bar where Eleanor had sung her last song. Recalling what the bartender had told him, he straightened. "Actually..."

Lindsey perked up. "What is it?"

Trick pointed with his fork. "The bar where she worked. The owner said the night before Eleanor disappeared, she sang her set then met up with some friends. They had some drinks, and left, supposedly to go home."

"Who were they?" asked Ben. "Did he say?"

"No," said Trick. "I don't think he knew."

"We need to find out." Ben pushed his plate to the side. "It's possible one of the people she was with was the hybrid."

Garret swiveled in his seat toward them. "It's also possible they didn't go home, and instead hit more bars. She could have met up with the wrong person, gone home with him or her, and ended up a craver."

Ben stared off as if contemplating their next move. "Then that's where we start." He set his napkin on the table. "Lindsey and Garret, you keep watch at Eleanor's apartment. If she shows, I want you two to be ready. Marcy, listen for any other suspicious deaths or homicides, monitor the alerts and stay in communication with Lindsey and Garret, and Trey, get the status on what the police have. I want to be sure those two detectives don't get in the way. And be prepared to divert them if necessary." He paused. "And tomorrow, Trick Brooks," He pointed at Trick, "you're going back to that bar."

Chapter Twenty-Five

MASON WALKED INTO SCOPE, tossed his hat on the sofa and went to grab a bottled water. Sitting at her desk, Mikey spoke on the phone and waved. Cracking the water bottle, Mason noted Trick's empty chair and wondered where he was.

Mikey ended the call and hung up. "That's one less appointment. Matt Bilson canceled for tomorrow. Says he has rats, not ghosts."

"Good, I think. At least it gives us a free afternoon."

Mikey typed on the keyboard and studied her screen.

"Where's Trick?"

"He's running late. Said he overslept."

Mason checked the time. "It's almost noon."

Mikey shrugged. "What do you want me to tell you?"

"How much you want to bet he didn't go home after he called me yesterday? Probably hit the bars, drank too much, and got home late." Mason shook his head. "He's pissed he didn't find Eleanor."

"And avoiding doing any consultations," added Mikey.

"Probably." Mason pulled out his phone to call his partner.

Mikey stopped typing. "How was your meeting with the Fields?"

"Good. I've set up a home visit. I put it on the calendar." Mason dialed Trick, heard the phone ring and go to voicemail. He left a message.

"Great," said Mikey. She put her elbows on the desk and interlaced her fingers. "Can I ask you something?"

Wondering what was up with Trick, Mason returned his phone to his pocket. "Sure."

Mikey hesitated. "What would you say if I told you I wanted to try again with Dad?"

Mason sighed and approached the desk. "What brought this on?"

"My phone call with Rem."

Mason nodded, recalling Mikey's excitement that Rem had called her. "Let me guess. His advice was to tell Dad how you feel in case Dad dies."

"Something like that. He told me he regrets not doing it with his own father."

Mason walked to the couch and sat.

Mikey stood and joined him. "What do you think?"

"Personally, I think it's a waste of time. I've said all I've have to say to the man."

"You're okay with leaving things as they are?"

"I've come to terms with Dad being who he is and him not changing. He isn't going to accept me, and I don't have to accept him."

Mikey hung her head.

"But if you want to try again, go for it. I won't stop you."

Mikey looked up. "I think I do. I just can't shake the feeling that he may not have long, and I don't like the way I left it the other day."

Mason shifted toward her. "Then do what you have to do, but don't expect much in return."

"No. I know."

Mason heard the outer door open. "That must be Trick."

Mikey leaned and peeked at the computer monitors. "It is."

Mason sipped some water and waited.

The inner door opened, and Trick entered. "Hey." He walked to his desk, took his hat off, hooked it on the edge of his chair, and sat.

"Hey," said Mason. "You enjoy your morning?"

Trick nodded and shook his mouse. His computer screen brightened. "Sorry about that. Slept later than I planned." He studied his screen.

"What happened after I talked to you yesterday?" asked Mason. "Did you go home?"

"Uh, no. I didn't." Trick flipped to a screen and stared at it.

Mason frowned. His usually verbose partner had little to say.

"What did you do?" asked Mikey. "Did you keep looking for Eleanor?"

Trick shook his head. "No." He paused. "I just hung out."

"Hung out?" asked Mason. "Did this hanging out involve a lot of drinking?"

"I stayed out longer than I planned," said Trick, fiddling with a pen on his desk.

Mikey eyed Mason. "Everything okay, Trickster?" asked Mikey.

"Sure. Everything's great." He looked away from the screen. "But I can't give up on Eleanor just yet. I'm going to keep looking."

Mason studied his friend. "We agreed if you couldn't find her, you'd contact Mrs. Trammel and leave Eleanor to the police."

Trick nodded. "Sure. I know, but I have a new lead." He bounced his knee.

"What lead?" asked Mason.

"I found the bar where she worked. They said Eleanor was hanging out with friends before she disappeared. I'm going to see if I can find the friends."

"How do you plan on doing that?" asked Mason.

"I'll go back to the bar and ask around. Hopefully someone knows who Eleanor went off with." He grabbed his hat. "But first I want to go see Kyle."

"You're going now?" asked Mason. "You just walked in the door."

"Have you eaten?" asked Mikey. "I was going to get sandwiches."

Trick waved her off. "I'm fine. Not hungry." He stood.

"Whoa," said Mason. "Maybe we should discuss this."

"Discuss what?" asked Trick.

Mikey's cell rang and she jumped up to get it. Seeing who it was, her eyes widened. "It's Vicki." She nodded toward the door. "I'll take it in here." She answered and walked into the outer office.

"I hope everything's okay with your dad," said Trick. "You heard anything since you saw him?"

Mason got the impression Trick wanted to change the subject. "Nothing. Mikey's worried about him, though. Still wants to make amends."

Trick ran his fingers over the brim of his hat. "Makes sense. Hopefully Vicki's calling to do the same."

"I'm not counting on it."

Trick put his hat on. "I should get going."

Mason stood and walked around the couch. "You sure everything is okay? You're acting strange."

Trick shot a grin at Mason. "I'm great." He adjusted his hat. "I should have just gone straight to the hospital. Would have saved some time."

Mason pointed. "What's that?" Trick's sleeve had pulled up and Mason saw the edge of some gauze wrapped around Trick's wrist. "Are you hurt?"

Trick pulled his sleeve down. "It's nothing. Just dropped a beer. The glass cut me, but I bandaged it up. It's fine."

"Did you go to a doctor?"

"No need," said Trick, hastily, "It wasn't that bad."

Mason reached toward Trick's wrist. "Let me see it."

Trick pulled away. "It's fine, Red. You worry too much."

Mason noted the tension around his friend's mouth and eyes. "What's up with you?"

Trick sighed and looked away. "It's nothing. I guess I'm just antsy about finding Eleanor. I know you want me to give up on it, but she almost killed Kyle. I think I should keep looking."

"If she almost killed Kyle, she could almost kill you. I'm just worried about your safety." Mason sensed that this was about more than Eleanor.

"I'll be fine. I'll call you if I need you."

Mason started to respond when Mikey returned, holding and speaking into the phone. "Let me get a pencil." She walked to the desk, found some paper and a pen. "I'm ready." She wrote on the paper. "I got it. I'll wait for you to call." She listened and nodded. "And thanks for getting in touch. I appreciate it." She paused. "Okay. Bye." She hung up.

"Everything okay?" asked Trick.

"Is it Dad?" asked Mason.

Mikey set her phone down. "He's not doing so hot. Vicki says he's weaker and she's worried. She feels bad about what happened, too, when we visited Dad. Says she wants to talk."

"Talk?" asked Mason. "About what?"

"She would like to meet with both of us, but not at the hospital. She wants to tell us something about why she and Dad visited that Dad didn't want to mention. She gave me an address of where to meet. After the cardiologist stops by to discuss Dad's test results, she can leave, but she's not sure when he'll get there. She'll call when she's free."

Mason recalled his schedule. "I have my appointment with Tarina this afternoon."

"That's fine. If she calls while you're out, I'll tell her we'll meet with her when you're done."

"Sounds cryptic," said Trick.

"I know. She hopes it will clarify some things." Mikey checked the address on the paper and added it to her phone. "I told her I'd like to try and talk to Dad again. She thought that was a good idea. But we should meet first."

"Where's this address?" asked Mason.

"It's a house. It's not far from the hospital. That's all I know." Mikey put her phone down.

"I hope whatever it is she wants to tell you helps," said Trick.

"I hope so, too," said Mikey. "I'm tired of this fighting."

"I'm sure you are." Trick headed to the door. "I should go if I'm going to swing by and see Kyle."

Mikey cocked her head. "Actually, can I join you? We can take two cars. I can get the sandwiches on the way back." She reached for her purse.

Trick stilled. "If it's okay, I'd like to go on my own. Nothing personal. I'd just like to talk to Kyle about what happened now that he's stronger. It would be better if it were just us."

Mikey held her purse. "Oh. Sure. I understand." She put her purse down. "I'll go see him later, maybe after we see Vicki."

"Sorry," said Trick. "I'll tell him you plan to drop by though." He opened the door. "I'll see you two later. Tell Vicki I said hi."

Mason watched his friend disappear and heard the outer door open and close.

Mikey stared at the exit. "What was that about?"

Mason's mind raced. "He's lying."

"About seeing Kyle?"

"It's about more than Kyle."

"I always thought Trick was a better liar than that."

"Oh, he's a damn good liar, when he wants to be. It's when he doesn't want to be that he goes off the rails. He can't look you in the eye, changes the subject, and says stupid things."

"You mean to tell Vicki he said hi? I thought that was odd."

Mason put his hands on his hips. "The question is, what's he hiding?"

"It must have something to do with Eleanor, don't you think?"

"He's got an injury. His wrist is bandaged." Mason couldn't help but worry. "Whatever happened last night, I hope to hell he knows what he's doing."

Mikey frowned. "Could it have something to do with Margaret? I told you what Rem said. Could she be watching Trick, too?"

"No. If that were true, he'd be sticking to us like glue and he'd notify the whole force."

"Should we do something?"

"I'll talk to him later. The good news is that once I call him on it, he'll usually come clean. After we see Vicki, I'll get in touch with him." Mason hoped his friend would be ready to talk. "And he better be prepared to tell me the truth."

·•••••••••

Trick sat in the family room on Kyle's floor in the hospital, nursing a cold coffee and trying to gather his thoughts. After seeing Kyle, Trick had been amazed by his improvement. Kyle had told him the doctors might let him go home in a couple of days. Trick had been thrilled and Kyle had asked about Eleanor and the progress of the case. Trick had told him the obligatory information but little else, and when Kyle's mother showed, Trick had left. Not sure where to go next, he'd stopped in the lounge to get a coffee.

Having barely slept and with only a piece of toast in his stomach, he needed to think. After his few bites of chicken and macaroni the previous night, Ben had given him a burner phone, telling him to use it only for emergencies and to dump it if needed to prevent discovery. Trick had taken it and followed Lindsey upstairs and back to the car. Still hesitant to trust him despite signing the rules, Lindsey had covered his eyes again, he'd laid down in the back seat, and she'd returned him to his truck. She'd told him they'd be in touch if there was any sign of Eleanor and for him to call if he had luck finding the hybrid.

Trick had gone home and tossed and turned the rest of the night. He'd avoided SCOPE for as long as possible and had almost not gone in at all. He hated the idea of lying to Red and Mikey, but knew he had to put in an appearance. He realized his mistake, though, the moment he'd entered the office. Struggling with their questions, he'd started to sweat and knew he had to get out of there. The bar where Eleanor had worked didn't open until later and he'd planned to kill some time at SCOPE, see Kyle and then start his search. Cursing at himself and sipping his coffee, he wished he'd called in sick. But even that would have been difficult. Mikey and Red would have checked in on him. At least this way, they might be suspicious, but he could do his thing without their interference. Once they found Eleanor and the hybrid, then he would figure out what to do. One thing he realized was that he couldn't continue lying, which meant he'd have to turn in his CU badge and Ben would have to find another civilian source to help. Unless he could tell Red the truth, Trick figured it would be the logical choice.

Checking the time, he decided he couldn't sit in the family room all day. He patted his pocket, feeling the burner phone. No one had contacted him so Eleanor must not have yet returned to her apartment. Trick stood, tossed his coffee and headed for the elevators. The doors opened and he stepped inside, wondering where to go. He had more time to kill but couldn't return to SCOPE. Thinking of Mikey, he felt bad that he'd ditched her but there was no way he could have spent any more time with her. The pressure of hiding his secrets would have been too difficult.

The elevator stopped at a floor, the doors opened, and a man stepped inside. Trick eyed the floor number and realized it was Martin Redstone's floor. He hesitated but before the doors could close again, he stepped off. Mason and Mikey had been struggling with their dad's presence since his arrival and Trick had seen Martin only once when he'd showed at SCOPE. Thinking he ought to say hello just in case the man didn't pull through, he decided to visit. He, like Mikey, didn't like to end things on bad terms, and in some part of his brain, he wanted to put in a good word for the Redstone kids. Not that his opinion would matter much, but knowing he'd made the effort would help.

Walking down the hall, he found the room number and stopped outside the door. He took a breath and knocked softly. Not hearing a response, he pushed the door open. He spotted Martin lying in bed, his eyes closed. Vicki sat beside him. The chair had been pulled up and she was holding his hand and resting her head on his arm, which sported an IV. Trick wondered if she was asleep.

She must have heard him though because she raised her head and sniffed, then turned and wiped her face. Trick could see the tissue in her hand. "Is this a bad time?" he asked.

She blotted her face and glanced at him. "Sorry. I must have dozed off." She let go of Martin's hand. "Come on in," she whispered.

Trick entered and the door closed behind him. "How is he?" He approached the bed.

"Sleeping. He does that a lot now." She stood and faced Trick.

Trick eyed the pale man in the bed. No longer healthy and robust, he looked frail and underweight. A heart monitor beeped and the IV pole stood beside the bed. "I'm sorry he's not doing so hot. How are you?"

She fiddled with the tissue. "Not so great." Tears filled her eyes.

"What do the doctors say?"

She shook her head and dabbed her eyes. "Not much. They keep thinking they know the cause and then they do another test and change their minds. It's so frustrating. Then Martin will rebound and feel better and think he's going home, only to crash again a few hours later. And then he gets so upset." She pointed toward his arm. "He yanked out his IV yesterday. They had to sedate him to put it back in. It was awful."

Trick eyed the older man's arm, seeing the bruises. "I bet he's hating every minute of this."

She scoffed. "He's not an easy patient. I keep telling him to rest and take it easy. Let the doctors do their thing, but does he listen?"

"It's the Redstone obstinate gene. It runs strong in their family."

"It sure does."

Trick wasn't sure what else to say. "I just wanted to stop by and check in. I know we don't know each other well, but despite whatever differences there may be within the family, I don't harbor Martin any ill will. I just wish he could see his kids the way I do."

Vicki nodded her head. "I understand. I wish I knew how to handle it." She paused. "I guess you and I are the outsiders looking in, wishing we could help in some way."

"I guess so. It's harder for you, though. You've been playing peacekeeper."

"And doing a lousy job." She sniffed. "I didn't handle Mikey's visit too well. But Martin can't handle any stress right now."

"Mikey gets it."

"Does she? I got the impression she was mad." She sighed. "I called her today. Told her I thought we should meet."

"I heard." Trick debated his next words. "You should know that despite what Martin has told you, Red and Mikey are good people. I know they may not have taken the path Martin wanted them to, and they've taken issue with Martin's parenting, but there's no one I trust more. Red and Mikey are like my own family."

Vicki nodded. "I know. And I know Martin was not a stellar dad. It's hard to repair long-standing damage. I don't know if it's even possible." She swiped at her eye. "But he's sick and if it's going to happen, it has to be now. It's why I called Mikey. I wanted to tell her and Mason something and I'm not sure what they'll think about it."

"Mikey said you're meeting at a house? Not here?"

"There's a reason I want to meet there."

"Who's house is it?"

"It was my mother's. She owned it for ten years. Never lived in it, though. Always rented it. She died last year and left the house to me. I've spent the last several months getting the house back from occupants who haven't paid a dime in rent for a while." She closed her eyes and rubbed her neck.

Trick gestured toward a built-in sofa along the wall. "Why don't you sit? You look tired."

She glanced at it and nodded. "I am." Vicki walked over and sat, and Trick sat beside her. "The house is one of the reasons Martin and I came to visit. Now that it's vacant, I have to decide what to do with it. The problem is, it's a mess. It hasn't been taken care of and it needs work. A lot of it."

"What do Red and Mikey have to do with the house?"

She clutched her tissue. "I've been staying there the last few nights. I couldn't afford to remain in the hotel and the house is close by. I cleaned up the bedroom and kitchen enough for me to manage. It's still not ideal but it will do for now."

Trick frowned. "You've been staying there? Is it safe?"

"Safe enough, I guess. To be honest, I'm only there to sleep. But the electricity and water work and as long as I can take a shower and lie down in a bed, it's all I need. But I got to thinking about Martin…"

Trick glanced at the sleeping man in the bed. "What about him?"

Vicki stared at the tissue in her hands. "He's not strong enough to travel. Once the doctors let him leave, I could take him to the house. He could recover there, see his doctors, get stronger. He'll hate it, of course."

"You want him to stay in California?" Trick widened his eyes, wondering how Red and Mikey would handle that news.

"Just for now. It would be better for him. I'm not worried about Max. I think he'll be fine with it, but Mason and Mikey might disapprove."

Trick pursed his lips. "Are you expecting some level of involvement from them?"

She rubbed her temples. "It would be nice. It's going to be hard being his only caregiver. But I'll understand if they say no."

"What if Martin says no?"

Vicki shrugged. "He may not have a choice. At this point, he's barely strong enough to walk. This is a sensible solution, but I'd need to get the home cleaned and ready for him. That's going to take time and a lot of work."

Trick tried to imagine Red and Mikey's reaction. "I have to tell you, Vicki, I wouldn't expect an outpouring of support, especially from Red. Mikey might be different, but I can't promise that either."

"I know, but I have to ask. I may not get their help, but at least they'll know my plan and they can't say I didn't discuss it with them." She groaned. "That's a big problem with this family. Nobody talks to each other."

"I would argue that there's plenty of talking, just not enough listening."

She glanced at him. "You seem to know what you're talking about. I'm guessing you have your own family issues?"

Trick thought of his mom and her variety of problems. "Enough to make this situation seem easy."

"I'm sorry to hear that."

Trick leaned back against the sofa. "What about Margaret?"

He caught Vicki stiffen. "What about her?" she asked.

"You expect her to visit, too?"

"No."

Trick raised a brow. "You know Martin will."

"Martin is barely coherent. Let's just take one problem at a time. The bigger issue is getting him into the house in the first place."

"And then keeping him there."

She nodded. "You understand, then."

"More than you know."

"Can you at least talk to Mason and Mikey, after I do? Help them adjust to their father living nearby? Maybe help smooth the waters?"

Trick sighed. "I can't promise anything, Vicki."

"I realize that." She eyed Martin in the bed. "Maybe I've got blinders on, but some part of me hopes this will help."

"Or it will drive the wedge deeper." He raised a brow. "This isn't just about Red and Mikey though. If you expect change, Martin is going to have to do his part."

"My hope is that once he starts to improve, I can work on that. He's just stubborn. He likes to be right."

"Don't we all?"

Holding her tissue, Vicki wrung her hands. "All I can do is try."

Trick shifted in his seat. "For someone who's only known Martin for a short period of time, you certainly are doing a lot for him."

Vicki tensed. "That's something else I needed to mention to Mikey and Mason." She bit her lip. "I haven't told anyone else."

Trick frowned, feeling uneasy. "I get the feeling you're about to tell me?"

"Do you mind? I have to tell someone. But you have to keep it to yourself, at least until I talk to Mikey and Mason."

Trick hesitated but gave in. "What is it?"

Vicki took a breath and sat up. "Martin and I got married. Three days ago."

Trick dropped his jaw.

"Here. In this room. I can't make decisions for him unless I'm his wife, and we both decided it made sense. A chaplain performed the ceremony and a nurse witnessed it. It was all very quick."

"And you didn't see the need to tell any of the kids?"

"Martin said no."

Trick blew out a gust of air. "Well, that's a bit of news." He figured Mikey and Red would either be angry or wouldn't care. "I wish I could tell you what to expect but I have no idea." He paused. "But I wish you luck this afternoon. Something tells me you're going to need it."

"You're welcome to join us." She made a face as if hoping he'd say yes.

Trick almost chuckled. "I appreciate the offer, but you're on your own for this one. Besides, I've got some other things to take care of."

She fiddled with her tissue again. "I thought I'd ask, just in case."

Trick empathized with her. "It will be fine. Just bring ear plugs. I suspect Red might do some yelling."

She smiled.

"I'm not joking."

Her smile fell.

Trick almost patted her on the arm when the burner phone in his pocket buzzed. He froze and straightened. "I should go." He pulled it out and it buzzed again.

"I'm sorry. I've dumped a lot on you and you're obviously busy." She stood.

Trick stood, too. "I apologize, but I need to take this."

She nodded. "I'm glad you stopped by. It was nice to speak with you."

"You, too, Vicki. And good luck with your talk today."

"Thanks," she said.

Trick headed for the door. "And congratulations to you and Martin."

"I appreciate it. Somehow, I think you'll be the only one saying that."

His phone buzzing, Trick smiled and opened the door. "I hope not." He waved. "See you." She waved back and he stepped out and answered. "Hello?"

Lindsey responded. "We have activity."

Chapter Twenty-Six

Talking, Trick held the phone to his ear and headed toward the elevators. "Is it Eleanor?"

"Garret and I spotted her returning to her apartment. When we went in though, she was gone."

Trick hit the elevator button. "Gone where?"

"We gave her a few minutes, thinking she'd relax and sleep. But when we went in, the place was empty. Trey watched the video and saw her enter, then go to her room. She didn't come out."

The elevator dinged and the doors opened. Trick stepped inside. "Where did she go?"

Lindsey sighed over the phone. "Garret and I went into her bedroom. Her window was open and there were clothes strewn across the bed and the shower was wet. I think she went in, cleaned up, changed clothes, and jumped out the window."

Trick watched the illuminated floor numbers descend. "But she's on the second story."

"I know. And she's being careful. It's extremely rare for a new craver. She's far more advanced than most at her level. It's almost as if she's been warned. And she's moving around during the day. Also very unusual."

"Where do you think she went last night?"

"No idea. And we have no idea where she is now, which is a big problem. She may be advanced, but she can't hide her hunger. We didn't hear of any attacks last night and if she hasn't fed, she will soon."

"Maybe she did feed, and the victim hasn't been found." The elevator stopped and the doors opened. Trick stepped out and walked through the lobby.

"You saw the crime scene at the overlook. That's hard to miss."

"I see your point, but it's still possible."

"Well, until we know for sure, we have to assume she hasn't, which means she could kill at any time. Have you spoken to anyone at the bar where Eleanor worked?"

"No. They don't open for a couple of hours. But I'll head over now. Maybe someone is there I can talk to."

"We've got to find her before someone else does. Especially those detectives. That would be a disaster."

"What are you going to do?" Trick left the lobby and headed toward his truck.

"Trey will keep watching the video in case she returns to her apartment. We'll stay in the area and look around. It's possible she didn't go far and found a quiet place to hide."

Trick stopped as a car drove past in the parking lot. "You be careful. She catches you by surprise, you may not go home."

"You, too. There's a possibility she could return to the bar since it's familiar to her. She knows your scent, so stay alert at all times."

Trick's heart thudded. "If I see her, I'll contact you." He had no desire to take on Eleanor alone again.

"No," said Lindsey. "You see her, you run. Because if you don't, you're a dead man."

Trick got to his truck, got in and slumped in his seat. "Great."

"Stick to crowds as much as possible. She'll avoid them, so she probably won't be at the bar, but she's already defying expectations, so stay aware."

"Okay. I'll be careful."

"Call us when you know something, or if anything seems off or suspicious."

Trick started up his truck. "Like what?"

"You'll know it when you feel it."

"You mean like that decay smell?"

"You smell that and you're already dead." She paused. "Just trust your gut and don't assume anything."

"Okay. I'll let you know what I find out, and you do the same."

"I will."

"And don't get dead."

There was a pause. "You, too."

Trick nodded and heard a click when Lindsey hung up.

· · • • · • • · ·

Mikey read the news article on her phone. The headline had caught her eye and surprised, she'd quickly read it again. Mason had left earlier for his appointment with Tarina, and Vicki had not yet called. Mikey had caught up with her work, made some coffee and had sat on the sofa at SCOPE to wait. Flipping through her phone, she'd spotted the article and a name that gave her chills. A local news site had picked up the story and a blog post writer had followed up and mentioned it in his blog.

After reading both the article and the blog post, Mikey swallowed and gripped her phone, wondering what it meant, if anything. Her mind wandering, she jumped when the door opened, and Mason walked in.

He set his hat on the couch. "Hey," he said.

Mikey lowered her phone. "Hey. How's Tarina?"

"Direct as ever." He pointed toward the coffee pot. "Is that fresh?"

"It is."

Mason headed toward it. "I'm tempted to add some of Trick's bourbon." He grabbed a mug and poured some coffee into it. "You hear from Vicki?"

"Not yet." Mikey eyed the article, wondering whether to tell Mason.

"Anything from Trick?" Mason returned the pot and sipped some coffee.

"Nothing."

"Maybe I should call him." He pulled out his phone.

"Mason," Mikey started, but hesitated.

Mason had reached for his cell but stopped. He stared at Mikey. "What's wrong?"

Mikey nibbled her lip.

Mason walked over and sat beside her. "Is it Dad?"

"No." She held out her phone. "It's this."

Mason set his coffee down and took her cell. He read the article and his eyes widened.

"There's a blog about it, too." Mikey swiped at the screen.

Mason read that too and cursed. He handed the phone back to Mikey.

"What do you think?" asked Mikey.

"Unbelievable." Mason rubbed his eyes and groaned. "Ruben Montes has bought a downtown building and is converting it to low-income housing and a homeless shelter."

"Some people love it, others hate it."

"The building is not my issue."

"I know."

Mason glanced at her. "I don't like it. It's a reason for him to be in town."

"I can't believe the feds could never pin anything on him. After everything that happened at Windhaven and with his son, Rain."

"Ruben is slick. He knows what he's doing, and he's covered his bases. Rain may be awaiting trial for murder, but he's like his father. They're both dangerous, and this..." he gestured toward the phone. "...this sounds more to me like a threat."

"You think Ruben Montes bought a building in the city to send you a message? It seems extreme."

"It's Ruben's style. Use his wealth to demonstrate his altruism and show the world he's reformed while making sure I know he's around and hasn't forgotten."

Mikey shook her head. "Maybe not. Maybe this is just a homeless shelter."

"I told you what he said to me. Ruben is pissed. I exposed the conspiracy at Windhaven which led to the demise of the Montes family's pharmaceutical empire and Rain's arrest."

"Rain almost killed you and did kill others. He's in jail because of that. Not because of you."

"Ruben doesn't see it like that."

Mikey tucked her phone in her pocket. "What do you want to do?"

Mason stared off. "Nothing. Hopefully, Ruben will build whatever it is he's building, and he'll leave."

Mikey nodded.

"We have to be careful, though. He made a veiled threat against me and you. And he mentioned Margaret. That's got me nervous. It may have just been his way to scare me, but with Ruben, there's no way to be sure."

Mikey laid her head back on the couch. "Great. So now we have a mentally ill sister to look out for plus an evil philanthropist?" She looked over at her brother. "It's a lot."

"I hope it's nothing. But you're right. Ruben could just be helping the homeless."

Mikey could sense that Mason didn't believe it was nothing and it was definitely something. "I hear the Caribbean is nice this time of year."

Mason smiled and sighed. "I may check real estate prices."

Mikey patted her brother's arm when her phone buzzed. She pulled it out and read the text message. "It's Vicki. She says she's headed to the house. You ready?"

Mason groaned. "I didn't get to finish my coffee."

"I'll tell her we'll leave in ten minutes." Mikey texted Vicki back.

Mason stood. "You know. I may have a touch of Trick's bourbon. I think I'm going to need it."

Chapter Twenty-Seven

Trick sat in front of O'Rourke's bar waiting for someone to enter. He'd arrived an hour earlier, but no one had been there. Tapping the steering wheel, he thought of Lindsey who couldn't be far away, keeping an eye out for Eleanor in the area. He shuddered at the thought that Eleanor might be nearby. How far did his scent travel? Could she sneak up on him? If he did find her, what were the odds he could outrun her? He had to admit they were slim to none.

Groaning, he slid down in his seat, but sat back up again when he spotted a man walk up to the door of the bar, unlock it and enter. Trick got out of his truck and double-checking his surroundings, crossed the street and approached the entrance. He entered the bar.

The man was behind the counter and looked over when Trick walked up. Trick recognized him as the owner who he'd talked to on his previous visit.

"Sorry, dude," he said. "We're closed." He narrowed his eyes. "Do I know you?"

Trick nodded. "Yes. I was in here yesterday, asking about Eleanor." Yesterday felt like a million years ago.

"That's right. Did you find her?"

"Yes and no, but that's not why I'm here. You mentioned that on her last night Eleanor was with some friends. I'm wondering if you know who those friends were and how to find them?"

"Sorry. I wish I could help you. I didn't pay that much attention."

Trick deflated. "You're sure? It's important that I find them."

The owner shook his head. "You might talk to Katie. She waited on them that night. If anyone knows anything, it will be her. She should be in soon."

Hopeful, Trick perked up. "You mind if I wait?"

"Suit yourself. Can I get you a drink?"

Trick debated a shot of tequila. "Tempting but no, thank you."

"Have a seat. I've got some stuff to do in the back."

"Thanks. I appreciate it." He held his stomach. "You mind if I use your restroom?"

"No problem." The owner gestured down a hall, and Trick saw the bathroom sign. After drinking that coffee at the hospital and sitting in his car, Trick had started to get uncomfortable. He headed down the hall and after using the facilities, he washed and dried his hands. He left the bathroom, praying Katie would know something, when he heard voices. Recognizing them, he stopped cold and peered around the edge of the wall. Cursing inwardly, he recognized Bevins and Winkler. They were at the bar, their backs to Trick and speaking to the owner.

Trick listened and heard them mention that one of the patrons had seen the news footage and reported that they'd seen Eleanor at O'Rourke's. Trick could barely make out the owner's response but hoped he wouldn't mention Trick. He waited and sucked in a breath when he heard the owner tell them about Eleanor's apartment over the dress shop. Trick hastily pulled out his phone and typed out a fast text to Lindsey, telling her Eleanor's home was now on the police's radar and to be prepared.

Putting his phone away, he didn't even want to think about what would happen if Bevins and Winkler encountered Eleanor in her current state. The encounter would be over quick, and it would be bloody. He glanced back around the wall and was relieved to see the detectives leaving the bar. Ensuring they were gone, he stepped out and approached the counter.

The owner folded a towel and set it aside. "Looks like you've got company."

"Did you tell them about me?"

The owner shrugged. "They didn't ask. I just told them what I told you."

Trick exhaled a sigh of relief but realized finding Eleanor and the hybrid that created her was now even more crucial. "I appreciate that."

"You still want to talk to Katie?"

"I do."

"Then you're in luck." He bobbed his head toward the door. "She's here."

Trick turned to see a woman with stick straight red hair and a short skirt enter the bar. "Hey, Johnny," she said.

"Hey, Katie." Johnny arranged some liquor bottles. "Someone here wants to talk to you."

Katie walked over and Trick noted her heavy eye makeup and red lips. She looked Trick over. "What about?"

Trick introduced himself. "I'd like to ask about Eleanor Clyde. Johnny tells me you waited on her and her friends the last night she was here."

"Oh, that?" asked Katie.

"I'll be in the back if you need me," said Johnny and he disappeared behind a staff door.

"Yes, that," said Trick. "I'm trying to locate the people she was with on her last night. Did you talk to any of them?"

She stared off as if thinking. "Not really. It was busy that night."

"Can you tell me what you remember?"

Katie set her purse on the bar. "Let me see." She scrunched her face. "I remember Eleanor sang that night. She did well, too. Got good tips."

"Did you know her well?"

"Not really, but I liked her. She was a little shy but when she opened up, she was really sweet. She was naïve though. Trusted people she shouldn't have." She raised a brow. "I remember that after she sang, she went to the bar to get a drink, and some loser was hitting on her. You could tell she was trying to be nice, and the guy wasn't getting the hint. I was on the verge of saying something when a woman walked up. Got between Eleanor and the loser and told him off. She wasn't nice about it either. He started to get in her face, and she leaned in and said something to him. I couldn't hear it, but the guy's face changed. He paid his bill and took off. Then this woman started talking to Eleanor and invited her to her table."

Trick frowned. "Any idea who the woman was?"

"No. But I served their table the rest of the night. That lady Eleanor was with was something else. Men were like moths to her flame. Some would sit and drink with them and others would be told to get lost. Eleanor was getting a lot of free drinks. Even other women were approaching the table. Another lady joined them and before you knew it, it was closing time. They got up to leave and I checked on Eleanor. She said she was going home, and I wasn't too worried since I knew she lived close by and wouldn't have to drive."

"What about the men?" asked Trick. "Did Eleanor leave with one, or did anyone suspicious follow her out?"

"Not that I saw. But believe me, if anyone creepy was hanging around, they were put in their place fast. Those women didn't mess around."

"Those women?"

"Yeah. The lady Eleanor met at the bar and the other lady who joined them. They all left together."

Trick had to wonder if Eleanor had been targeted by someone and had been followed home. If that were true, they'd never find the hybrid. "Does this place have cameras?" He looked around.

"Not yet. Johnny's working on it though."

Trick gripped his temples, trying to think. "Okay." He looked up. "What about the women? Any idea who they are? Have they been in here since?"

"Not that I've seen. They were good tippers though. They didn't pay for a single drink, but they still left me some money."

"If you were to see them again, would you recognize them?"

Katie smirked. "Of course. I never forget a face. Especially the customers who know how to tip." She pointed a red fingernail at Trick. "I'd definitely know the woman who helped Eleanor with the guy at the bar. She had a unique look about her. Small but fierce, and the bluest eyes I've ever seen."

Trick froze and felt like he'd been dumped in a pool of ice. "Blue eyes?"

Katie nodded. "Yeah."

Trick blinked, wondering if what he was thinking was possible. He grabbed his phone, accessed his camera and flipped through his photos. He found the one he wanted and held it out. "Is that her?"

Katie studied it. "Well, she was more dressed up and wore make up, but yeah. That's her."

Trick gripped the phone, barely able to speak.

"You know her?"

Barely able to form words, Trick glanced at the mug shot of Margaret Redstone. "I sure as hell do."

• • • • • • • • • •

Mikey pulled up to the curb and parked in front of the two-story house.

"Are you sure this is it?" asked Mason.

"According to my navigation system, it is." Mikey had to admit, it wasn't the neighborhood she'd been expecting. It was older with large mature trees, but that was its only desirable feature. Many of the houses needed repair and plenty of paint. Lawns were overgrown and the cement in the driveways and street was cracked. Chain link fences surrounded most of the properties, including the one they were visiting. Looking at the house, Mikey saw the weeds in the flower beds and the windows were dirty. "It's not exactly Fifth Avenue, but with a little TLC, it could be really nice."

Mason undid his seatbelt. "I wonder why she wanted to meet here."

"Let's go find out." Mikey also undid her seatbelt. "There's a car in the driveway, so she must be inside."

They got out of the car and took the sidewalk to the fence. A neighbor's dog barked, and they walked through the gate and up to the front of the house. "Something about this is really strange," said Mason.

Mikey thought it was odd, too. "Let's just talk to her and then we can leave."

They approached the front steps and Mason hesitated. "Maybe we should—" The front door opened, and Vicki stood in the entrance.

"You made it," she said. She walked onto the creaky porch. She glanced at the exterior. "I know it wasn't what you were expecting, but I can explain." She gestured. "C'mon in."

Mikey glanced at Mason and gave him the *just give her five minutes* face. Mason shot her *the five minutes and that's it* look and they entered. The inside didn't look much better than the outside. The wallpaper was peeling, the laminate floor had cracked and buckled, and the furniture had seen better days.

Vicki closed the door. "I know it's not much, but I asked you here for a reason." She walked to the kitchen which sported a torn curtain over a cracked window above the sink. She opened an old refrigerator and took out two bottled waters. "Here. It's all I have in the house."

Mikey took her bottle and Mason took his. "Thanks," said Mikey.

"Have a seat," said Vicki, waving toward a lumpy stained couch.

Mikey walked over and sat. She looked around, seeing stairs leading to an upper floor and a door off a small hall which she guessed led to a bedroom. On the other side of the kitchen was an open door and Mikey could see stairs that led down to a basement.

Mason sat beside Mikey and Vicki sat in a rickety chair across from them. "Thank you again for coming," she said.

"Why are we here?" asked Mason.

Vicki stared at her hands. "There are a lot of reasons."

"Is this about Dad?" asked Mikey.

"Yes," she said. "And what's best for him...and me...and you."

"What does this house have to do with it?" asked Mason.

Vicki paused and then sat back. "The house is mine. It belonged to my mother who used it as a rental property. I inherited it when she passed. It's one of the reasons your father and I visited. To figure out what to do with it." She looked around. "As you can see, it needs a lot of work."

"That's putting it mildly," said Mason.

Mikey nudged him with her knee. "It's not terrible," she said. "But I can see your point."

Vicki nodded. "I've been staying here the last few nights since we can't afford to remain in the hotel."

Mikey frowned. "Staying here? Why didn't you tell me? I would have offered you my apartment."

"It's fine," said Vicki. "It's close to the hospital and I'm only here to sleep. I've cleaned it enough to make it habitable."

Mason sighed. "No offense, Vicki, but I wouldn't stay here alone at night. That lock on your door wouldn't stop a first-offense teenager looking for some place to smoke his weed."

"I'm getting the locks changed tomorrow." Vicki adjusted the cuff on the sleeve of her blouse. "Thankfully, I haven't had any issues."

"Are you going to sell the house?" asked Mikey. "Are you talking to realtors?" She still didn't understand why Vicki had wanted to meet at the home.

"No. Not yet, at least." Vicki stopped fiddling with her blouse and paused. "I'm thinking of bringing your dad here when he gets out of the hospital."

Mikey dropped her jaw. "Here?"

Mason narrowed his eyes. "Why?"

"Your father is too weak to travel. He'll need care when he leaves the hospital and until he's strong enough, he'll need a place to stay. I'll work on the house to make it livable. There's a downstairs bedroom so he doesn't have to use the stairs. It makes sense."

"What does Dad say about this?" asked Mikey.

"He doesn't know." Vicki wrung her hands. "He's too out of it for me to tell him. He won't like it, but I don't think we have a choice."

"Have you talked to Max?" asked Mason. "His house is plenty big."

Vicki shook her head. "I don't want to inconvenience anyone. It's a lot to ask. Plus, I don't know how long this will take. We could be here a while."

Mikey didn't know what to think. What Vicki was proposing was unexpected and surprising. "That's a lot for you to handle. Have you thought about that?"

"Especially for someone who hasn't known our father for long." Mason cracked his water bottle open. "If Dad disagrees, he's going to put up a fight." He stared at the bottle before looking up. "Who's discussing his care with his doctors?"

"I am," said Vicki.

Mikey glanced at Mason. It hadn't occurred to her to ask about who was making decisions for her dad. "Can you do that?" she asked.

Vicki hugged herself and looked between the two of them. "Your father and I got married at the hospital."

Mikey stilled and sensed Mason tensing beside her. "You did what?" asked Mikey.

"You didn't tell anyone?" asked Mason.

"Your father didn't want to," said Vicki.

"Of course he didn't," said Mason. He took a sip of his water.

Mikey sat quietly, not sure what to feel. "I don't know what to say."

"There's nothing to say," said Mason. "It looks like Vicki and Dad have it all figured out."

"I'm sorry you have to hear about it like this. I know I'm throwing a lot at you." Vicki leaned forward. "But I want you to know that you're always welcome here. I hope you can understand why we did what we did and why I've made the choice for your dad to stay here."

Mikey rubbed her head. "I hope you know what you're doing."

"I think I do," said Vicki. "And I'm hoping for your support."

Mason snorted. "Is that what this is about? You're hoping we'll stop by and help you clean this place up, and when he's here, we'll help you with his needs?"

Vicki eyed the floor. "I didn't know what to expect. I know you're not on good terms with your father, but he's still your dad."

"In name only." Mason set his jaw.

"What would you need?" asked Mikey.

Mason erupted. "Oh, hell, no. Don't you dare, Mikey. You know that if the situation were reversed, Dad wouldn't lift a finger to help."

"I think his illness will mellow him," said Vicki.

"It won't be the illness," said Mason. "It will be the drugs. And a lot of them." He recapped his water bottle. "No. You do this, you do it on your own. If Max wants to help, then let him, but we're out of it." He stood, his face red. "You ready, Mikey?"

Mikey understood her brother's anger but didn't like him deciding for her. She looked up at him. "Vicki never said anything about bathing, feeding, or clothing him. Dad would hate that anyway. But what if she needs to run an errand or needs food or supplies?"

"Call a delivery service," said Mason.

"All of this costs money, Mason," said Mikey. "How do you expect her to fly him to Texas when he's sick, then take care of him there without help?" She struggled to calm herself. "She's right. At least here he can recuperate, still be near his current doctors and whether you like it or not, we're nearby."

"This is a mistake, Mikey," said Mason. "You know it and I know it."

"Are you saying he's not sick?" asked Mikey. "That Dad did this deliberately? You know he'll hate this, too, but what choice is there?"

Mason ran a hand over his face. "That's exactly it. He'll hate all of it and he'll hate that we're here and end up taking out his frustrations on us. How are you going to feel when you bend over backwards to help and you don't get so much as a thank you from that man, and instead he berates you for your life choices?"

"Who said anything about bending over backwards?" asked Mikey. "I was offering to pick up some groceries or run errands."

"You start there and where does it stop?" Mason glared. "I'm sorry but I'm not going to be the dutiful son when he's never been the dutiful father. Vicki," he looked over at her, "you married him, so he's all yours."

Mikey stood. "Mason, listen…"

"You ready?" he asked. "Because I sure as hell am." He set his bottle of water on the floor. "Our five minutes is up."

Vicki stood, too. "I'm sorry I upset you. I was afraid this might happen."

Mikey wasn't sure what to do. She understood Mason's point, but this was still their father. "I think we need some time to think about this, Vicki. It's a lot to absorb."

Vicki crossed her arms. "You take all the time you need. Your father and I will be fine. You two are not the only siblings."

Mason snickered. "If you think Max is going to run over here every time you need milk, you're in for a shock. He's out of town most of the time, anyway. You might get lucky in the money department though. Maybe he'll buy you some new furniture and hopefully a new TV. You know how Martin likes his sports."

"Mason, stop it." Mikey took his elbow.

Mason eyed her and sighed. "I'm sorry, Mikey, but this is not our problem."

"No, it isn't," said Vicki. "But I still wanted to tell you. You needed to know. I can't say I'm not disappointed, though. I guess I'd hoped that this might make things better, but your sister told me not to expect much."

Startled, Mikey turned and gripped Mason's arm.

"What are you talking about?" asked Mason. His whole demeanor changed, and he straightened. "Have you spoken to Margaret?"

Vicki smiled. A shiver raced through Mikey and her hair raised. In that moment, Vicki revealed herself. "Vicki?" Mikey asked. "What are you up to?"

Vicki stepped over to the kitchen counter and leaned against it. "You two are so spoiled and ungrateful." She made a face. "Dad did this and Dad did that. He didn't treat me right. It's pathetic."

Mikey's skin prickled and she suddenly felt exposed. "I think we better leave."

"Right now," added Mason.

Vicki checked a nail. "Sure. Go ahead. Leave. It's what you two do best. Someone needs you, like your dad or your sister and you two head in the other direction."

Mikey shook her head, trying to understand. How had Vicki duped them so well? Mason took her arm and pulled her closer to him. "Let's go."

Mikey nodded and they started to leave when the bedroom door opened. Mikey stopped when a woman stepped out.

Mason stopped, too, and the color left his face. "No," he whispered.

Mikey gasped and backed up when Margaret walked toward them. She grinned and her blue eyes sparkled. "Oh, yes, little brother."

Chapter Twenty-Eight

TRICK RAN OUT OF the bar and back to his truck. He got behind the wheel and pulled out his burner phone to call Lindsey. Trying to catch his breath, he heard it ring twice before she picked up. "I got your text," she said. "Garret and I are in front of the apartment and the two detectives just arrived. The good news is Eleanor isn't here. Let's hope it stays that way."

Trick closed his eyes. "Margaret Redstone was with Eleanor during Eleanor's last night at the bar. She bought her drinks and was with her until closing."

"Margaret Redstone?" asked Lindsey after a pause. "Is that your partner's sister who escaped a psychiatric facility?"

The CU definitely did their research. "Yes," said Trick. "The question is why? What does she have to do with all this?" He smacked the steering wheel with his palm. "And how does a woman wanted by the authorities who had her face splashed all over the headlines less than four months ago walk into a bar, let people buy her drinks, and leave with no one recognizing her?"

"Like you said. It's been months. Nobody remembers any of that beyond a week unless her face continues to be splashed on the news."

Trick cursed. "Why would she have been with Eleanor, of all people?"

"Could she be the hybrid?"

Trick couldn't help but laugh. "I know Margaret's father and knew her mother. Trust me. Neither one is or was a craver, although her dad might be mistaken for one."

"Then think," said Lindsey. "You know the Redstone family and you've learned some things about Eleanor. What is Margaret's game? What does she want?"

Trick tried to collect his thoughts. "She wants to hurt Mason and Mikey."

"How does Eleanor help her do that?"

Frustrated, Trick raised his voice. "How the hell should I know?"

"Getting pissed at me isn't going to help." She paused and Trick took a breath to settle himself. "What else did you learn at the bar?" asked Lindsey.

Trick loosened his grip on the phone. "Eleanor got hit on by some pushy guy and Margaret told him to get lost. She invited Eleanor to her table where they drank and talked to men and other patrons. Somebody else joined them until closing and then they all left. Eleanor supposedly went home."

"Who was the other person that joined them?"

"I don't know. Nobody else did either."

"Odds are, that person is our hybrid."

Trick sighed. "Why do you say that?"

"Think about it. Eleanor is an easy target. Margaret helps her out and befriends her. They have some fun and someone else shows up and they hang out and all leave together. My guess is that the hybrid is your third person. They helped get Eleanor drunk and probably walked her home where the hybrid attacked."

"I thought you said they weren't normally hostile."

"Absolutely nothing is normal about this situation. What's really going to get you is when you realize Margaret lured Eleanor as much as the hybrid did, which means Margaret knew this person was a hybrid, too. They were on the hunt that night, and Margaret likely played a role in convincing the hybrid to create a craver."

"But why would she do that?" asked Trick. "Wouldn't that put her at risk?"

"Not at first. A new craver is confused and disoriented. If Margaret befriended Eleanor after she was turned and offered to help, Eleanor would look to her as a friend and might even protect her, for a while at least, until the illness took over. The same would apply to the hybrid."

Trick cursed. "How would Margaret even know about any of this?"

"From what I understand, she traveled in interesting circles. There's no telling who she met or what she learned."

Finding all of this hard to believe, Trick shook his head. "Why would she want to create a craver?"

Lindsey went silent for a moment. "What does your gut tell you?"

Trick's stomach twisted and he knew immediately. "She's going after Mason and Mikey."

"You need to contact them."

"Hold on." Trick set the burner phone down and pulled out his own phone. He dialed Red's number, but his voicemail picked up. The same happened with Mikey's number and he called the SCOPE office line, but the voicemail picked up there, too. Scared, he picked the burner cell back up. "They're not answering."

"You know where they went?"

Trick fought to recall his conversation with Mason and Mikey from earlier. "Uhm, something about meeting Vicki, their dad's new wife. But I don't know where." He bounced his foot. "It's at a house. Maybe they have bad cell reception."

"Who's Vicki? How well do you know her?"

"She married their dad at the hospital. It's a long story. He showed up unexpectedly with a fiancé. He's been estranged from Mikey and Mason for a while. Then before he went home, he got sick, and he's been in the hospital ever since."

"Sick how?"

Trick attempted not to lose his patience. "What the hell does that matter?"

"Does he sleep a lot? Has bouts of pain and weakness? Doctors don't know what it is?"

Trick swallowed. "I suppose."

"How was he when you first saw him after he arrived in town?"

Trick held his head, still confused by the questions. "He was fine. In fact, he was better than fine. He looked great. He'd lost weight, had good color, thick hair. I wondered what—"

"We found her."

"We found who?"

"His wife, Vicki."

"What about her?"

"Listen to me," said Lindsey. "When a hybrid begins to feed on human blood, the host initially benefits from it. They're stronger, healthier, they lose weight and have loads of energy."

Trick's heart thumped.

"But after that initial phase, if the hybrid continues to feed, the host's health declines rapidly with various issues, most of which doctors can't explain. If the hybrid isn't stopped, they'll either create a new craver, or the host will die on his own." She paused again. "Does he have unexplained bruises?"

Trick recalled Martin's bruised forearm. "She said it was from the IV."

"It's not from the IV."

Understanding, Trick sat up and gripped the steering wheel. "Are you telling me Vicki is a hybrid that turned Eleanor and is feeding off of Martin Redstone?"

"She probably turned Eleanor with Margaret Redstone's help. They're working together." She paused. "You need to find Mason and Mikey and you need to find them now."

"Shit." Trick started up the truck and took off into traffic, ignoring the blare of a horn. "I know where they went but the address is at SCOPE."

He couldn't help but think the worse. "You think Eleanor is with Margaret and Vicki?"

"There's no way to know. We'll wait here to be sure the detectives get out safely, but you call me as soon as you get the address, and we'll meet you there."

Trick turned a corner, his tires squealing.

Chapter Twenty-Nine

MASON PULLED MIKEY BEHIND him and felt her grip his shirt. Margaret walked further into the room and stood between them and the door. He considered escaping out the back, but something told him they'd planned for that. "Call nine-one-one, Mikey," he said.

Margaret continued to smile. She was much the same as Mason remembered her. Her long dark hair fell across her shoulders and her blue eyes glittered.

"Yes, Mikey," said Margaret. "Call nine-one-one. Maybe Detective Remalla will run to save you." Her face fell. "Oh, wait. That's right. He's not a detective anymore." She sighed. "Poor man. The travails he's faced. He's been through so much." Her expression hardened. "Too bad he can't save you now. Nobody can."

Mikey dialed and put the phone to her ear but then shook her head. "It's not working."

"Don't worry, though," Margaret continued. "After you're dead and Remalla grieves, I'll be there for him." She paused. "He and I will get reacquainted." She smirked. "I'm looking forward to it. Watching him at the zoo is getting boring. I mean, how often can a man shovel shit before he's had enough?" She made a *tsk tsk* sound and lowered her voice. "He's meant for so much more. I'll have to remind him of that."

Mason pulled out his own phone and realized it was unusable. "You're jamming the cell signal."

"Pretty simple," said Vicki, still looking relaxed. "You can buy a jammer online. Your sister taught me that."

"Vicki," said Mikey, her voice shaky. "You can't trust Margaret. Don't listen to her."

Margaret tipped her head, and Vicki smiled and spoke. "Margaret has been more of a friend to me than you two have. We've known each other for years, ever since the days of Victor D'Mato. I entrusted her with my secrets which she's kept to herself all these years. And when she got out of that stupid facility, she came to see me and your father. Which is more than you two have done."

"She's using you, Vicki," said Mikey. "Can't you see that?"

"Don't bother, Mikey," said Mason. "There's no point." He reached low, pulled up his pant leg, and grabbed his gun. He aimed it at Margaret. "Mikey and I are leaving. Right now."

Mikey sucked in a breath, and Margaret shot a steely gaze at him. "What are you going to do, Mason? Shoot your sister?" She chuckled. "Go for it. I imagine once you do though, you'll be back in one of those drug rehab centers in no time. The guilt and shock will weigh on you forever and you'll never be the same. You'll likely graduate from the pills to the hard stuff and one day, they'll find your body in some alley, dead from an overdose." She glared. "That may be even more satisfying than what's about to happen today." She took a step toward him. "So go ahead. Shoot me."

Mason held the gun but couldn't pull the trigger.

"I should warn you, though," said Margaret. "You might want to save the bullets. I think you're going to need them."

Vicki snickered.

Mikey pulled on his arm. "Let's just walk out, Mason."

"The door locked when I closed it." Vicki held up a key. "The lock isn't great, as you say, but it will do for our purposes."

Still holding the gun, Mason kept talking. "Why are we really here?" Vicki and Margaret, while dangerous, certainly weren't enough to overtake him and Mikey.

"You're about to find out," said Vicki.

"What about Dad?" Mikey spoke to Vicki. "Did you ever really love him?"

Vicki shrugged. "Your father is a good man. Margaret did introduce us, but he also served a far greater need. One I urgently required. Your sister understands that. She understands my true self and potential. She helps me see my strength, where before I felt weak and small. But not anymore."

"Vicki is a powerful woman," said Margaret. "It didn't take me long to realize how we could work together to serve each other."

"Vicki," said Mikey. "Don't do this. You know she'll kill you when she's done with you."

"Shut up, Mikey," said Margaret. "Your voice is getting on my nerves." She shook her head and scowled. "I had hopes for you once. But you were my one rare mistake."

"Marge, listen to yourself," Mikey stammered. "You're free. You could be anywhere in the world right now. Why don't you just go and forget us? You've never loved anyone, anyway, so why do you care?"

Margaret straightened and Mason's mind whirled with how to get out unharmed. If he could get past her, he could use his bulk to break the lock on the door. His only worry was Mikey. He had to get her out of the house safely.

"The only people incapable of love are you two," said Margaret. "Max isn't much better."

"Mom loved you," said Mikey. "She wouldn't want you to do this."

Margaret set her jaw. "And you both killed her."

"Victor killed her," said Mason. "You know that. You made that box, didn't you? The one Victor sent Mom to make her sick. Just like you cursed that statue that almost killed Detective Daniels. And something tells me the reason for Dad's decline is not just Vicki. You made him a target." He focused his aim. "So don't stand there and act all innocent when the reason for our grief and pain is you, not us. You're not a saint or hero, Margaret, and you never were, despite whatever illusions you're under."

"And Rem doesn't want you and he never will," added Mikey.

Margaret stared at them, but Mason could sense her seething fury eager to erupt. He braced himself, prepared to fight both women to protect Mikey. If he could get her out of the house, he'd sacrifice himself to keep her alive.

A bump upstairs broke the moment and Vicki's sense of assurance vanished. "She's awake."

Margaret continued to glare.

"We should go," said Vicki. She walked toward the door but kept her eyes on the stairs.

Mikey heard the sound of footsteps and a door creaked open from above.

"Margaret," said Vicki, holding the key.

Margaret's glare softened and she relaxed. "I'm feeling oh so satisfied with my decision now." She took a step back and eyed the stairs.

Mason heard a stair squeak.

"Who's here?" asked Mikey.

"You're about to find out," said Margaret. She moved closer to the door where Vicki waited. Vicki unlocked the door and Margaret sneered at them. "I'll give you a word of advice only because I relish the thought of you simmering in fear."

The stairs squeaked again, and Mason saw bare feet walking down them. His heart thumped and his skin raised in chill bumps. They were in trouble but from what, he didn't know.

"Who is that?" asked Mikey. She moved closer to Mason, who still held the gun.

Margaret stood beside Vicki, who opened the door. Her face pale, Vicki didn't take her eyes off the stairs. "You can try and shoot," said Margaret, "but make sure you hit the target. If you don't, it will only slow her down but not by much.

Mason, starting to sweat, watched the feet descend and turn at the landing.

"Don't try to run outside, because you won't make it. I'd head for the basement," said Margaret, her eyes sparkling. "It will hold her off, but not for long."

The feet descended and legs came into view, then a short skirt.

Margaret looked over. "Hello, Eleanor."

Vicki paled even more.

Hearing the name, Mason held his breath. "Eleanor?"

"She attacked Kyle," said Mikey.

Margaret didn't bother to look at them. She simply smiled. "As I promised, dinner is served."

Terror ran up Mason's spine, and he stepped away and aimed the gun toward the stairs. The legs became a torso, and a woman came into view. Her short blue skirt fluttered above her knees but that was the only thing normal about her. Her t-shirt was rumpled and dirty, her hair was unkempt and hung in her face and when she reached the bottom of the stairs and turned, Mason saw her eyes were the worst. They were wild and empty. He pushed Mikey back and aimed his gun at Eleanor.

Vicki stepped outside. "Let's go."

Margaret hesitated at the door and Mason sensed she was appreciating the moment. "I'd wish you well," she said, "but that would be cruel." She stepped outside with her hand on the knob. "And don't worry about Dad. I'll keep an eye on him. Max, too." She glanced at Mikey. "And I'll check in on Rem. I can't wait to visit him, too." She smiled again, chuckled, and closed the door.

Eleanor stood in the room, not moving and blocking their exit. Mason sensed the pent-up energy in her and knew he and Mikey would die if they didn't do something. "Move," he whispered to Mikey. "Toward the basement."

He heard Mikey's uneven breathing, but she took a sidestep. "You come with me," she whispered back.

"I will, but you need to go. I'll hold her off."

"No," said Mikey. "You can't."

He raised his voice. "Go, Mikey. Now."

His command made Eleanor straighten, and her focus narrowed. "I'm so tired," she said. Her voice was scratchy and low.

Mikey took a step and Eleanor turned her head toward her.

"Look at me, Eleanor," said Mason, praying to distract her. While this woman was small in stature and of average weight, Mason knew what she'd done to Kyle. She oozed a raw animalistic nature and he assumed she had to be on drugs. "You don't want her. You want me."

"No, Mason," said Mikey.

"Keep going," said Mason.

Eleanor's gaze settled on Mason, and she took a step. "I'm hungry."

Mason held his gun on her and aimed it at her chest. A strong odor began to fill the room. "Just stay calm," he said. "No one wants to hurt you." He took a step toward the basement. "If you're hungry we can get you some food." In his peripheral vision, he saw Mikey reach the basement entry.

Eleanor didn't seem to comprehend his words. She looked him over with a curious look. "You're handsome." Her eyes darkened and Mason shuddered. The odor became a stench and Mason grimaced.

Mikey stood at the door. "Mason—"

Before he could respond, Eleanor opened her mouth, shrieked and bolted toward him. He fired but she was so fast, he only hit her in the shoulder. She slowed briefly and he fired again, hitting her in the leg. Eleanor stumbled, Mikey screamed, and racing for the basement door, Mason fired again but his hands shook, and the bullet only grazed Eleanor's arm. Mikey scrambled down the stairs and Mason reached them and turned to grab the handle. Eleanor was back up and running at him and he barely had enough time to fire another round. She buckled, and he slammed the door shut before she could reach it. Breathing fast and shaking, he fumbled for the lock.

"Oh, my God." Mikey was behind him. "Are you hurt?" He heard her patting the wall. "Where's the light?"

A light came on, and Mason managed to flip the bolt. He backed up and almost pushed Mikey down the stairs into a dank and dark room. There was minimal light and no window. All he saw was a washer and dryer and a shelf with some detergent.

Mikey grabbed onto him, and he put his arm around her. Breathing hard, they both shook and stayed quiet, listening for any sounds from above.

After a few seconds, Mikey spoke. "Did you hit her? Is she dead?" Her voice trembled.

Mason's heart pounded against his chest, and he tried to make sense of what he'd seen. Eleanor had taken three bullets and had kept coming. "I hit her." His only hope was that his third bullet had been fatal. "Try your phone."

Her fingers shaking, Mikey pulled out her cell and tried to use it. "Still doesn't work." She put it away and held onto him again. "I'm scared."

"Me, too." He looked around the room, hoping to find something they could use, but the room had little in it.

"Nobody knows we're here," said Mikey.

Mason had come to the same conclusion. "Trick knows we went to see Vicki. You wrote the address down. He'll find us."

"But when?"

Mason had hoped she wouldn't ask that. "Soon." He hated the lie but had to say something. "We'll wait here until he comes. She can't get in."

Mikey squeezed him harder, and he pulled her back to the wall where they huddled together. "You sure about that?" asked Mikey.

Before he could answer, Mason heard a loud bang. Mikey jumped and so did he. The bang came again, even louder than the first. The basement door creaked but held.

"She's trying to break the door in," said Mikey.

Mason checked his gun, noting his remaining bullets. If Eleanor gained entry, their only hope would be a kill shot but if he missed, they'd die. He'd have to put himself between Eleanor and Mikey so Mikey could get out.

"She's going to kill us, isn't she?" asked Mikey.

The bang came again, and Mason cursed.

· · · • · • · • · · ·

Trick raced up the stairs, taking two at a time, and ran to the door of SCOPE. He unlocked it and sprinted inside to Mikey's desk. Her scribbled address was still on the notepad. He ripped it off and ran back out, grabbing his phone and calling Lindsey on his way back to his truck. He put the phone on speaker, started his truck, and plugged the address into his truck's navigation system.

She answered.

"I've got the address," he said, breathless. He read it to her.

"Got it," she said. "The detectives left Eleanor's safely. We're on our way."

Trick gunned the engine and tore out of the parking lot.

Lindsey hardened her tone. "Do not, under any circumstances, go in without me and Garret, you understand?"

Trick blew through a stop sign.

"Trick? You hear me? You can't do this alone. You'll all wind up dead."

Trick raced down the street, dodging cars and praying he'd get to Mason and Mikey in time.

"Trick. Promise me. Remember the rules. You have to do as I say."

"I'll see you soon." Trick checked the route again and hung up the phone.

Chapter Thirty

THE BANGING CONTINUED FOR several minutes, and Mason searched the basement, looking for a way out or anything to use as a weapon. He found a screwdriver and handed it to Mikey, who jumped again when another bang shook the walls.

"What am I supposed to do with this?" asked Mikey.

"If she gets in, use it however you need to," said Mason. "Go for her throat if you can."

"Are you serious?"

Another bang sounded from above. "Mikey, I don't know what drugs this woman is on, but she literally feels no pain. You need to do as much damage as you can."

"What about you?"

"I have my gun, but I don't know if that will stop her. If she breaks through the door..."

Mikey stared. "What are you saying?"

Mason sighed. "If she gets down here, I'll distract her. I want you to run up the stairs and get out of the house."

"I can't leave you here with her. She'll kill you."

Mason took her shoulders. "You'll do exactly as I say. I want you to run and don't worry about me."

Mikey shook her head. "I can't. I'll stay and fight her."

Mason squeezed her arms. "No. You won't. I'll do what I can to keep her off of me while you go get help."

"Mason, you saw the state she's in. You won't be able to stop her. We know what she did to Jackson and Kyle. She'll do the same to you."

The door shook with another bang and Mason pulled Mikey to the side of the stairs. "Listen to me. It's my job to protect you. I need you to do as I say. Promise me you'll leave me behind and get out of the house. Your survival is crucial. If you get to the street, your phone should work. Call for help."

Mikey gripped his wrists. "I will never forgive myself is something happens to you. Don't ask me to do this."

"I can and I will. Your safety is paramount."

"So is yours."

Mason cursed and jumped when another bang blasted the room. "Please, Mikey."

Mikey hugged him and he held her. "Maybe she won't get in," she said and jumped when there was another bang.

Mason heard the sound of splintering and pulled away. He peered up the stairs and his stomach turned when he saw the wood begin to buckle. Eleanor banged again and the wood splintered more. He wondered what she could be hitting the door with that would hold up to so much force. There was another slam and Mason realized their time was short. They had to prepare.

He pushed Mikey against the wall beside the stairs to keep her in darkness and out of Eleanor's sight for as long as possible. "When you see your opportunity, run."

Mikey started to argue again, but he ignored her, pulled his weapon and went to the base of the stairs. He swallowed and braced himself. Another loud bang sounded, the wood gave way, and a long wooden implement broke through the door. It looked like a heavy table leg and Mason wondered if Margaret had ensured Eleanor would have a tool to use if Mason and Mikey successfully made it to the basement.

The wood was yanked back out and then slammed back into the door. More wood splintered and broke and Mason saw a hand reach in and unlock the door. It was done with such ease that he guessed Eleanor knew exactly where the lock was located and how to unlatch it. The door swung open, and telling himself to stay strong, Mason raised his gun. Eleanor stood at the top of the stairs. Sweat shone on her skin and her hair hung in her eyes. Breathing hard, she stared with fury and with a wild screech, she raced down the stairs at Mason.

Mason fired and he heard Mikey scream. Eleanor was so fast though, that he barely had time to move and fire again before she was on top of him. The gun was knocked from his hand, and he fell backward onto the ground. He grabbed her hands to hold her off and tried to push her away, but she was too strong. Eleanor used her teeth to go for his neck and he squirmed to keep her from reaching him. She writhed and used her legs to pull up and away. Mason lost his grip on her, but she was off of him, and he scrambled away. He prayed Mikey had escaped but didn't have time to check before Eleanor slashed out at him with her ragged and sharp nails, slicing him across his chest. He gasped from the pain, and she came at him again. He raised his hands in defense, preparing for the attack when she shrieked and pulled back.

Stunned, Mason watched in horror as Eleanor faltered and almost fell. Mikey stood behind her, her face white with shock and Mason saw the screwdriver in Eleanor's back, between her shoulder blades. Eleanor tried to reach it, but instead of weakening she only got angrier.

Giving up on removing the screwdriver, she snarled. Mikey stood at the foot of the stairs, unmoving. "Get away from him," she screamed.

Terrified, Mason screamed back. "Mikey. Run."

Eleanor rose up to her full height and turned toward Mikey.

"No," Mason fought to get to his feet. "Me. Take me."

But Eleanor ignored him.

• • • • • • • • •

Seeing Mikey's car, Trick drove up to the house and squealed to a stop. Before the truck had even stopped moving, he jumped out and raced up to the front door. He swung it open but saw no one. "Mikey. Mason," he yelled. Desperate to find them, but smelling the familiar odor of death, he almost ran up the stairs when he heard a scream and then Mason's voice. Seeing a broken splintered door near the kitchen, his heart slammed against his ribs, and he ran toward it. A stairwell led down into a basement, and he saw Eleanor at the bottom of the stairs and Mikey standing near her, backed up against the banister. Eleanor ran at her and Mikey ducked just as Eleanor reached her.

Trick raced down a few steps. "Eleanor. Stop."

Mikey fell backward, holding her arm and Eleanor froze and lifted her head. She seemed to sniff the air and turned toward Trick.

Trick's heart surprised him when it sped up even faster. "Remember me?" he asked.

Eleanor's eyes glittered and sneering, she took a step toward him.

"Trick," said Mason from somewhere in the basement. "Don't."

Trick backed up. "This bitch doesn't scare me," he said, lying. He took another step and so did Eleanor. "Come and get me." He turned and fled the basement, hearing Eleanor's thunderous footsteps behind him. Running as fast as he could, he flew through the living room and was almost outside when he felt her land on his back. The force of her weight slammed him to the ground, his head hit the wooden floor hard, and he saw stars and a stinging sensation ripped across his back. He shoved up and twisted to fling her off, but she was too strong. Expecting the fatal blow at any moment, he hoped he'd bought some time for Mason and Mikey to get away. She yanked on his arm, and he was flipped to his back like he was a pancake. She hissed at him, her teeth bared, and drew back a hand. He flinched, raised his hands, and waited for the sharp pain of his skin being slashed open. But as fast as the attack itself had occurred, the weight of her against him was suddenly gone. His head spinning from her assault, he heard a wail and a horrendous scream, and he turned to see Garret on top of Eleanor. A knife was in her stomach, but she still fought hard against him. Garret held her down as Lindsey raised a wicked knife and brought it down fast toward Eleanor's throat. Trick shut his eyes before he could see the result, but he heard a wet sound and a guttural gasp. The sound came once more, and then it all went quiet.

Chapter Thirty-One

MIKEY SAT IN THE waiting area of the emergency room. Her throbbing shoulder was bandaged, and she held a water bottle but didn't drink from it. Still in shock from Eleanor's attack, she took deep breaths to calm herself.

Mason and Trick were still in the ER. They both required more stitches than Mikey did, and Trick had a bump on his head. She'd called Max, who was an hour away at a business meeting. She'd assured him they were okay, and he said he'd leave and head to the hospital. Valerie had arrived earlier and was with Mason, and Daniels and Manetti had also come to the ER to question them about the assault. Mikey hadn't spoken to anyone yet, but after she'd been treated for her injured shoulder, she'd told Mason and Trick she'd stay in the waiting room until they could all go home together.

While staring at her water bottle, Eleanor's eyes flashed in Mikey's mind, and she shuttered.

"Mikey?"

Mikey looked up to see Rem enter the waiting area. He ran over and sat beside her. "Daniels called me, and I came as fast as I could." His eyes wide, he looked her over and saw the bandage and the blood on her shirt. "What the hell happened? Are you okay?"

Mikey shivered and he put his arm around her. She snuggled into his side and took a long breath. "I've been better." Her voice still trembled.

"Where's Mason and Trick?"

"Being treated, but the doctors say they can go home. I'm just waiting. Daniels and Manetti are talking to them, I think." Margaret's face flashed in her brain and Mikey closed her eyes.

"Just take it easy. You need anything?"

She swallowed and opened her eyes. "I'm just glad you're here."

Avoiding her injured shoulder, he rubbed her arm. "Me, too."

The ER door opened, and Daniels emerged. He saw them and headed over.

"Hey," said Rem. "What the hell is going on?"

Daniels sat across from Mikey. "You okay?" he asked her.

"I'll live," said Mikey. "How are Mason and Trick?"

"They'll live, too, but they're pretty shaken up. Like you." Daniels eyed Rem. "Good to see you. Mikey needs some company and I need to question her."

"I'm glad you called," said Rem. He took Mikey's hand and spoke to her. "Are you up to talking?"

Mikey nodded and straightened. "I'll do my best although I'm not sure how much help I can be. Everything happened so fast."

"Where's Manetti?" asked Rem.

"Talking to Trick," said Daniels. He looked at Mikey. "And if your account is as crazy as his and Mason's, this is one hell of a mess."

"Where're Bevins and Winkler?" asked Rem. "Aren't they assigned to this?"

"At the crime scene," said Daniels. "Lozano asked me and Manetti to assist." He paused. "Apparently, it's as big of a mess there as it is here."

Shivering, Mikey bit her lip, recalling leaving the basement and seeing Eleanor's body. Rem squeezed her hand.

"Can you start from the beginning?" asked Daniels. "Why were you and Mason at that house?"

Mikey took a deep breath and dove in. She told Daniels about Vicki and her dad and how Vicki had contacted them and asked to meet with her and

Mason. She went over Vicki's story about the home and her plans to use it while their dad recuperated.

Getting to the part where Vicki's demeanor had changed and Margaret had appeared, she steeled herself. When she mentioned Margaret, she felt Rem tense against her.

"Margaret was there?" he asked.

Mikey nodded. "Yes."

"What happened then?" asked Daniels, frowning.

Recalling the rest, she gripped Rem's fingers. She told Daniels what Margaret had said, how she and Vicki had worked together and then about Eleanor.

"How far had Trick gotten in his search for Eleanor?" asked Daniels.

"Well, we told you he was investigating Jackson Trammel's death. They started looking for Eleanor and that's when Kyle was attacked, we think by Eleanor. But she disappeared and Trick kept looking. He got a lead when he found the bar where she worked."

Daniels pulled out a notepad and pencil and took some notes. "So, Trick was after Eleanor, who allegedly attacked Kyle and possibly Jackson, and you and Mason went to meet Vicki but found Margaret and Eleanor instead."

"This sounds complicated," said Rem. "What do Margaret and Vicki have to do with Eleanor?

"That's a great question," said Daniels. He spoke to Mikey. "What happened when Eleanor appeared?"

Mikey trembled at the memory. "It was awful. Something was wrong with her. Margaret and Vicki knew it and purposely left us with her. Eleanor's eyes...they were...wrong. She was wrong. It was like she was a blank slate and the only thing she wanted to do was kill." She held her head with her free hand. "Mason, he told me to head for the basement stairs and I did, and then Eleanor attacked him, and he fired. I think he hit her. It slowed her down long enough for us to get to the basement and shut and lock the door, but she kept coming." Mikey had to take a second to catch her breath.

"Take it slow," said Rem. "Have a sip of water." Mikey had set a bottle of water beside the chair, and he reached for it and handed it to her. Her fingers still trembling, Mikey took a drink.

Rem spoke to Daniels. "Are Mason and Trick as spooked as she is?"

"If not more," said Daniels. "They're as pale as their bed sheets." He scribbled something in his notes. "You okay to keep going?" he asked Mikey.

Mikey took another sip and nodded. "I'm okay." Rem took the water and set it on a side table.

"What happened after you got to the basement?" asked Daniels.

Mikey wished she didn't have to remember. "She started banging something against the door to get in. It was terrifying. It went on for what felt like forever. Mason found a screwdriver and gave it to me to use as a weapon and tried to convince me to run if she got in." Mikey paused to compose herself. "I couldn't do that though. I couldn't leave Mason behind."

Rem rubbed her arm. "You're doing great."

Mikey kept talking. "She kept banging on the damn door and it started to give way, and she got into the basement. She ran at Mason, and he fired but I think he missed, and she tackled him." Mikey stopped at the memory. Nothing had been more frightening then seeing her brother go down with Eleanor on top of him. "I stabbed her in the back with the screwdriver, but that only made her mad." She paused, recalling Eleanor's ugly gaze on her. "I thought that was it." She swallowed. "She came at me and that's when she caught my shoulder. She would have done worse, but Trick showed. He diverted her and she chased him out of the basement." Her stomach turned and she held it. "Mason was hurt, and I thought he might die. I just ran to him and held him. He was just as worried about me. But we had to get to Trick. I helped Mason up, but he was bleeding a lot." She shook her head. "I didn't know what to do. I wanted to help Mason and Trick, but

I was terrified Eleanor was still in the house. And I was afraid of what I'd find once we got up the stairs." She stammered. "I...I...was sure Trick was going to be dead." Her breath caught and she put her hand over her eyes.

Rem pulled her closer. "Take some deep breaths."

Mikey swiped at her eyes and tried to pull it together, but the memory was intense. "That's when Trick returned." She blew out a heavy breath. "It was such a relief that he was alive. He came down to make sure we were okay, but he was injured too. His jacket was slashed, and his back was bleeding. We all needed medical attention." Getting past the worst of the story, Mikey sniffed. "Trick told us Eleanor was dead, and we had to leave. We went up the stairs and I saw her." Mikey paused. "Her...her throat was slashed. There...there was blood everywhere. I barely had time to process any of it before Trick got us out. Everything is sort of a blur after that. The police arrived and then we were at the hospital."

Rem leaned, reached for a tissue on an end table across from him, and handed it to Mikey. Mikey took it and dabbed her eyes.

Daniels lowered his notepad. "Did Trick say anything about what happened to Eleanor?"

Mikey tried to think. She'd been in such shock at the time and so relieved that they'd all survived, she hadn't even cared how Eleanor had died. She'd just been happy that she was no longer a threat. "I...I don't know. I didn't even ask."

"Do you think Trick killed her?" asked Daniels.

Mikey couldn't even consider that. "No. Did you see his back? She almost killed him."

"Then who did it?" asked Daniels.

"What's Ibrahim's initial cause of death?" asked Rem.

"I talked to Winkler a few minutes ago." Daniels sighed. "Like Mikey said. Eleanor's throat was cut, plus she had three bullet wounds. One in the shoulder, one in the thigh and one in the calf, which matches Mason's account that he shot her, plus the screwdriver between her shoulder blades.

But she also appears to have a knife wound in her abdomen." He sat back. "Problem is, there's no knife."

"So someone stabbed her in the stomach, slashed her throat, and took off with the weapon?" asked Rem. "What does Trick say?"

Daniels rubbed his eyes and blinked. "Manetti's going over his story again, but from what I've gathered, Eleanor attacked him from behind, Trick went down and hit his head. Said he blacked out. When he came to, Eleanor was dead. He got up, found Mason and Mikey, and they got the hell out of the house."

Rem narrowed his eyes. "He didn't see anything? He doesn't know what happened to her?"

Daniels shook his head. "Nope."

"Does he have a concussion?" asked Rem.

"Doc says it's a bump on the head but stopped short of saying it was a concussion."

Mikey caught the look between them. "You think he's not telling you everything?"

Daniels rubbed his face. "You don't normally blackout without having a concussion."

"But why would Trick lie?" asked Mikey, sitting up. "He saved our lives. If he hadn't shown when he did, Mason and I would be dead."

"Nobody's saying he's lying," said Daniels.

"But he may not be telling the whole truth," added Rem. He knitted his brow. "How did Trick know Mikey and Mason were in trouble?"

Mikey perked up at the question, curious to know the answer.

"I asked him that," said Daniels. "He said he went back to the bar where Eleanor worked to find the friends she'd hung out with that last night before she disappeared. He talked to a waitress named Katie who served Eleanor and her friends. Katie identified one of the friends as Margaret."

Rem stared in surprise. "Eleanor was hanging out with Margaret?"

"Apparently, Margaret may have targeted Eleanor," said Daniels. "Eleanor left with Margaret and another woman. Katie's description of the other woman matched the description of Vicki."

"Wait a minute," said Rem. "Why would Trick assume it was Vicki?"

"He didn't at first, but then he recalled how Martin and Vicki had been in touch with Margaret when they'd arrived in California. He wondered if Vicki had more involvement with Margaret than she'd admitted to. He called the hospital and talked to a nurse who told him Vicki had left. Then he tried Mason and Mikey, but they didn't answer. He began to worry that Vicki's meeting had more to do with Margaret than Martin, so he drove back to SCOPE, found the address and headed to the house. He went in and heard screaming from the basement, which is when he found Eleanor attacking you two." Daniels gestured toward Mikey.

Mikey's skin prickled and she had a distinct memory of Trick standing on the basement steps. He'd called out Eleanor's name and had asked *Remember me?* Had he been referring to Kyle's attack, or something else? She recalled Trick showing up late that morning at SCOPE. He'd been distracted and not himself, and Mason had said he'd had an injured wrist. Did that have something to do with Eleanor?

"That sounds a bit sketchy," said Rem. "But not impossible."

"I thought so, too," said Daniels. "Especially when you combine that with a good Samaritan who shows up at the perfect time to kill a woman who's about to kill you."

"Did anyone see this good Samaritan come or go?" asked Rem.

"Winkler said they're canvasing but so far, no. I get the impression the neighborhood isn't too forthcoming when it comes to the police." Daniels crossed his arms. "What's Trick hiding, Mikey? Has he done anything recently that seemed odd, especially when it comes to finding Eleanor?"

Mikey kept her face flat and shook her head. "Not that I know of, but this is Trick we're talking about. Nothing he does is normal."

Daniels studied her and Mikey eyed the floor. She wished Mason were there and wondered what he'd told Daniels about Trick's behavior.

"Obviously, something tipped him off about Vicki," said Rem. "I'm more curious about Eleanor, though. Who the hell killed her if it wasn't Trick?"

"If it was Trick," said Daniels, "then, considering Eleanor's wounds, you'd think he'd have Eleanor's blood on him. His back is bloody but nothing else. We'll check it, but I think he's telling the truth about that much. Plus, even if he did kill her, why hide the knife, especially since it was obviously self-defense." He closed his notepad and put it back in his pocket. "Whoever did it knew what they were doing, though. They took her down as if they knew she was dangerous."

"That's another thing," said Rem. "Why was she so dangerous? Was she on something?"

"Had to be a hallucinogen. We'll see what the tox screen says." Daniels put the pencil away, too.

"Did Trick say anything about Eleanor using drugs?" asked Rem.

"No," said Mikey. "Doesn't mean she wasn't on them, though. It's the only explanation." Another possibility occurred to her. "Unless Margaret dosed her with something." Mikey widened her eyes. "What if that was Margaret's plan? Find and use the last person anyone would ever suspect to try and kill me and Mason."

"It seems like a hard way to go about it," said Daniels. "Also risky."

"That would be Margaret," said Mikey. "Nothing is ever simple with her." Finally catching her breath and starting to think clearly, she thought of Vicki. "Oh, hell. What about Vicki? Has anyone found her?" She straightened. "And Dad. Is he okay? Is anyone watching him?"

Daniels nodded. "Don't worry. After I talked to Mason, I requested an officer to watch your dad's room. I've also requested another patrol on your house, and yours." He pointed at Rem. "Now that we know she's been watching you."

Rem blanched. "And I thought it was my imagination."

"We've got an APB out on Vicki," said Daniels, "but so far, there's been no sightings of her."

Exhausted, Mikey leaned back in her seat. "She and Margaret will go to ground and stay out of sight. And the patrol cars won't matter. Margaret will just wait them out like she did before." She rubbed her tired eyes. "I need to check on Dad. Somebody needs to tell him about Vicki." She hated the thought of telling her father Vicki had duped him, especially when he was sick.

"Mason should be out soon, if you want to wait," said Daniels. "You two can tell him together. And Manetti and I will need to talk to your father, too, but we'll wait for you and Mason to give him the news."

"I'd appreciate that." Mikey hung her head. "I hope he's strong enough to hear it."

"He's a Redstone," said Rem. "Something tells me he is."

Daniels stretched his neck and stood. "I'll go find Manetti. Maybe he's pulled something out of Trick that's helpful." He hesitated before leaving and eyed Mikey. "And if you learn anything we should know, call me."

Mikey bobbed her head up and down. "I will."

Daniels eyed her as if gauging her honesty. "I'll go check on Mason. He's worried about you, too."

"Thanks," said Mikey, wringing her hands.

Daniels walked away and Rem grabbed her water and handed it back to her. "Take another drink. I think you need it."

Mikey took it and had a sip.

"You think Trick's telling Daniels and Manetti everything he knows?" asked Rem, his brow raised.

Mikey took another sip and didn't answer.

Rem rested his arm on the back of Mikey's chair and stared off. "Neither do I."

Chapter Thirty-Two

After talking to Max on the phone, Mason leaned back on the sofa at SCOPE, twirling a pen through his fingers and thinking over the past three days. They had been long and strenuous ones. After being cleared to leave the hospital, he and Mikey had stopped in their dad's room to tell him about Vicki. It had been a difficult conversation and their dad had been belligerent, refusing to believe them. They'd had to bring in Daniels and Manetti to explain the situation and confirm what had occurred with Vicki and Margaret.

Although tired and struggling to stay awake, their dad had stopped arguing and there had been a moment where Mason had seen the truth seep in. For a rare second, his father had looked lost and vulnerable, and for the first time, Mason had felt empathy for him. After he'd drifted to sleep, Mikey and Mason had left, and Valerie had driven them home since Mikey's car was still at Vicki's.

Remalla had stayed long enough to ensure they were okay but had promised to check in, which he had done each day since. Now that Margaret was back on the radar, it seemed important to stay in touch, and Mason could see how the renewed conversation between Rem and Mikey was helping Mikey. She needed someone to talk to besides him and Mason was glad it could be Rem.

Trick had gone home to recuperate but had said little about the attack. He hadn't yet returned to SCOPE and when Mason made any attempt to talk to him about that day in the house, Trick changed the subject or refused to discuss it. Bevins and Winkler had questioned him more than once about the attack, but he'd stuck to his story about an unknown stranger killing Eleanor. The knife had still not been found and there was no clear evidence that Trick had been the one to attack her. Trick had at least been able to tell Mrs. Trammel that Eleanor had been the one to murder her son. The only explanation he could give her was that Eleanor had likely been on drugs or had suffered a psychotic episode.

Mason realized his friend wasn't telling everything he knew. He had to have witnessed the assault and maybe was too traumatized to recall it. Mason hoped, with time, that his friend would come clean. The attack was still fresh though, and they were all shaken and recuperating, so Mason had chosen not to push it. For now.

Their father remained in the hospital and although he'd gained some strength and seemed to be improving, he still had a long way to go. After talking to his doctors, Mason, Mikey and Max realized his recovery would take time and it had become obvious he'd need full-time care. It's what Mason had been talking to Max about on their phone call – what to do with their dad. Dad wanted to return to Texas and Max had been checking into facilities that could take him, but they weren't cheap. Dad had some money, but not much. Max said he could handle it, but his business was still bouncing back after the false murder accusations against him earlier in the year. He could afford a decent place but nothing opulent. Mason wanted to contribute too, since he didn't want the financial responsibility to fall solely on Max. Mikey had also asked to help. Between the three of them, they hoped they could provide their father with something affordable they could all agree on. Their dad would be the one to convince though. He remained stuck on returning to his home and taking care of himself, which was the one thing he couldn't do.

Mikey had tried speaking to him and she'd made some headway. Mason had to agree that the difficult situation had mellowed Dad a little. Realizing he had nowhere else to go and that his children were the only people he could turn to, his dad had eased up on the insults and had even told Mikey thank you before she'd left him the other day. It wasn't huge, but it was progress, and that's all that Mason could ask for.

Max had found a potential place for Dad to live and was on his way to the hospital to talk to Dad about it. Mason had spoken to Max on his drive over, wished him luck and told him to keep him updated.

Adjusting his position on the couch, he grimaced when his stitches pulled. Eleanor had slashed him across the midsection, but he'd gotten lucky. Any deeper and he would have ended up in surgery, but all he'd needed were several stitches and plenty of rest. Unfortunately, pain pills were not an option, but he'd gritted it out. Trick had sustained a similar injury to his back, but he'd said he was doing fine and planned to be back in the office soon.

The door opened and Mikey walked in, carrying the mail. Her shoulder was still bandaged but Mason had been more concerned about her mental state. They'd all been rattled by Eleanor's attack and Margaret's role in it. A police cruiser was back on patrol and while that offered some comfort, Mason knew it didn't matter much. Mikey had told Mason she'd been feeling better and to stop worrying, but it had taken a visit to Tarina to help Mason gather himself. The attack had been a close call for all of them and he'd struggled to sleep. His talk with Tarina had helped, and he'd made another appointment for the following day. The last thing he needed was to turn to pills to cope.

"You shouldn't go to the mailbox by yourself," he said.

Mikey rolled her eyes. "I am perfectly capable of going downstairs to get the mail. Margaret is not lying in wait for me in the lobby of the building."

"Did you expect her to come after you with a drugged, rage-filled woman who, a week earlier, would have been too shy to introduce herself?"

Mikey sighed. "You have a point. But they didn't find drugs in her system."

"Then they missed something. Or Margaret gave her a drug they don't test for." Daniels had been in touch the day before, telling them that Eleanor's toxicology screen had come back negative. The most she'd been suffering from was a fever and a viral infection. The only other explanation for her aggression had to be mental illness, but from everything they'd learned about her, that had not been indicated. As of now, they had no explanation for her attack and no leads on who could have killed her after Trick had been knocked out. He'd stopped short of saying Trick was lying, which Mason appreciated, but he'd sensed the underlying suspicion because he felt it himself.

"You okay?" asked Mikey, flipping through the mail. "You look tired."

"I am tired."

"Sleeping any better?"

"A little."

"I had a nightmare last night of Eleanor chasing us through the basement. I woke up sweaty and out of breath." She shook off the memory and pulled out an envelope. "This is for you." She frowned. "There's no return address or stamp."

Mikey walked over and handed the letter to Mason, who took it. She put the rest of the mail on the coffee table and sat beside him. "I'd feel better if they could find Vicki," she said. "You think she went back to Texas?"

"The authorities have been notified. If she shows, they'll find her." Mason studied the envelope, wondering who'd dropped it into the slot.

"Can I ask you something?" asked Mikey.

Mason lowered the letter. "Sure. What is it?"

Mikey hesitated. "Why do you think I didn't pick up on Vicki's lies? It's been bugging me. I should have seen right through her."

Mason debated how to answer since he'd wondered the same about himself. He considered how Tarina would respond. "I wouldn't be too hard on yourself. We can't sense everything, Mikey, no matter how much we want to. I've told you before. We aren't superheroes."

"But you did sense it. Remember how you felt sick when we met Vicki for dinner? I think you were picking up on her deceit."

Mason recalled feeling ill during their meeting with Vicki the day Dad went to the hospital. "Maybe. Or maybe I was picking up on Dad's health issues. Either way, it doesn't matter. I ignored it." He remembered the funny feeling he'd had when he and Mikey had been about to enter Vicki's house. "Besides, we were dealing with Dad. That's enough to throw anyone off their game."

Mikey scratched at a spot on her jeans. "I guess. It just pisses me off that I didn't see through her."

"And what would you have done? Told Dad? He wouldn't have believed you. And Vicki was very good at playing sweet and innocent. Margaret taught her well." He patted Mikey on her knee. "Go easy on yourself. We may have missed the signs, but we were doing our best with what we knew at the time."

Mikey glanced at him. "You were doing your best? Because you were a giant pain in the you-know-what."

Mason shrugged. "I may have not seen Vicki's true colors, but Dad's never changed. That was never in question."

Mikey smiled softly. "You've done better the last few days, though. You didn't gripe once when we saw Dad yesterday. I'm proud of you."

"Yeah, well," Mason eyed the letter again. "Even I can feel bad for a man whose health is declining and whose wife lied to and left him, and who tried to kill his kids." He ticked up an eyebrow at Mikey. "I'm not a total monster."

"No, you're not," said Mikey. "You're more of a hamster, you just like to act like a monster sometimes."

Mason chuckled. "It doesn't scare off the people who love me."

Mikey narrowed her gaze at him. "Not yet, anyway." She fluffed the cushion behind her. "Oh, and by the way, I brought the razor from home. I figure you can shave your mustache sometime today."

Mason gaped at her. "Excuse me?"

"The bet, remember? You said if Dad and Vicki got married, you'd shave your mustache."

He sucked in a breath and almost choked. "The hell that's happening."

Mikey's eyes widened. "You're going back on your word?"

"My word?" Mason pointed at her with the letter. "I didn't promise a thing. And if you think I'm going to shave anything after that woman's lies and what she did to us and Dad, you've got—" He caught Mikey's grin.

"I'm just kidding." She shoved his arm. "I couldn't resist."

Mason relaxed but glared. "That's not funny."

"Consider it payback for putting up with you last week."

Mason bit back an unhelpful retort. "Fine. Then we're even."

"You could use a trim though."

Mason eyed her, glad she could joke with him and was no longer beating herself up over Vicki. He started to open the letter when his phone rang. He saw Max's name on the display and could only imagine it was about their dad and his dislike of Max's choice of senior living. "Can you get that?" Mason asked Mikey. "I'm sure it's about Dad." He opened the envelope and pulled out a piece of paper with a handwritten note.

Mikey picked up Mason's phone and answered. "Hey, Max. It's Mikey."

She listened while Mason read the note. His heart began to race, and he sat up.

"What?" asked Mikey. "What do you mean Dad's not there?" Her face fell. "He what? He checked himself out?" She glanced at Mason. "But why? How? He's not strong enough."

Mason read the rest of the note in disbelief and lowered the paper.

"Max. That's crazy. Where did he go?" She listened. "Back to Texas? How in the hell did he get back to Texas?" She listened again. "Well, talk to the doctors and nurses. Somebody knows something." Mikey went quiet and her jaw dropped. "They wheeled him out? What the hell is going on down there?"

Mason stared at the note, still not sure he believed it.

"Well, see what you can find out. I'll tell Mason. Did you call Dad?" She scoffed. "Figures. Okay. Call me back." She hung up. "You are not going to believe this."

Mason handed her the note. "Dad checked out and has gone back to Texas. A car picked him up and took him to the airport."

Mikey stared in surprise. "How the hell did you know that?" She took the note. "What's this?"

"Read it."

Looking dubious, Mikey raised the paper and read it. Her eyes widened. "You've got to be kidding." She finished reading. "Is this for real?"

Mason sat up and cursed. He rubbed his face and tried to think. The note was from Ruben Montes, who'd personally written to Mason to let him know he'd heard of Mason's recent troubles with Margaret and his father's plight. Glad he and Mikey had survived and wanting to be of help, he'd stopped by to visit Martin. After a pleasant conversation where Martin and Ruben had talked at length about family and their relationship to Mason, Ruben had offered to assist with Martin's medical needs. Martin, of course, had jumped at the offer and couldn't wait to leave. Ruben had made immediate arrangements. He'd booked a limo ride to the airport and travel in his personal jet to Texas. Once they landed, Martin would be taken to a hospital where he'd be fully evaluated and then transferred to a rehabilitation facility where he'd remain until strong enough to return home. Once home, he'd have full-time nursing and a cook. Ruben had wanted to discuss it with Mason, but Martin had argued against it, anticipating push back from the siblings. Ruben ended the letter stating that he hoped this would help take the burden off the Redstones and allow Mason more time to pursue their sister Margaret and bring her to justice. He'd signed it *Your friend, Ruben*. Mason had half expected a smiley face after the salutation.

Despite his attempts to think, Mason had no answers. "I'd say after your conversation with Max, that yes. It's for real."

Slack jawed, Mikey reread the note. "Dad went off with Ruben Montes? I don't believe this. We have to talk to Dad."

"And what do you plan to say?"

Mikey stammered. "I...I don't know, but we have to say something. Ruben just highjacked our father."

Mason held his head. "He's done worse than that. He's using him."

"Then that's what we tell Dad."

"You think he'll listen? He's just been offered everything he wants and more on a silver platter. You think he'll reject it because we ask him to?"

"We can't let Ruben do this."

"How do you propose we stop him? He's not breaking the law." Mason thought of his father with regret. The slim chance their relationship had of improving had just been yanked out from under them. "Ruben's going after Dad to get to me. And he knows there's nothing I can do about it."

"What are you saying? That one day Ruben's going to expect something in return? And if you don't do it, he'll leave Dad with nothing?"

"Or worse," said Mason. "He blames me for Rain, so this is his retaliation."

Mikey just stared, and Mason sensed her shock. "We have to do something, Mason," she whispered.

Mason sighed. "When you figure out what, you let me know."

Mikey dropped Ruben's letter on the table, fell back against the cushions and stared at the ceiling. "When will this shit ever end?"

Mason almost laughed. "Look on the bright side. How much crazier can it get?"

The door to SCOPE opened and Trick entered, but not by himself. A tall older man, and a younger blonde woman followed him in.

Surprised by the visitors, Mason stood along with Mikey. "Trick?" he asked. "Everything okay?" He eyed the man and woman warily and thought the woman looked familiar.

Trick dropped his hat onto the back of the couch. "Sorry for the unexpected visit, but it's necessary." He paused. "Mikey. Mason." He gestured toward the visitors. "I'd like you to meet Ben and Lindsey."

• • • • • • • • • •

A short time later, the five of them sat around the coffee table, each with a coffee in hand. Trick bounced his foot, Mikey stared with uncertainty and Ben and Lindsey waited. Mason eyed the sheet of paper in front of him, which detailed a set of rules to follow if he wanted to find out what the hell was going on with Trick, and he guessed would explain Eleanor's strange affliction and death. He didn't just investigate spirits.

"It's fine if you don't want to sign," said Ben. "Lindsey and I will leave, and you'll never hear from us again."

His mind raced and he tried to make sense of it. Who were these people, and could they be trusted? What exactly had happened with Eleanor? Was it true that it had nothing to do with drugs, and if not, then what could explain her rapid unraveling, superior strength and violent rage? A past case as a Texas Ranger flashed in his mind and a small voice in his head told him to expand his horizons

"You signed this, Trick?" asked Mikey.

"I did." Trick sat back, still bouncing his knee. "But if you two don't, I'll understand." He glanced at Mason. "What do you think, Red?"

Mason stared at his coffee, his mind reflecting back. "You remember a year into our partnership, Trick, when we made a visit to a house outside Dallas to question a suspect supposedly connected to a Mexican drug cartel? His name was Devin Torrance."

Trick frowned. "I do. Vividly. The guy lost it. We busted in to find him attacking his girlfriend." He blanched. "Grisly."

"Not attacking," said Mason. "Her neck was slashed, and he was on top of her, his mouth at her throat."

"I remember," replied Trick. "He saw us and took off. You chased him and I stayed to help the girlfriend, who didn't make it."

"Devin didn't make it either. He was too fast, and I lost him in the alley, but they found him the next day, not far from where he disappeared. His throat had been cut, like Eleanor's. They never found the killer."

Ben began to smile.

"What does this have to do with…?" Trick frowned and glanced at Ben. "Wait a minute…"

"Let me take a guess," said Mason. "Did Devin suffer from the same affliction as Eleanor?"

"Sign that paper and you'll find out," said Lindsey.

Mikey shook her head. "I don't understand. What happened to Eleanor has happened before?" She eyed Ben and Lindsey. "And you two can explain it?"

Ben chuckled.

"They can't say anything," said Trick. "Not unless you sign."

Ben studied his hands for a moment and then looked up. "You're a smart man, Mason."

"Thank you, Ben," said Mason. "Am I on the right track?"

"You are," said Ben.

Mason relaxed in his seat. "You know all about us, don't you? SCOPE and what we do here?"

"We do," said Ben. "You're an intriguing group."

"As are you," said Mason. "Why all the secrecy, though? I'm out in the open. Why aren't you?"

"There's a lot of answers to that question. One is we have superiors who wisely prefer secrecy. Most of what we do would frighten the public. As far as other reasons…" Ben eyed Lindsey, who raised a brow at him. "Let's just say we've made some enemies along the way and it's best not to draw their attention."

Mason eyed Ruben's letter on the table. "I can imagine."

"It's better we stay off the grid," said Ben. "Staying on it could be detrimental to all of us. And protecting my family is paramount."

"I understand," said Mason. "I feel the same." He paused. "You know about our sister Margaret and her issues?"

"We are aware," said Ben. "I'd offer to help, but her afflictions are more mainstream, so we can't help you much there. As they say, that's not in our wheelhouse."

"Mainstream," said Mikey. "Not a word I would have ever used for Margaret."

"Just as long as you know that the Redstones come with some baggage," replied Mason.

"Don't we all?" asked Ben. "Doing what we do, risk is inherent. And I don't know anyone who has a normal family. I gave up on normal a long time ago."

Mason nodded. "So did I."

Ben smiled softly. "You and I are much alike."

Mason sensed that was true. Despite the need for secrecy and their unexpected introduction, Ben had a natural charisma about him that was hard to ignore. Lindsey appeared more guarded, and he sensed she had secrets of her own. He wondered what they were.

Trick glanced between the two men. "You're handling this way better than me, Red."

"That's for sure," said Lindsey.

Trick scoffed. "Must have something to do with the presentation."

Lindsey narrowed her eyes. "I doubt it."

Mason studied his partner and then spoke to Ben. "If I sign this, what assurances do I have that you're telling me the truth and that Mikey and I are safe?"

Ben didn't hesitate. "You have no assurances at all. Just good old-fash-ioned trust."

"There isn't much of that left nowadays," said Mason.

"I wouldn't have brought them here if I didn't trust them, Red," said Trick.

"I'll offer you this much," said Ben. He eyed Mikey and Mason. "You don't have to worry about Vicki. She won't be bothering you or your family anymore."

Mikey dropped her jaw and Mason frowned.

"She's no longer a threat," said Lindsey.

"What happened?" asked Mikey.

"Vicki possessed unique skills that she used improperly and had to be dealt with. And the rest is need-to-know," said Ben. "And only if you sign the paper will you need to know. Trust goes both ways. You help us and we help you," said Ben. "Don't you agree, Mason?"

"I do," said Mason, wondering about Vicki's unique skills. He tapped his fingers on his knee and considered his options. Something told him joining forces with Ben could open up a slew of new problems but also might create a whole new side to the business he'd be curious to explore. Other than spirits, he'd had some experience with the unexplained and maybe it was time to learn more. Thinking of Ruben, he glanced again at the letter. "Where I come from Ben, in Texas, a handshake is as good as your word." He sat up. "You agree?"

Ben grinned. "I do." He gestured at the unsigned rules. "I've never been a fan of paperwork."

Lindsey nudged him. "Dad," she whispered. "You sure about this?"

"I am," said Ben.

"Mason?" asked Mikey. "Are *you* sure about this?"

He looked at her. "You're not?"

Mikey focused on Ben and Lindsey and Mason suspected she was tuning into them. "I'm not picking up any bad smells," she said.

Trick squirmed in his seat. "Thank God for that."

Mikey sighed and spoke to Mason. "I trust your decision. I go where you go."

Mason nodded at her. "Good. Because I think we're all here for a reason." He spoke to Ben. "Just know that Mikey, Trick and I come as a team."

"I expected as much," said Ben.

Mason stood. "I think this could be the start of an interesting relationship." He held out his hand.

Ben stood, too. He glanced at the group. "I couldn't agree more." He shook Mason's hand, then held his hand out to Mikey.

Mikey hesitated, but then stood and shook Ben's hand.

Ben beamed a wide grin. "Welcome to the fold, Mason and Mikey Redstone."

What Happens Next?

Get ready for *Lost Lives*, book five in *The Redstone Chronicles*. Tempted by an offer they can't refuse, Mason and Mikey, along with Trick, and Daniels and Remalla, agree to a getaway that promises fun and easy money, but all is not what it seems. When they find themselves stranded in the mountains, and at the mercy of an ancient evil, they'll have to use their shared wits and abilities to survive. Will they all make it out alive?

Enjoy on excerpt below.

Reading Detectives Daniels and Remalla?

After the events of *Lost Hope*, the story continues with Daniels and Remalla in *Of Love and Loss*. The threat grows when Margaret targets both detectives who are coping with difficult losses. When Margaret uses their struggles against them with a shocking attack, Rem must decide whether to fight for his life and his love for Mikey, or leave it all behind.

Will Margaret finally seek her vengeance or face retribution? There's only one way to find out.

Enjoy an excerpt below.

Note: Because the Daniels and Remalla books and The Redstone Chronicles are a spinoff and crossover series, they share an overarching story, and the characters from each are mentioned or appear in all the books, so reading both is ideal. The books published alternate between both series. A list of books in chronological order follows below.

Want more from J. T. Bishop?

Sign up for her newsletter at jtbishopauthor.com. Get the Daniels and Remalla prequel novellas, *The Girl and the Gunshot and The Magic of Murder,* for free, in addition to extra content, plus opportunities for more free books.

How did it all begin with Daniels and Remalla?

Check out the four-book *Family or Foe* saga, which introduces the charismatic detective duo. A killer with powerful abilities is out for revenge against the family he believes wronged him. But his devastating secrets aren't limited to family, and Daniels and Remalla find themselves caught up in his shocking revelations. Can the killer be caught before he exacts his vengeance and destroys them all?

New to Daniels and Remalla?

Then dive into *Haunted River,* book one in the series. The ghost of a woman whose murder remains unsolved haunts a small town where she lived and died. When another woman turns up dead years later, are Daniels and Remalla next?

Or start with *Murder Unveiled*, the prequel novel to *Haunted River*. A prominent art dealer is found murdered after the unveiling of a famous, but cursed, painting. When Daniels and Rem are assigned to investigate, they'll learn that a curse may prove more deadly than a killer and they could be the next targets.

Or go big and enjoy the omnibus, *Shadows and Secrets,* which includes the first three books in the detectives series, *Haunted River, Of Breath and Blood* and *Of Body and Bone.*

Do you like light sci-fi with urban fantasy and a delicious romance thrown in?

Check out Bishop's first series, *The Red-Line Trilogy*. One woman holds the key to unlocking a secret that will ensure the existence of a secret community. One man, assigned to protect her, will risk everything to keep her alive, but when he falls for her, will their destiny be enough to save them both?

And the Red-Line series continues with the sister series to the trilogy, *The Fletcher Family Saga*. A distant but deadly threat risks the lives of three unique siblings, but life can't stop because of who they are. They'll endure love, loss and a dangerous enemy determined to destroy them.

Either the trilogy or sister series can be read first. Take your pick. Boxed sets are available, too!

A Note from J.T.

I LOVE TO HEAR from my fans about my books and I hope you enjoyed *Lost Hope*. This book took off in a direction I did not anticipate. Mason's past exploits have always involved ghosts and spirits, but the name of his firm is SCOPE, which stands for the Study of Cryptids and Paranormal Entities. Since cryptids are part of his business, I figured it was time to explore more of this subject. As I developed the idea for this book, I found myself being pulled toward exploring the vampire theme. Who (other than my mom), doesn't love a great vampire movie? I'm a huge fan of Dracula and if you haven't watched the TV series *Midnight Mass*, then you're missing out. So, I figured why not come up with my own take on the vampire story. Thus, the CU was born.

I like calling them the Cryptid Unit because that leaves the door open for other cryptids to make an appearance and for the CU to get involved and work with the Redstones. Lindsay and her family are great new characters that allow more opportunities to dive deeper into their history and maybe give Trick a love interest that will keep him on his toes. I've been wondering about the kind of woman he might fall for, and I think Lindsay is the perfect candidate. We'll see where it leads.

And, of course, Daniels and Remalla will continue to play a pivotal role in the Redstones lives, especially since Rem and Mikey have their own smoldering attraction for each other. Want to see what happens next with them? Then read *Of Love and Loss*. You won't be disappointed.

Reviews are a huge plus and big help for an author and potential readers. I would love it if you could please take a couple of minutes to leave a quick review for *Lost Hope* And if you'd like, please leave a few comments, too.

As always, thank you for your time and readership. It is deeply valued and appreciated.

Now, on to the next book!

Books in Chronological Order

Although recommended but not required, in case you prefer to read in order...

Red-Line: Prelude to The Shift, a short story (subscribers only)
Red-Line: The Shift
Red-Line: Mirrors
Red-Line: Trust Destiny
Curse Breaker
High Child
Spark
Forged Lines
**
The Girl and the Gunshot, a novella (subscribers only)
A Hamburger Christmas, a novella
The Magic of Murder, a novella (subscribers only)
First Cut
Second Slice
Third Blow
Fourth Strike
Murder Unveiled
Haunted River
Of Breath and Blood

Lost Souls
Of Body and Bone
Lost Dreams
Of Mind and Madness
Lost Chances
Of Power and Pain
Lost Hope
Of Love and Loss
Lost Lives
Dominion
Lost Time
Illusions
Lost Love
Vendetta
Black Bird

Acknowledgements

ANOTHER BOOK IS COMPLETE, and again, I have many to thank. This doesn't happen alone, and I am indebted to family and friends for their help, support and encouragement. It is truly appreciated.

I also want to thank my Beta and ARC teams. You guys keep me on my toes, ensure I write a great story, and help with early reviews. Thank you for being honest and offering your guidance.

I love writing about the bonds between loving family, deep friendships and the ties that hold them together. Plus, my fascination with the unknown thrown into the mix makes for a satisfying story and hopefully, adds a little more thrill for my readers.

I especially want to thank my fans. Hearing from you and knowing that you're enjoying my books makes all the hard work worthwhile. None of this would matter without your tremendous support. If I can help you escape from this crazy world for a short period each day, then I've done my job.

Here's to more stories, more fun, and more time for yourself. If you can have a little of that each day, you're on the right track.

Enjoy an excerpt from Of Love and Loss, Book Six in Detectives Daniels and Remalla

MIKEY REDSTONE PULLED THE frozen lasagna out of the freezer in the garage and carried into the kitchen. She opened the refrigerator, slid it onto a shelf and closed the fridge. Her brother Mason walked into the kitchen, looking dapper in an ironed navy shirt, pressed jeans, boots, and his wavy hair combed back. His handlebar mustache had been trimmed and he smoothed it with his fingers. "How do I look?" he asked.

"You look great. Valerie will be suitably impressed."

He paused. "You're sure you're okay with me going out tonight?"

"Of course. You and Val have had this planned for a while. You can't cancel because of me."

"It's not you. It's the first night in two weeks without someone watching the house."

Mikey sighed and pulled on her snug black jeans. "If you want to stay home because you're going to worry, that's up to you. But if you value your relationship, you should go. Valerie's getting an award. You should be there. I'll be fine. I doubt Margaret is going to strike the first night no one's watching. You and I both know she'll hang back until we relax. Give it a couple of weeks, then you can worry."

"I don't think we should assume anything when it comes to our sister."

"Like you've said before, we can't hide. I'll set the alarm and have you on speed dial, but I'm sure it will be fine."

Mason nodded but raised a brow. "Why don't you invite Rem over? You two can order in your gross tacos, watch a movie, and hang out."

Mikey smiled. "Stop playing matchmaker. You know I'm not pushing it with him. He asked to go slow and I'm honoring that."

"It's tacos and a movie. I didn't ask you to take advantage of him." He paused. "Maybe just a kiss." He smirked.

Mikey scoffed. "You and Trick. Between the two of you, I'm going to need counseling sessions myself."

"I know a great therapist," said Mason.

Mikey shook her head, knowing he referred to Tarina, his addiction counselor. "I'm aware." She tipped her head. "Besides, I just pulled out the lasagna from the freezer to thaw for dinner tomorrow. I figure I'll ask Rem over then. You know he can't resist lasagna."

"Especially mom's lasagna. What's the occasion?"

Mikey shrugged and tucked a strand of her pinkish, purple-tipped brown hair behind her ear. "I don't know. It just felt like a good idea. We haven't had lasagna in a while and I thought we could invite Daniels, too. Ask Val when you see her, and I'll text Trick. It would be nice to get together and have a meal. Especially after all that's happened."

Mason nodded. "It's a great idea. We can stop and get some garlic bread and a good couple bottles of wine tomorrow."

"Sounds great."

Mason eyed the time. "I should go. You sure you're okay to stay alone?"

"Totally okay." Her cell rang and she pulled it out of her pocket. "Speak of the devil. It's Rem."

Mason grabbed his keys and headed for the door. "You can still ask him over. There's nothing wrong with seeing him two nights in a row." He winked at her.

"Stop worrying about me. I'll see you later." Mikey answered as Mason left.

"Hey," she said, walking to the door. She bolted it and set the alarm.

"Hey," answered Rem. "I'm on my way home and thought I'd check in. How was your first day without the patrol?"

Mikey smiled. Rem had been doing a much better job with staying in touch after she'd called him on it a few weeks earlier and certainly after Margaret's attack on her and Mason. "So far, so good. How about you?"

"Nothing suspicious. Not yet, at least."

"Good. Let's hope it stays that way. How was work?"

They talked for a few minutes about their uneventful days and Mikey took a breath and invited him for lasagna the next night. Regardless of her brother's light-hearted suggestion that she invite Rem over, every time she'd asked since Chloe's death he'd declined. Before Chloe's death, she and Rem had expressed their attraction for each other, but Rem feared a romantic relationship between him and Mikey would only put them at greater risk. Mikey had disagreed but she'd told him she'd be willing to wait. But then Allison had been murdered along with Chloe, and he'd left the force. He'd pulled back from her and Daniels and certainly from anything suggesting that he and Mikey spend time together. The last two weeks, though, she'd sensed less resistance and maybe a willingness to take the next step. "It's okay if you don't want to," she added. "No pressure."

He went quiet for a second before he spoke. "Your mom's lasagna, huh?"

"Yeah. I made a batch and froze it, but figured it was time to eat it. We'll have wine and garlic bread, too. Mason will be here and I'm going to invite Trick, Daniels and Val, too, so no worries about anything romantic."

He chuckled and paused again. She could hear him breathing and wondered what he was thinking.

"I'd like that," he said. "When do you want me there?"

Mikey's heart fluttered. *Finally* she thought to herself. *The cracks are starting to widen.* Mason was right. It would just take time.

Grinning, she told him when to arrive.

• • • • • • • • • •

Rem pulled into his driveway and parked his car. He said goodbye to Mikey and hung up, looking forward to a social dinner and feeling oddly happy. He hadn't felt that in a while and had to attribute that to Mikey. Since he'd resumed his conversations with her, he'd felt better. Talking to Daniels always helped but that was a given. Having someone outside of his partnership to talk to who knew almost as much as Daniels did was guiding him out of the darkness. He had to wonder at what point he'd assume the risk and take the next step. The thought of it excited him but at the same time, the possibility of giving his heart to someone again only to have it ripped back out terrified him. He pushed the thought of taking the next step with Mikey out of his mind as he got out of the car and went to check his mail.

He pulled it out of the box and sighed when there was no letter from the lab. Eyeing his surroundings and the street, he looked for anyone suspicious who could be watching but saw no one. The house across the road from his had been vacant since the incident with Oswald Fry. Rem wondered if anyone would rent or buy it again. The place held too many ugly scars. He wished the owner would raze it and start over. An empty house across the street was a good spot for anyone to break in and watch Rem and his house. He'd met the owner though, not long after what happened with Oswald, and the owner had assured him the house would be locked up tight with cameras and alarms. No one would be on the property without his knowledge. Rem didn't have much of a choice but to live with it, unless he wanted to move, but he hadn't reached that point. Not yet, anyway.

Holding his mail, he walked up to his front door, unlocked it, and went inside. The alarm beeped and he turned it off, closed the door and relocked it.

He dropped the mail on the front table and headed into the kitchen when his phone rang. He pulled it out of his pocket and saw it was Daniels. He answered. "Hey. Don't tell me you want to get a beer. I just got home."

"You're home?" Daniels asked, his voice clipped. "Good. I need to stop by. I'm headed that way."

Rem heard the concern in his friend's voice. "Everything okay?"

Daniels paused. "Not sure, but we can discuss it when I get there. You got any food in the house?"

"Uh, not much. Was just going to get a hot dog. But I can check the pantry. Maybe I can cook up some pasta if you're hungry."

"Just so long as you don't serve anything raw."

"Huh?"

"Never mind. If nothing else, we'll order pizza and have a beer. I think we're going to need it."

Rem wondered what Daniels meant. "Now I'm curious."

"Join the club. I'll be there in ten."

"Okay. See you."

"See you." Rem hung up, wondering what Daniels had on his mind. He set the phone down on his counter and wondering about the pasta, he walked to his pantry and opened it. Something swung out and bounced against one of the shelves that hung from the door. It took a second for Rem to register what it was, but when he did, his stomach lurched, he fell backwards onto the floor and scooted back until he hit the kitchen cabinet. Holding his stomach, he fought back the urge to be sick and stared at the pantry. A dead chipmunk, it's torso red with blood, was hanging by its tail from the spice rack.

Enjoy an Excerpt of Lost Lives, Book Five in The Redstone Chronicles

JONATHON TILLERMAN STUMBLED, AND his foot slid on the rocky gravel. His knee hit the ground, and catching himself with his hand, he grunted.

"Dad? You okay?" His son, Gary, jogged up behind him.

Jonathon pushed up, ignoring the flare of pain in his knee. He brushed the dirt off his pants. "I'm fine. Just slipped. Watch the rocks here. They're loose."

"How's your knee?"

"Knee's fine. Don't worry."

"You just had surgery on it, Dad. You should take it easy."

"Son, I need you to stop worrying. That's why we came out here." He took a full breath. "To get out of town, get some fresh air, and relax." He stretched out his arms and turned toward the mountains. "Look at that view." He faced the trees. "And these beautiful woods."

"I'm not complaining. I'm happy we came. This camping trip was a great idea. I just don't want you to push yourself. It's hard to enjoy hiking if you're hurting. You sure you don't want to go back to the camp? We've been out here a while."

Jonathon put a hand on Gary's shoulder. "I'll let you know when I've had enough, okay? Let's go a little farther and then we'll turn back." He took another deep breath. "Let's go into the woods a bit. Enjoy the shade."

"You sure?" Gary eyed the trees dubiously.

Jonathon chuckled. "We're safe, Gary. Those noises we hear at night are wildlife. They're curious just like we are. There's nothing to be afraid of."

"It's the bears that spook me."

"You've got your bear spray, and we make plenty of noise, so they know we're coming. And I have my gun if we need it. Just relax." He started walking again.

"Okay," said Gary. "I'll follow you. Let's head back soon though. I'm getting hungry."

"Eat your protein bar."

"I ate that an hour ago."

Jonathon patted his jacket pocket. "You can have mine if you want it." He reached the edge of the woods and stepped into the trees.

"I can wait." Gary followed, and Jonathon admired the beauty around him. Tall spiring trees reached high up into the sky, their thick leaves providing ample shade. A light, cool breeze blew, and a woodpecker pecked away on a nearby branch. A hawk flew over, and a squirrel raced across a fallen log and up another tree.

Jonathon took it all in. Nature energized him and no knee surgery was going to stop him from his outdoor excursions, especially with his son.

Gary had recently gone off to college and this was their first camping trip in two years. Now that Gary was older, their time together had dwindled, so Jonathon embraced the moments they shared, knowing they would only dwindle more.

Adjusting his backpack, he moved deeper into the forest. Gary walked beside him but said little. Jonathon appreciated the quiet. Nothing was more peaceful than hiking through the woods, listening only to the sounds of nature. Jonathon could hear a babbling brook, and a crow squawked from above.

Gary pointed toward the bird. "Isn't that an omen?"

"The crow?" said Jonathon, looking up. He sighed. "What exactly are they teaching you at school?"

The bird flew off. "It's not school. My roommate's girlfriend is into all that stuff. Signs, astrology, Ouija boards, spirits. She's very woo-woo."

"Sounds to me like someone's off their meds." He stopped. "That bird is no more of a sign than that rabbit." He gestured to a rabbit hopping through an area of high grass. "You could assign meaning to anything." He turned and kept walking.

"I suppose." Gary fell into step beside him. "You should have heard her before I left, telling me to be careful. That all sorts of creatures live in the woods, some not so nice."

Jonathon grunted. "Maybe you should reconsider the company you keep. She's obviously a city girl. She needs to get outside more."

"Maybe. She is a little bit dramatic. She does these deep breathing exercises and has fainted during them more than once, and she takes ice baths. Says it clears her head and toughens her immune system."

"Proves my point. She could come out here for all of that. Fainting and freezing aren't required."

"She told me she has visions just before she faints." He paused. "She had a vision about us, out here, and told me to be careful. She said to stay away from the obelisk, whatever that means."

"Obelisk? What the hell is she talking about? You seen any obelisks?"

Gary smiled. "Can't say that I have."

"Then I guess we're safe."

"Guess so."

"How about you ignore her and just appreciate hanging with your old man. Who knows how many trips we have left in us?"

Gary nodded. "I know, and you're right. I'm having fun, Dad. This has been a great trip."

"I'm having fun too, kid."

"Just be careful with that knee of yours. I don't want to carry you back. You're not as slim as you used to be."

Jonathon glared. "Watch it, or that protein bar is all mine."

Gary jumped over a rock. "Just kidding. You look great. You've got the energy of a man half your age."

Jonathon patted his stomach. "Not sure about half, but maybe three quarters."

They walked passed the babbling brook and reached a clearing. They stopped and Jonathon shared his protein bar with his son before deciding to return to camp. After eating their snack and drinking some water, they took some photos out in the woods and started the hike back.

Jonathon varied the route to admire more of the scenery. Watching his step in a patch of loose rocks, he caught a whiff of decay in the air and stopped.

Gary sniffed and grimaced. "Smells like something died."

"Probably a kill from a bear or mountain lion." He followed the scent.

"Where are you going?"

"It's not far. Judging by the stench, it's been dead a while and whatever killed it is long gone."

"Do we really have to find it?"

"I'm curious. Aren't you?"

"Not really, no."

"Did your roommate's girlfriend warn you about stinky animals?" He stepped over a fallen log.

"No, but nothing that smells this bad can mean anything good." Gary put a hand over his mouth and nose.

"We won't go much—" Jonathon stopped when he almost kicked the rotted head of a deer. The smell hit him, and his stomach tightened. "What in the..." He squatted and eyed the remains. What was left of its glassy black eyes stared back at him and its lips were twisted and withered. Jonathon wondered why the eyes and lips remained. They were usually food for smaller animals who foraged after the dominant predator left. "Where's the rest of it?" He'd never seen an animal decapitated before.

"Ugh. That's gross," said Gary. "And it stinks. Can we go back now?"

Jonathon looked around and spotted something on the ground a few yards away. He straightened and walked toward it. His stomach lurched again when he saw entrails sprawled over the ground. "What animal would do this?"

Gary approached. "That's weird and disgusting."

Jonathon followed the blood trail.

"Dad, I really think we should head back."

"C'mon, kid. Let's look." He kept walking, thinking the rest of the deer must have been dragged away and eaten when he stepped past a large tree and stopped cold again. Lying on a pile of rocks were the remains of the carcass. Its stomach was split open revealing the empty abdominal and chest cavity. Its heart and other organs were gone but Jonathon could see the animal's spine and ribs. Meat remained on the bones and maggots covered the flesh. Confused, he shook his head. "A bear or lion wouldn't do this." Seeing the rocks beneath and around the animal, he frowned. "It looks like some sort of sacrifice." He walked closer.

"Dad, let's go."

"You think some college kids came up here?" asked Jonathon. "Maybe the kind who'd be friends with your roommate's girlfriend?" He touched a hoof. "This is sick."

"Dad, we should leave. Right now."

Hearing the anxiety in his son's voice, Jonathon looked up. "What's wrong?"

"Look. Over there."

Jonathon followed Gary's stare and widened his eyes when just beyond the rocks, almost hidden by the trees, was a tall narrow stone structure that was about eight feet high and came to a point at the top.

"That's an obelisk," said Gary, his voice quiet.

"It can't be," said Jonathon. "Why would there be an obelisk out here? It's probably just a—"

A high-pitched wail pierced the quiet of the woods and faded. Jonathon froze and Gary paled. "What was that?" asked Gary.

Jonathon listened but heard nothing but silence, which bothered him. The normal sounds of the woods had vanished. All he could hear was the breeze. He stared at the obelisk and his heart thumped. Uneasy, he grabbed his phone, snapped some photos, and returned it to his pocket. "Let's go."

"Right behind you," said Gary. He turned and followed Jonathon.

The wail came again, only closer, and Jonathon froze again. A cold spike of fear sliced through him, and he had the terrifying sensation that they were being watched.

"What is it, Dad?" asked Gary, his gaze darting around the area.

Jonathon slowly reached for his weapon. "Get your bear spray."

Gary gaped at him, bit his lip, and fumbled for the spray in his pocket. He pulled it out and gripped it.

"Just walk slowly and stay beside me."

Gary nodded and Jonathon could sense his fear. He suspected a nearby predator could, too.

"Stay calm. Take deep breaths. We're going to walk out of here, slow, and easy." Staying alert, Jonathon walked away from the obelisk and the bizarre kill. The woods remained quiet, and the wail didn't come again.

Getting farther away, Jonathon began to breathe easier when the wail blared from directly behind them. They whirled and Jonathon expected to see whatever was tracking them, but there was nothing there.

"Wha...what is it?" asked Gary. "What's following us?" He held out the bear spray, his hand shaking.

Jonathon narrowed his gaze. "I don't know." Sensing they needed to move fast, he turned back. "C'mon. Hurry."

They picked up their pace. Jonathon's knee began to ache, but he wouldn't let it slow him down. They passed more trees and the babbling brook. They stepped over a large log, but that was a problem. He thought they'd already crossed the same log several minutes back. Looking around,

Jonathon realized they were going in circles. His sense of direction, which he could always rely on, had deserted him.

Gary, breathing hard, studied his surroundings. "Where are we?"

Jonathon spied what he thought was the way out. "This way."

"Dad, are you sure—"

A wail pierced the air, and they spun toward the sound. The sun had dropped lower in the sky, creating eerie shadows that cast irregular shapes on the ground. Movement caught his eye, and Jonathon raised his gun.

"Dad...?"

"Just stay still. Don't move," he whispered.

"What is it?" He held out his spray, his knuckles white with his grip.

A dark mass moved behind a tree, and Jonathon aimed and tightened his finger on the trigger. "It's over there."

"Where?"

A low growl echoed, breaking the silence, and Jonathon's attempts to control his fear failed. He didn't know what type of predator would stalk them like this. The deep growl came again, and the figure moved. For a brief second, Jonathon saw what looked like a fur-covered hand with wicked claws grip a tree trunk near its base. The animal straightened, and a head with a long snout emerged. Jonathon couldn't fathom what he was seeing and before he pulled the trigger, the beast bared its teeth, growled again, jumped from the trees, and ran straight toward them.

Gary screamed and Jonathon fired.